CHANDELIER

BEN HAWKEN

Hardcover ISBN: 979-8-9913994-1-8
Paperback ISBN: 979-8-9913994-0-1
eBook ISBN: 979-8-9913994-2-5

First Edition: September 2024

Printed in the United States of America

For my grandmother, Carmen Riley,
who would have done all of this first.

CHANDELIER

Antennae

For nine years this room was the most closely guarded secret in the world.

No president, prime minister, or general knew of its existence until 30 years after it had been disassembled and the pieces incinerated.

The room was domed, well lit, and arranged in a semicircle that directed all of its attention to a single folding chair. The floor was covered with neatly coiled cables carrying power, transferring data, and connecting the array of sensors studying every move, heartbeat, and murmur from a nearby ten-year-old who sat deep in thought.

Sienna Barrett leaned forward in the chair, her eyes closed tightly. It was the 10th of April 1991.

Her head tilted from one side to the other, and her brow cycled between furrowed and flat – as if she were searching for the right word or the name of an obscure world capitol. Her long hair fell in front of her shoulders, and seven careful scientists stared silently into a dozen different screens scattered across the long plastic tables you might see at a potluck. Most of these screens were following her biometrics and neurology – in particular the electrical activity of her brain and the faint magnetic fields of a few specific brain regions. Months earlier she'd seen the technical names of these sensors stenciled onto the boxes they were stored in – "electroencephalogram" and "magnetoencephalogram," among others – and made a point of quizzing the operators on the spelling. The two monitors in the back of the room had a rotating lineup of star chats, satellite images, and a variety of readouts from across the electromagnetic spectrum.

This room, referred to as the "research cabin," was one of a dozen small buildings spread across a campground built at the turn of the century as a summertime getaway for middle class families eager to escape the urban sprawl of San Francisco. The campsite had gone out of business decades earlier, but the cabins remained in this secluded thicket of trees, tucked up against Sugarloaf Mountain in San Mateo, California. The collection of children who currently lived here jokingly referred to this secretive site as "Camp Loaf" and called themselves "Campers."

Years later, when the existence and function of the Dark Antennae program was declassified, people who had lived at Camp Loaf would often begin their story by noting that this setting was nothing like the sterile and eerie underground lab in "Stranger Things" or any number of cinematic thrillers where some wing of an American shadow government was training "gifted" children with blank faces and dead eyes to carry out some morally quanderous secret mission. Instead, Camp Loaf looked and operated like an actual summer camp that just happened to stay open year-round, and, off to one side, was a cabin where a small handful of friendly technicians operated a comical amount of oversized 1980s-era computer equipment. For all the national security that was allegedly at stake here, the leader of this project, Dr. Julius Torquemann, took the advice of the child psychologist attached to the program: Happy, balanced children in an environment without emotional or physical extremes would produce better results over the long term.

Decades later, when those children told their stories, there was a uniformly positive perception of Dr. Torquemann, even if they knew essentially nothing about him.

On this particular afternoon, the scientist sitting closest to the research cabin's back wall could hear the beginnings of an activity outside that would occupy the campers until dinner started: A game the kids called "Hammer Slaps." The exact origins of the game were unclear, but it seemed to revolve around an antique croquet set and draw rules arbitrarily from both softball and lawn darts. For a group of children with countless entertainment options, it was a source of amusement for the staff to see what activities they invented from scratch – and, in the case of Hammer Slaps, it probably helped that none of them knew how to play croquet.

Inside the cabin, however, things were still very quiet. Sienna leaned back in her chair, took a deep breath, and kept searching.

The atmosphere was serious, and, at times tense, but never anxious. Periodically she would speak quietly to herself, and the technician with the earpiece connected to the small microphone hanging from the ceiling above her chair would start typing. Often, when a keyboard somewhere in the room was clacked hard enough or fast enough, Sienna would crack open one eye, usually to tease them for their eagerness, but also, on afternoons like this one, when she felt on the verge of something big, to ask for silence.

Sienna always knew when *something* was really happening. It was the same thing all her roommates and friends here described – the warbling hum that would begin to rise inside her head. It would build and fall, flatten out, and then start crackling.

In the back of the room Dr. Torquemann leaned over the shoulder of a technician and stared at the rows of data coming back from the electrode on her temple, from the sensors in the canvas strap draped across her like a sash, and the dozen other machines pointing at her. The two men made eye contact and the specialist knew the question his boss was asking.

"Right now, it's only bits and pieces, but it's been a long time since we saw activity with this kind of structure from the Signal."

Dr. Torquemann had already reached the same conclusion, and he was afraid they weren't getting anywhere with this opportunity. Before he had time to ask the next obvious question, he noticed that Sienna's face had changed from quizzical to furrowed, and now she was starting to scowl.

Suddenly her eyes flickered open. The hum had dipped suddenly and then vanished, and she knew from experience that, when you lost the Signal like this, it was gone until you had a good, long reset. She was disappointed but not despondent. Torquemann gestured to two other scientists and called out, "Let's wrap it up for the day."

Sienna removed the electrodes and the sensors with familiar ease, hung them over the back of the chair, and stood to leave. "I'll see you tomorrow, Torchy!" she called out to Dr. Torquemann. She waved to the two specialists closest to the door, and soon joined the game that was already in progress. The score was tied at "Blue."

As she waited for her turn, she reminded herself of what Dr. Torquemann had told her countless times: "This research isn't about hitting a homerun every time; what we need are small, incremental steps. And I need you to not beat yourself up if sometimes you just plain miss."

Today had been a miss despite having started out strong. But, on the positive side, she had arrived just as the game was getting good.

Back in the research cabin, Torquemann leaned back in his chair until it creaked and then groaned, and he took his glasses off before rubbing his face for several long seconds. He opened his eyes and saw seven different scientists quietly waiting to tell him what he already knew, but from the perspective of a wide variety of scientific fields. This cabin was a listening post more than a research lab, but, over the last nine years, most sessions ended a lot like this one – and nine years was a long time to puzzle over the pixels of a much larger picture.

"While the Signal is this strong, I want us to stay sharp and stay ready to capture whatever data we can pick up," he said. He could tell the team was sensing a missed opportunity. "You guys, I will say this much again: I am perfectly happy to shovel through days when we miss what we're aiming at if it means eventually striking the motherlode."

He looked around the room and noticed again how bad he was at pep talks.

One of the scientists finally spoke up – it was Dr. Carney, who was a psychiatrist on top of specializing in magnetoencephalography. "In terms of good news, the kids remain in great spirits. I guess that alone keeps the program from falling apart."

Across the room, Dr. Fierst, a favorite of the campers, laughed. "I'd be in great spirits too if I lived at a summer camp and wasn't in school and just spied on Russians all day."

"Hey, woah," Torquemann objected through a laugh, "they do go to school." He paused to check his watch. "Let's call it for today. Our first session back here tomorrow is 9:30 with Michael, and then we have a block of time with Lydia at 11:00."

The last of the monitors were turned off, bags were packed, today's data was packaged up, and, after everyone was gone, Dr. Hamza Tunis hung back with Torquemann to switch off the last of the lights.

As Torquemann reached the door, reading a printout with inconclusive results, he stopped and let out a long sigh.

Tunis cleared his throat, "What are we going to do when..." he trailed off. This question had been weighing on him for two years, and now probably wasn't the best time to ask it. Torquemann looked up from the sheet and stopped halfway out the door when he saw how concerned his normally stoic friend had become.

"What are we going to do the first time a kid notices something unusual?"

Torquemann had thought of this. The senior officers he reported to had also thought of this. This had been the subject of the first meetings he'd ever had about this project – long before he'd gotten around to digging into the science itself.

"Well, Hamza, that would require the kids to speak or read Russian, and the government goes to pretty extreme lengths to keep track of the number of fluent Russian speakers we have traveling freely around the country."

Tunis took this in and let out a long breath. "I think I would have figured it out by now."

"Well, yeah," said Torquemann with a smile as he stepped out into the breeze, "but you're 42."

1989

1   Discovery

19 SEPTEMBER

Today was the second time Sienna had visited the neurologist. Ten days earlier she'd been in this same office for an MRI. The follow up visit had been scheduled for a week later, but the office called and asked to delay until they could clear up a "small issue with the insurance company," and the next available date was today.

All of this had started almost six weeks earlier when Ginny brought Sienna to see the family doctor after a month of intermittent complaints about seeing and hearing things that she described, to the best of her eight-year-old abilities, "flickers." That appointment generated a referral to a neurologist at the Walnut Creek Medical Center. The family doctor had said this could be something as simple as allergies or the nerves between the brain and the optical nerve having a growth spurt – and the neurologist agreed that half those were possibilities, but an MRI was needed to see what exactly might be happening. Today's appointment was to discuss the results.

Sienna sat in the waiting room with both parents, flipped through an issue of "Highlights" magazine she had already seen at school, and ended up staring into the fish tank. It was fun to miss school in the middle of the day, but there were better reasons to miss school than this. She watched the puffer fish in the tank swim in slow corkscrewing loops, and caught her reflection in the glass; her hair was short enough that she could just barely tuck it behind her ears, and on her wrist she had braided one bracelet for each color in the rainbow.

When a nurse finally brought the Barrett's back to the exam room, she sat on a padded chair that looked suspiciously like it had come from her dentist's office. The nurse took her temperature and listened to her heart, and Sienna noticed that her parents were both trying and failing to act nonchalant.

There was finally a knock at the door, and a doctor that she didn't recognize poked his head into the room.

"Hello," he said with a big smile, "you must be Sienna. My name is Dr. Torquemann."

Sienna said hello, and he greeted Mike and Ginny with the same big smile. In his hand was a file folder with her name on the tab. He was friendly and polite, and he was immediately likable, but all three Barrett's would later agree that it was obvious Dr. Torquemann did not belong at this hospital and that he wasn't the "medical type" of doctor.

It was Sienna who asked the first obvious question.

"Is Dr. Besharti not here today?"

Dr. Torquemann smiled again, placed his folder on the small exam table, and sat down on a stool that he rolled over from underneath the sink.

"Your neurologist will be here in just a second, but, before he comes in to tell you that everything is fine – and, to be clear, everything up here is definitely 100% fine," he tapped the top of her head with a click pen and they both laughed. "But, before he comes in, I just asked him if I could meet with you for one quick second first. Is that ok?"

Sienna nodded automatically, but he still repeated the question to mom and dad just to make sure. Mike and Ginny shared glances; Mike shrugged in a way that indicated everyone was curious and a little worried to find out what was so important, and Torquemann took those reactions as a "yes." Sienna was especially curious – this doctor wore the standard white lab coat, but there was no name stitched into it like every other doctor she had met, and he was wearing Nike basketball shoes instead of the church shoes every other doctor wore.

"Well, like I said, nothing is wrong with your brain – I just want to emphasize that again. And there isn't a 'but' coming – like where I might tell you that 'something horrible is happening 'but' it's not really that bad.' Everything is actually fine. Totally, totally fine. The explanation for why I'm here, however, is going to sound kind of crazy, so I'm just going to tell you right up front that I work for the National Reconnaissance Office. If you've never heard of it, that's kind of the point. We are kind of like the spy agency that's responsible for all the secrets that are so secret that all the people who get to know 'Top Secret' things aren't allowed to know what we know."

He smiled at Sienna, "Cool, right?" She smiled again, and he continued.

He looked over at Ginny and Mike, "I know this is a pretty insane way for a stranger to introduce himself, so if at any time you want me to leave, I'll stand up and walk right out that door and I'll keep apologizing for wasting your time until it slams shut. And right here at the outset, I'll show you my ID," he handed them a bifold wallet holding a plastic card with his name and information on it. "I'm also going to leave you with a card that has a phone number on it. That number will work one time and I promise someone will pick up no matter what time you call. You tell them who you are, and they'll verify where I'm from. Or you can go to the San Francisco Federal Building right across the bridge from here, it's downtown on Mission Street, about two blocks away from Civic Plaza. That's the highest-ranking government building west of the Mississippi. You can walk in there any time it's open and tell the person at the front desk you want to talk to the 'Special Agent for Defense Affairs.' Asking for that will get you a free ticket to a back office where an escort will bring you to sit in a conference room for a few minutes, and when that special agent finally comes to meet you, just tell him my name, or just tell him your name. He'll have both pieces of information already, and he can verify that this is real, that I'm real, that I'm a real scientist, and we're doing real stuff that can't really be talked about out in the open. He won't know who I am or what I do, but he will have enough information to confirm or deny what's happening. To be safe, he'll probably show you a couple pictures and ask you which of them is the person you met; one of the pictures will be me, but if they throw in a wild card, like adding a picture of Lionel Richie or something, you can try pointing at him just to see what the agent does, but I wouldn't recommend it. They don't really build those guys with senses of humor."

Ginny took the card and handed back the wallet. This was enough verification to at least finish this conversation, but things were certainly far stranger than expected – even for a neurology appointment. With that part settled and some basic trust established, Torquemann continued.

"I'm here today because I lead a very special project at the National Reconnaissance Office that, like most projects at the NRO, doesn't officially exist, and I want to tell you about it for a couple reasons that will become clear shortly. But I will say, one last time, that, after we talk, if you don't want to meet ever again, then that's fine – you can rest assured that, as far as the government is concerned, this conversation never happened and the four of us will go on with the rest of our lives, no problem.

"So, now that you know where I'm from, the reason I'm here is, well... there are a ton of reasons, and one of them is tachyons. I know that sounds like something from Star Trek, or maybe something you get at a craft store, or maybe it sounds like the name of a tiny particle that is so small and fast that most scientists don't think it can technically exist because it would defy all the known laws of physics and the Universe.

"But," he said leaning closer to Sienna for a moment and talking in a faux whisper, "if you did guess it was that third option then *you* are even smarter than I thought – because, much like me, these tiny particles might not *technically* exist but they do, in fact, actually exist right here on this planet." This got another laugh. He was on a roll with the younger part of the room, but the adults were growing more skeptical rather than less.

"Now, don't get me wrong, even though a small group of us in the scientific community know that tachyons definitely exist, we don't know nearly as much about them as we hoped we would by now, and the things we do know don't make any sense. Like, we know that they can travel faster than the speed of light which is technically supposed to be impossible, and yet they do it anyway and we don't know how they do it. They also don't have any mass or weight, which is weird. Let's see, what else," he said, trailing off as he thought through other facts which might interest a child. "Oh yeah, we know that as they run out of energy, they start going faster instead of slower, and we know that if you wanted to slow just one of them down so that it's only moving at the exact speed of light, that would take more energy than exists in the whole galaxy. Why is that, you may ask? We don't know. If you can't tell, my job is very hard sometimes."

Even the parents smiled at that one, so he was making progress.

"And the weirdest thing about tachyons is that when we do all the math on these different calculations that try and study them, well, we see that as these tachyons are flying around back and forth all the time, sometimes they change direction – but not change direction like go up instead of down, I mean that they change 'direction' and travel backwards along the timeline which brought them here."

He paused and there were a few moments of silence. Torquemann had had this discussion enough times with enough skeptical families to know that this was a good spot to let the information sit for a moment and wash over everyone. Ginny was the first one to break the silence. "And you said these tackios are where?"

"That's a great question. For better or for worse, we've discovered that tachyons move in waves across the entire Universe. In some ways there are whole oceans of these waves that cover everything out there, but really, considering that they move fast enough to be everywhere all the time, it's like one big wave that covers the galaxy. This wave is moving in the background the same way that there are radio waves right here in this room. They don't really affect things, but we know they're here. We know for certain that tachyons are a foundational part of the makeup of the Universe, but the list of things we know about them can be explained to an eight-year-old in," he paused to check his watch, "about seven minutes."

"That's all you know?" Sienna asked, expecting the story to end with a big breakthrough.

"Well, over the last few years – since the mid-1960s, actually – a couple universities have done some very interesting research, but none of them have gotten anywhere close to the big picture. The fact we can't ever hope to see them doesn't help."

"Why can't you see them," Mike asked.

"It's actually kind of funny – since tachyons travel faster than light, you can't really see them coming or going because they're moving past you faster than the light bouncing off of them can reach your eyes."

Mike would spend the entire drive home trying to explain this phenomenon to himself.

Ginny took a long look at her daughter and her mind raced trying to figure out the connection between a mystery particle and her daughter. Right on cue, Torquemann continued. "I mentioned radio waves a second ago, you know what those are, right?" Sienna nodded in a way that told him she had heard the term but couldn't explain the electromagnetic radiation spectrum yet.

"Well, radio waves are one part of a big family of waves that come in lots of different sizes – almost all of them are invisible, and they're all around us. It starts with waves that are really big, like the ones that bring music to your radio. Then there are medium-sized waves, these ones are just the right size for your eye to see and these are the ones that carry photons to the back of your eyeball so you can see things. Right after that there are X-rays – and they're so tiny that they can see through your body right down to your bones. And then the very tiniest of the waves are called gamma rays, and you only get those from big explosions like supernovas and stuff like that."

This had started to sound more like a 7th grade science class and less like a rationale for why this topic was so secret.

"And the way those radio waves can bring a song to the stereo in your car is that whenever the radio station plays music, they create a wave of their own that's the exact same shape as one of those natural radio waves, and then that song just rides piggyback on the wave until it gets to your radio. And this is where I finally bring this conversation back around to tachyons. We discovered a couple years ago – and we were *very* surprised by this, believe me – that someone is having their message ride piggyback on those tachyon waves, just like a radio."

"Who is it and what's it playing?" Sienna interrupted grinning. She was oblivious to how skeptical her parents had become; this sudden plot point in the story was perfect for sweeping up the imagination of a curious 2nd grader.

"We know for certain that it's the Soviet Union, and we think they're using it to communicate with their army and their spies around the world. And you have to give them credit – using a particle that no one thinks is real to communicate is very clever and very secret. Whoever designed this over there has probably been given every medal you can get and an extra potato."

For Sienna, this was like a sci-fi movie, mixed with a spy movie, mixed with a PBS special about how the galaxy works.

"All we really know for sure," Torquemann continued, "is that the Signal we're detecting is very important to them and all kinds of important information is moving through it. The bad news is that right now we can only pick up bits and pieces of it – we'll get some parts of sentences, and there's stray pieces of images here and there – but that's it."

At this point there was a knock on the door and another person she didn't recognize stepped into the room. Dr. Torquemann smiled and gestured for him to come in and pull up a stool. "This is Dr. Hamza Tunis, and, unlike me, he actually is a neurologist, and a very talented one at that."

"What's the difference between a good neurologist and a bad one?" Mike asked.

Dr. Torquemann laughed, patted Dr. Tunis on the back and said, "It depends where you fall on a scale of '1 to Very Good at Brains' – and he is as close to a 10 as you can get."

Torquemann told Dr. Tunis that they had just been talking about secret Soviet radio stations, and then turned back to the family as if to say that everything they'd discussed thus far was leading up to this moment.

"So, everything I've told you so far is leading up to this: We can't detect the Signal with an antenna like the one on your car. Believe me, we have really tried, but the technology we have right now just can't do it. We can't even come close to doing it. But we can detect it with the brain – or, to be more clear, a very small part of the brain, and only a very, very small number of brains."

Sienna looked at her parents. This doctor had been aiming them at a strange and unpredictable target for several minutes, and now it seemed they were about to hit it.

At this point, Dr. Tunis took over.

"Sienna, do you know what braille is? You know, those dots that blind people use to read?"

She nodded.

"Well, imagine if there were braille dots all around a blind person but that person couldn't reach them. Even if those dots were out of reach by just the width of a hair, it's the same as those dots not existing at all because they'd be impossible to read. But now imagine if just one blind person had a bump on the end of their finger – just a tiny bump that you might need a magnifying glass to even notice, but it's enough to make their finger touch the braille dots. *Now* that person can suddenly read everything even though no one around them even knows that information exists."

He, too, had learned when to leave the occasional strategic pause to let people catch up, and this was an important one.

"Dr. Torquemann and I are here today because your brain, quite randomly and quite harmlessly, has a tiny bump on it that lets you touch a dot that no one else can. The flashes and the flickers you've been seeing are your brain occasionally touching the Signal."

Mike and Ginny took deep breaths in tandem; they were now holding hands and staring at Dr. Tunis as he spoke. Sienna was thinking, too, but she also had a smile creeping across her face.

"So, Sienna," Torquemann asked, "what questions can we answer for you?"

"So that wart on the end of a finger..."

"It's more of just a tiny bump, like some extra skin cells on the tip of your finger," Torquemann interrupted.

"Sounds like a wart," Sienna continued, "and you're telling me that I have a wart on my brain that is an antenna for this Signal? What does it look like?"

So far this one's personality seems like a match, both men thought. "Precocious" was an overused word that got used a lot during the recruitment phase to describe a positive personality trait to look for in potential campers.

Dr. Tunis flipped through a few pages in her file, found a film of Sienna's MRI, and put it up on the lightboard for everyone to see. There on screen was a cross section of her brain, looking at it from the top down.

"It's right here" and he circled an area toward the back with a dry erase marker. This reminded him of another picture from the scan and he pulled it from the folder. "Here's another angle, that is zoomed in by about 150 times" and he pointed at an area between two folds of the brain.

"This is the image that made it to the office where Dr. Tunis and I work," Torquemann explained. "A few years ago we had researchers start paying attention to the patient notes every doctor typed up in their office computer, and if their notes had words like 'child' and 'seeing images' or 'hearing sounds,' and if those notes also had an MRI that showed anything in this area," he tapped the circle he had drawn on the film "then those researchers send us a copy of the file."

Mike spoke up again, "Aren't there laws against that?"

"Oh, yeah, definitely. Tons," Torquemann replied with a shrug as he sorted through the other images in the folder.

With everyone still staring at a grainy picture of a brain, Dr. Tunis went back to his explanation.

"This spot I've circled here on the back of your brain is an area where the cerebral cortex – that's the part of your brain that controls our ability to understand language – bumps up against the occipital lobe, which is the part of the brain that controls vision. It's a very powerful area and, in some *extremely* rare cases, there's just the tiniest bit of overlap between them. And, in exceptionally rare cases, there is a brain like *yours* where that overlap has *this*," and he pointed again to the grainy black and white picture of a brain.

Dr. Tunis knew that it didn't look like much.

"I know it doesn't look like much, but what I've circled here is something that acts the same as that bump on the end of the finger. If you look closely, you can see a little line right here on the picture. It's a tiny buildup of cells that gives you something that almost no other human being has. Dr. Torquemann and I have seen pretty much every brain in the Western Hemisphere that has something like this, and it's not a very long list."

"What makes those specific cells in that picture so special?" Ginny asked. Mike was quick to follow up: "And how did the Russians figure this out before us? And did they build some futuristic type of radio?"

Torquemann nodded and rubbed his chin, which he had been told is an effective way to demonstrate you're listening and thinking about the answer to a question you've given a hundred previous times.

"Those are both great questions; I'll start with yours, Mike: We have no idea. We're just happy we discovered that they're doing it, and, with some luck of our own, we'll figure out the science behind it as we keep listening to what they're discussing and how those messages are moving. The technology you would need to do this has existed since the second World War, but it's the *way* they are using it and the way that they've pieced together so many disparate scientific disciplines that is so ingenious and so darned clever – and that's what we're trying to figure out."

He turned to Ginny, "As for those cells, what makes them so important is the exact point they're at on the brain. That tiny ridge of neurons is unusually dense, but they aren't hardwired into the rest of the brain in the typical way – they're just kind of sitting there on that tiny area where the cortex and the occipital lobe overlap. And because those neurons are absorbing the Signal without a place to send it, that information just kind of radiates out to those parts of your brain that control vision and language. We think that the combination of what's in the Signal plus the areas it's hitting is why certain kids can see or hear it."

Torquemann could tell the parents were relieved their daughter wasn't ill, but they seemed to sense this new information would have an outsized impact on her nonetheless.

"What all this means, Sienna," Dr. Tunis concluded, "is that this small group of cells in your brain – I mean, this ridge is about 1.5 millimeters tall and 3.5 millimeters long, and, for reference, 1.5 millimeters is about the width of 12 human hairs – and just that tiny extra amount is what allows you to read or hear or see things that no one else can."

"So, if you're the brain wart expert," Sienna said pointing at Tunis, "then what do you do?" and she poked a finger in the air towards Torquemann.

Torquemann smiled. He liked this one's spirit.

"My job is to figure out what's in that Signal and where exactly it's coming from. And I think if you come help us with this research at a place I've set up, we can do it."

9 OCTOBER

Less than three weeks after meeting Dr. Torquemann, Sienna was saying goodbye to her friends and telling a story that was simple enough to repeat without any suspicious variations: She had been accepted to a private school and was going to go there for a couple years. Part of the story that her parents would help tell was that the school was hundreds of miles away in southern California, so Sienna wouldn't be back every week, but they'd still go visit and plan fun stuff to do on breaks. This put her far enough away to discourage casual visitors, but not so distant that it felt like some remote boarding school.

It was still warm on the San Francisco Peninsula the day Sienna arrived with her parents and a suitcase. The orientation meeting was mesmerizing: Every kid in the 1980s knew enough to be terrified of the Russians, and everyone was wondering if there was some point in the future when America would have to do the bold thing necessary to finally defeat them. The idea that she, *Sienna Barrett*, could contribute to this effort was akin to being told that it was time to collaborate with the action heroes from the cartoons. Sure, most of those shows weren't really her thing, but her older brothers played the TV at an absurd volume, and she had unintentionally absorbed all the stories and overarching plotlines.

It made perfect sense to her why this work was so important and treated with such secrecy. In her mind, there was no question why this had to be shrouded in mystery, why she needed to tell a story to everyone back home, and why this work had to be done. Anyone even slightly patriotic could get on board with this – and Mike and Ginny Barrett were the highly patriotic type. And Sienna had unintentionally absorbed some of that, too.

Shortly after pulling up to the gate, pausing for a moment while a video camera panned back and forth, and then driving through when it rolled open, they saw Dr. Torquemann waiting to greet them as they parked outside the dining hall.

"It's very good to see you again, Sienna," he said. "Dr. Tunis wanted to be here to say 'hello' but he's wrapping up some work right now, so we'll see him a little later. Let's walk around and I'll show you Camp Loaf."

That name got the expected reaction. "This is called 'Camp Loaf?'" she laughed, "Why?"

Torquemann laughed, too. "I know," he explained, "that's the name our original campers called this place. That's Sugar Loaf Mountain," he said pointing up at the peak of a nearby hill, "or Sugar Loaf Hill, depending on who you're talking to. There is a much bigger mountain with the same name in Brazil, of course, but my guess is someone who used to be on the San Mateo city council was Brazilian, or liked Brazil, or both, or who knows. So, anyway, Camp Loaf is what we ended up with."

They walked past a small cluster of cabins, including one with a thick tube running to it, and they made their way to the open area in the middle of camp. They passed other campers while they walked and Dr. Torquemann paused to make introductions. Everyone was nice, and everyone looked very normal. The former was a relief, the latter was surprising, and the combination was auspicious.

"This cabin over here," he said gesturing to the one with the tube, "is where we do most of our research with the Signal, that weird tube you see has a couple dozen different cables inside it carrying power and information. Dr. Tunis is in there right now going through some data."

"Somebody else with a brain wart, huh?" Sienna asked.

"Like I said," Torquemann said with a smile, "it's easier to think of it like a bump no one else has."

"Still sounds like a wart."

Just as they were about to turn around and head back to Torquemann's office above the dining hall, Dr. Tunis and Adams opened the door to the research cabin and came over to say hello.

"There's our resident wart expert now," Torquemann said, just loud enough to avoid being heard.

"I knew it. This is so gross," Sienna whispered back.

After a few more pleasantries they got an impromptu introduction to Dr. Adams and the work she did with the electroencephalogram. As she explained it, her job was to study the electrical signals moving around inside the brain. This was the first time any of the Barretts had heard that the brain is actively producing electricity whenever information passes between neurons, and, as Dr. Adams explained it, that electricity is what makes up our thoughts, emotions, and tells our muscles to move. Sienna had a lot of questions about this that she would save for later.

As they walked back to Dr. Torquemann's office, Mike started in with questions he still had from their first meeting.

"How exactly does this work, again? Like, with how the Soviets are creating this Signal?"

This question had a remarkably wide spectrum of possible answers – it included responses that were "official" to "less official" to "completely truthful" – and Torquemann had some leeway, up to a point, in determining where on the spectrum his response should land. In this case, his answer was essentially accurate in relation to its intended purpose of reassuring these parents that their daughter was safe and doing important work.

"Our best guess is that the Russians have a transmitter tower deep inside the country that is malfunctioning – not malfunctioning so much that they notice or that their own communications are suffering – but malfunctioning in the sense that they are sending out a wider signal than they intend, and that extra width is bleeding over onto just the tiniest edges of that electromagnetic spectrum we talked about last time. But that bleed over is so tiny that they don't even notice it or, perhaps, they can't measure it. But we *are* measuring it and listening to it, and we are getting really good at it." That explanation seemed to make sense. "And with Sienna's help, we might get even better at listening to the Signal so we can have more to show for all the work we're doing here."

"How did the Russians figure out how to do this before us?" Ginny asked.

"That's another great question, and I can tell you that this made a bunch of our scientists just sick when they saw it. It's one of those breakthroughs that you can't believe you didn't have yourself, and then, when you see someone else do it, it's like a slap in the face every time you look at it. But the short answer is that we have no idea yet, but there are a lot of theories. One of the scientists we'll meet later on, Dr. Gustafson, is our resident expert on piggybacking information onto waves and particles, so he's losing sleep over your exact question all the time."

By now they were in his office up in the rafters above the dining area, and the next phase of the conversation happened. This discussion happened with every family at some point, and it was an important one.

Somewhat unexpectedly, Sienna kicked it off.

"Has anyone ever talked about what you do here? Like, after they leave the camp?"

"No," he said after pretending to pause and think about it, "not really."

This surprised Mike. He assumed there must be government agents standing by to silence people who were less patriotic than him and who might start selling secrets.

"Never?" he asked.

"Nope," Torquemann said, this time without the fake pause. "The reason for that has a lot to do with how much differently we do things with this program. First, as you had explained to you at the Federal Building, we have moved some money around so that you guys get sent a nice little lump sum every year for the rest of your natural lives. It's not a life-changing amount, but it's enough that it would hurt to lose. Since that money is hidden inside the income tax refund you get every year, no one will ever see you get the money, and it will just keep showing up like clockwork. But let's say you think you could get even more money with this information – sure, you could try to sell it to some foreign government, but good luck spending rubles at the mall, and good luck trying to hide where it came from considering someone sitting behind a desk in the CIA's spy hunting department will be sporadically checking in on your bank account and your spending habits, just as a precaution, forever. But, sure, all of that probably isn't enough to stop someone who's the type to get bored and tell a reporter or another government what goes on here. To protect against that, it's up to my organization to psychologically evaluate all three of you very carefully to see if you're the type of person who can get that bored or greedy. And that's a process that has to happen pretty fast since we usually have a narrow window of time between when you get your first MRI and when you have the follow up visit. It helps that my organization can ensure that a few critical pieces of paperwork can get lost or misplaced within any insurance company and thus slow things down just enough for us to finish our evaluations."

Ginny was shaking her head before he even finished, "We haven't met with any psychologists, so how come we're here?"

As per usual, Torquemann feigned a look of surprise when he heard this, and said, "Well, I suppose, things do tend to get busy this time of year."

The Barretts couldn't help but wonder what it might have been like to be psychologically evaluated for a program like this. What Mike didn't consider at the time – or any point thereafter – was the long talk he'd had with a friendly and loquacious stranger when his plane was "delayed" three hours for maintenance at O'Hare Airport and his airline had unexpectedly given him a voucher to the first-class lounge while the repairs were made. Mike and "Jim from Tampa" had sat at the bar, ordered complimentary drinks, and talked about life, and politics, and goals, and dreams, and fears. Mike loved to talk, Jim had some great stories of his own, and, when the intercom announced the flight back to Oakland was ready to board, Mike had left to get his bag and Jim excused himself to make a quick phone call he had forgotten about.

For her part, Ginny also failed to make the connection to the chiropractor she had visited after waking up with a sore neck a few days in a row. "Shelly" was a new employee at the clinic, and they talked throughout the appointment, in between the cracks and groans. Ginny would recommend Shelly to a friend a few weeks later, and she appreciated that the people at those holistic clinics really did like discussing all the deep questions about life.

Sienna also didn't think twice about the interim school counselor who had come to her elementary school for a few weeks to replace the substitute who was filling in while Mrs. Saunders was on maternity leave. The substitute left when she got an offer for a full-time job in another school district, so a substitute-substitute then stepped in. This new counselor was warm and funny, and she had administered a long "standardized test" to a handful of kids in Sienna's grade. The sub chose kids at random, and Sienna happened to be chosen first. The test, she explained, covered "the full brain" – and that must have been the reason why all the questions were about your outlook on life and personal beliefs, instead of math or science.

Dr. Torquemann knew there was very little chance they'd make these connections, at least not if the field agents from the PsyOp team did their jobs right, but every so often a parent would say something like, "Wait, a second! Is Martin at the gym a secret psychologist?" So far, no one had identified an agent correctly. At least not out loud. And that amount of uncertainty was considered more than enough to keep a suspicious mouth closed long enough for this project to eventually and quietly fade out of existence.

If money was the carrot for this secrecy, Torquemann also felt it was important to explain the stick.

"So, the money is one thing, and there's the intermittent monitoring that goes with it, and there's the fact that you volunteered to be here and part of that volunteering was the promise you made to keep these things a secret – and that secrecy is why it goes without saying that there's one other good reason not to talk, and that reason is formally known as Title 18 of the United States Code, otherwise known as the Espionage Act. In Section 793, and then again in 798, the Espionage Act explains that if you were to reveal anything you've heard so far or anything you will hear in the future... Well, things get incredibly ugly. And when you take what the Espionage Act says and add to it the penalties laid out in the Classified Information Procedures Act... *then* the punishments start to be worse than any amount of money could be good."

This had the desired effect of making everyone tense, with perhaps the slightest hint of second guessing.

"I know hearing this can make you start second guessing what you're doing or begin wondering if this is a horrible idea on account of what 'could' happen if you ever chose to start telling people about it, but", he said, turning to the only person who really mattered now in this discussion, "Sienna, think of it this way: If you walk into an ice cream shop tomorrow and hit someone on the head with a big pointy stick, you are probably going to go to some kind of jail for bad kids, right? And I get it, you're not a bad kid, but you did just do a bad thing, so now you gotta get locked up – that's fair. But, come on, let's be honest, what are the odds you're really going to start hitting people with pointy sticks all of a sudden? I mean, seriously?"

"I wouldn't," she said with a mix of earnestness and amusement at the mental image.

"Right, of course not. That's just not something you're ever going to do. Doing that isn't *in* you. Sure, if you ever did – boom, jail. But that isn't ever going to happen. You wouldn't be here if that was possible. So, instead of worrying about hypothetical punishments for crimes you won't ever commit, let's just do something great here. You, me, mom, dad, the Wart Doctor, the rest of the doctors – *this is the team.*"

"This is the team," she said, looking him in the eye.

Then to his surprise, she extended her hand like someone far older might do to close a deal that had been months in the making. Torquemann shook it, looked at Mike and Ginny, and knew the program had succeeded in finding another camper.

"Well then, let's drop off your suitcase and meet some of your fellow campers, then we can walk through the kitchen before dinner. Watching these guys chop stuff up is pretty fascinating – they are professionals."

"Professional chefs?" Mike asked, impressed.

"They are multitalented, to say the least," Torquemann said over his shoulder as he led the Barretts back across camp to a nearby cabin that had been outfitted for the comfort of these carefully selected children.

PRESENT DAY

18 JUNE

The Department of Defense was contained, almost entirely, in a single building. It had the distinction of being the single largest office building in the world, and its fairly uncreative name was derived from its pentagon shape.

The hallways in this building stretched 800 uninterrupted feet, and none of them had the moving sidewalks which featured prominently at the commuter airport located two miles away. The orientation video shown to everyone on their first day claimed you could get between any two points inside the 30-acre complex in just 10 minutes, but that assumed you were willing to run in full uniform.

Major Carl Horn had worked at the Pentagon for eleven years and, as of a year ago, had finally committed to memory each of the building's five rings, office layouts, and the unofficial number of basement levels. He might have figured it out much sooner, but the majority of his time was spent in the secure sub-basement which housed his organization's operations center – a place everyone called the Black Hole. In this room, information constantly entered, and the idea was that none of it should ever leave in any form except direct orders. From here, Major Horn monitored, influenced, anticipated, and subverted the movements, provocations, escalations, and retaliations of foreign governments and their puppets all over the world. If there was a black op happening somewhere – on behalf of his own government or any of the others his government was watching – that information almost always arrived here first.

His official title was "Director" of the "Global Operations Center" – but all four of those words were formalities behind which a far more nuanced range of responsibilities could operate unseen.

Today, the reports were more numerous than usual, but none of them were necessarily more volatile than average. But, in this line of work, volume was its own kind of volatility – and today's reports showed too much tension simultaneously creeping across all the wrong areas, and, most alarmingly, it all centered around the same subject.

The first briefing he'd received during the 33-minute ride to the office – having a driver was the most essential perk accompanying his unique kind of seniority – had to do with chatter amongst the leadership of the Chinese military regarding its neighbors in Russia. Once he reached his office in the Pentagon's A-Ring long enough to put his bag through another scanner, he traveled 80 feet down to the Black Hole where the next briefing began as soon as he arrived. This update covered how, 1,500 miles southeast of the situation in Beijing (北京), the Indian Ministry of Defence (रक्षा मंत्रालय) was furious about what it believed it could prove Pakistan was doing at their airfield outside Karachi (کراچی). General Gupta, the commanding officer of the entire Indian army disliked what he saw so much that he had already recalled two generals who had been on leave to celebrate Ratha Yatra (रथ यात्रा) on the other side of the country – and both of them were expected to be back at the South Block military headquarters in New Delhi (नई दिल्ली) before the end of the day. One of these officers supervised the country's special forces, and the other was a senior Air Marshall in their Strategic Forces Command (सामरिक बल कमान) named Akash Chatterjee (आकाश चटर्जी).

Chatterjee led a wing of the Indian Air Force (भारतीय वायुसेना) that coordinated all the search and rescue operations for high value ordinance and individuals. He'd first come to Horn's attention when he redesigned the Indian military's Churaya Trishul (त्रिशूल चोरी हो गया) program and turned it into what was, arguably, the world's most sophisticated and responsive. The same type of program existed in the U.S., but here the term for it was "Broken Arrow."

The U.S. military used the term Broken Arrow to describe the accidental loss or theft of a nuclear weapon while in transit from the factory where it was built to the missile silo where it would spend the rest of its life. Any report of a Broken Arrow immediately set in motion a four-inch-thick handbook of protocols – and a cross-departmental task force of exhaustively trained engineers, investigators, and special operators were immediately deployed to track and restore the package. Such an action was something equal parts delicate and frantic, and it called for the careful use of countless sensors to reacquire the device, and a variety of automatic weapons to unacquire its captors.

Seeing Chatterjee's name moved this topic from "mildly interesting" to "worthy of his ongoing attention."

Within 10 minutes Horn had received an update with information from a source the CIA had within the Indian military: It seemed the Ministry of Defence was reacting to what they believed was evidence of a pending cyber attack of massive proportions, and the only country with both the means and motive to do this was their traditional enemy in Pakistan. The report explained that the scientific wing of the Indian military, formally known as the Defence Research and Development Organization (रक्षा अनुसंधान एवं विकास संगठन), had, at first, been investigating reports of unusual influxes of noise in the sensor arrays it used to study the electromagnetic spectrum. When this noise, while still barely perceptible, was subsequently found creeping into telecommunications networks, the military's cyber warfare department got involved because such interference had preceded a particularly exotic digital attack 11 months earlier. For the time being, this effect-preceding-the-cause conclusion was the prevailing theory explaining these strange readings, and the DRDO was convinced that this attack was already quietly underway.

The report ended with a note that, within the next hour – which made it very late in New Delhi – the Prime Minister was going to be briefed on options to counter this threat.

The officer who delivered the report added that, in the opinion of the Pentagon's resident specialists, the electromagnetic interference the Indians were seeing was actually the software in their sensors misinterpreting the very coincidental simultaneity of a major magma displacement on the ocean floor lining up with an above average amount of magnetic activity in the atmosphere thanks to an ongoing solar flare. Having both of these things happen at the same time was more than enough to throw entire networks of sensors into disarray, and it had happened before.

The consistently heightened tensions between India and Pakistan presented a seemingly endless number of opportunities for flare ups, but India's rapid military growth over the last decade had dramatically reduced its willingness to absorb unprovoked attacks of any kind. This fact was the basis of where the situation's truly problematic nature presented itself: Any moment now a young intelligence officer was going to walk through the blast-proof doors on the opposite side of this room with the first draft of an analyst report explaining how any action taken by a dominant India against Pakistan would get Iran's full attention and, almost certainly, a response would follow. Pakistan and Iran were not the tightest of allies, but ever since Pakistan stayed neutral during the Iran-Iraq war and hosted peace talks between the two nations, things had consistently, if very slowly, warmed up; now they even collaborated on border security and had a joint task force to interdict drug trafficking. In this scenario, Iran would be very unlikely to let an attack on Pakistan go entirely unretaliated, and if Iran made a move – especially a move across international borders – things were going to get very tense inside the headquarters of their bitter enemies at the Royal Saudi Land Forces (القوات البرية الملكية السعودية) in Riyadh (الرياض). And anytime the Saudi military and the Iranian military do anything – much less do it simultaneously – Israel starts rolling crates of missiles out to their fighters and loading cases of ammunition into troop carriers. The Israelis were, out of necessity, the best F-16 pilots on the planet, and their infantry had all been training in krav maga (קרב מגע) since childhood – and both of these things boded poorly for enemy combatants, regardless of numerical superiority. After decades of existential crises Israel had become exceptionally adept at identifying existential threats, and it did not require a major provocation before it started shooting back.

It also went without saying, but Horn knew it would be in the report anyway: Once Israel was involved, the U.S. would be involved. And once Israel was busy with Iran and the Saudis, all its traditional enemies in the region would very likely start to consider what they could do to a distracted adversary. There was certainly precedence for this – in 1967 Egypt, Syria, and Jordan launched a sneak attack during a sacred Jewish holiday with the intent to erase Israel from the map while it was busy celebrating. That attack, which came to be known as the Six-Day War, was now a carefully studied event for officers at the

U.S. War College due to how swiftly Israel repelled and then obliterated its attackers. By the end of those six fateful days the combined armies of three countries were frantically running home as fast as their bullet-riddled transports and officers could take them.

Horn would read the report anyway just to see the baseline of knowledge his team was working with, but, over the next 48 to 72 hours, things could get hot very fast.

That thought was interrupted by a vibration on his wrist. It had been 60 minutes since he'd eaten, and it was time to take one of the pills in his front pocket. He fished it out along with a gnarled fragment of metal, about the size of a house key.

This object was a subject of ongoing conjecture around this office, but no one had ever asked him about it directly. Horn would commonly place it on the table in front of him during meetings, and he carried it in his pocket everywhere he went – inside and outside this building. It was small enough that you might not notice it next to his phone or notebook, but it was nearly always there. When a situation the GOC was navigating became particularly dire, or when a decision fraught with especially problematic circumstances had to be made, he would pick it up off the table and squeeze it in his fist, or he might tap one of its twisted edges on the expensive grain of the tabletop. Other times he would stare at it, or through it, before he began to talk – and, quite often, whatever he had to say meant that somewhere quiet on the other side of the world would suddenly become very loud, or that people with dreams and ambitions were soon relegated to stories told about martyrs.

Discreet onlookers referred to it as "the shard," and this wasn't entirely inaccurate, but, more specifically, it was shrapnel.

It had passed through the body of his roommate from OTS before ripping a hole between his ninth and tenth ribs and finally embedding itself behind the pelvic bone on the opposite side of his body. He might never have known the route this fragment had taken if his blood test in a hospital two days later hadn't shown trace amounts of an antibiotic Dorian had been taking in the days leading up to the mission.

At the time Horn's torso was unexpectedly ventilated he was commanding an assault group in Delta Force's Bravo Squadron. He was an eager young officer with a West Point degree and a bottomless interest in the infinitely arcane minutia which came with planning combat operations.

Six years earlier he and Dorian Kay had been the only two graduates out of the 191 people invited to Delta Force Selection, and, six months prior to that, no one from a group of 203 were selected. Both of them did well on their new teams, their first several deployments were successful, and, within a couple months of each other, both were put in command of their own unit. This was a well-established career path for smart, inexhaustible, and pragmatic warfighters – and the two friends aggressively tried to one-up each other with new stories whenever their paths crossed.

The shrapnel found both of them on a mission to a small corner of the world so horrible that it was probably what the residents of Hell were threatened with whenever they misbehaved. This expedition called for their two assault groups to pair up, and they planned the operation together, with Horn taking the lead on submitting the plan for review and leading the operation on the ground. Later, when the long debrief began, there were less than half as many people to explain what went wrong than Horn had stood in front of to explain what to expect. The final verdict was that, considering the circumstances, the fact that this many people had survived was miraculous – but those were a collection of words which, strung together in that order, meant very little to the young captain with the ugly trail of stitches zig-zagging up each side of his torso. Long before those stitches were removed, Horn knew that somewhere an "After-Action Review" memo had reduced the entire operation to a short series of bullets about that day's long series of bullets. The first bullet probably said something like, "Local assets compromised immediately prior to arrival." The second and third covered things like, "Disproportionate and previously unobserved offensive capabilities relative to the size of the outpost" and "Resulting malfunctions from a lightning strike after disembarking the Black Hawk." The fourth bullet was likely, "Unbeknownst to local recon, at the time of arrival the enemy was amassed at the LZ in preparation to build a new garrison and took concealed offensive positions when inbound teams were spotted."

The firefight had erupted on all sides and all at once. The Deltas knew what to do in these situations, but the horrible weather – which should have been working to their advantage quickly turned against them – and when the surprisingly good local intel turned out to be surprisingly bad, the predetermined alternate routes to the objective and the corresponding fallback positions were all unusable. The fact that the source of that local intel had been captured once they were in the air and had gone dark on comms ensured all the details which might go wrong did. Horn called for suppressing fire on an area to the southwest where he saw the fewest muzzle flashes, and he led a bounding-overwatch attack on the position. It was textbook CQB, and they had soon secured the position and were returning fire while the teams regrouped. Horn was calling in these details and requesting an adjustment to the extraction plan when the rest of the outpost they were targeting began chewing apart their area with mortar fire. This onslaught was intended to soften up their position so that the small fleet of pickup trucks headed their way could finish them off.

Dorian's team included a sniper who he put in position to ensure the chain guns rarely had an operator, and he cleared the rampart of the outpost so that the commanders couldn't offer any help directing troop movements. There was more than enough enemy manpower and horsepower still coming their way, however. The following 90 minutes were, in the aftermath, considered a master class in "tactical repositioning" during a "firefight with disproportional enemy advantages." This was all a way of saying he had called for a retreat at the right moment while putting his soldiers in position to inflict maximum damage on hostile forces, therefore reducing the likelihood of their ongoing pursuit of his injured men.

By the time he had called for that retreat, Horn was already leaking from a few new places, and it took several requests over the radio to find his fellow commander. Unsurprisingly, Dorian was covering his squad's retreat by himself 200 feet south. Over the comms Dorian called out that the target they had come for had made the mistake of getting in one of the pickups, and he was now nearly within range.

"We gotta head out, D!" Horn barked into the radio.

"Negative, the big fella is inbound with a crowd of his personal guards."

"How sure are you?"

"Tall and ugly with a big scar on his forehead, right?"

"Stand by."

Horn muted his mic and cursed. He gave his remaining officers the bearing to take with the wounded and gave them the coordinates for their new extraction, and he took the two remaining men with him to assist Dorian. They moved quickly through the thick woods and, as soon as they arrived Horn instructed them to carry away the dead sniper and the badly injured medic who had taken a ricocheted fifty-caliber round to the chest plate of his body armor. Dorian was working the sniper rifle to disable engines in the wave of trucks while he waited for a clear shot at their target. Once within range, the round he fired grazed the leader's lower jaw, and he dropped out of sight. They would later learn that his face had been mangled to the point of being unrecognizable, but he had survived and would keep living another eight weeks until being murdered by a member of his inner circle. In this region of the world, this was a way of saying that a council had determined his medical condition rendered him unfit for ongoing leadership.

After seeing his target fall backwards into the bed of a truck, Dorian got up to join the retreat – but he'd barely started running when one of the remaining mortars hit the ground less than 20 feet away. The shell sent a concussive wave of metal fragments in every direction; 30 of them made their way to Dorian, and one found Horn who had just turned to check on his friend's progress. Without stopping to assess this new flash of pain in his side, Horn scooped up his old friend and carried him the entire 11 kilometers to the evac site.

Horn kept him talking as they moved, and the regular trickle of blood across his wrist showed that this particular warrior was still fighting.

"How you feeling, D?" Horn asked.

"It's not great, man."

"You picked the worst time to stand up, dude. Like, the *worst*."

"I'm hit bad, like, real, real bad."

"It's not that bad."

"My ankle got it bad – I can't even feel my foot; my stomach is bad, I can feel my shoulder grinding…"

"Ok, I'll be honest D, it's easier to list the places you aren't hit."

Dorian burst out laughing, and he was so strong that it started to make him bounce on Horn's shoulder.

"Damn, it hurts to laugh."

"I'm just saying."

"I think I got hit in my stomach, too."

"Nah, that's just my shoulder digging into your gut."

Dorian hated himself for being out of commission. He hated the jeopardy in which this put his friend. He hated the way it looked.

"I'm never going to hear the end of this, am I?"

"I won't tell anyone if you won't."

"Oh, I won't," Dorian said with another groan.

"I *am* going to tell Marta, though."

"The last thing a woman *that* pregnant needs is this image in her head."

"If you're really the father, then she's already seen worse things than this."

By now they were climbing through a steep ravine in order to get to the river on the other side. Horn shifted his friend's weight about halfway up and kept climbing once he saw a sign left behind by the rest of the squad confirming that this was the route they had taken.

"Am I getting heavy?"

"No, but I'm starting to think you were hit a lot more times than you wanna admit."

"What? Why?"

"Cuz it feels like you took on about 95 pounds of frag."

"You're just lucky I'm in such good shape."

"You're lucky *I'm* in such good shape."

Horn couldn't talk for a few minutes as he reached the steeper top of this channel. It had been 7 kilometers so far, and too much of it had been uphill; he was in agony, but he knew things were much worse for Dorian.

"Do you remember when we were in SERE school?" Horn asked. "Those woods looked a lot like this."

"That week was a picnic, dude."

"The instructor said he'd never seen someone with so much diarrhea after barely eating for a week."

"Barely eating? I ate like a king. I was finding –"

"I don't think you found a non-poisonous plant."

"Bro, I was the only one who didn't get found."

"They only found me because you were in the bushes with your colon turned inside out."

"I can't believe we still graduated," Dorian said with some pride.

"I can't believe you graduated."

"I had good instincts in those woods."

"The instructor said the way you smelled when you finally came in – and I'm quoting – was 'un-Christian.'"

"Not true."

"I still don't even know what that means, but he wasn't wrong."

By now the responses began to take longer, Dorian's speech slowed, and, every once in a while, he'd miss a question entirely.

"I was proud of us for finishing that course," Dorian said finally.

"Talk about another thing Marta should never know about you."

"Oh, I told her about that."

"I'm sure you told her you finished the course. I doubt she knows that those bushes needed an exorcist."

Dorian started to laugh but couldn't. He was quiet for a long moment.

"You know this is our last conversation, right? You picked a good one."

"Nah, but this is definitely the last time I carry you anywhere."

"Please, I've carried you before. I carried you back from that place we went in Croatia."

"That tiny bar? That wasn't me, that was Jansen."

"Oh, right."

"Freaking Jansen."

This time they both tried to laugh but neither one could.

"But thank you, man. I love you for this."

"You can thank me once we plug all these new holes you got."

"Do you remember the interrogation training at the end of the SERE course?"

"Do I remember being stripped naked and sprayed with a firehose of ice water? Yes, Dorian, I recall."

"We did it though."

"You started laughing."

"It was funny – like, it was absurd what we were doing. Absurd is funny."

"You made it so much worse for all of us."

"Worse?!"

"The jacked black dude, down in the stress position, stark naked and laughing maniacally? Those instructors made it their mission to make you stop, and they dished it out to all of us just in case we were in on it."

"That's right, they did do that."

"So, yes – much worse."

"They loved it."

Now Dorian was barely whispering the words. His eyes hadn't been open for a while. This was the end.

"I can't believe you got promoted a year later," Horn added. "How did that not end up in your file?"

"Oh, it's in there. Anderson told me it's in the file."

"Sometimes this is the dumbest profession in the world."

"It's pretty good usually, though."

Eventually, three questions in a row went unanswered, and then Dorian stopped bleeding. And Horn knew his brother was gone.

Eventually the group arrived at a river which they floated down, in total darkness, to their extraction point. Horn carried Dorian into the helicopter, and he passed out shortly after they turned north and entered friendlier territory. He woke up in an operating room where five other stretchers had white sheets pulled over them. On the cart next to him was the stainless-steel basin holding the shard, still attached to a tangle of viscera. He reached over to take it and concealed it in his fist until after he was sent back to the States.

Every second of this operation remained classified to this day, and large parts of it were so secretive that they were never committed to writing in the subsequent reports – so, just out of habit, he even sifted those parts out of these recollections. What was on the record, however, was that Horn was awarded the Distinguished Service Cross for his actions to preserve the lives of his men, rescue wounded soldiers, pursue the objectives of the mission, and for "acts of heroism which involved great personal risk."

He denied the invitation to accept the award twice before being ordered to attend.

Like many special operators, Horn did not care for recognition, and, in his particular case, the extra space it took up on his formal uniform was an inversely incarnate representation of the great weight of living with so little to show for his dead teammates. He saw to it that Dorian received the same honor, and he personally delivered it to Marta three days before she went into labor.

A sense of obligation led him to return to duty long before he was done healing, but his alacrity for combat had left him. It was impossible not to notice that his demeanor and his sense of humor had gone with it. It had drained out of him somewhere in those woods, never to return. Those who met him subsequently could not picture the animated and contagiously funny young man his colleagues had worked with for so many years.

A senior Delta commander took him aside one afternoon, a week after his return, and offered an exceptionally hard truth to this exceptionally hard soldier.

"The types of missions we're asked to lead – the types *you* have to go lead – never come to us with everything mapped out just perfectly so that all you gotta do is go color inside all those perfect little lines."

"I know, sir. Thank you, sir."

"Do you know? Because the problems that don't require any hard decisions – the kinds with all the thick black lines drawn out ahead of time that make it obvious how you're supposed to color it – those are the types of problems you give to mall cops or the Coast Guard. What we're doing here is calligraphy, soldier. It's art, it's technique, it's patience, and the lines cross, and they bend at stupid angles, and the outcome can seem pretty subjective if anyone but an expert is looking at it. We chose violence as a profession, and every one of us accepts the outcomes which accompany that."

"Yes, sir. Thank you, sir."

"This outfit cannot tolerate mistakes. And it also cannot try and pretend that accidents do not happen in our work. I accept both of those realities, and so did both squads you led out there. And we both know that there is unfinished business, even if you can't be there to wrap it up."

"Sir?"

"You won't be the last commander who deals with the grief of feeling like there's blood on his hands by washing it off with some more."

This was how Carl Horn transitioned to his mastery of global strategy and operation. His sapped interest in live combat exercises in the field offered him the opportunity to pursue an expanded proficiency of the methods and means by which situations could be analyzed, understood, controlled, and mitigated long before any direct action became necessary – and, when that action was required, to make the preparations behind those actions essentially foolproof. His creativity in devising these systems of information gathering and situational control hinted at what could only be described as a preternatural ability, and his acumen for this quickly exceeded his well-deserved reputation as a commander out in the field. This unique combination of abilities was impossible to miss further up the chain of command, and when the invitation from the Pentagon came to set up a worldwide version of what he had built for the Deltas, no one was surprised.

What was never far from his mind, from the moment he assumed his expanded role with the Deltas, up through today at the Pentagon, was that a mission he planned had left his friend and seven other operators dead, and in return he got a promotion because he knew how to fix the problem. He had returned to Fort Bragg with his stitches still bleeding and fully expecting to be relieved of his command, if not expelled from special operations entirely. Instead, his debrief at Bragg went down in history. For six hours a panel of senior officers listened to his fury boil over as he leveled a litany of critiques which had led to this mission's disaster, and he was unsentimental in explaining what ought to be dismantled, ripped out, and replaced to ensure this could never happen again. By the end there was no adjudication about his future, but, in the days following, instead of banishing him, the leadership put him in charge of addressing everything he had so furiously attacked.

And now he was here. He had failed out in the field that day; he had succeeded in transforming the profession. Extreme aptitude for an impossibly difficult job was a strange way to avoid the consequences of your actions. Such treatment was usually reserved for athletes and celebrities. What he accomplished in the Pentagon was unlikely to provide any consolation to the grieving families created that day, and he had yet to feel any satisfaction from his successes.

Since establishing the GOC, this quiet man receded even further into the sub-rosan nature of such a role. Years ago he had ensured his name and his organization's did not appear on any office doors, internal memos, or line-items in budget reports and HR files. The door to the GOC simply had "No Access" stenciled on it.

For the dozens of people working within the all-consuming environment of GOC it was a way of life. Horn was economical with his words and precise in every action, no matter how casual or unobserved. In this operations center there was something monastic about his isolation and the focus that came with it, and things were unmistakably hellish for who or what drew his attention.

He was still holding the shrapnel in his hand when he noticed the black phone hooked to a cryptographic box start ringing across the room. That was going to be at least one of the Joint Chiefs on the other end. He dropped the shard back into his pocket and watched as one of his aides lifted the phone.

The potential for a domino effect back here in the present was very, very real. This burgeoning conflict had all the right ingredients and anxieties needed to sweep up China, Russia, India, Pakistan, and the U.S. – just for starters. When you factored in their allies, that number got much bigger. And when you factored in other international ties, the number at least quadrupled.

The first thing he'd say into that encrypted phone, after listening quietly for the first 60 seconds, was that he agreed things need to get defused ASAP. He'd also agree with their assessment that defusing a tense engagement between two superpowers is indeed possible – if only barely – and if this wasn't handled with sufficient subtlety and nuance, they'd soon have to defuse a lot more.

He would also act surprised when the Joint Chiefs told him the information one of his senior officers had just shown him: The Secretary of Defense, the executive in charge of everything that happened in the Pentagon and the worldwide military, had just tipped the first domino by asking for assessments on the readiness of the carrier groups, submarine fleet, and air power. In parallel with this, he asked to see a first draft of a message that could potentially be sent out to the ambassadors of the three dozen countries who could get swept up in this about what to say to their respective heads of state regarding the value of cooler heads prevailing.

Horn had seen many times that the diplomatic process could be quite helpful, right up until the moment it wasn't. And that moment was usually a gunshot.

18 JUNE

On the opposite side of the country from Major Horn's bunker, at about the same time his car had reached the South Parking Lot near his office, Sienna Barrett woke up.

For the last 19 years it had been "Sienna Barrett Riley," which was a lot to write on forms or spell out over the phone, and most of those years had been spent in the quiet, heavily forested Seattle suburb of Sammamish, Washington.

She checked her phone to make sure nothing crazy had happened at work overnight, and then let the dog outside and found her shoes while she brushed her teeth. Five minutes and one Wordle solution later she was on the trail down the street from her house jogging towards a scenic ridge line 2 miles away. Forty minutes later she was home just in time to start hearing alarm clocks go off in different rooms upstairs.

Her oldest daughter, Calista, was already downstairs making pancakes – a Wednesday tradition that this very independent 12-year-old had started years earlier. In the beginning, this tradition seemed to put more batter on the countertop than the griddle, but she was a quick learner and now her siblings started looking forward to it days in advance. Upstairs the water was running, and that meant her oldest, Blaise, who was 14, was already in the shower. The last alarms she could hear belonged to Scarlett and Josephine, nine and seven – and they were taking their time getting up. If today were like any other, Scarlett would be laying on her face with a pillow over her head, and Josie would have made it halfway to her closet before laying back down on the carpet.

Once Sienna reminded Scarlett and Josie that there were pancakes downstairs, things started to move a bit faster. Josie crawled to the door, sniffed the air, and was convinced this story about pancakes was not a trick designed to get her to put on clothes. Sienna couldn't hear weights clanging in the garage anymore, so that meant her husband was done working out and would soon be inside to supervise the loosely organized chaos in the kitchen while lunches were packed and the dishwasher was unloaded.

Fifteen minutes later Sienna was out of the shower, pulling on a t-shirt, and putting the lanyard holding her work ID into a pocket. On her way down the hall, she checked on Blaise, who was still doing his hair in the bathroom. "Blazer, don't forget to brush your teeth before the orthodontist today; I think you're getting something tightened." Downstairs, Jordan was scrambling Scarlett an egg to go with the pancakes while a Zoom call on his phone droned away on mute off to the side. She kissed him goodbye, slapped him on the butt loud enough to make the kids groan, and gave everyone a hug on the way out.

Life for Sienna Riley was good, it was very normal, and she had no complaints.

Her time spent at Camp Loaf was a very distant memory, and she would often go weeks without thinking about it. Every couple of years she'd see a familiar face show up on a podcast talking about Cold War experiments and what that person may or may not have seen or done at a mysterious government location, but these conversations never got much further than Reddit, and they were treated like a type of storytelling you might describe as "fairy tales for adults." Sienna had never found it difficult to keep this secret, and, with some very minor exceptions, this perspective seemed universal amongst her fellow camp alumni.

She drove due east towards the mountains for 20 minutes, and at about the time the road started pitching upward she exited the freeway and headed down a long road where the forest grew right up to the edge of the concrete, and long branches a hundred feet above her cast heavy shade from the canopy. She showed her ID to the guard at the front gate, parked, showed the ID to another guard at the front door, and then walked down a long, mostly blank hallway. She made two right turns and finally reached a door where she swiped that same ID again and entered a room where a group of middle school-aged students sat at desks in matching jumpsuits. She said hello to the pair of guards standing in the back, greeted the kids, and made her way to the front of the room. The group was particularly dour looking today, and she noticed that almost everyone was trading glances and looking past her at the table which sat in front of the whiteboard.

She followed their gaze, saw the envelope, and walked over to it. This led to a few laughs and more shushes, and she read the handwritten scrawl on the outside of the letter. She looked back at the guards and the big one, Mason, nodded his head and said, "I already checked it."

Technically speaking, these kids were never supposed to approach the front of the room, but a little leeway was not the end of the world. She held up the envelope and read: "To the best English teacher at this school."

The classroom erupted in laughter. Somewhere in the back a voice rang out, "Cuz you're the *only* English teacher at this school!"

There was never a dull moment at the Washington State Center for Violent Juvenile Rehabilitation.

The WSCVJR did not have a name that was particularly beautiful compared to other middle schools in the region – with names like Mountain View, Pine Lake, and Cascade Crest – but this was not exactly a place where beautiful things happened. It was also a place that was almost invisible to the rest of the education system. Every student here, despite the fact that most of them were under 16 years old, had at one point committed a crime so exceptionally repugnant that they simply had to be incarcerated to ensure the ongoing safety of the people around them. Every state had at least one facility like this, and Washington's was here – tucked out of the way, at the end of a long road, existing anonymously halfway between downtown Seattle and the mountain pass where Sienna and her family skied in the winter.

Sienna had taught public school for years before having children, then spent several years at home with them, and, then, when the time came to go back to the classroom, she took a long look at where students were getting the least from the education system and what types of students needed the most help. It didn't take long to see how desperately teachers were needed in the places where children had reached the very bottom of the criminal justice system. She didn't and couldn't overlook or excuse the things they had done in order to get here, but she had seen enough of human nature to know that these children were victims of their environments long before they made victims of anyone else. Had any of her gentle, goofy, usually pleasant children grown up in the same infernal conditions that produced her 9:00 am class – they would be right there in the front row offering to do stick-and-poke tattoos in exchange for candy bars.

She waited for the roaring laughter to subside, and waved off the guards when they barked at the two big kids in the back who were pounding their desks a little too hard. She re-read the line on the envelope in the predictably wobbly handwriting – full-sized pencils were easy weapons, so students were issued miniature golf pencils to write with, and those did not lend themselves to fine motor functions.

"That's a good joke, boys, nice work," she said, rolling her eyes and getting another laugh from a room that appreciated she was going to engage with this particular joke. As she tore open the top of the envelope and pulled out the letter, a long-term resident named Kenny turned and shouted toward the back of the class, "Nah, that joke sucked, but Roger said we couldn't cuss or say anything nasty, so we had to clean it up." Sienna looked back at the other guard and smiled, "Thank you, Roger."

The letter had a full page of text on it, and, as she began to read, Kenny's cellmate, Marquiss, produced a handwritten copy. He passed it to the left and each contributor began reading the section of the letter they had written. Sienna was impressed that they had collaborated with each other on a project without a fist fight breaking out – or at least no one's face seemed to indicate a recent fist fight – and each section of the letter listed what they hated least about this year's class.

Perhaps on purpose, the reading of the letter took up the majority of the class time, and, at the end, the two students who hadn't contributed were arguing about why they weren't included. Tyler was mad no one had let him add something. Then Mario pointed out they'd worked on it during the three days he had escaped. Max claimed to have had a lot he wanted to add but didn't – and this explanation was interrupted by Miguel shouting across the room, "Because you don't know how to write, bro!" Now Max was on his feet and needed a warning from both guards before he sat back down.

The last line of the letter was written by Cameron. He was, by a fairly wide margin, one of the most gifted students, and, during his years at the school, he had responded particularly well to therapy and the structured routines of the facility. His past was especially violent, even by the standards of his fellow classmates, so his academic successes were not the subject of as much teasing as they might have been otherwise. When the letter made its way to him, he read: "During this school year, I learned things I never expected to learn at a prison like this. You always say, 'hurt people are the ones that hurt people,' and even though we're all pretty sure you got that from a TV show, you do treat us like real human beings, rather than Mr. Dougherty who sucks at teaching math and sucks as a person. I always figured that coming to a school like this would just teach me how to be a better criminal. But, when I got here, I discovered that this was completely true. I am probably way better at crime now, but I have limited ways to find out for sure. But a man can dream. Also, the other day during laundry duty, Craig said he had a dream about you once, and you know that dude is a pervert."

The entire room and one of the guards were now laughing hysterically. Craig was in shock.

"Ok, Cameron, thank you for that," Sienna said, trying desperately not to laugh in front of the class.

"Ok, ok, wait, I'm almost done," Cameron pleaded. Sienna used this as an opportunity to smile and cover up the laughter she could no longer hold in.

Cameron cleared his throat, took a very long deep breath, and continued, "Have a great summer." And he sat down.

"Thank you, everyone, that was very nice. I will see all of you again in September when class begins again; please be nice to Roger and Mason until then."

Four classes later – each of them segmented by the crime committed, except for the girls who were all lumped together in a single class – Sienna was back in her car and headed home. There were strange moments, every so often, when something in her classroom reminded her of Camp Loaf. There were not many similarities between her fellow campers 34 years ago and these current students, but there were times when her heart ached at the sight of these children, in a place they didn't understand, sent here because of actions they were too young to be fully accountable for but because of which they no longer had a place out in the world that suited them.

She promised each student who finished their sentence and left the facility that she would travel any distance across the state to attend their high school graduation, and she wrote back to every e-mail she got from students who had moved home, got a job, and started over. Sienna knew how hard it was to transition back to a normal life after a couple of years spent in the woods.

1989

5 Orientation

The first morning at Camp Loaf was relaxed, and three surprisingly large guys who didn't look like cooks were making breakfast. Each of the cooks were operating multiple waffle makers simultaneously to keep every plate full, and the campers ate together with the scientists at a long table. A sparrow flew in and out of the wide doors and through the rafters, and Sienna had the benefit of already knowing three of the fellow campers from the night before when they spent the evening helping get her set up in the cabin.

The campers went from breakfast to an hour of free time before class started, and Sienna felt very grown up now that she had fun roommates at a place she lived without her parents. The four of them walked the grounds of the camp showing Sienna the tree with a squirrel nest, the library in the barn, the heavily stocked snack bar right next to that, and the video games that would have put any mall arcade to shame. An earlier generation of girls at the camp had once lobbied for supplies to build a fort for their own purposes; when Dr. Torquemann had asked what purpose a fort would serve at a camp already filled with cabins, his question was dismissed immediately as ridiculous, and a list of required supplies was presented in lieu of an answer. Now the fort existed in a small ravine about 200 yards away from the dining hall, with a collection of boards making the walls and using two Blue Oaks and a Pacific Madrone as the anchor points for each corner. The roof was low, the gaps between the planks making up the wall were frequent and uneven, and it was a tight fit for more than six or seven people – but the long afternoons, weekends, and occasional star watching that took place at Fort Torch were the happiest memories of Sienna's childhood.

The campers were all very proud of the people who had come before them for convincing Torchy to let them build it. "Torchy," Sienna was told on the first day, was the fondly playful nickname every camper used for Dr. Torquemann. Up until that clarification, she had just assumed there was yet another scientist she hadn't yet met. The explanation, according to the story she heard, at least, was that early on in the program, one of the campers had mangled the pronunciation of the first syllable of the doctor's name so badly that his incredibly unique elocution stuck immediately.

During the mid-morning break from school, Torchy – Sienna knew she was going to start calling him this but didn't know how to do it for the first time – stopped by the class to bring Sienna over for a tour of the research cabin.

As they walked, the wind coming off the Bay picked up and both stuck their hands deep into their pockets to stay warm. As Torchy asked about her first day, Sienna interrupted with a question of her own. Ever since their first meeting back at the neurologist's office, Sienna had been reading books in her elementary school library about radios and radio waves, and what she learned had only added to the reasons she found this whole process so exciting.

Her question was roundabout enough that it never presented a specifically cogent point of inquiry, but he loved that she was thinking about this deeply enough to go seek out information on her own, and he particularly liked that she understood that ordinary messages took time to travel from one place to another, even if that principle didn't seem to apply to the Signal. Rather than continue to talk about hypothetical particles, he tried to explain the interplay of time, space, and information in terms he felt had a better chance of resonating with someone her age.

"The way information travels can do some strange things to our perception of time," he explained. "For example, Candlestick Park, where the Giants play, is about 10 miles that direction," he said pointing to the north. "And have you ever been to a game there and sat in the outfield seats – the ones really far away from home plate?" She nodded. She had actually been there for her birthday the year before, and she had eaten two whole boxes of Red Vines and then thrown up on the car ride home. "Well, when you are sitting in those outfield seats and you see the batter hit the ball, did you notice how when you see him take a swing it takes a second to finally hear the crack of the bat?" She nodded again. There had been two home runs at her birthday party game, but there had also been those two boxes of Red Vines, and, as a result, she had not noticed either hit. But that seemed unnecessary to explain right now.

"So what this tells us is that information can travel in different ways and at different speeds even when things are all happening at the same time. You saw the batter swing because light particles bouncing off the batter reached your eye, and those particles were bringing you that image at the speed of light, which is about 167 million miles per hour. The sound of the bat traveled to you as a sound wave, and that moves through the air at the speed of sound, which is about 767 miles per hour. That's why you see the swing before you hear the swing. But what's really interesting is what happens for all the people listening to the game on the radio. Because, just a couple feet away from the batter is a camera and a microphone – and, as soon as he swings, the sound wave reaches that microphone, travels as a radio wave from the ballpark to a stereo, and then someone listening 50 miles away hears it. The weird part is that because radio waves travel at the speed of light, the person listening on the radio is going to hear the crack of the bat before you do."

"The person 50 miles away hears it before the stadium?"

"Well, if you're in those faraway seats the sound has to travel about 400 feet to get to you, but for the people listening at home, the sound has to travel about 10 feet to the microphone, then it travels basically instantly to their radio, and then the sound moves another 10 feet from the radio to their ear. So, yeah, they hear it a lot sooner than you do."

Sienna had initially been unsure where this story was heading, but now her ten-year-old mind began to grasp the extent to which time and information could slide past each other on a scale.

"There's a few extra details to consider if you want to get really technical, but those are the main points," Torquemann concluded with a wave of his hand. "Some other time we'll talk about how everything I just said changes if that baseball game is being played on a giant spaceship traveling close to the speed light – because, in that case whether you're sitting on the ship or outside it changes what you see happen. But that's a conversation for a different day, and probably a different decade of your life."

A little over a decade later Sienna was at a baseball game and witnessed another homerun, which reminded her of this conversation. Later that night she spent an hour online researching the spaceship stadium scenario and found, as promised, that things would indeed get much weirder on a spaceship traveling 166.999999 million miles an hour. The Theory of Special Relativity apparently stipulated that if the ball was hit in the direction the spaceship was traveling at a speed of 167 miles per hour – which was apparently possible in the vacuum of space – then a person sitting on the ship watching this game would see something very different from someone watching this game as the spaceship went past. Specifically, the person inside would watch the ball arc through the air until it landed on the ground, and the person outside the ship would watch it freeze in spacetime for eternity the moment it hit the bat – and while all this was happening the person watching from outside would age 31 years relative to the person on the ship. Or something like that.

But that Pandora's box of partially understood theoretical physics was still very far away as Torchy and Sienna climbed the two small steps onto the porch of the research cabin. Torchy held open the door, and Sienna entered a well-lit room with a domed roof, a comfortable looking chair that seemed to be the center of attention, and, around that, horseshoe-shaped rows of desks covered with screens and machines. There were several pieces of equipment in this room which, much like tachyons, were still theoretical to most of the scientific world, although almost all of them would be in hospitals and observatories within 15 years.

Torquemann was never quite sure how to introduce this room, but he also didn't want any of the kids to feel like lab rats. The NRO's child psychologists had demonstrated that the children would feel more at ease in a room where they had been introduced to every piece of equipment and none of the machinery felt unknown or foreign; Torchy took that suggestion to heart and he had grown adept at explaining this impossibly complex setup to children.

"Let's start in the front row, shall we?" he said, gesturing to a large screen as if it were a distant relative whose hand she was supposed to shake. "This screen is Computerized Axial Tomographer. You've heard of CAT scans right? It's like one of those except we've made a few upgrades so that you don't have to lay on your back in a big tube – instead we've put all the pieces of the tube up in the dome above the chair. This lets us see really detailed cross-section pictures of your brain, without us having to go open up your head to see those cross-sections for ourselves." He pretended to karate chop her on the forehead, and this got a laugh, so he moved on to the next box.

"This is a Near-infrared Spectroscope and it measures the levels of oxygen and blood flow to your brain. Your brain needs both of those things, and the levels can change based on what kind of stress you're feeling, or if you're overstimulated, or if you fall asleep and start snoring while we're working on something important."

They moved on to the third machine which, like usual, was vibrating a little.

"This is a Diffusion Tensor Imager, and, as you can see, we have it hooked up to this other machine which is a High Angular Resolution Diffusion Imager. All of these seemingly random words mean that this is one of those pieces of equipment that probably won't make it to your average hospital until you have grandkids, but what it does is track the water molecules moving around inside your brain so that we can better understand how the electricity and other materials are bouncing around in there. So this machine also saves us the need to karate chop your head open. It's kind of a bummer because karate chopping is fun, but it's good because Dr. Tunis is the one who has to clean up all that mess, and he's tired of it."

In the next row was a box that looked like it had a spotlight bolted to the top. "This is an Intrinsic Optical Imager, and it sends light waves at you that get absorbed by your optical nerve, and then we watch how these specific light waves enter your brain. This helps us map the changes your brain goes through while you're thinking about something and the connections that are made along the way."

"What if I think of something really crazy and it freaks you out?" she said with a grin.

"Luckily for me, it doesn't show us what you're thinking about, but it helps us understand *how* you're thinking about whatever it is. This machine right next to the mind reader is an Electroencephalogram machine. All the early models make you wear this net on your head made out of sensors, but we just built those into the chair – this way your hair won't get messed up, so you're welcome. This shows us how that electricity in your brain is moving around or bunching up in one spot, or both.

A few machines later they were in the third row where she was shown a Single-photon Emission Computed Tomographer. "You remember us talking about gamma rays, right?"

"Yup," she lied.

"Well, this machine uses them to create a 3D picture of your brain at any given moment so that we can see how things are going in there – from the molecular level all the way up to the lobes." This shared a table with a Magnetoencephalogram, which, Torchy explained, was able to study the brain functions that happen very fast, like sensory perception and language processing. "This way, when you're hearing or seeing or even feeling things from the Signal, the MEG can help keep track of how your brain is absorbing it."

The rest of the third row and all of the back row were dedicated to machines measuring readings from deep space and cross-referencing that information with what was being picked up from inside the brain. If a tachyon could move anywhere and do it faster than light, then Torchy wanted to see where in the observable universe it was bouncing around before or after it passed through this cabin or some frozen outpost in the Soviet Union. So far, they hadn't seen much on these deep-space maps, but they were still looking.

In addition to the astronomical equipment you could find at any well-funded observatory, there was also gravitational wave detectors, cosmic ray detectors, interferometers, a direct link to a gamma ray telescope, an Extragalactic Cosmic Microwave Background Polarimeter, and two devices which were new enough to remain unnamed, although a future generation of stellar cartographers would refer to them as a neutrino detector and a quantum interferometer, respectively.

This much equipment made the room perpetually warm, which was pleasant for about half the year, and it also gave this cabin the distinction of being among the most expensive wooden structures to ever stand on planet Earth. On several occasions the scientists had recreationally tallied up the cost of what had been packed into the room, but it was difficult to put a price tag on half a dozen pieces of machinery which wouldn't enter civilian use this century.

Sienna was very curious to see how this was all used and to see it in use, but Torchy explained that today's visit was just a meet and greet. He took her back outside and across the common area so she could return to class.

"Tomorrow, after lunch, let's meet back at the research cabin and see what we can find in the Signal, ok?"

They arrived back at class just as the teacher was starting a lesson about what the sun was made out of. This lesson turned out to be her first experience with the way nearly every lesson at this school ended up going down deep, winding, and fascinating rabbit holes instead of staying on topic.

Today's lesson began simply enough with the teacher commenting, "The light you see from stars is the oldest thing you will ever see – in some cases, that light has been traveling for 2,500 years through space before you look up and see it."

This was clearly something the class had never considered.

"Some of those stars you're looking at are 10 trillion miles away, and there are planets circulating around those stars, and the light you're seeing today is the light those planets saw two millennia ago – and it flew right past them and has been moving toward us ever since."

"Which light is the oldest?" asked Sam.

"I have no idea which one it is exactly, but remember the star we talked about yesterday from the constellation Orion – the one called Betelgeuse – that one is 700 light-years away. So, when you see it twinkling tonight just think about how those twinkles used to be sunlight shining down on the planets revolving around it back when the Magna Carta was getting signed, and the Mongols were invading Poland here on Earth. And just now it's finally getting here. It's kind of amazing to think about those photons traveling through empty space for all these years and then hitting your eye on some random night."

"It's sort of like time travel," Jamie said.

"It is a glimpse into the past," the teacher agreed.

"So, time travel does kind of exist?" Leah asked.

"You have to keep one key fact about time travel in mind," the teacher said, leaning back against the edge of his desk. "We know it doesn't exist in the future because no one has ever come back to tell us about it."

This insight kicked off a discussion which included one student wondering out loud if, perhaps, the reason no time travelers had arrived yet was because "no one in the past had invented it yet either." This comment caused the teacher to exaggeratedly stumble backwards, suppress a smile, put his hand over his forehead, and ask for a moment to sort out what he had just heard. The class howled with laughter and the guards in the building next door looked up from their game of pinochle to listen for a moment before determining everything was ok.

"I can't figure out if what you just said is brilliant or maybe the dumbest string of words ever uttered in a classroom setting."

The class kept laughing.

"That question assumes so many things about the nature of time, general relativity, and the quantum state of the Universe. Like, you're assuming that the past and future exist as pre-built states which already exist in the space-time continuum and that you are simply projecting your consciousness into this current instance of reality – but, at a future state, certain technological breakthroughs are occurring. It also assumes that your consciousness is the predominating arbiter of both reality and time, so any future inventions are reliant on you entering that timeframe in order for 'the future' to 'finally happen' despite you remaining at this moment in time."

Obviously, none of the kids knew what 90% of this meant, but they knew it was funny – and Sienna beamed with pride at having successfully moved the classroom discussion to this fevered pitch. This teacher would later be recognized as one of the great physics researchers of his era, but the four months spent at this camp and in this classroom was something he would think about with a smile and a shake of the head whenever a new accolade was added to his top-secret resume.

* * * * *

That afternoon, after classes but before dinner, Sienna had the first of many conversations about what her fellow campers had seen or heard in the Signal that day. Since her first crackle, since her first trip to the neurologist, and since arriving at camp, she had kept seeing or hearing peripheral sights and sounds – and she learned, to her relief, that this was pretty normal for everyone at camp, and no one was particularly bothered by it. There was comfort to be found in knowing it was a Russian radio and not a tumor.

The other girls in her cabin filled her in on one of the details she had missed while staring into the various screens and pretending to type on the polarimeter earlier that day: The entire research cabin was lined with a material that focused the Signal down onto that point where the chair was sitting – kind of like how you could focus light with a magnifying glass to burn a leaf. Fortunately, a focused tachyon couldn't set things on fire. At least not people. At least not yet. At least not at this camp. At least not to anyone these kids had met. At least not yet.

6 Focus

11 OCTOBER

Sienna woke up that morning with her turn in the research cabin already on her mind.

Her roommates were positive and reassuring, as was everyone in class. When the time came, she strolled to the cabin with Dr. Tunis, walked up to the chair like she'd done it countless times before, and sat down with all the confidence she could muster. Every scientist in the room noticed the performance, and they preferred it to timidity.

The night before, Torquemann had invited her to watch a research session with one of her roommates, so she felt fairly confident about what to expect and what to do. From the outside it looked like a lot of sitting and concentrating and trying to see or hear what was in those flashes rather than being startled and blurting out "What the heck was that?" in the middle of a piano lesson – which had been her reaction the first time it happened.

Earlier that day, right after breakfast, she and Dr. Torquemann had walked a couple laps around the camp to talk about the process of sitting and listening in the chair. They strolled along the edge of the camp, close enough for Sienna to run her fingers along the unusually thick chain links while she walked.

After a few minutes of walking, two of the security guys wandered up from the cabin where they lived next to the barn – a location that, not coincidentally, had ideal snack proximity. Dr. Torquemann waved as they came up the hill and kept walking. One of the guards started walking about 75 feet ahead, and the other trailed the same distance behind. They each held a rifle close to their chest, and their heads never stopped looking back and forth while they walked. As they approached, they both said one of the many combinations of "hey, kid" and "what's up boss" and "hello, ma'am" and "hey dudes" that they used to greet any camper they crossed paths with during the day. In so many other settings, it would have been unbearably uncomfortable to always have characters this big and mean-looking hovering nearby, but there was something unmistakable in their demeanor that made it obvious that they were here to protect the camp and everyone in it. This made their presence genuinely comforting – and it helped that they smiled when they talked to the kids, that they all joked amongst each other, and that they could be coaxed into telling cleaner versions of those jokes to the kids. It also helped that, on any given day, the campers saw them making French toast or pancakes in the morning, and then, later on in the evening, they could be observed telling incredible lies like, "I made you guys this lasagna from scratch" when it was obviously a frozen entree from Costco.

"There are a thousand things about the Signal we don't entirely understand yet," he admitted for the third or fourth time. "And everything your fellow campers have got from it so far has been just bits and pieces of information – like, a few words but not a sentence; fragments of images but never a complete picture; and the feelings are always pretty despondent."

This was also the third or fourth time he'd mentioned the way the campers felt while they were listening to the Signal.

"Why does the Signal make them feel sad?" she asked. "Is the stuff they're seeing really sad?"

That was another of the inevitable questions the campers asked, and he was betting the other unavoidable question was coming up next.

"The emotional part of the Signal is one of the things we never expected at the beginning. At first we thought that the initial group of kids in the program were just overwhelmed by what they were seeing or maybe they were homesick – but, when they'd talk with the psychologist we have here, they were all pretty excited about what they were seeing, not depressed. So, it was quite a while later that we discovered that there are properties of tachyon-based communication that embed the state of mind of the communicator into the message."

It was clear this part wasn't making sense yet.

"Think of it like this: You know how your brain is full of electrical impulses? And you know how all the emotions you're feeling are, at any given moment, a very complex combination of electricity, right?"

Sienna nodded. This much she understood.

"Well, from what we can tell, when the tachyons move from the sender of the message to the receiver of that message, they don't just move the information itself – they also bring along an imprint of the electrical state of the sender's brain, and that tells you pretty much exactly how the sender is feeling at the time the message is sent."

He looked down at Sienna and could tell she was still trying to sort this out.

"Weird," she finally said.

"Yeah, pretty weird. I'm sure the Russians didn't plan on this being a part of their radio."

"And every message in the Signal is sad?"

"Yes."

"Every single one?"

"All of them."

They walked in silence for a moment.

"All of the ones with words in them, at least. The pictures are just pictures."

They walked for another minute in silence while Sienna turned this over in her mind. Then came the other expected question:

"If this comes from Russia, why can we understand it? None of my roommates speak Russian, and none of the girls at Fort Torch do either?"

"Oh, you've been to Fort Torch?" he said, laughing, and briefly changing the subject.

They both laughed, and then he brought things back around.

"That's another good question, and I don't think you're going to love the answer. In much the same way that communication with tachyons can copy the state of mind of the person sending something, it also appears to break down the message into concepts or ideas rather than a collection of words."

Sienna scrunched up her face and stared back at him like he was speaking gibberish. In a sense, he was.

The answers to both of these questions strayed so far outside of what science presently understood about the properties of the Universe that answers like these could only address "what" was happening without even attempting to explain the "how" or "why." If Sienna were eight or nine years older, he would try explaining how quantum entanglement was a phenomenon that had been proven to exist but a satisfying explanation for *why* it existed was still entirely beyond the grasp of the best theoretical physicists. But someone with a brain developed enough to understand *that* would have no place *here*.

"Maybe it helps to think back to that radio tower again," he said hopefully. "When the tower sends a song to your car, it isn't sending musical notes through the air – it's sending a bunch of tiny pieces of electrical information to your radio with instructions that are kind of like a recipe for what sound the speakers should make. And that recipe is the song you're hearing."

Sienna stared straight ahead. She had no idea listening to music in the car was this complicated. It made the idea of her dad listening to the news seem even more boring.

"This comparison isn't perfect," Torchy conceded, "but when words are said on one side of the Signal, there is something about the process of breaking it down into pieces tiny enough to be carried by a tachyon that strips away the vocabulary and leaves only the intention of what was said. That's why, when the Signal gets to your brain and it's reassembled into something intelligible, you understand it in whatever words you already have that match its intention."

"That brain wart is doing a lot of work," Sienna said deadpan.

"It is," Torquemann agreed. "It took us a long time to develop a clear idea of how this might be working, but we're pretty certain that the way the Signal hits that ridge of neurons helps the information radiate out into those two overlapping areas of your brain where you're processing language, visual perception, and just perception in general – so you end up getting the *feeling* of the message, and you also get the intellectual *substance* of the message."

"And that's what the recipe makes," Sienna said, staring at a strange animal eating grass under a nearby bush. "Like a cake."

"A what?"

"The things everyone in camp feels and hears, that's the cake – the Signal has a recipe in it, and our brain makes a cake out of it."

He smiled. "I suppose that's about right," he agreed, and sidestepped a gopher hole. "That's a pocket gopher back there, by the way," he said, "I think it's the mascot of a high school around here, or something."

He called ahead to the security guard – the one that the kids all called "Bob" for no reason whatsoever – and indicated they were going to start heading back down toward the cabins.

As they walked down the gentle switchbacks Torchy said, "I'll see you after school gets out, just come down to the research cabin when you're ready."

* * * * *

Three hours later all the doctors, scientists, and other technicians were standing by when she arrived.

Every machine was already stirring, and they were ready to begin – and, for reasons that would have made sense to no one else, the concept of the cake she was there to make had given her an extra sense of swagger.

She took her seat on the chair, just like she had seen her roommate do the day before. Above her in the dome was a hum that was barely audible but still unmistakable to the point of being something which might be distracting to all this listening that was about to happen. Someone off to the side dimmed the lights, and the room was now mostly dark aside from the small beam of light coming from the machine meant to do some version of reading her thoughts.

Dr. Torquemann walked up, rested his foot on the light-gray ring that looked like a gigantic, 10-foot-wide hula-hoop around the chair, and leaned in to reach her eye level. This ring, she was told later, was connected to all the machinery up in the ceiling.

"How are you feeling, my friend? You want to see what there is to see today?"

She pointed to her ear, "I'm getting a kind of..." She struggled to pick just the right way to explain it in a way that sounded scientific enough since this was, after all, the research cabin.

"It's already humming?" he asked, obviously delighted.

"Yes," she replied, kicking herself for not just saying that.

He smiled and turned to the back of the room, "Hamza, she's

already got it!"

She was confused, but, after a moment, he turned back around to explain.

"So, now that you have the Signal, why don't you clear your mind, relax, close your eyes if you want, and start listening."

Now the meditation classes Torchy had everyone attend in the afternoons made sense. The story she had heard about the materials in the ceiling focusing the Signal were also apparently very true.

It took less than a minute of stillness for the first flash to enter her mind.

What had, during that fateful piano lesson with Mrs. Martinez, felt so jarring now made a lot more sense. Instead of reeling from the impact of it, now it felt like she was chasing it back into the oblivion from where it had emerged in order to get a better look at it. The moment that image crackled in and out of view she could hear, like it was happening in another room, the sound of machines suddenly whirring to life. She could hear the fans on multiple computers begin spinning and then straining, and the giant plotting machine on the back wall began to sweep from side to side, as if it were chasing the same thing she was. The slow cadence of beeps in that distant room was now a regular set of staccato chirps, and she could hear half a dozen sets of hands on keyboards with unnecessarily sharp clicks at the bottom of each keystroke.

The next image began to take shape slowly, and, with her eyes squeezed shut, she leaned forward instinctively to get a better look. The focus sharpened for a moment, and she could suddenly hear the words as if they were coming from underwater.

This is another attempt.
The following information –

She gasped.

She remembered the instruction to repeat whatever she heard, and, in the distance she could hear that everyone was now typing much faster. The words seemed to echo for a moment and then disappear. As soon as they were gone, she sensed something else coming.

There is currently a –

There was a hard stop.

And silence.

She opened her eyes to check the room. Her eyes took a second to adjust to the light, and she saw Dr. Torquemann step towards her.

"How are you feeling, kiddo? That was kind of interesting, right? Do you want to call it a day?"

"I'm good" she reassured him, anxious to get back to it.

She closed her eyes again, and on this attempt needed less than half the time to catch a glimpse of a sphere that seemed stretched or warped into a new shape – but it seemed caught in between two phases, so she couldn't tell what the new shape would be. As instructed the day before, she explained everything she saw as best she could. The typing continued, the fans on the computers and processors around the room kept spinning. The thought occurred to her that no one here probably knew any of the rap songs her brothers played at home constantly, so she could just start reciting lyrics and blow everyone's mind. As that thought began to take root, everything went dark again.

"Oh," she thought to herself, "that's why they say you gotta focus."

A moment later she was back, the hum in her mind rose and fell, but other than a handful of more crackles, and just a piece of the first words she had already heard, the following 25 minutes of this research session were uneventful. It was as if she had tuned in just as the interesting stuff was wrapping up, and then that day's broadcast was over. She would soon learn that the substance of what any of the campers could see or hear in the Signal was inconsistent and sporadic, even for the few in camp who seemed to come across the most information.

When the time was up, every one of the researchers in the room came up to shake her hand and to congratulate her on a great first session.

Dr. Torquemann and Dr. Carney walked with her back to the barn where they knew her friends would be, and when they arrived she ran off to discuss everything that had happened. It was unlikely she heard their reminder to at least get a start on reading the book that had been assigned in class today. A week later an earthquake would rattle the camp – a seismic event made particularly historic because it happened during the local World Series – but it would be this half hour that would stand out in her memory as the most significant moment of that autumn.

"I think that was a productive enough first day for our new

camper," he said.

"Speaking strictly as a child psychologist, I'm very happy with her attitude and the way she rolled with it in a proactive and creative way, considering that this is an objectively very weird thing to do."

"Yeah, I thought that was great," he agreed.

"It does take a lot of work out in the field to determine if a 10 or 11-year-old with a perfectly shaped brain is also highly adventurous and emotionally resilient – and then, on top of that, if they're inclined toward diving into the unknown rather than running from it."

Torquemann nodded and asked, "So, if the psychiatrist part of you liked it, what does the magnetoencephalogramist part think?"

"Her brain lit up in all the standard ways when she heard those first words. It was nothing revolutionary, but she was definitely right in the thick of the Signal."

"I can work with that," he said. "All we need is to break through once."

PRESENT DAY

18 JUNE

Sienna pulled into the garage just before 4pm and immediately began working to extract her phone from the impossible place it had fallen between the seat and the center console. By this time the three girls would be home from school, and Blaise would be somewhere between the Starbucks across the street from his middle school and lacrosse practice.

Once she got inside everything looked normal: Josephine was lying upside down on the living room couch, with her head resting on the carpet and her feet up on the pillows, reading a book and petting the dog. Outside she could hear a hammer pummeling something into oblivion, and she walked out onto the back deck to find Scarlett finishing work on an impromptu fort that seemed, even by child-sized standards, small.

"It's for the squirrels to use against the raccoons," she replied when asked about the size.

"Are the squirrels and raccoons fighting? Do they do that?"

"Mom, we've been over this."

"Do they even eat the same food?"

"I know, mom, it's all very sad; there's enough resources in this forest for everyone, but you know how raccoons can be."

This was all explained very matter-of-factly by someone who had spent Christmas break reading a three-foot-tall stack of *National Geographic* magazines which had been found in the "free" pile of a nearby garage sale. There must have been something in that stack about North American forest creatures.

On the other side of the house, Calista had something baking even though the sink still needed help recovering from all the pancake batter earlier that morning. This smelled like the second batch she had produced this week, and it was only Wednesday. Most people would be surprised by how quickly a 50-pound bag of flour can be emptied, but Sienna had learned all it took was about two months, one passionate baker, and an additional five willing eaters.

By this time in the afternoon Jordan would, hopefully, be getting close to wrapping up meetings with his team on the east coast, and that meant he'd wander upstairs to cook whatever he had planned for dinner. It was his week to cook, but, even when it wasn't his turn, he could always be counted on to fill in a couple times. There were enough differing perspectives on food in this family to make just about any meal the subject of withering scrutiny from at least one person, but, overall, his batting average was very good.

Sienna had always thought the term "super dad" was painfully corny and worthy of sustained mockery, perhaps because Mike had been disinterested in the title, but Jordan was certainly in the ballpark for this categorization – even if the kids were quick to point out each of the things they thought qualified as demerits. It was his own fault for introducing them to the phrase "we only roast the ones we love." Well-deserved demerits aside, he was, without question, a dad whose heart was set on his kids, and they, in turn, regularly invented reasons throughout the day to knock on the door of his basement office just to hang out. The kids thought he was hilarious, and he thought he was even funnier than they did, and almost all of his sense of humor was lost on Sienna. But she liked that he liked that they liked it.

This place and the people in it were Sienna's joy. This was everything she had ever wanted. She loved her children in a way and with a fierceness that only mothers could summon, and this small group of humans was what filled her heart and drove her crazy and brought her peace and kept her awake.

But, as was the fashion, things that shined brightly when placed in the best possible light were often not entirely realistic.

Sienna, in quiet, honest moments, knew she was too hard on her children. Any introductory textbook on child psychology will spend dozens of pages examining the many ways in which a child who is burdened with intense feelings of failure due to unmet expectations will carry that complex assortment of emotions into adulthood – and then, in their own subsequent parenting, this potent, unresolved melancholy will often present itself as unnecessary pressure to excel. She was self-aware enough to know this about herself and to understand where it came from, and, after reading through what seemed like half the parenting books on Amazon, she had come to temper this urge fairly effectively, with a few exceptions which then offered her a chance to show her children how to admit mistakes and apologize.

Her marriage was highly functional, if not entirely blissful. She had married young enough to be romantic about it, but not quite old enough to be practical. The wedding was beautiful and a truly happy core memory: Friends and family at a beachside ceremony on a quiet cove, even the seabirds and waves seemingly drawing silent for a few precious moments of vows and professions, and then the excitement which comes with taking life's major steps. The subsequent years had presented a veritable cornucopia of bumps and other difficulties, particularly during those earliest years, but there was nothing that had presented itself as ultimately insurmountable.

The loyalty promised in those vows remained intact, but now it most often took the form of duty and convention, rather than the rom-com concepts of sentiment and devotion.

It wasn't until years afterward, when the stress of raising three kids under five-years-old plus an infant had subsided, and when they had both fallen into the steady routine of raising kids that she began to have the distance necessary to understand the source of her chronic frustration with Jordan during those early years. The short version of a very long story was fairly simple: As a young adult, Jordan introduced regular doses of unintentional chaos thanks to his near-complete inability to plan for the future. While he could certainly operate in the present and take into account the needs of the near-term, in those early years together Jordan avoided anything that would require him to think beyond the arc of the horizon right in front of him – his relationship with Sienna notwithstanding. And, for a planner and an organizer and a list-maker and a worrier like Sienna, this radically different approach to the world was the biggest possible disconnect with her spouse.

The early years of marriage bring challenges to any couple, but

Jordan's shortcomings in this department brought more than usual. Particular strain came from the multiple attempts he needed to get his career off the ground, and the unemployed periods between those reboots caused the predictable friction, and, perhaps, a little doubt for both of them. At the time, Sienna viewed his immaturity and these failures as *weakness* rather than his ultimate maturation and subsequent successes as *perseverance*. Jordan had been a speculative investment that, financially at least, had certainly paid off after those protracted initial stumbles, but it had required a lot of work and even more patience to reach that point. He ultimately came away from those many years of living with a frustrated wife readily willing to admit that he had contributed far more than his fair share to it, but also with the conclusion that what he had assumed was a bottomless source of strength inside of her was, perhaps, just an infinite hardness.

All of these conclusions, as misguided and misinformed as many of them were, had long ago made their way into the fundamental beliefs upon which they each built – and, like so many architectural foundations, it spent most of its time out of sight and out of mind. It was important to consider, however, a secret every construction foreman knows but never says out loud for fear of its slippery slope: A foundation with a few imperfect stones and a few sloppy areas of concrete could still be counted on to hold up a beautiful building, especially if the rest of that structure is built by craftsmen who get progressively more talented over time.

The metaphor didn't hold up perfectly, but, had it ever been said out loud, it would have made sense to both of them.

Everything else about their relationship had turned out, in a word, average. And that outcome was acceptable and sustainable – and it would have been a dramatic improvement for millions of other marriages. But, a pessimist might point out, no one dreams of average or wishes for more of it. A marriage counselor would say that most marriages, including the good ones, took this form eventually, and that what a couple and a family require from marriage are bonds that are both strong and do not inadvertently harm the things inside or around them. Instead, what that family requires from a marriage is a protected place filled with love and opportunities to grow. By any measure, this met the definition of the family Sienna and Jordan had built. Although "built," as any couple knows, is a strong word; so much of what constitutes a relationship – in particular, theirs – is simply something you find yourself with as the cumulative amalgamation of thousands of tiny decisions, actions, and interactions.

Sienna had spent many years trying to be a strong and self-contained person that did not require external emotional inputs or the validation of others in order to be happy – and she expected the same from Jordan. What both of them knew but would never put into words is that Jordan loved her more than she loved him. And both of them accepted that. If hooked up to a polygraph machine and asked if she loved her husband, Sienna would pass with flying colors. If a linguist or a behavioral psychologist then began exploring how she defined and lived through that word, that's where things might get interesting. Jordan, on the other hand, believed that he had always liked women who played hard to get, but really it was much simpler than that: His own backstory made it nearly impossible to take anyone who liked him seriously. Unsurprisingly, Sienna's aloofness made him adore her even more. And this was the strange, but not terribly rare, ground where they met and built something beautiful.

Sienna and Jordan each carried stories with them that went undivulged but which shaped them and their relationship, nonetheless. They were not stories that fell into the category of "deep and dark," but they had been sufficiently character-shaping at long-distant points in life, and they were foundational enough that they were very rarely reflected upon.

For Jordan it was the fact that everything about adulthood was unforeseen and unexpected. Adulthood hadn't caught him off guard because he was ignorant, but because he had been led to believe it would never happen.

The year before Jordan was born, his father, Robert, had joined a small religious movement which believed the end of the world would very likely arrive within the next 15 to 20 years. In the meantime, the adherents were encouraged to be upstanding members of society and live normally – but with the understanding that, at any moment, they would finally be called to gather in the geographic center of the country and witness the cataclysmic moment wherein something nebulously defined would happen to both reward them for their obedience and usher them into heaven.

Robert was smitten by his new-found faith, and devoted himself to it, and, like any dutiful convert, he taught it to his family. Friends who knew Robert and his kids would not have described any of them as particularly unusual, even if Robert was a bit overbearing and opinionated when discussing current events. But, in his defense, he simply lived 30 years before having a "hot take" on poorly understood topics was considered an acceptable way to communicate. But what never came up in conversation, however, even with close friends and relatives, was Robert's understanding that eventually his family would be called to this gathering, and, at this point, they would drop everything, load up the car, and head east. Chances were, Robert explained to his children, that by this time the world would be in such dire straits that the car would only take them so far before gas shortages and other calamities forced them to walk the rest of the way – and they would all happily do so with righteous pride in their hearts while the sun and this wicked planet sank out of sight behind them.

This topic did not come up often, but whenever it did, it was discussed as a matter of fact.

Considering how infrequently this tenet of the religion was discussed, it had an incredible effect on Jordan. Because he had been taught in no uncertain terms that his mid-teen years would be spent walking to greet the world's end, Jordan never spent a single moment thinking about reaching adulthood, or being in his 20s, or having a real job. Doing so would have seemed like a ridiculous mental exercise, and it seemed sacrilegious and irreverent to expect to reach such an advanced age. Jordan never gave any thought to what he wanted to be when he grew up, he never wondered about what to study in college, he never thought about where he'd like to live, and he never considered falling in love, starting a family, or growing old.

By the time Jordan was 14 his father had drifted away from the church, but the family never had a discussion about the fact that the future was now probably going to happen. Jordan had always felt the idea of the mass gathering seemed unlikely, but somehow the message about not having a future stuck with him. By the time high school started, he was impervious to the pressure to ace tests, prepare for SATs, and research colleges. And, as high school progressed, he noticed far too late the horrible corner that this worldview had painted him into. But *that* was another set of memories altogether.

The reconstruction of Jordan's belief in the future took a long time, and the extent to which it was incomplete continued to rear its head for years. One of the earliest arguments he and Sienna had was about how much of their salaries to set aside for retirement or a rainy-day fund. Jordan found both ideas preposterous because, he reasoned, "Shouldn't we might as well spend it now?" When an incredulous Sienna overlooked the grammar and instead just asked him why, Jordan was horrified to notice that the reason which leapt to the forefront of his mind was: "Because, obviously, none of us are even going to be here when we reach retirement age."

Jordan hadn't thought about or believed in the need to walk to the middle of the country for years by that point, but here it was impacting his opinions on creating a 401(k). It was purely ridiculous, and he loathed it about himself. But, if a silver-lined cloud could be found anywhere in this thunderstorm, it was that every new phase of life was now a beautiful and preciously unexpected gift. For a guy who once saw the far-distant expiration date on a credit card and thought "yeah right," there was something enchanting about seeing his retirement fund grow and thinking of ways to spend his free time someday.

Sienna, perhaps ironically for a teacher, had her own foundational moment *outside* of a school – or at least "outside" of a school she might have attended.

While she was away at Camp Loaf the construction of a new grade school had been completed, and it was set to open the following autumn after she returned home. This particular school was set to include her school district's "gifted program," and, of course, Ginny signed Sienna up to take the aptitude test for prospective students. The program and the test were both things Ginny had heard about from the other moms in the neighborhood, and two other girls from down the street were there when Sienna showed up for the test.

Sienna liked the sound of a program like this, and she took the test with the commensurate level of seriousness. She was in the living room watching cartoons three weeks later when the phone rang, and she watched her mother take the call on the old rotary phone attached to the kitchen wall. For some reason, perhaps it was just the way the phone happened to ring that day, or maybe it was the fact that the Barrett's got so few phone calls, but Sienna suspected correctly that it was from the people assessing her test.

It only took about two seconds of body language from Ginny for Sienna to know the results.

She listened for about 20 seconds, said "Yep, ok" a couple times, then said, "Thanks," and then hung up.

She craned her neck to see across the room, met Sienna's gaze, rolled her eyes, and said, "Well, that settles that."

And it was never spoken about ever again, like the entire thing had never happened.

Sienna was a perfectly good student before and after that, with nothing particularly spectacular to report or correct, but her experience cruising beneath the bar set by that test was always somewhere in the back of her mind. Under any set of normal circumstances, it's possible she would have forgotten about this entirely – but, as fate would have it, it was not that simple. The corner where Sienna stood every morning to take the bus two miles north to school was situated directly across the street from where the two girls from her neighborhood stood to catch the bus to the gifted program three miles to the west.

Every morning she would stand there, gripping the straps of her backpack, looking in every direction except straight across at the smart kids waiting to be taken somewhere she did not qualify to attend. There wasn't even any righteous indignation she could summon – she hadn't done anything wrong, per se, and those girls hadn't done anything "right." This separation was simply a matter of who she was as a person and the intellect that the crapshoot of genetics and biology had given her. And thus, every single day of school began with this small, quick reminder. This was all, of course, petty, strange, and even a bit pathetic – but children are generally not capable of choosing the way they process the reminders they get each day, especially when they would really rather not get them at all.

At multiple stages Sienna was left to rebuild her life while carrying a secret that defied categorization. World leaders had historically sent hundreds of thousands to their deaths for things that were comparatively worthless. Jordan also rebuilt himself, but with precious few tools and with no value to offer anyone.

Jordan did this by finding friends and building an identity that could fall in line with what he wanted to be.

Within those first days of returning home from Camp Loaf, the *new* Sienna was already under construction. She sought out hopeless causes where she could volunteer, found the bus route to take her there and back, and showed up with a forged permission slip from Ginny. She signed up for the clubs at school with the least attention but the highest potential. She wanted to be meaningful and anonymous and useful, and she wanted to do something worthy of love and gratitude without ever getting close enough to the recipients of her hard work and thus risk being told to her face how much she mattered.

When she met Jordan years later, her personal construction project had not lost any of its willpower or energy, and the contrast of his total inability to plan for a future or even conceive of doing so was, at first, mistaken by her as a refreshingly lighthearted approach to the stresses of early adulthood. They fell in love and began to talk about a future together – much sooner and faster than either anticipated – and so much of that velocity came from Sienna's desperation to build a future that could overshadow a past that was too painful to use as a launchpad.

They would have made a passionate combination as teenage sweethearts who could enjoy all the ways that opposites attract at that age, but they were a poor match as adults. What each of them discovered in the other were converse personality traits which were so foreign that they were misunderstood as endearing quirks. But, despite being so different, there were strengths each of them needed from their partner but neither possessed.

Early on it was Sienna who had the most to offer – a fact she resented since what she wanted most was a partner who was a source of stability in those difficult early years of adulthood. Yet, in time, Jordan grew into all of his potential, and he became many of those things she needed most, and they became true equals – which was only possible because they finally became true opposites.

It was difficult to know Jordan or Sienna without understanding their reactions to their own personal crucibles or their particular path up to the point wherein their trajectories collided, but so many of these were tales neither husband nor wife ever told. These formative moments had happened far enough in the past as to seem inconsequential to the present. These stories were, however, the impetus for so much of the wall-building both of them had done to protect themselves from ever suffering through those feelings again, and they had grown so accustomed to those fortifications that they never considered tearing them down and using the raw materials to build a bridge. And, in lieu of that bridge, many years were spent on opposite banks, looking at the river instead of each other.

Despite all the things they lacked, what they did have was a stunningly effective small business that catered to the hopes, dreams, hobbies, and interests of their kids and the stability that every young mind craves. It was something that was impossible without two equal partners committed to accomplishing such an enterprise, and its relative success was the source of considerable pride. Amidst the number of childrearing mistakes they both made and the various missteps that would have made a pediatric psychologist cringe, their house was a happy place.

There was enough that was unusual and unspoken about Sienna's childhood that what she appreciated about her own family was the distinctive normalness of it – even if it was filled with so many small, hilarious, eccentric, nice, mean, and beautiful participants.

And, as she paused just long enough to consider each of these facets and express quiet gratitude for what she had, Scarlett emerged from the makeshift art room in the basement with intricately designed shields and helmets that she would leave at the foot of a tree for the squirrels to use. It was a bad day to be a raccoon.

18 JUNE

Despite having several of the biggest cities on Earth and a gigantic, albeit shrinking, population, China was still a mostly rural country, and, among its many remote regions, few were quite so remote as its northeastern corner where the Chaoyangchuan Air Base (朝阳川) patrolled the skies above a critical geopolitical juncture where the borders of China, Russia, and North Korea all met – an area known as the "Tripoint."

Multiple mountain ranges surrounded the area, with barren, rolling foothills in between. This entire area had been unpopulated until the mid-1800's when the Qing Dynasty (大清) forced people to relocate there just to keep Russian settlers from moving in, and it was still entirely inhospitable and almost always freezing.

Chaoyangchuan was a bright spot for the People's Liberation Army Air Force (中国人民解放军空军), however, because it had been the home of an entire squadron of Chengdu J-10C fighters ever since they entered service in 2018. The J-10 was known as the "Vigorous Dragon," and it was considered the single best thing their country had ever put in the sky – regardless of how much praise was heaped on the stealthy J-20.

First Lieutenant Wáng Xuěméi (王雪梅) had been at Chaoyangchuan since graduating from the Air Force Aviation University (空军航空大学), which happened to be located in the next closest city 270 miles away. She had spent seven years prior to that as an engineer specializing in the design of the J-10's wings, and, perhaps as a result of her time spent on airbases studying the J-10 in action, she eventually married a test pilot of the J-10C. Her path to becoming a pilot herself had been unorthodox in an organization that revered orthodoxy, but, upon graduation, her merits earned her the opportunity to become the second female pilot selected to fly the J-10C she and her husband had pioneered. By the time she reached the cockpit there were already five female pilots flying the J-11, but this posting represented the unique honor of flying an aircraft which was an entirely homegrown product of her nation's Air Force.

The 22 pilots of the 61st Fighter Brigade at Chaoyangchuan were immensely proud of their aircraft, and they took great pride in their maintenance of air superiority in this unique area of the world. Just 220 miles to the south of their main runway was the famous Tripoint on the eastern bank of the Tumen River (图们江). In another unique geographic quirk, Russia also happened to surround this corner of China – Russian territory was not only due south, but it was also directly north and east as well. Although few officers dreamed of a deployment in such an isolated place with a smaller-than-average detachment of jets, it required extreme discipline and focus to fly near so many international boundaries at high speed.

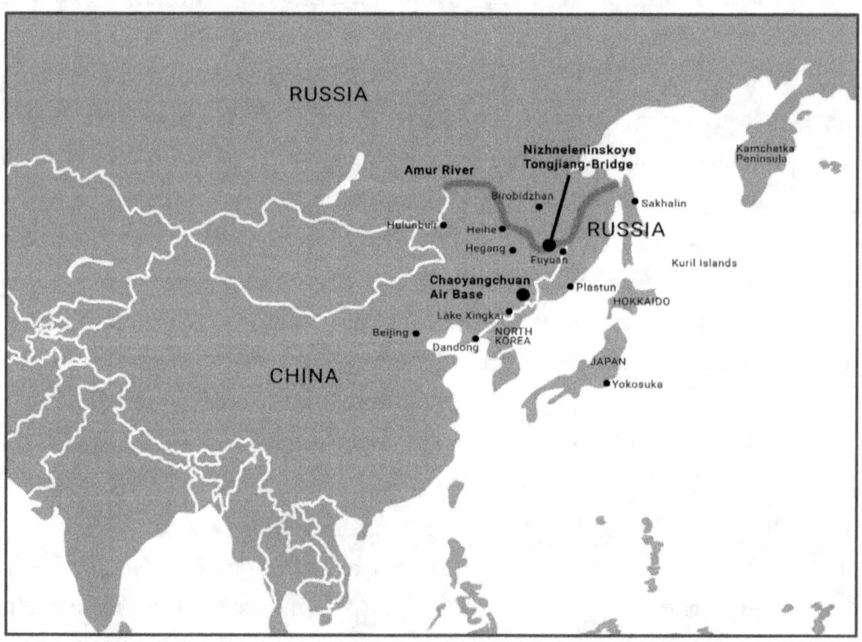

This morning a series of training flights had been canceled in favor of a briefing with their commander and the base's political officer. Yáng Péngfēi (鹏飞) was the lieutenant colonel – or Zhong Xiao (空军中校) as they called it in the Air Force – responsible for this squadron and the 1,100 support personnel who kept these jets in the air. He had assumed command of this air base the year before after several years teaching at the Aviation University where he had slowly overcome his prejudices about female pilots after watching Xuěméi train there for five years. He respected pilots that could combine a quiet, restrained demeanor with airborne lethality, and the fact that she was several years older than anyone else in her class made her an outlier within a group of outliers. She walked on what their ancestors, three thousand years earlier, called "Wu Shi Dao" (武士道) – the "the warrior's path." Xuěméi had taught him the extreme degree to which that path was gender neutral inside a $65 million aircraft.

Yáng began the briefing with the unnecessary reminder that due to the incredibly sensitive nature of what he was about to share, the most extreme secrecy must be maintained regarding everything they were about to hear. The information, he went on to explain, would remain restricted to just his senior staff, the political officers, and the pilots, and it had arrived from the Central Military Commission (中央军事委员会) overnight following a presentation of this data by the army's Intelligence Bureau (中央军委联合参谋部情报局) which had stretched late into the evening. The data had further been vetted by the Ministry of State Security (国家安全部), and their insignia on the opening slide of this briefing meant it came with the seal of approval from Beijing's most senior leaders.

"Our leaders in Beijing are facing what appears to be a grave situation, and very likely the prelude to a serious attack" Yáng explained. "Our scientists have discovered electromagnetic interference at listening posts along the Russian border, and since first appearing on sensors along the Russian frontier, the same interference had been seen in similar devices monitoring the perimeter of our African naval base in Djibouti (驻吉布提保障基地)."

Yáng paused to glance over at the political officer, or the Commissar (政治委员) as he was formally called, who nodded approvingly.

"Our Intelligence services believe that the sensors along the Russian border are older and not as sensitive as those surrounding our naval bases and civilian areas – therefore it is impossible to know at this time if this interference has arrived simultaneously or began in one place and spread."

What went unsaid but hung heavy in the room was the question of what it would mean if those sensors along the Russian frontier were functioning properly. In that case, it would indicate that the source of the electromagnetic interference was both coming from inside Russia and in relatively close proximity to the border with China. The fact that an overnight meeting in Beijing was followed by an early morning briefing at an airbase so close to Russia indicated that this conclusion had already been reached by the leadership. The only truly open-ended question was whether or not this same meeting was taking place at the other bases along the long border with Russia or if Chaoyangchuan was just lucky.

"Right now," Yáng explained, "we have a job of paramount importance. We must keep a sharp eye on that Russian border until the electronic surveillance specialists have a chance to compare the sensors from the border, the interior, and Djibouti to see if this is simply a malfunction."

The way he said it made it clear that he had already heard someone else say it in a way which made it clear this wouldn't end up being a hardware problem.

"It will take a week to get all three of those devices in the same room, and, until then, we are the best sensors available to our leaders in the Joint Staff Department (中央军委联合参谋部) and they have recalibrated the mission of Chaoyangchuan to focus entirely on this until further notice."

The job of watching the border was a truly monumental task in terms of sheer mileage. Xuěméi still remembered the class project in 3rd grade that charted each of the 100 rivers straddling that border, to say nothing of the multiple mountain ranges, a few million square miles of forest, and, for good measure, there was steppe and tundra. "In other words," she thought to herself, "regular grass and frozen grass." She figured there were at least seven other squadrons just like this one getting the same briefing; China's border with Russia stretched over 2,600 miles and that meant near-constant flight time from dozens of aircraft to keep a meaningfully close eye on all of it.

What also went unsaid in this briefing – but it was probably said out loud in Beijing – was the dramatic nature of misunderstandings between nuclear powers under the best of circumstances, and, in the event some kind of incursion or aggressive act was discovered, the next step was often to start assigning targets to the type of people with the type of training found in this room.

"Our job here in the northeast is particularly important," Yáng reminded them, "since Russian territory happens to be in every direction." This got a couple laughs, but it did not come with the guarantee of conflict that most fighter pilots craved. As if to temper any hopes of a dogfight, he emphasized one final point before dismissing the squadron to catch up on their missed morning training: "The Central Military Commission is clear that within our new mission there should be no engagement with foreign forces along the border and that you are to avoid potential conflicts at this time. Until further instructions arrive, we are watching, we are keeping the cameras rolling while we fly, and we're reporting back every time we notice a stone along the border has moved."

After being dismissed, Xuěméi stopped to talk with a few officers about plans for that morning's training schedule, and then, on her walk back to the hanger, spent several minutes instructing one of the maintenance technicians about an adjustment she wanted double checked on the engine nozzle of her jet. By the time she reached the hanger her commanding officer was already charting daily patrol routes and possible schedules for her team of six pilots. Chén Wěiqiáng (陈伟强) was ten years older than her and a strong aerial tactician, and his long-term deployment at Chaoyangchuan made planning these routes simple, as long as the geopolitics could be put aside – which, in a situation like this, you did at your peril. The routes were clear enough, however: Long oval-shaped patrols originating from the airfield and reaching as far north as the city of Heihe (黑河市), then following the Amur River south and east until reaching the far northeastern corner of the country – the town of Fuyuan (抚远), near the famous Nizhneleninskoye-Tongjiang Bridge (宁斯科耶-通江大橋) that famously connected Russia and China with regular commercial rail traffic back in 2022. From there they'd turn south again, clip the edge of Lake Xingkai (兴凯湖) – which actually had the Russian-Chinese border running through the middle of it – and end up within a couple hundred miles of the Tripoint before heading back. For good measure they could even skirt the northern edge of North Korea just to make sure things were quiet there, too – the trip to Dandong (丹东) on the opposite side of that border was only 326 miles away. The 1,150 mile range of the Vigorous Dragon gave them the ability to cast a wide net, and the ability to travel 1,500 miles per hour meant they could see it all quickly.

She paused for a moment to consider the river. Most maps used the Russian name for it, "Amur" (река Амур), but on all their maps it was listed with its Chinese name – the Heilong (黑龙江) or "Black Dragon River."

To avoid making it obvious that their patrols were looking for something, Chen was going to propose that all these surveillance flights happen individually rather than in groups of two or three. Stepping back to observe the dozens of tightly organized, overlapping routes on the map, he paused to think out loud.

"Honestly, the chances are that we see nothing, we engage with nothing, and sooner than we think, this blows over and we're back to regular operations."

Xuěméi agreed, both because she was expected to do so and because he was almost certainly right. But she knew this would all be taken very seriously until that interference could either be explained or proven to not be Russian.

The assembled pilots were dismissed. Xuěméi had three hours until her patrol, and she made her way back to her quarters. She locked the door and walked to her desk where she took the small leather calendar book from an otherwise empty drawer. It had a spiral binding, and each page was split into sections, each one representing a day. It was something a businessman in Shanghai (上海) or Dongguan (东莞市) would have carried to keep track of appointments back before a smartphone took its place.

Most days there was something short and simple written on each square.

Today it said: "Sat up by himself."

She took a sheet of paper and started to write a note.

As her pen touched the paper she paused and closed her eyes. She wanted to first see the moment in her mind.

But her mind went all the way back instead.

She had met her husband on a base just like this one, on another edge of the world far from here but indistinguishable in ways that mattered. Zhang Jun (张军) was a brilliant pilot no matter what he was flying, and she was a young aerodynamics engineer working on the next generation of the J-10 . She spent as much time in laboratories and wind tunnels as she did in a simulator noting all the imperceptible ways the aircraft reacted to the changes she made to the leading edge of the wing, and Jun had noticed that she logged almost as many simulator hours as him. "Not that the simulator counts as real flying," he would always point out with a smile.

They first crossed paths when Xuěméi, newly promoted to explore extensions to the leading edge of the J-10's wings, delivered a briefing on these new components to the assembled test pilots. It had gone poorly. She dreaded public speaking and it showed, and, worse yet, her fellow scientists attributed it to something she did not even know at the time: One of the pilots sitting near the back of the room was the son of a party official of above-average importance back in Beijing. When she was later told to not let this minor celebrity rattle her in future briefings, she made a point of avoiding him. This daughter of a truck driver did not feel any need to impress the scion of a family with a revered last name and outsized political influence, and she bristled at the idea that anyone would think *that* was why she struggled discussing wing design. But her plan to keep a contemptuous distance was ill-fated considering he was among the best pilots and the new aircraft's wings needed a lot of attention. She spent countless hours instructing him on what to expect from each new adjustment to the prototype aircraft before flights, and he would sit with her from the moment he landed until late into the night debriefing on everything he had learned in the air.

Two people who cared so much about fighter jets soon cared for each other. She told him every granular detail of aeronautical engineering in case he ever needed it at 60,000 feet, and, on quiet weekends or very late nights, he would take her out in a spare J-10S training jet so she could learn what real aerial combat flying felt like and know personally what pilots needed from those wings when Mach 2 tried to tear the fuselage apart. The flights in the trainer jet could have gotten them both thrown in prison, but Jun was old friends with the flight controller for this base, and the idea of earning a couple favors from the son of a man everyone knew from television didn't hurt, either.

Xuĕméi was a quick study in a real cockpit, and soon she was executing every maneuver the Aviation University expected from its graduates; Jun, for his part, was exceptionally adept at looking fascinated when she explained the unique metallurgy she was using to improve the J-10's ailerons.

Long before either one dared speak a single heartfelt word, the J-10C prototype became the child they brought into the world together. It was something beautiful on a dangerous planet; it was the single greatest thing two people could create; and, in the labyrinthine wilderness of their lives, they found each other.

Less than a year after that early morning briefing, they were married, and less than a year after that they had a son, Mínghuī (明辉). When he was three weeks old his grandmother sent a furry winter coat with small brown ears sewn to the hood, and after he put it on, they hardly used his real name ever again – to them he was just *Little Bear* (小的熊).

When Mínghuī was two years old, he and Jun died when a rockslide pushed their car off the road alongside a canyon near the base. Jun had used his day off from instructing new pilots to take Mínghuī to see a herd of milu deer (麋鹿) who lived along the river.

On a large wall calendar in their apartment, Xuĕméi had made a note of every milestone or notable occurrence in Mínghuī's life, and now that story traveled with her in the small, black book.

Her pen started moving again and she watched the words.

> *Little Bear, today you pulled yourself up when you saw me coming to bring you a snack. You had just started getting the hang of crawling, but today you sat right up all by yourself. I was so impressed, and you laughed and laughed when you saw me clap for you.*
>
> *I cannot believe I have not held you for almost nine years. I can still feel your head under my chin whenever I hear a child's voice. Sometimes when I am walking I drop my arm down by*

my side just in case I can feel you reach up to grab it with your small hand.

Last night it was so quiet here that when the wind was still I heard you roll over in your crib two times. You were always so bored in your crib, and even when I was exhausted, I just wanted to see your tiny face as it slept.

I hope you are taking good care of your dad. I hope he has shown you how to be strong until I get there. I hope your grandmother has taught you how to sing. I wish I was with you every day. I wish I could have ridden with you. I would have helped you count the deer.

Xuǎméi knew what grief counseling and duty had to say about accepting this loss, but nothing in those concepts offered anything of value to her. Her son had spent the final seconds of his life terrified, and he had left this world screaming. There was nothing on earth or the Tian (天) of her ancestors to heal her.

There was nothing left but the aircraft. And there was nothing left to do but what that aircraft did. The J10 was her last family member, and she was ready to fly it anywhere that might lead back to them. And this, she knew, was what made her such an exceptional pilot; there was nothing quite so empty and dangerous as someone who had nothing.

She sat for another moment, her eyes shut tight again, and she saw Mínghuī' sitting there on the rug. She saw the way he teetered when he laughed and then caught himself. She held onto it, and then set the pen down. She folded the note in half and placed it on the ceramic incense tray (接香盘). When it was done burning, she put the calendar book back in its drawer, dried her face, and walked the long way to her hangar.

1990

6 FEBRUARY

Four months passed in quick succession for Sienna. The breaks at Thanksgiving and Christmas helped the time pass, but Sienna was enamored with the work she was doing. This was the most exciting opportunity a child of the 80's with bottomless curiosity could be offered, and every moment in that chair was spent eagerly hunting within the great emptiness and scouring the inside of her mind as if set loose on a scavenger hunt of heroism.

This attitude was very common amongst her classmates, and this, combined with the culture and tone set by Dr. Torquemann, made it easy for this collective of like-minded and like-purposed campers to get along more often than not.

The campers traded notes about what they saw and heard, despite the fact this would almost certainly taint the data in any other experimental project, and the typical juvenile exaggerations were kept to a minimum since it was impossible to claim to have spotted something big without there being a corresponding spike on a dozen different sensors monitoring your brain.

That morning in class a new teacher introduced herself as "a strategist" from the National Security Agency. The class was currently in the middle of a unit on ecosystems, and most of yesterday was spent walking back and forth across Sugar Loaf Mountain to find leaves and insects to put in a jar and label it as something representing a "Lower Woodland" biome.

The new teacher found this exercise particularly exciting because, as she explained it, the specific nature of her work had to do with astrobiology – or, said another way, her research was focused on how to detect from thousands of light years away if there might be life on distant planets.

Eventually the class would learn enough to understand that her specialty was designing the technology and methodology that astronomers used when looking through a telescope at the ring of light surrounding a distant planet's silhouette – and then, when they analyzed how the light refracted through that planet's atmosphere, certain conclusions could be reached about what was happening on the surface. For example, if the light refracted a very specific way, it meant there were specific chemicals in the atmosphere and the presence of certain chemicals was evidence of minerals being burned. And a certain type of burnt mineral could indicate an intelligent civilization heating its homes or powering its factories.

Hypothetically, at least.

Today's class discussion quickly became a hybrid of the ongoing ecosystems unit and her own study of how life began and then thrived – whether here on Earth or anywhere else her technology might someday detect it.

"What kind of life are you trying to find on other planets?" Kelsi asked.

"The only thing we really know," she explained, "is that if there's anything out there at all, then there are about a million different shapes it can take – and that can be anything from slime to stuff that flies, or anything in between."

"So, you don't think aliens would look a lot like us, but just with some weird ridge on their forehead?" Sam asked, hoping to find some validation for his critique that all the "Star Trek" aliens were lame because they were all obviously humans with extra makeup and some rubber knobs glued to their faces.

The teacher laughed and said she agreed, and this was the jumping off point for something along the lines of: "The first thing to understand about how any lifeform evolves is that evolution is entirely dependent on the ecosystem where that organism is doing its evolving. This is a pretty simple principle, but it gets overlooked a lot. I mean, for example, the animals here on Earth – ourselves included – evolved so that they could better make their way around the specific ecosystem where they lived, and they developed bodies and brains that would help them do that. And those bodies and brains were meant to not just help them survive wherever it was they were living, but also to help them survive the things in their environment that wanted to eat them. So, over time, those brains and bodies grew to thrive in that ecosystem's temperature, to be able to move across its unique type of land, and to eat or use all the plants in that area. So, after a couple hundred thousand years, everything on that animal is affected by where it lives – from the shape of its stomach, to how it sleeps, to the way muscle wraps across its skeleton. And its brain and instincts are built to take advantage of the most common threats and opportunities it comes across every day."

This left the class thinking about their own unique physical variations and what could have happened in some ancient ecosystem that bestowed them with the ability to listen to Russian radio stations.

"And even our brains were changed by where our ancestors lived?" Sienna asked.

The teacher nodded, started to grab a piece of chalk, and then decided to just explain it instead.

"It sounds kind of weird to think that the type of wild landscape where your ancestors evolved can impact how you think or act today, but if you follow our trail back through history, that's what you end up finding. Now, don't get me wrong – you can't blame your decisions on where your ancestors evolved. But all the pathways in your brain that your thoughts and your reasoning take in order to reach all the conclusions that we believe in and seem so very carefully studied – those things were established a long time ago based on what your ancestors needed to survive their ecosystem. That doesn't mean all your choices are made for you, but what you do have to recognize is that all your thinking is done with equipment which was built a long time ago with the intention of doing a small number of basic tasks, like build forts and find food. And because our brains were constructed with such limited usage in mind, we're left with the sobering reality that there are types of thoughts and kinds of conclusions our brains simply cannot ever reach. And, well, I don't know if you've ever watched the news, but being able to come up with a few extra ideas would be really helpful. But even if your brain can only reach a limited number of conclusions, it's still up to you to make good choices and be a good person."

Sienna's mind was racing at what this implied about the

astrobiology they'd discussed earlier.

"So aliens are thinking different things than us."

"That's right. We have no idea *what* they're thinking, but they will have evolved in a completely different ecosystem that has given them a different brain, and that means they have completely different thoughts, and come up with different ideas, and reach different conclusions."

The teacher considered for a moment which direction to take this next, and she wondered if she should ruin the genre of science fiction for them.

"Based on our discussion today, what is the flaw in every book or movie about aliens showing up and taking over the planet? And I'll give you a hint: It's not that aliens arrived here in the first place."

The class was silent.

Sienna loved the next part of the discussion, but she could never repeat it back as well as this "strategist" from some organization within an organization that didn't formally have a name. It was something like: "The problem with that alien takeover plot is that all those stories are written by a human brain, and it's just projecting human ideas onto the aliens in their story. The urge to conquer things is deeply wired into human beings because we evolved on a planet with so many hostile environments and temperatures and predators – so we evolved in a place where we were often hungry and usually in danger, and the only way to survive was to kill things and conquer things until we were no longer hungry and our enemies were gone. But what if – hypothetically – something or someone else evolved on a planet where food grew abundantly right there on the ground, and what if all the other animals in that ecosystem were small or harmless? Someone that evolved on that planet would be *very* different from us. The wiring of their brain would have evolved very differently because they faced very different challenges and had very different needs than us – and those very different brains would have very different thoughts. And all of that different thinking would lead them to value different things – and that means their priorities would be different and the things that were important to them might seem strange to us."

She paused in case there were questions, but there was only more bewildered silence.

"So, that's why those sci-fi movies are a bit silly. It's just humans writing about what we would do if we found some less technological planet full of living things. But any alien civilization that can reach us is going to have very different motivations for coming this far. Conquering and fighting and starting wars might not even occur to them. Our ancestors crossed a relatively tiny ocean because of an indefatigable compulsion to accumulate materials they believed would help them survive – largely because they evolved in an ecosystem where scarcity was the paramount danger. But any alien civilization that is technologically sophisticated enough to cross the enormous emptiness of the universe to reach this planet doesn't need anything we have. They wouldn't need our 'natural resources' because anything we have here on Earth – there's a lot more of it already floating out there in space. They wouldn't need us for slaves because they already have enough technology and robots and whatever else to do anything they need done. So a human trying to write a book about aliens we cannot possibly understand is like a jellyfish writing a novel about orangutans. There is simply no circumstance where one of those creatures could summon the slightest idea of how the other thinks."

The teacher had been talking for a long time at this point, so she paused again and invited questions. The discussion continued for another 40 minutes until it was time to break for lunch – and by that time they had covered what other possible body types could exist throughout the Universe, what different types of air could be breathable based on what your body was made out of, and how many times our tectonic plates had erased everything on the Earth's surface.

* * * * *

During these first few months Sienna had experienced a bit of a slow start after that first burst of information in session number one.

Dr. Torquemann and his team were careful to never openly praise a camper for exceptional performance – and this, too, helped maintain the esprit de corps that kept things harmonious – but their meticulous analysis of every single second a camper spent in the research cabin made it obvious where the greatest amount of usable Signal data was being captured. Sienna was within the performance bell curve, albeit toward the bottom end. This wasn't to say she had seen or heard nothing at all, however. Right after Thanksgiving break she had caught a glimpse of a few different reflective surfaces, and a very long study had followed of what exactly was caught in that reflection. An instrument panel? A pattern of lights? A grid of circuitry? There had also been a long burst of "characters" which might have been letters, numbers, or shapes – or maybe just lights – that sped past in a line as if it was being typed at an incredible speed. The sad voice, or at least the melancholy that came with it, had also made a small number of appearances. Her third session had rendered the words

Repeat and process again

as clear as if someone in the room had said it, followed by a long stream of what sounded like one of the dot matrix printers in the back of the cabin echoing at the bottom of a metal tube. Two weeks ago, after getting nothing but a garbled hiss and flashes of a huge, unremarkable metallic surface for days, she faintly picked out:

This process has been replaced.

January and into February found Sienna in the midst of another dry streak.

She was frustrated by it, but the concerns the scientists had about her output were something they all had the discipline to never insinuate around her. Today, at the end of her session, Torchy invited her to stick around and look at some of the readings they had gathered that day. The specific technology was never explained in any great detail to the campers, and hardly any of them ever showed a huge amount of interest in seeing it after walking around the cabin a few times early in their tenure. She looked at the three-dimensional constructions of her brain on the screen and saw the path the Signal had taken through it, along with the way individual tachyons had scattered and spun away in different directions along its route. She could see the star charts monitoring the flow of those particle waves and the way they twisted and turned like a churning river current across observable space. But, of course, she recognized this at only the most cursory of levels, and she wondered what the men and women who leaned so close to these screens found interesting *outside* of work when squinting at those tedious green pixels was no longer required.

As the research team collated all the printouts and began packaging up the data for further processing – there was an entire floor of Cray supercomputers in a basement outside of Washington D.C. that analyzed each day's information for countless hours – Torchy and Dr. Tunis swiveled around in their chairs to answer a question she'd asked earlier that day.

"If everyone here has the same brain-finger-bump that I do," she had asked, "why is it just kids here? Why aren't there any teenagers or grownups doing this?"

"That's a great question," Torquemann said. He was known to say this to almost any question that was even remotely novel or unique. "And the short answer has to do with how your brain is growing – and how it will keep growing until quite a while after the rest of your body stops. For example, your brain doesn't finish growing its prefrontal cortex, which is the part you use for all the really intensive thinking and difficult decision making, until you're about 24. And by then, a lot of your biggest decisions will already be made – so, thanks a lot for *that* evolution. But, as for the rest of your question, well, I really think Dr. Tunis can do a better job of explaining this."

Dr. Tunis laughed in a way that showed how much he loved discussing this. "Dr. Torquemann is right that your brain is always growing at this current stage of your life, and that the structures of your brain are growing right along with the rest of your body."

Right on cue, and not for the first time, Sienna flexed her arm, kissed her bicep and said, "That's what's up." The pull up contests the campers had been having were taken surprisingly seriously.

"So what that means, Schwarzenegger, is that the way your brain is shaped right now, and the way the two different lobes of your brain are overlapping in just the right way, and the way you have such an ideal position of the ridge..."

"The brain wart," she corrected, right on cue.

"...the tiny ridge on your occipital lobe – well, right now all of that growth means that the way the ridge and lobes line up is in motion. At the moment, the way your brain is shaped means that it picks up the

Signal very effectively, but, as you keep growing, those things will get out of alignment."

Dr. Hamza said this all so matter-of-factly that it took a moment for her to process what this meant.

"And then I won't be able to hear the Signal at all. So, then what happens to the ridge?"

"The ridge will likely just be reabsorbed back into the brain tissue, or perhaps atrophy from never being used. If, for example, this program didn't exist, you probably would have kept seeing flashes of things, you would have gone to half a dozen different neurologists, and they would have told you to wait and monitor how things progressed, and then when you grew out of it, they would have just assumed that the most recent treatment they gave you was the one that solved it."

"So, what this means," Torchy concluded, "is that by the time any of you kids turn, at the latest, 12 or 13 years old, your brain has grown enough that you just go back to having a normal brain that doesn't happen to be tuned to a frequency that's playing the hits from a hypothetical particle radio station."

Sienna thought about this. "Then I want what Margo and Andrew both have."

Torchy and Tunis shared a look. This was not information that was supposed to be circulating quite so broadly.

"Let me explain what Margo has," Dr. Tunis offered, hoping it would seem strange enough to make Sienna reconsider this option. "What she has is, essentially, an extension of that ridge on her brain – it's like we built a satellite dish on top of that little hill. But, to be clear, getting this means having a procedure that physically goes in and places that dish on that hill."

In a reaction unique to precocious children and naive adults, Sienna already knew this existed but was amazed it was real.

"And then what changes?"

"You essentially have a longer, more efficient antenna that can theoretically pick up more of the Signal," Torquemann explained.

"Longer?" she asked, incredulously, "'Longer brains' is the answer here?"

"No," Tunis cut in, "it is still highly experimental, and, although the early results are very promising, I want to advise against it because the procedure is unpleasant. The technical term for it is an endoscopic endonasal surgery – and what we do is go in through your right nostril, up through your nasal passage, at which point we're already pretty deep inside your head, and then with an endoscope, which is a really thin tube with a camera and light on it, I make a couple of holes so I can reach your brain. And then, at *that* point, I have to keep maneuvering a bit more until I make my way back to your ridge."

He paused and walked over to a shelf that ran along the back wall of the cabin, and he came back holding a small glass bottle.

"And then I place this right over the spot where the MRI showed us that ridge on your brain."

Inside the glass jar was a tiny, dark gray wisp of metal. He unscrewed the jar and slid the item out onto a white sheet of paper to make it easier to see. Sienna, who was equal parts grossed out by the endoscope story and fascinated by the idea of a tiny satellite dish, leaned in to see it. She nudged it with her little finger to try and understand its weight – and even next to her nine-year-old hands it was tiny. It looked like a heavy eyelash, but not nearly that long. It was something you would brush off the table while wiping it clean without even thinking about it. "It's called an Epicortical Surface Reflector or ESR," Tunis explained.

She was relieved it was so small considering she'd already decided to put it in her skull.

She stood up, looked back at Tunis and Torquemann, and made her intentions clear.

"So after I do this, how much changes the next time I'm in that chair," she said, gesturing over her shoulder.

"We've put an ESR on top of the hill 22 previous times," Dr. Tunis said, "and about half the time we've seen a difference in how they capture the Signal."

"What else does it affect besides the Signal?"

Torquemann could guess what she meant by this. "It will not change how you think, or who you are, or…"

"But…?" she interrupted hopefully.

"And there is no possibility that it will give you mental powers."

This had been a long shot, but she had to ask.

"Technically, it's not even *inside* your brain – it's just right on top. And when you're done here at camp, and when that ridge melts into the background as your brain keeps growing, it will be like the ESR isn't even there. It's small enough to not cause any problems, it has no hard edge, so it's not going to rub up against anything and make your tongue go numb or make you forget your name or something, so the long-term side effects are essentially zero. Chances are your body will naturally surround it with goo, and that will be the end of the story."

"Ok, gross, but what if I ever get my head scanned or I walk past some strong magnet like at a junkyard and this thing gets pulled out through my skull?"

Now it was Dr. Tunis' turn to laugh.

"No, the ESR is made from a non-metallic substance. It won't even show up if you ever get your head scanned. We don't have a name that everyone can agree on for the substance it's made out of, but it definitely doesn't show up on scans. And, considering it was built inside a Non-Zero Particle Field, it kind of doesn't even exist at a physical level – at least in terms of how you would normally describe if a thing exists or not."

Dr. Torquemann leaned back in his chair and let out a long sigh.

Tunis had just signed them up for a minimum of 15 more minutes of questions with that answer. There were so many times when saying "Haha, nope" was a sufficient response. But now, just a split second after giving a real answer, Sienna would already be forming a very predictable list of questions, things like: "What on Earth does that mean?" and "What is a Non-Zero whatever you said?" and also "What 'terms' are you guys using for what does or doesn't exist?" What Torquemann couldn't know was that 22 years later another group of scientists would also discover the existence of a Non-Zero Particle Field and rename it a Higgs Field.

"So, explain it. You can answer those questions in whatever order you like."

"Well," Torquemann said letting out another deep breath, "there are different 'fields' that hold the Universe together in different ways, like a gravitational field is what keeps the moon and the Earth close together, and an electrical field is why you can screw in a lightbulb and it works, and a magnetic field is why magnets stick to your fridge or a compass works – and these fields don't really have any substance to them that you can pick up and touch, and so particles can just fly through them without even slowing down. Those are called 'zero-fields' – as in they have zero things in them that would stop a particle from flying right through the middle of them. But a few years back – actually, more than a few – a scientist like me, working for a group a lot like mine, named Carol Baltazar, discovered a 'field' that is *more* than zero."

"Non-zero," she figured out.

"Right, so this non-zero field is actually pretty much everywhere – it's like a big net stretched over the whole Universe, and when Dr. Baltazar recreated this field in her lab, she discovered that even though all kinds of particles fly right through an electromagnetic field without even noticing it, well, when they hit a concentrated Baltazar Field, they slow down – like, *way* down. And as part of that slowing down, they pick up stuff – kind of like a snowball rolling down a snowy hill and getting bigger as it goes. And, after some more research, Dr. Baltazar found that this is essentially how all the atoms in the Universe were once made, and she noticed that every time she sent an atom through that Baltazar Field it came out the other side a little bigger with new stuff attached to it.

"What does this have to do with the brain antenna?"

"Well, it didn't take long for Dr. Baltazar to notice that her field was capturing all types of stuff there in the lab, and one of those things caught in that little net were tachyons. In a weird and unexpected way, the Baltazar Field was kind of like a tachyon magnet – it pulled them in, compressed them, and any object you put in that field seemed to keep attracting tachyons once you took it out. It's kind of like when you connect a magnet to a battery and it temporarily becomes even more magnetic."

"Wait a second" she interrupted, "what do you mean, 'put it in' the field? Is this like an oven?"

The girl was sharp.

"The machine that generated the Baltazar Field looks like a gigantic dryer – like the ones you see at the laundromat with that spin really fast and they have the window in the door so you can see everything dancing around inside. The way Dr. Baltazar built hers was with a tiny window on a giant door about the size of a garbage truck, and you could see this pulse of light inside, and that was the spherical Baltazar Field that was drawing in energy and particles from several layers of space all at once. Well, probably several layers – but, actually, you know what, nevermind. So, yes, you actually could just 'put something' inside that big dryer-looking thing. You'd put it in, close the door really tight, then turn it on so the field would generate, and then let whatever it is you put in just sit there and absorb tachyons for a while."

Now they were finally getting back to the previous point.

"So, the ESR was very carefully molded with some very tiny tools right there inside the containment chamber of the Baltazar Field," Dr. Tunis explained, "and then it sat in there for several days just getting pelted with tachyons – and, just like that magnet you hook up to a battery, now it is just pulling in tachyons from all over, and it will stay that way for quite a while."

Sienna sat and thought through this avalanche of new information. Dr. Torquemann started to slide the ESR pack into its jar.

"I want to do this, but I want it to make me good at math."

"You are already good at math," Torquemann pointed out.

"But I want it to stop being hard."

"No deal, but, tomorrow morning, after breakfast, come find us at the cabin next door – the same one you went to when you rolled your ankle. We'll be ready."

Later that night, Torquemann and Tunis would discuss this next step Sienna had decided to pursue. In recent months the volume of material she'd intercepted from the Signal had not been particularly remarkable, but she did seem to have an inherent feel for finding things in it, even if she didn't get her arms around them very often. What she did have was an indomitable and indefatigable desire to pull something great from those stray bursts and flashes of information. More than anyone else in camp, and maybe more than anyone who had ever been in the program, she wanted to find something important and provide something meaningful. She was driven independent of the goals of the program itself, and if she were older, the staff psychiatrist would have already pulled her aside and asked questions which were too deep for a nine-year-old, like, "Is your intense desire to do something important here a symptom of your belief that you will never have a chance to do something important ever again?" Or maybe, "Are worried that this is your one opportunity to be meaningful in a world which might permanently overlook your value?"

Torquemann hated that the answers to those questions were so easy to anticipate from this otherwise lovable, feisty, funny, and unintentionally charming child.

"Ok, last question: How bad is this surgery going to be?"

"You lay down, you fall asleep, Dr. Tunis moves his light and camera around in there for about an hour, and then he stitches things up. After that, you wake up and lay on the couch in your cabin with a headache and eat ice cream for 2 or 3 days. Past that, it's like nothing ever happened. The security guys will get you any flavors you want, or you can get a secret flavor that doesn't even officially exist yet from one of our agents who is spying on Häagen-Dazs."

"What? Really?!" she shouted looking at Tunis to see if he knew about this.

"Nope, but you can order whatever you want until you feel well enough to go back to class."

Twenty-four hours later she was propped up in bed, digging the peanut butter cups out of a carton of ice cream, and watching "Teenage Mutant Ninja Turtles" and "Tremors" on VHS even though both movies were still in theaters.

PRESENT DAY

10 Hemisphere

19 JUNE

Yesterday's call with the Joint Chiefs had gone as expected, and so did the following two calls Horn had with them later that day, as well as the early morning meeting he'd just wrapped up with all six members of the formal Joint Chiefs of Staff and the Secretary of Defense.

The SecDef's presence at the meeting made things very, very serious. This meant the President was now getting briefed on this situation as it developed, and controlling those ongoing developments were now Major Horn's sole responsibility.

Based on the decisions made during this last meeting, the next steps were straightforward but still incredibly unusual to see put into motion. Now 20 different military bases around the world had been quietly instructed to prepare their troops and equipment to move if and when a call arrived within the next 10 to 14 days.

This order had to be very carefully managed by the base commanders since a large military installation could not suddenly jump to a state of advanced readiness without it being noticed by other governments. It was considerably easier to do this with a floating air base, however.

The USS George Washington was currently far away from its headquarters and homeport of Yokosuka, Japan (横須賀海軍施設) – a city on the eastern coast, about 90 minutes south of Tokyo. The George was in the middle of a semi-annual tour through the outer reaches of the South Pacific, and was, at the moment, at the southernmost point of its circuit – a short visit to the city of Tauranga on New Zealand's appropriately named North Island.

The visit allowed the sailors to go ashore after an intense week of joint exercises with the New Zealand and Australian navies, and it gave a few local dignitaries the chance to come aboard and take pictures with Captain Paul Goral before it set off on its trip home the following morning.

Far to the north, a brand-new carrier, the USS John F. Kennedy, had just wrapped up a deployment in the Persian Gulf and was heading towards a rendezvous with the Indian Navy for three days of training when new orders from Horn arrived.

The Kennedy was told to keep its present course, but to be prepared to break off and take action on additional instructions at any time, such as the need to turn 180 degrees and race back up the Arabian Sea to park somewhere near the beach in Pakistan. The Kennedy's captain was also informed that two different Virginia-class hunter submarines were being dispatched to the area to keep an eye on any Indian vessels who might have a first strike on their minds.

The odd man out in this setup was the George, who, as of 26 minutes ago, seemed too far away from anything to play a part.

Twenty-five minutes ago, however, Horn had been updated on a report detailing a sudden and severe escalation in tensions at military headquarters in Beijing. The CIA source who sent this information apparently had first-hand knowledge of an extremely agitated group of generals who believed their borders were being tested by the Russian military in preparation for a clandestine operation against some target inside the Chinese homeland. The source didn't say if the Chinese had any guesses about what the target on their homeland would be, but the working theory amongst the leadership was that the attack would come across the Nizhneleninskoye-Tongjiang Bridge, albeit in a currently unidentified way. This much uncertainty, according to the spy, added additional hostility to types of counter-actions Beijing was willing to consider.

Horn's job required him to develop the means to physically intercede in the event one side suddenly escalated in a way that future historians might describe as having "marked the beginning of the global conflagration." The only viable or acceptable way to do this would be to control the airspace around the bridge, and, unless this control was taken without Russia or China knowing it had happened, this entire situation would immediately cascade into that dreaded conflagration.

Taking control of the airspace above two countries with established air forces and anti-air defenses – and to do it without either country knowing... Horn was certain he was the first person to ever need to do this. To do this would require stealth, speed, firepower, and they would have to park somewhere so far away that neither country would think to look there. This meant that the control of the air would be sporadic and dependent upon long round trips, but, if they were stealthy enough, it might not matter.

Horn looked at the map, overlaid with the placement and operational range of available U.S. assets, and calculated in his head what could be put to use in the event there was an option or an opportunity to intervene and prevent a shooting match between superpowers. The George was unlikely to get there within a week, even at maximum speed, but he would have them try. There was also Misawa Air Force Base (三沢飛行場) in northern Japan, which was home to the 5th Air Force and the 35th Operations Group. The Russian-Chinese border was out of reach for most of the offensive aircraft at Misawa and, in the event a conflict arose, both countries would keep a close eye on that exact runway to ensure there were no interdiction attempts from the U.S. But, even if the situation did call for it, there wasn't anything currently available at Misawa with enough stealth to get close enough to make a difference. This left the U.S. without a readily available option to defuse or deflect an attack inside the continent at a moment's notice.

Besides Alaska, that is.

"No," he said to himself before he could finish the thought, "that is insane."

He had spent the previous day thinking through the potential domino effects of India and Pakistan getting into a shoving match. This development in China made things infinitely worse. Now there was the potential for the U.S. to get pulled into at least one – and possibly three – different regional wars. "But," he corrected himself, "this wouldn't be three wars – it would be us fighting on three fronts in one gigantic world war." In this case, however, the group of countries fighting would feature populations that were 20 times larger than those involved in World War 2. But at least Germany would be neutral this time. Probably? Or maybe even fight for the good guys. Maybe?

Maybe.

Right on cue his watch began to vibrate again, and he made his way over to the small bottle zipped into his bag.

The bottle said "Erlotinib," but there were a few extra things in each tablet besides that already complex compound. A career like his came with the benefit of being connected with a handful of people who could get you access to medicine that was still deep in the experimental phase but nonetheless promising enough to give you a leg up on a terminal diagnosis. His diagnosis in particular did not yet have any survivors to use as inspiration, and, unfortunately, there was no chance that he might be the first.

It had been eight weeks since a young doctor with a furrowed brow and a low voice had delivered the news. If this medicine did its job he had somewhere between six and slightly more than six months left. There were no other options available, alternate treatment plans did not exist, and the homeopathic remedies could only promise you'd die smelling like lavender.

"Many people with a diagnosis like this find it incredibly helpful to meet with others dealing with the same news," the doctor had explained, "and there is a group which meets here twice a week."

Horn nodded and thanked him for the information, but politely declined the pamphlet with times and locations of future meetings.

"Are you sure you wouldn't like to meet with the group, Mr. Horn?"

"Yes, thank you," he said, already starting to stand up.

"I understand, it's just that research shows that many people…"

He sat back down.

"Son, I can accept the parameters of any given situation without trying to bend reality with my feelings."

This response had been a bit unfair and a bit out of character to reveal so much to a relative stranger, but he was, at that time, still reeling.

His decades of training in life-or-death situations had prepared him exceptionally well to deal with the realistic effects of his diagnosis, but what he still struggled with were the more ephemeral elements of this information. He had encountered something that years of leading a Delta squadron had never presented: What a terrible thing it was to contemplate no longer existing.

He had very suddenly discovered how ill equipped the human mind was to grasp this, and he was surprised by how much he was surprised.

A couple-hundred-thousand years of human evolution had, it turns out, built a brain that was fine-tuned to end quickly and unexpectedly; it was designed to be intensely focused on the present – like how to escape this lion or evade that enemy tribe – right up until the *last* moment. And, in those cases, that brain wouldn't even know when the end came. An arrow or claws or a falling rock would simply turn out the lights. It was up to everyone else – not the brain in question – to process the death.

These sudden ends did have the unexpectedly positive byproduct of evolving a complex set of neurological pathways in the surviving families and villagers such that Homo sapiens, despite their high intelligence, long memories, and unremitting emotional bonds, became exceptionally effective at coping with tragedy, accepting loss, and then moving on. After all, a dead husband or child did not change the fact that roots and berries still needed to be gathered and that the fort needed a taller wall. Evolution had discovered that being left with your grief was a form of poison and our minds had found a way to save us from it.

But the modern world, or at least modern medicine, did something entirely unexpected. It was something we were not prepared for or capable of managing, and cognitive evolution was caught entirely off guard by it: Being shown the exact path death would take to find you, and then having a polite doctor tell you when it would arrive.

When Horn got a second opinion from an old connection he knew from his days in JSOC, he was told that his condition was "very advanced in its development."

Horn rolled his eyes. "Well, hell, Howard, when you say it like that it sounds like this thing deserves some sort of congratulations."

But Howard had, at least, connected him with a steady supply of those small, orange bottles of pills – and that kept the violent nausea and debilitating pain off the table during work hours. This disease could now eat him alive in peace right up until the moment its claws put out the lights.

* * * * *

In New Delhi, 7,500 miles away and nine hours ahead of the command center where Horn was taking his pills without water,

General Mukund Gupta (मुकुंद गुप्ता), the Chairman of the Chiefs of Staff Committee of the Indian Armed Forces (भारतीय सशस्त्र बलों के चीफ ऑफ स्टाफ कमेटी के अध्यक्ष), set his glasses on a marble tabletop and rubbed his eyes.

That title put him in charge of the vast Indian armed forces – the army, navy, air force, everything. He had been a young officer during the Indo-Pakistani War of 1971 and had caught shrapnel across his neck and the right side of his face in a firefight on the second-to-last day of the conflict. A lifetime of fighting – both covertly and overtly – against Pakistan had followed, and the scars ensured that every time he looked in the mirror, he knew who and what his job demanded. There had been many times when the bloodshed had been existential, and at other times it had been cravenly political – and both those things were necessary bullets on the resume of an ambitious political operator.

In a career spent parrying threats and delivering reprisals, he believed he had seen every possible permutation of combat, but the report he had just heard was unusually strange.

He knew all his counterparts in the Pakistani military and intelligence services – he knew which ones did which jobs, he knew what was dangerous about each one, and he knew what things they considered most threatening about him. He also knew that there were good men in the Pak Army (پاکستان فوج) who, much like himself, often found themselves compromised by political or populist pressures. He respected the job they had to do, even if his job was, so often, to neutralize it.

Now he held a dispatch from the science division that spiked his blood pressure instantly. He caught himself before he did or said anything reactionary.

"What was that phrase Rahul always taunted me with?" he thought to himself.

It was from one of the German philosophers. Nietzsche, perhaps? Schopenhauer? Captain Rahul, his longtime adjutant had so often said it when gently chastising him for having so much anger roiling beneath the surface of a calm and poised exterior. He was almost certainly quoting it out of context, but it did sound profound, and he accepted the reminder each time he got it.

"Oh General," Rahul would say with an arched eyebrow and zero eye contact, "I suppose 'There are no beautiful surfaces without a terrible depth.'"

And right now, those terrible depths were churning.

The military's chief scientists had confirmed that the structured, almost imperceptible interference that had recently been detected in their satellite network was something other than atmospheric noise. It was, in the studied opinion of multiple agencies who co-signed this report, the byproduct of a carefully hidden datastream moving through their military networks. Six of the seven senior analysts who reviewed this report reached the same conclusion: Pakistan was the only player in the region with both the motive and ability to infiltrate the military's network, and the considerable level of stealth currently being used indicated the prelude to an attack, or an ongoing exfiltration of data, or both.

General Gupta thought through the recent sequence of events. At first it was assumed that this interference was something as mundane as a random cosmic occurrence that would recede as quickly as it arrived, but when the Indian Space Research Organization (भारतीय अंतरिक्ष अनुसंधान संगठन) did not report any problems with their space-based telescopes, the investigation turned its attention to the ways in which this sudden interference of unknown origin was also adding microscopic levels of noise to fiber optic lines. It was as if someone or something invisible had just entered the network and was now sitting there quietly breathing. And watching. This situation presented a perfect opportunity to overreact dreadfully, and Gupta paused again to gather himself. The most pressing issue now was determining the degree to which this interference may have already compromised his military's initial ability to detect and assess the threat, and now it appeared the threat was testing its ability to impact their communications by introducing what it thought was an imperceptible amount of noise – with the opportunity to then introduce a lot of noise in the future when it needed to scramble their network. In the guidebook for preemptive strikes, all that was left to do was compromise the enemy's ability to respond and react.

With all due respect for statesmanship and diplomacy, Gupta was not going to wait to see how those latter steps unfolded.

"If a snake is coiling around us," he explained to his senior staff, "we must do two things: Know where it is going to bite and kill it before it does." He knew he was demanding answers from a group of officers who hadn't slept since they found this information, and likely wouldn't sleep again until they started making definitive claims. This also went for the hundreds of people reporting to those men.

He ran his hand across the top of his head, and down the back of his neck, his fingers followed the lines and grooves of scar tissue along the way, and he looked around the room, waiting for his mind to seize upon a detail buried in this new information. This "situation room" where he spent so much time had always been strange to him. It had been built at a time when the best way to make decisions was to have as many experts as possible available to you in one place. That explained the tiered seating and the polished wood tabletops in long half circles around a central bank of projection screens on the opposite wall. It looked like NASA's mission control in the 1970s. But now all that marble and wood was covered with neatly organized cables running to screens that could call up any datapoint or any single person or remote team you needed.

General Gupta's challenge was to navigate an entire military apparatus – arguably the second largest in the world, depending on how and what you were counting – along a razor's edge of international relations. His country had hostile or semi-hostile relations with every single country it bordered, with Pakistan traditionally topping the list of antagonists – but, in addition to having a "challenging" relationship along every inch of its 9,400 miles of shared borders, there was also the matter of how many different types of land his army had to protect. In the north there was the world's largest mountain range, in the south was dense tropical rainforest, and in the west was a vast desert. It was strange to say that a country of 1.4 billion people was isolated, but India had no friendly military alliances, it lacked cordial relations with other regional powers, and it completely lacked cultural similarities with its neighbors. This left India uniquely and unmistakably alone on the world stage.

The General knew this made India an easy target for international scrutiny, but it also meant his country could pursue particularly obtuse agendas since there was so little reason for them to carefully weigh how friends or allies might react. For this reason, India could choose to act purely in its own self-interest, and the motivations for some of these self-serving actions were not always obvious. From the perspective of their enemies, this made Gupta's military very difficult to predict.

Gupta was an expert at using that uncertainty to his advantage, and he loved exploiting that gray area to draw blood where and when he needed it. What he did not like was the uncertainty that was now foisted upon him. Part of what unsettled him was the very real possibility that he and his senior officers were diagnosing this potential attack based on the order in which it had been discovered, not necessarily the order it had happened. He knew that a barrage of tests had been administered to check for this blind spot, but the results, in his estimation, seemed ambivalent. Now that he had intel about the source of this threat, he was ready to rely on his training: He was expected to determine where attacks might come from, identify a pattern, and then reach a conclusion on how to counteract whatever was coming. He had spent his entire career staring across the border, waiting to detect and neutralize Pakistan's next attack, and then respond. That didn't even take into account the proactive maneuvers he had so often put in place. This was the best way he knew how to maintain the safety of an entire subcontinent – and now, with a very vaguely understood weapon pointed at him, he was tasked with orchestrating an operation which existed firmly within a strategic and ethical gray area. Would this operation qualify as a preemptive strike since Pakistan had not yet harmed any Indian people or assets? Or would this be retaliation since the early stages of the attack had, apparently, already begun?

This differentiation would certainly not matter once he pulled the trigger on an operation and the entire region plunged into something approximating chaos.

At some point very soon the electronic warfare specialists would admit that the exact source of this interference would be impossible to track down in a timeframe that left India intact by the time their investigation was complete, and, for that reason, the ability to create such a thing had to be eradicated in a way that made it impossible for it ever regroup and attack again. The word everyone would be hinting at but unwilling to be the first to say out loud, was "EMP."

The rationale for an electromagnetic pulse, he knew, would be presented like this: "The interference in our networks is clear evidence of a first strike of some kind, in particular a cyber weapon. To prevent this weapon from being used, we need to shut off Pakistan's ability to use electronics of any kind, and we need to do this in such a way that, even if the source of this weapon is shielded against a pulse, all the wiring, power lines, routers, cell towers, transformers, and substations that distributed power and internet connections throughout the country would be rendered useless, effectively stranding this weapon wherever it is being developed."

Gupta had already received a call from a friend on the Defence Planning Committee (रक्षा योजना समिति) that the Prime Minister had inquired about the EMP option independently of a military recommendation, and this meant that the Nuclear Command Authority (परमाणु कमान प्राधिकरण) would already be looking into how soon they could facilitate this option outside of his own chain of command. But it was still far, far too soon to be discussing EMP's. He knew he was probably within 36 hours, maybe less, of having a very difficult discussion with the Prime Minister about what an EMP meant, and he had started planning how to have that conversation.

"Sir," he would begin, "I would, respectfully, ask you to consider the reaction from the international community in the event we were to use an electromagnetic pulse weapon in a non-combat scenario. Preemptive strikes bring considerable ethical concerns with them and using a weapon like this in a preventative capacity – especially considering what's in its warhead – presents a moral quandary of the highest order."

This, he figured, was a respectful enough intro to the topic, but it still had enough force to jar the Prime Minister just enough to ask his most senior military commander to elaborate. There was also a small chance it would get him thrown out of the room preemptively – in the same way Truman had thrown Oppenheimer out of the Oval Office when he foolishly attempted to have a similar conversation retroactively.

So, if the Prime Minister responded the way he hoped, he'd continue: "The first thing you have to consider is that, even though you've heard an EMP weapon is non-lethal to humans, it *still* has a nuclear warhead attached to it. That nuclear device is designed to detonate in a way that sends out a giant wave of electricity in the form of radio waves and microwaves – but its explosion is controlled so that it doesn't produce enough energy to create the type of radiation that kills everyone in its path."

He wasn't sure if that distinction would make a difference or not. Sending a nuclear bomb up into the atmosphere was a major step regardless of whether or not it could kill anyone on the ground.

Maybe he could add this: "Even without all the radiation and fallout, an EMP is still *massively* destructive. It will fry every single electrical object within its range instantaneously – that means, computers, refrigerators, the entire power grid, radios, any car made after 1955, alarm clocks, traffic lights, airplanes, the pumps that bring water to your house, toasters, telecommunications, databases, and every medical device invented after the stethoscope – the list goes on. Anything with a wire or a circuit board is unfixable."

The Prime Minister was intelligent and curious, and wise enough to ask good questions when topics strayed outside her various areas of expertise; Gupta hoped this would lead to more questions about how easily an EMP could roll back the centuries on its target. "It may interest you to know that the United States war-gamed all of this back in the 1960s, and the standard measurement they developed was this: If a relatively small 1.4 megaton warhead on an EMP device detonated in the upper atmosphere, about 250 miles above their state of Kansas to be precise, the resulting pulse would be enough to wipe out every electronic object in the entire country, most of Mexico, and a big chunk of Canada – all at once. Considering the continental U.S. is ten times bigger than Pakistan, we wouldn't require a warhead anywhere near that size, or we could just detonate it much closer to the ground. And, for reference, a modern 1.4 megaton warhead could fit inside your briefcase with room to spare."

If nothing else, he could paint a picture of the aftermath: "There are going to be military assets and a few commercial or industrial setups that have shielded their electronics from an electromagnetic pulse, but an overwhelming percentage of Pakistan – something likely exceeding 95% – will be directly affected by this. While the international community will almost certainly rally to their aid while simultaneously denouncing us with the most inflammatory rhetoric possible, Pakistan will effectively be sent back to the Stone Age for the next 20 to 25 years while their power and communications grids are rebuilt from scratch. The economic collapse following the pulse will be laid at our doorstep, as will every story of a child who dies because a simple medical procedure was impossible without functioning equipment."

This would put him in the unenviable but not uncommon position of having to order something terrible to happen on behalf of someone else – and with the understanding that his role in the military spanned a lifetime, whereas a prime minister's term in office lasted just five years. Long after the next election was over, or even the election after that, he would still be navigating the national security threats which come from transforming a neighboring country full of mostly innocent civilians into a paleolithic nightmare.

He had recalled Air Marshall Chatterjee from his scheduled vacation last night when these discussions began, just on the hunch that the EMP conversation would present itself. In retrospect, that reasoning for Chatterjee's return didn't make any sense. It struck him, much to his surprise, that he'd taken that action at something resembling a subconscious level – he knew the EMP was going to happen, and his solution was to engage a low-impact, low-destruction, minimally geopolitically fatal way to do it. This option might even be deniable enough to blame on a rogue faction.

The plan his psyche had set in motion – he couldn't help but laugh at framing it in this way – was to have his military's expert at recovering lost nuclear weapons reverse engineer that process: A nuclear device needed to arrive at a location in an enemy's territory after being removed from his own country's arsenal – and, in the investigation that both countries and international inspectors would conduct afterward, there could never be any record of a device going missing, or of a stockpile being short by one warhead, or that a nuclear device was given a routine inspection but never returned to its secure housing. This mission required Chatterjee to move a nuclear device through the gaps that were not supposed to exist in his perfectly secure program. But, General Gupta thought to himself, who better to find those gaps than the man tasked with eliminating them?

The next step would be to find the correct target to neutralize.

Gupta knew where this attack was being built, and if his intelligence service wasn't ready to say it definitively yet, he knew it was coming: The Pakistani cyber warfare program had operated for years on the grounds of the massive Masroor Air Base (مسرور ائیر بیس),

just across the Lyari River (دریائے لیاری) from Karachi, and they used this proximity to one of the 10 biggest cities in the world to tap into its tech sector or any other specialization they needed. The cyber weapon group was situated in a large hangar on the northern edge of the airfield that butted up against a canal with an austere, ancient cemetery on the other side. He'd stared at the roof of that building for years in satellite photos whenever another report had arrived with details of his military's databases being probed by military hackers, and he'd often wondered if he'd be in this post long enough to address this persistent problem. The current attack had enough of the hallmarks of past attacks to paint a bullseye clearly on this airbase.

But that dusty rooftop was only half the target. He also had to disrupt all the routes their cyberwarfare team would use to move the weapon's payload outside the country. And there were a lot of wires going in a lot of directions to and from a facility like this.

He paused again to refocus his thoughts. After a moment his mind wandered until it came to rest on a memory of a small, nondescript room he had sat in years ago. Two promotions ago, to be exact.

He had just been nominated to take command of an expansive portion of the military, including supervision of the nuclear weapons program, and, before he could be presented to the Indian Parliament (भारतीय संसद) for confirmation, he underwent three days of psychological tests to ascertain the precise mental state and emotional makeup of a man about to be given such a job. This final appointment was very different from the rigor and mental bombardment of the previous sessions; this time he was introduced to a short, soft-spoken woman who, during the initial exchange of pleasantries, seemed like the ideal person to meet with a sensitive child or forlorn teenager.

The session was scheduled to last just 40 minutes, and he would learn after his confirmation was complete that this meeting was the type which only happened if every other evaluator had already reached a satisfactory verdict – and that this was the single evaluation which could block the promotion if anything problematic was discovered.

"Mukund, I'm not going to ask you how you balance your conflicting priorities or how you manage stress or check your ambition on behalf of the 'greater good' – I know my colleagues spent the last two days asking you about that in every possible way they could think to do it."

He politely gave half a smile and nodded.

"Your service record shows a career that can only be described as 'spectacular' when it comes to your success rate at accomplishing the very difficult tasks placed in front of you."

He suppressed the unconscious urge to nod again while he waited for the question to arrive.

"But what isn't captured in reports like these is what your reaction is up here," she tapped the side of her head, "when you first lay eyes on your orders and see something that is, in your estimation, morally questionable."

Still no question.

"I understand your premise."

"Ok, so how do you personally reconcile your commitment and your loyalties when you are given an order that you disagree with?"

"At the earliest stages of training every soldier is taught how problematic it is to question orders, and, unlike when I was young, now we even explain to them the many reasons why doing so is counterproductive."

"And what about when you were young?"

"At the time, anyone insolent enough to demand a reason ran the risk of being shot."

"I see, but I know that someone of your current and future rank does have the latitude to ask a few good questions about orders – so wouldn't you welcome those same questions from the officers who report to you?"

"I would not," he said with clipped certitude, nearly stepping on the end of her question.

She waited a moment to see if he had anything to add to such an adamant response. The moments passed in silence.

"I'm a bit surprised by that, Mukund, and I wonder if you're saying what you've either been trained to say or, perhaps, what you think you're supposed to say."

Yet again, there was no question, so he waited.

"I genuinely am curious, how do you balance those demands of loyalty and personal ethics?"

"The latitude you asked about is found in the ways I choose to execute the task I am given, what I do not get to choose is the outcome

I have been instructed to achieve."

"So you can control how you reach an objective but not the objective itself."

"That is the nature of military discipline."

"But I suppose there are many cases where there are very few available ways that an unpleasant outcome can be achieved, and, in those cases, any of the paths you might take to get there are problematic."

"Your example is hypothetical, but I will agree with your characterization that there are tasks which cannot avoid an unpleasant process of rectification. Hypothetically, of course."

"And that doesn't bother you?"

"My role in this military's leadership is to make exceptionally difficult choices and then be personally responsible for the totality of the outcome. That is a responsibility that I accept."

"But that does not prevent you from critically evaluating the moral and ethical implications of the actions that you order."

"Correct."

"And so why don't you feel the need to push back on orders that you deem to be morally repugnant?"

"I can't adequately conjure a specific answer from such a generalized starting point, but I can tell you this: The institution tasked with protecting our democracy is not itself democratic. I do not get to vote on the orders I am given, and I do not solicit votes on the orders I give. I also don't believe any single mission or engagement is indicative of the philosophic totality of my career or the nuance of this military as a whole."

"That is a good answer, Mukund, but I suspect there is a great deal more you could say if you didn't think every word of this was being recorded, which I can assure you it is not."

There was another extended pause, and this one lasted long enough for him to notice that the air from a nearby vent was quietly circulating again.

"If you were stripped of your rank tomorrow and suddenly found yourself outside of the military, what would you do without the trappings of the power and prestige your rank affords you?"

"I have never considered that before."

"That doesn't surprise me, and it's ok that it hasn't crossed your mind. But, now that it has, I'm curious how you react to it."

"Every career choice I've made since I was 13 has been done with the intention of leading soldiers and protecting this country. I haven't started thinking about what I will do after the military."

"I didn't ask what you wanted to do when you retired, I asked what you'd do if you were removed from the military."

"I don't have a plan for that, either."

"I see. One last question, Mukund, and then I suppose the next time I see you will be when I spot your picture in the newspaper breezing through your confirmation."

This got a laugh from the general who was not looking forward to the confirmation process, but who was now very eager for this session to end. Each of the questions had caught him just a few small degrees off guard, and now, after almost 40 minutes, the cumulative effect was remarkable.

"Two different times you've been very badly wounded in combat."

"Yes."

"In both cases the reports indicate that you returned to duty early, you immediately took on increased responsibilities, and you continued your way up the ladder, as it were."

"There is an old saying that the fastest way to add stars to your epaulette is by catching bullets."

"Did you find that to be the case?"

"I might have preferred to avoid the injuries."

"Elusive until the end," she said, glancing at the clock. "But I am curious, Mukund, what do you make of the fact that people who have had their blood spilled and their bones broken find themselves drawn to *fix* things?"

"I make of it that those of us who have had that happen are keenly eager to find ways to keep it from happening again."

"To yourselves."

"To anyone."

"Do you feel like your experience being wounded gave you a level of insight you could not have reached otherwise?"

"No one is surprised when a soldier dies – that is as much a part of the job as the bad food and the long hours. And no commander deploys expecting that every single one of his soldiers will walk back out of that combat zone when it's time to rotate home. But what will wake up a good officer in the middle of the night is the thought of the people who died because he was indecisive at a critical moment, or because he trusted bad information, or because he miscalculated the correct portions of violence and restraint."

"And that is what you are known for, is it not? Your unique approach to that alchemy of violence and restraint?"

"I won't speculate on the component parts of my reputation."

"And doesn't having a reputation for restraint certainly offer you a considerable benefit of the doubt when the time does come to choose violence?"

"Violence comes in many forms, and the very worst kinds available to a general do not require a military."

Now it was her turn to feel the sudden churn of discomfort that accompanies a glimpse into a dark room which is much larger and far more crowded than you ever imagined. And, right on cue, the meeting with this promising general was over.

22 JUNE

At 2 pm local time First Lieutenant Wáng Xuěméi was traveling the exact same route along China's northeastern border for the third day in a row.

After takeoff she climbed at a steady 60-degree angle and very quickly left the nearby city of Jilin (吉林省) behind, dipping out of sight as she climbed above the foothills and into the persistent cloud cover. Right on schedule she swung her Vigorous Dragon northwest to skirt the Mongolian border for several hundred miles before turning northeast once she reached Hulun Lake (呼伦湖). After two hours in the air, she refueled high above Hulunbuir (呼伦贝尔市) and continued due north. Shortly after detaching from the fuel tanker, she reached the Greater Khingan mountain range (大兴安岭), a 750-mile stretch of volcanic peaks that extended all the way to the country's northernmost corner. None of these mountains were huge – the tallest was just shy of 7,000 feet, which was tiny compared to the mountains on China's western border which averaged 20,000 feet – but what these mountains lacked in size they made up for in sharp peaks and impassable valleys carved by multiple rivers. It was no wonder that this area had been completely unexplored until the 20th century – and only then to build a railroad for logging.

Just as she reached the northernmost point of mainland China, the Amur River came into view, and she began a slow U-turn to follow this famous waterway until she reached the city of Heihe 370 miles to the southeast. While holding a steady speed of just below Mach 1, and cruising at a conservative 51,000 feet, she could see nearly 300 miles in every direction, including about 200 into the interior of Russia. At this point she was looking into the Khingan Nature Reserve (Хинганский заповедник), a protected area created to preserve, among other things, the endangered Red-crowned Crane.

Once she spotted Heihi out the left side of the cockpit window she adjusted slightly and turned due south to return to the airfield where all of this had begun a few hours earlier. The Amur River slowly hooked to the east where it would continue its role as natural boundary between China and Russia until turning north – which, she noted, was something that didn't seem to happen very often – before dumping out in the Gulf of Tartary (Татарский пролив) in the Pacific Ocean. This nearly unheard-of river was actually the 10th longest in the world and, notably, filled with monsters like the 18-foot, 2,000-pound predatory kaluga (Калуга).

Starting tomorrow her patrol was shifting to follow the river all the way to the Pacific Coast, through the Manchurian heartland. This was territory that every major empire in this region had fought over and owned at one point in history; the Mongols, Koreans, Japanese, Russians, and Han had all bled on this ground, and the resulting mixture of cultures found in various isolated pockets were each proud to be something resembling none of those while still featuring pieces of each. That route would take her up into the country's furthest east corner, past the politically significant – and, arguably, therefore delicate – Nizhneleninskoye-Tongjiang Bridge over the Amur River. After passing the bridge, the route traced the edge of the North Korean border before heading home.

She knew that the two pilots who flew the patrol through the Manchurian territory yesterday were in near-constant contact with the base's intelligence officers, and, at several points, the pilots were certain they recognized the voices of leaders from Beijing that no one here had ever actually met, but who had been seen on countless video broadcasts from the Ministry of Defence. At least this extremely elevated level of stress made the flights more interesting, although they didn't make the scenery any less boring. There were several pilots in this squadron who had been scrambled on previous occasions when the leadership in Beijing suddenly got uncomfortable about something happening along a distant border. Her regular wingman, Chén Wěiqiáng (陈伟强), had previously been stationed at an airbase near the Altai Mountains (阿尔泰山脉) mountains, and, on multiple occasions, he had spent several hours flying uncomfortably close to peaks straddling the China-Russia border just to see Russian glaciologists pulling ice cores, rather than Russian special forces taking the least logical route to invade his homeland.

Yesterday Wěiqiáng had been asked to take a second pass over the Nizhneleninskoye-Tongjiang Bridge so the camera equipment mounted near the nosecone of his J-10 could pick up additional data. This Amur River bridge was heavily traveled, and, since its opening in 2021, it had been a regional source of pride – as well as a source of much diplomatic high-fiving in both Beijing and Moscow. The purpose of its construction had been to take advantage of the intensive farming and mining done on the Russian side of the border and transport it to the Chinese side for processing and manufacture. The bridge was 7,300 feet long and cost $360 million – all for just two train tracks, one in each direction. Winter temperatures in this area regularly reached -40C, and that must have made the construction process miserable

The bridge also did something besides move 21 million tons of raw materials every year – it also connected the Trans-Siberian Railway with the Eastern China Railroad, and this was a very important part of the Central Committee's plan to connect Beijing and England by rail before the end of the decade. That assumed, of course, that anyone would want to make a 9,000-mile trip on a train that, at best, would occasionally reach 100 miles per hour. Xuěméi had done the math in her head – even if the train was moving 24 hours a day at that speed, it would still be a five-week trip. No thanks.

This particular point about Chinese excellence relative to their Russian neighbors had once been a common topic of conversation with her father-in-law. After a career spent amongst the ambassadorial ranks and, later supervising the manufacturing sector, he had no illusions about which superpower had the upper hand. "Russia may be 10 times larger," he would explain, "but all that space is just bears and permafrost – we have twice the population and all the passion!" This particular bridge was also a favorite topic of his. "You know that during construction Russia and China were each responsible for building their own half of the bridge – and do you know how long our half of it was?" Even if you offered the answer, he would always repeat it. "Yes, our 'half' was 6,200 feet, and we finished our section three years before the Russians finished their 1,100 feet." Jun never missed a chance to congratulate his father for this, and the fact that he hadn't been involved in the construction did not remotely dampen his pride. "That bridge tells you absolutely everything you need to know about what makes our two countries different."

Her husband lacked his father's passion for politics and public works, but he was a good son and adept at appearing fascinated by the constant analysis of international relations as seen through the lens of Party doctrine. Xuěméi was even less interested – which is to say she had zero interest – in such dynamics. The fact that the ephemeral nature of politics was of no interest to a scientist was all very stereotypical and predictable; she saw politics as an inelegant and exceedingly convenient way to repackage reality in exchange for short-term gains – and this made it inherently fake and intrinsically useless. This was not a surprising conclusion for a scientist to reach, but she knew enough about history to know the fate of thousands of Chinese scientists who said similarly rational things in the decades before she was born, as well as some of the decades after. So, out of pragmatism, but more out of a desire to have a genuinely positive relationship with her husband's very kind father, she also listened and nodded and smiled during his analysis.

This willingness to listen and her accompanying eagerness to demonstrate the prized Chinese ethic of filial piety (孝) quickly led to a close bond with both her in-laws. She, Jun, and Mínghuī spent many happy family gatherings in Beidaihe (北戴河区), a resort town frequented by senior Party officials on the coast of the Bohai Sea (渤海). Almost immediately she was the long-lost daughter to a proud father of two sons.

After Jun's death, his father saw to it that Xuěméi was offered a job as a consultant in the government's foreign affairs department advising on aeronautical trends and areas of investment. It was a job that would require her to do nothing but pay lavishly nonetheless – and it would allow her to live comfortably in the same luxury building as him. It was an exceptional gesture and, even for someone of his status, it had been exceptionally hard to arrange.

She shocked him by refusing.

Instead, she asked him for something even more difficult to deliver:

She wanted to attend the Air Force Aviation University and train as a fighter pilot.

This request was wildly unreasonable for someone of her age and gender, but it was the only future her present could picture. Jun's father was so blinded by his grief – and so anxious for anything which might assuage it – that he called the cabinet member responsible for the military academies and promised him a future favor of any kind in return. Such open-ended, blank-check promises are the most valuable commodity in any totalitarian bureaucracy, and the offer was readily accepted since it was assumed this grief-stricken wife could not possibly qualify for admission. Xuěméi was informed she would be allowed to take one flight with a university instructor to demonstrate her aptitude for the aircraft, and, after that, she and her father-in-law would accept the decision of the school without any questions.

Four weeks later she taxied the tandem J-10 she knew so well onto the runway in Jilin. Within seven minutes she was streaking past the peaks she now knew so well from her patrols of the border. A little over 90 minutes later she had landed and, right there on the tarmac, Training Officer (訓練人員) Yáng Péngfēi congratulated her on a successful admissions exam. That spring she entered the university.

Now, so many years later, she was something very different than what had stood at the site of that rockslide, staring deep into the crevasse below, searching for some sign of her former life. The politics which had never interested her now bled into her work, and she resented that such machinations were afoot; it did not occur to her that similar processes were responsible for her seat at the academy.

But now she knew enough to understand that the political value of this border crossing did not change the fact that a heavily traveled stretch of railroad like this made for a very porous international border. No matter how carefully watched a crossing like this was, it presented a tempting type of target to a particular type of malicious interest. If the Central Military Commission was suspicious about something happening inside Russia and ending up in China, then it made sense to put this area at the top of their watchlist.

There was certainly nothing else to watch here.

* * * * *

About 6,000 miles away, bobbing gently in the ambiguous corridor of water where the Arabian Sea slowly becomes the Indian Ocean, the USS John F. Kennedy had just arrived to conduct three days of training and international coordination with the Indian navy.

The captain, a man large enough to have only barely fit within the 6'5" maximum height requirement for Navy fighter pilots was on the bridge as his First Officer briefed the senior staff on the expectations for the upcoming exercises with the flagship of the Indian maritime force. This flagship, the INS Vikramaditya, was a carrier the Indians had bought from Russia in 2004, and it had originally been built in 1978 by the Soviet Union. As the captain listened, a young intelligence officer walked up, saluted, and handed him a dispatch that was still warm from the printer.

This printout came adorned with the highest possible security designations and had been sent directly from the Pentagon, by orders of a "Major Carl Horn, GOC." Captain Samuel Guillory knew just enough about the way secret messages were sent at times when secret problems needed to be dealt with to know that any time you saw this insignia on a document a few smoking craters were likely in somebody's very near future. Both recipients of this message were apprised of an unusually ugly sounding development: A sudden spike in tensions in the Chinese intelligence services happened to coincide with the Indian Minister of Defence sending all types of chatter through their channels about the idea of possible incoming threats from Pakistan.

"Either of those situations can go sideways in a hurry," Guillory thought, "and having both percolating at the same time was a lot worse."

The dispatch asked Captain Guillory to be prepared to respond to further instructions at a moment's notice. The battlegroup attached to his carrier consisted of the standard complement of seven other ships – two cruisers, three destroyers, a supply ship, and a Virginia-class fast attack submarine just to add an extra layer of danger to anyone or anything attempting to get too close – and the dispatch made it clear that, in the event of any escalations, the Kennedy was to break off from the planned exercises and travel at the highest possible speed to a point on the shared coastline of India and Pakistan. By the looks of it on the map, this would place them somewhere off the coast of the Keti Wildlife Sanctuary (کیٹی بندر وائلڈ لائف سینچری) – which, if memory served, was just full of flamingos. Or something.

For the past week his engineers had been planning to power down one of the reactors for routine maintenance, but racing up the coast meant both reactors would need to be primed to travel at or beyond their still-classified top speed. Guillory was also instructed to be ready to launch interceptor missiles in the event that either military puts anything in the air that needs to be put back down on the ground.

The other recipient of the message was about 688 feet below him and reading the same thing.

Captain Desmond O'Shea commanded the USS Arizona SSN-803, one of the Navy's new generation of fast-attack submarines, and an object of dread and terror amongst every other navy on earth. O'Shea was instructed to break contact with the carrier group immediately and begin patrolling the coastline for any and all Indian vessels – surface or submersible – capable of launching a cruise missile attack. Giving Captain O'Shea a task like this was to put a new piece of wreckage on the ocean floor. Desmond O'Shea was quite possibly the hardest man in the Navy – a title which hundreds of others had tried and failed to achieve, even if few consciously recognized they were competing for such a thing. But O'Shea knew. Had he lived a century and a half earlier, he would have almost certainly done his part to add to the mythos of Old West gunfighters who were wildly colorful in the retellings but unsentimental when it came time to reach for their revolver. This temperament made him a unique presence in the otherwise bland officer core of the United States Navy. There was something to be said for a man in a 460-foot steel tube with an itchy trigger finger. He had been the first choice for a command of the new 5th generation of Virginia-class attack subs, and the Arizona was, as planned, the most technologically advanced killing machine currently attached to a periscope. He had previously commanded one of the 2nd generation Virginia-class vessels, and before that one of the old Seawolfs.

O'Shea was not the man who was going to tinker with the code in the sonar visualizer, and he couldn't do the advanced calculus in his head to plot firing solutions, and he only knew the bare minimum about the inner workings of that S9G reactor that was pulsing 150 feet behind him – but he had senior officers on the bridge for all of that. What set him apart in this profession was much simpler: He was the last person any other U.S. or allied submarine wanted hunting them in a training exercise. He could sense the dead spot beneath a thermocline layer to lie in wait, he could listen to the barely audible rotation of a propeller blade and know who it was and what it was doing, and he innately understood how to use a target's greatest strengths against them. In 22 years of war games, Captain O'Shea had displayed an ability to track, close, and destroy that was coldly preternatural. Officers who had worked for him all used the same phrase to summarize the most dangerous man underwater: "All killer, no filler."

1991

10 APRIL

Fresh off her mid-afternoon session with the research team, Sienna was relieved to be done – "and even better to be done a bit early, *all things considered*" she said to herself. This was a phrase she had recently heard in context well enough to start using it, but not enough to use it in the *correct* context.

She walked across the campsite to the barn that had been outfitted with every available amusement for children between the ages of eight and 12.

She made her way to one of the couches occupying the front porch of the barn and slumped down next to two friends she'd made during her first week at the camp. Nora was reading a magazine about penguins, and Naomi had a handheld video game that beeped constantly. The beeping was so loud Sienna was suspicious that beeping might be the entire point of the game. Sienna leaned her head all the way back and stared up at the planks in the sloped roof shading the porch. In the background she could hear a game show on the TV.

"Did you get anything today?" she asked.

Nora didn't even look up from the penguins. "Yeah," she said, "a couple small things. A lot of it was the same as the last three days. I keep getting this 'Please confirm' and then it's 'Repeat and confirm,' and then there are all these blueprints or plans and blah, blah, blah." Naomi's game stopped beeping for a split second, and she used the gap to add, "I got the same thing, I think I was actually the first one to get that."

Nora rolled her eyes and laughed, "You're hilarious. My old roommate Tiff had that back before either one of us even got here."

Sienna stretched her legs straight out in front of her and held them there in the air. Just as she was pushing today's shortcoming from her mind, Naomi added: "I actually got a couple of things out of those 'blah, blah, blahs' you flew past."

This was hopeful. "Yeah," Sienna said, "I was pretty sure I had something there for a split second. I could see a design for something, but it was from a bad angle, so I couldn't make anything of it."

Naomi was back at her game by now, but still listening. "Oh, yeah, I went over that this morning. It's not that it's a bad angle, it's just that it's appearing across a curved surface. Torchy thinks it's a design – he calls it a 'schematic' – of some Russian machine or something."

"A curved surface?" she said, squinting her eyes and trying to picture it again in her mind. "Yikes, I missed that entirely."

She stared up at Sugarloaf Mountain or Hill or whatever it was called. The patches of blue oaks were rippling in the breeze, and behind them the haze that had started drifting out to sea. It was quiet for a long time before Nora tossed her magazine about penguins into a basket and picked up a new one with Vanilla Ice on the cover. As she searched for the photos of Vanilla she asked, "You're hanging out with your parents this weekend, right?"

"Tomorrow after lunch is what Dr. Carney told me."

Sienna was fortunate that her family lived in nearby Walnut Creek – about an hour away, on the other side of the San Francisco Bay. Her fellow campers came from all over the country and didn't get to see their parents on a weekly basis, although the NRO did have a lot of planes and flew parents in on a fairly regular basis.

"He really is pretty cute," Nora said offhandedly.

"What?"

"Vanilla."

"You just call him 'Vanilla' now?" Sienna asked, laughing while she leaned over to see the magazine.

"Well, 'Mr. Ice' seems a bit too formal," Nora explained.

Now Naomi was leaning in, and together they flipped approvingly through a few more pages while debating the merits of shaving lines in your eyebrows. Soon enough, Sienna's mind drifted back to the pending visit.

"By now they've spent the last two days telling their friends about how they're coming to," she made big air quotes with her fingers, "'parents' weekend' at 'the boarding school.'"

Naomi's game stopped beeping completely, and she checked the batteries. "My parents left last night," she said while trying to pry the battery compartment open with a fingernail. "They hung out forever just eating the snacks and watching Pay Per View. This is a dream situation for my dad – for him, having a kid that works here is like being James Bonds' dad."

Naomi and Sienna's dads were eerily similar – because this was also exactly how Mike Barrett saw himself.

"I also heard we're getting two new kids first thing next week," Nora said.

"Well, Martin went home last week, and Amaya went home on Saturday," Naomi added.

Sienna's stomach dropped. The idea of going home before finding something big in the Signal terrified her.

* * * * *

Walking across the common area in the middle of the campsite, Dr. Torquemann said hello to each of the campers he passed and kicked a soccer ball back to a group of boys chasing an errant pass. He reached the large, open floor plan dining hall and climbed the stairs to his office tucked in the rafters above where everyone would be eating dinner in about an hour.

This was the official headquarters of Operation Dark Antennae, a project so secret that, at its height, less than 10 people outside the camp perimeter knew it existed. As the decades passed after the conclusion of the program, that number would shrink as information about its existence was deliberately placed far outside the reach of FOIA requests or Oversight Committee inquiries.

In the small-but-still-crowded world of clandestine agencies, the National Reconnaissance Office was a strange beast – it did not have the most well-known acronym, but it did, by a very wide margin, have the largest budget. The unbelievable level of funding made its relative anonymity all the more impressive – or perhaps that kind of anonymity is something you can buy with so much money. The NRO was expected to solve problems and know things and take actions that no one else wanted to know about or even know were possible to exist – and that is where the gargantuan amount of money began to seem like a bargain: Because everyone in D.C. ultimately saw the NRO budget as downright affordable in exchange for getting to believe the type of problems they solved didn't really exist.

He dropped his bag on his desk and started reading through the messages that had accumulated during the several hours he'd been at the research cabin. Down below he could hear the security team putting together tonight's meal. Whichever three guys from the team were in charge of dinner tonight sounded like they were working fast.

Even though the security detail doubled as cooks, he knew that this was as secure a place as anywhere on the planet. The eight guys on the security team were all former special operators who now worked for the National Security Agency providing security at safe houses, laboratories, and other places that did not and would not ever officially exist. They were stationed here in rotating groups and, although each of them would admit being a few years past a prime spent wiping out enemy commandos and HALO jumping behind enemy lines, they all remained unparalleled in their mastery of violence. Even now, in semi-retirement and on a deployment that was considered recreational compared to normal, each of them were still purely lethal; any of them could still run at a flat sprint for three miles and then draw their newly issued M4 carbine rifles and hit a quarter 19 out of 20 times from 100 yards. Anything bigger than a barstool would get hit 20 out of 20 times from 300 yards, without exception. The camp was small enough that they could fan out across it in a matter of seconds if a sensor from the reinforced perimeter fence ever caught something it didn't like or went offline unexpectedly – and they had arranged and endlessly rehearsed protection protocols for every possible entry point, from any angle, from any conveyance, and this was cross-referenced with contingency plans for what to do if this happened during the day or night, if students were in classes or out in the yard, and if backup was available or if it wasn't.

And backup was always available.

Shortly after this campsite was selected as the home of Dark Antennae, a mid-level planning committee within the Department of Defense was guided to establish a pre-deployment foreign language training center for Army Rangers in the hills above nearby Montara

State Beach. The preexisting plan for this training center was then modestly expanded to include a second school to teach advanced avionics and instrumentation to helicopter pilots that were expected to operate in combat zones. "It is true," said a quietly imposing major from a Pentagon department that went unnamed when he appeared before the committee to present this addition to the plan, "that the 160th Special Operations Aviation Regiment has one of these facilities in Kentucky, but a West Coast alternative is important for pilots who will be operating in and around the Pacific theater." Later, no one at the new language training center ever noticed that each class of Rangers selected for the Montara Language Readiness Program always reflected the exact ratio of specialties present in a nine-member Ranger assault team, and everyone just assumed it was normal for a hangar of pristinely maintained Black Hawk helicopters to sit idle at a school dedicated to studying electronics. The commandant of this school was the only soldier on campus who had any idea that the facility also had a secondary mission.

Each new MLRP commandant was met at some point during their first 24 hours on the job by a NRO representative and an officer from military intelligence in order to learn the very specific details relating to this secondary mission. The meeting was always very brief and provided only the barest and most basic details, but it was nonetheless always overwhelming for the new supervisor of the facility.

"First, Colonel," the intelligence officer would begin, "we need you to ensure that at any given time two of the bungalows housing your students here on campus are always assigned in such a way that the group of Rangers in each unit happen to fit every role in a traditional assault squad. You also need to do the same with two complete crews of Black Hawk pilots."

The commandants throughout the years would always think to themselves that this seemed overly specific but easy enough to accommodate.

"The second item, sir, is that each of the Black Hawks in the hangars must always be flight ready at any time and pre-loaded with a Ranger fire team's standard outfit of infantry weapons, helmets, and frags."

This would also seem overly detailed, but easy to do, especially with the crew of mechanics who took several of the classes with the pilots.

Before the third item of this briefing was explained, the silent NRO representative would slide a satellite phone across the commandant's desk, at which point the intelligence officer would continue his overview.

"Colonel, there is only one reason this phone will ever ring, and when it does you will recognize that the moment has arrived because the display screen identifying the incoming caller will simply read '&&&&&.' In the event of that call, you will notice that a call will also be coming through the main switchboard here in the administrative offices in such a way that it automatically cuts off every other ongoing phone call in order to make it impossible to miss that call. And, also at that same time, the phone on the wall of your personal quarters – the one without a keypad on it – that phone will also begin ringing. All three of these will be going off simultaneously. It will be the same caller on each of them. And when this occurs your only duty is to subordinate any other action you are taking in order to answer that call."

The commandant would nod, but their heart would be pounding.

"To be exceptionally clear, sir: There is no situation, under any circumstances, where that satellite phone will not be on your person at all times."

By this point the commandant, who would have been selected based on a sterling reputation and a flawless history of noteworthy military service, would have grown rigid and exceptionally attentive as he processed the gravity of this "secondary" mission that was, quite obviously, the facility's primary mission.

By this point, everything the military intelligence officer could or would ever know about this setup had been covered, and the NRO representative who had never offered his name would finally speak for the first time.

"Sir, no matter what you hear on the other end of that call, you will immediately use the facility's public address system to order both predetermined Ranger groups and flight crews to report to the hangar. You will tell them that this is a Tier-1 emergency and not a drill."

Without fail the commandant would confirm the order.

"There is nothing that you or this intelligence officer need to know about what ultimately happens, but I would like you to understand how the following few minutes will proceed after that call. First, the call itself is not intended to be a conversation – it exists only to set your next few steps in motion. The person calling will know that, although he may see fit to share a few quick details with you."

The NRO rep's tone was flat, and his voice never rose or fell.

"By maintaining the operational readiness of the Black Hawks here on campus, both birds should have no problem leaving the ground within six minutes of you receiving that phone call. I want to stress *unequivocally* that there cannot be exceptions to this timeframe. When the pilots reach those birds they will find, written in permanent marker on the control panel, the coordinates of their only destination. It is a wooded area 10.78 miles away."

The NRO rep knew that both the commandant and the intelligence officer would spend months and years staring at a map, trying to figure out where the hell those Black Hawks were supposed to go, but the odds of either one guessing correctly were essentially zero – there are 365 square miles of territory within a radius of that size.

"Once you order those teams to the helicopters, your final role in this process is to communicate three things to them. First, tell them that they will encounter an incredibly hot landing zone. Second, inform them that they absolutely *must* land in the prescribed area no matter what – regardless of what damage they take on the way in. Third, tell the Rangers to put on their helmets. And that's it."

By now, any commandant who hadn't gone pale was a fool.

The NRO rep would smile and thank the commandant for his time, but not before emphasizing that the likelihood of this situation ever developing was extremely low to the point of its odds being nonexistent. "This briefing, much like the process attached to it, is simply a carefully designed precaution against foreign forces interfering with a highly sensitive operation at a nearby site. The Rangers are intended to supplement the highly capable on-site security team in the event they require backup."

Torquemann knew about this plan, and he knew that in the unlikely event anyone ever knew this program existed, there were more guns available here than there were campers. The top speed of a Black Hawk meant those Rangers would be here in just over three minutes, and once those Rangers put on their helmets they'd be patched into a channel connecting them with the security team here at the camp, and they'd use that flight time to coordinate a plan.

He had watched the camp's security team train, and he shared their confidence that they could handle anything for nine minutes. To make things particularly unpleasant for any unplanned visitors, the guys cooking dinner downstairs had stashed M240 machine guns, rocket launchers, and extra grenades inside innocent looking objects at various locations all over the camp, and the pitch in the roof above his head had a ready-made sniper nest built into it.

Between the anonymity and the firepower, Torquemann never spent a moment worried about the physical safety of anyone at the camp, but he spent long hours worried about the project itself.

The paperwork he was required to share at regular intervals served as both a reminder of how minimal the progress looked on that paper, and it presented a consistent means to draw his focus away from the actual mission. The team he reported to at the NRO wanted regular updates and then weekly recaps of everything the campers had seen, heard, or felt in the Signal. They wanted to know what was contained in the visuals, what were the sounds, what were the impressions?

After typing a 421-page dissertation at Cal Tech, Torquemann had hoped to never lay eyes on another typewriter, but, without fail, he found himself back at this desk outlining the main points from today's research and the context in which it should be viewed. As he worked, the other specialists from the research cabin stopped by the office to drop off their summaries – things like biometric data that was worthy of notice, transcripts of key things the kids saw or heard, and the amalgam of art and science that attempted to cross-reference these readings from the electromagnetic spectrum and brain scan data with the best available multivariate star charts. At the moment, this last area of focus was squarely in the "cool idea" phase, and not yet ready to offer results that the NRO should know about.

There wasn't anything of note from Sienna's session, but both Scott and Evan before her had glimpsed a few key pieces. "This is all cumulative," he thought to himself again – repeating a mantra that had successfully kept him focused and optimistic about the health of the program and the opportunity it provided. He didn't think purely in terms of national security in the ways his superiors did, but he appreciated the opportunity to contribute to stability while pursuing pure astrophysics in the meantime.

But he really did need a breakthrough.
Six years was a long time for impatient people.

13 · Education

16 APRIL

The relaxed schedule enjoyed by the campers was not entirely free from structure. School, for example, was still held Monday through Friday to keep everyone up to date on the basic academics for their age group. The managers of Dark Antennae were incredibly thorough when it came to eliminating any chance that the project's shroud of secrecy could be disturbed, and they knew this program had a better chance of staying secret permanently if there were no academic deficiencies when each student returned to their regular lives.

It would be counterproductive to the priority of invisibility if an enterprising school counselor noticed that a former camper was struggling with grade-level material during their first few years back in public school and subsequently feel the need to investigate this private academy which had so poorly served this student.

The program's managers also recognized the value of routine for children who were young enough to, if left to their own devices when outside one of the research cabins, run around like crazy people. Thus, class started every day at 9:30 am, lunch was at noon, and school was usually done a little after 2:00 pm. There were a lot of breaks throughout the day, the NSA snack budget was simply unmatched by any other government agency, and the rotating group of teachers who visited Camp Loaf were all remarkable in their own unique ways. They often punctuated lessons about grade school math and biology with stories about experimental aircraft, the pros and cons of spy makeup, and space-age weapons that they may or may not have used to shoot stuff.

The only element that would have seemed out of place was when the intercom would chirp and ask for one of the students to meet up with Dr. Torquemann in the research cabin. Whenever this happened the student would be gone for an hour – 90 minutes at the absolute max – and then come right back to class, often finishing off an Otter Pop or Capri Sun as they entered the room. For anyone familiar with public school, this didn't look much different than seeing someone get picked up for a dentist appointment. And, sometimes, that call over the intercom actually was for a dentist appointment. Torquemann was always surprised that even kids this unique still didn't brush their teeth nearly often enough. But, regardless of the reason, every time a camper was plucked from class the others would envy their serendipitous evasion of yet another writing assignment or math quiz.

The research schedule for each camper had them visit the cabin roughly every other day, with plenty of exceptions and days off – but the occasional back-to-back visit was common enough, especially if things were going well or some particularly interesting information was in the Signal at that moment. The sessions themselves did not tend to take a physical toll on the campers, and Torquemann never let things get tense in the way outsiders might have expected from a dystopian sci-fi movie where reluctant children were relentlessly castigated to produce results like proper lab rats.

If the program had a hard deadline or even a clear and concise mission statement, the kids knew nothing about it. The official purpose for all this camping was made clear to Torquemann's staff: Identify the specific source of the Signal and catalog the information within it. As far as the NRO was concerned, this primary mission was a fine cover for the far larger objective which was known only to Torquemann and the people he reported to: Determine the purpose of the Signal.

The Signal itself had first been detected in late 1976 or early 1977, depending on what dataset you were using. Prior to its official documentation, it had, at first, been the source of confusion – and, later, great interest – amongst a small, international community of researchers studying the behavior of pulsars. It was a member of this community who brought this data to the attention of a young Julius Torquemann.

Years earlier, Torquemann had helped his post-doc advisor fact check the arcane mathematics undergirding a research paper about pulsar activity, and, although Torquemanns' area of focus was Astroparticle Physics, with a particular emphasis on the oscillation of tau neutrinos, the advisor had been impressed by his mastery of Vector Calculus, Partial Differential Equations, and especially Fourier Analysis – the latter of those items being an esoteric corner of the mathematical world which was used to disassemble complex waveforms into simpler components.

At the time, pulsars were still only partially understood, and describing them could make you sound crazy: Deep in space are stars so huge that once all their fuel is burnt off, they collapse under their own weight – and the weight of a star like this is so unthinkably massive that all of its positively charged protons and negatively charged electrons get crushed together to form electrically neutral particles called neutrons. Quite unexpectedly, this ultra-dense sphere begins rotating at incredible speeds – and now, instead of it taking a 24-hour period to rotate like the earth, a neutron star rotates several thousand times per second. What gets researchers particularly excited, however, is the way that a small, dense sphere of tightly packed particles can generate huge pulses of electromagnetic energy once it spins this fast. Hence the name "pulsar."

And, of particular interest to these astronomers, are the tiny gamma waves and the huge radio waves that pulsars blast out into the universe. Within the spectrum of electromagnetism, radio waves exist on the far-left edge, and gamma rays exist on the far-opposite side.

The goal of the research Julius had originally helped with was to compare and contrast the activity at both edges of the spectrum in order to better understand what happened at all points in between, as well as how to better track how energy moved along said spectrum. But, starting in October of 1976, a steady interference found on both spectral edges had begun tainting the data. A few months later, in the early months of 1977, the interference had steadily grown to the point that these researchers were crawling around inside their satellite dishes looking for hardware problems.

That February, Torquemann got a phone call from his old advisor. At the time, Julius was already at the NRO and was one of several dozen astrophysicists working in the Advanced Systems and Technology Directorate, or the "AS&T" as it was known. The small talk on the call was kept to a minimum since the advisor had consulted for the NRO enough times to not bother asking Julius what he'd been up to lately. Instead, the advisor recalled the work they'd done together previously, and he asked if he could mail some preliminary data gathered by another former student now working at the Arecibo Observatory in Puerto Rico.

A week later an oversized manilla envelope arrived in Torquemann's office.

Inside was a collection of printouts showing variations in electromagnetic radiation around the Earth at various times over the preceding 18 weeks. Clipped to each of these printouts were several pages of calculations which tried – and failed – to explain the slowly escalating interference along the edges of the spectrum. The calculations tried to account for the interference by overlaying them with what could be expected from naturally occurring factors like coronal mass ejections, geomagnetic storms, or, in the more exotic category, tidal distortions from a black hole causing LEO satellites to have their orbit determination systems go haywire. As he scanned through the data and the additional calculations which followed, he agreed that nothing in the math indicated that these naturally occurring phenomena were the culprit for the interference. Toward the bottom of the stack was a single sheet of paper that he instantly knew was the real reason for the initial phone call.

It was a printout of the Earth's current electromagnetic spectrum with corrective filters applied to sift out every natural phenomenon and to essentially turn down the sensitivity of all the regular sensors collecting this data.

And there it was.

The first time Julius Torquemann laid eyes on the Signal, he knew in his gut what it was.

The reduction in the sensitivity of the sensors had been an attempt by these pulsar researchers to, essentially, turn down the volume of their own music so they could better hear what weird noises were coming from the apartment next door. They could not have possibly imagined they would find *this*.

Right *there*, at the furthest edge along each side of the electromagnetic radiation spectrum was evidence of highly structured data seeping – just barely – into the edges of mankind's ability to detect. It was so tiny that, without the best possible equipment, it would have been undetectable.

It was obvious that this interference was operating actively in the areas of the electromagnetic spectrum beyond our ability to detect and they were just barely crossing over into the slice of it that current instrumentation could spot. There was an entire body of research dedicated to what could theoretically exist outside of the current understanding of the electromagnetic spectrum – and that research was beset with creative names like "Extremely Low Frequency Waves" and "Super High Frequency Waves" – but none of that explained or anticipated how to reach or read those exotic frequencies.

The few facts available at this early stage were: The Signal itself was structured and unambiguously inorganic, the way in which it was being sent demonstrated a remarkable level of technical sophistication, and it was invisible to anyone without the most sensitive Cherenkov Detectors or ELF Magnetometers.

His first move was to cross-reference this with the information he knew a nearby department at the NRO would have readily available. When he showed an astronomer from the Tactical Space Reconnaissance Program what he had been sent, she stared at it for several long seconds before looking up with a raised eyebrow to ask, "How long have you had this?"

Julius explained the connection with his old professor and the work they had done on pulsars, but she cut him off early as she scanned the spectral analysis and the underlying calculations. Dr. Maggie Walker was in a hurry now. "This has gotta be from Arecibo, right? Nothing else in the public domain can see through the ionosphere this cleanly."

Julius didn't respond, he was carefully watching her reaction and waiting to see if there was an explanation forthcoming about what he had found.

She measured a wave form on the same printout that had made Julius stop and stare, and then she stood up to leave.

"I want to show this to my team, but I'll be in touch."

Three minutes later Maggie was entering a large stellar cartography lab and wasted no time in announcing to the eight other experts in the room: "Puerto Rico has found it."

* * * * *

Back in the classroom, the discussion was as lively as ever.

The lesson for today was about the basics of Bernoulli's principle – the process in which air moves very fast over an airplane wing thus creating a pocket of low pressure that generates a force called "lift" and, ergo, airplanes can fly. The instructor had managed to keep the class on track all morning, and the kids were busy building their own model airplanes to see the principle in motion. At some point between drawing a diagram of airflow and finishing up with the glue guns, the teacher casually mentioned that all of the principles they were discussing today applied to normal airplanes, but the science was quite a bit different for the spy aircraft that have to fly three times higher and much faster than a normal plane. Now the questions began to pour in about spy planes and, in a misguided attempt to redirect the discussion back to today's lesson, he said something which guaranteed they wouldn't finish talking about Bernoulli today: "I really don't know that much about them, I've only been in one of those planes three or four times."

Now every hand in the class was raised; everyone needed more information about what it took to be a passenger on a spy plane. The instructor couldn't even hide behind the classified nature of his prior jobs because every camper was already living in a facility classified somewhere far above Top Secret with an unusually robust "Sensitive Compartmented Information" designation added on top of it.

After answering 15 minutes of questions, the teacher saw an opening to wrap up the discussion on wings and flight. But, lacking the experience of a full-time teacher, he restarted the lesson by mentioning, "So, in conclusion, Bernoulli's principle is really cool – even if no one understands how or why it works."

This got Sienna, who, for the first time in weeks, was hoping the intercom wouldn't interrupt with a call for her, to burst out laughing along with the rest of the class. She knew how to spot something that was about to go down in flames – and this discussion had just officially met the criteria.

"What do you mean no one knows how things fly?" she asked, her voice trailing off at the end in laughter.

This officer knew he'd made a mistake, but he was willing to roll with it – and, besides, there was probably a life lesson hidden somewhere within what he was about to tell them.

"Ok, consider a couple things: First, we know that 'lift' is a real thing because obviously planes can fly – but scientists don't know *why* lift happens. For example, like we talked about earlier, for lift to happen the air has to move faster over the top of the wing than it does the bottom of the wing – and we know that this is what's happening and that it's the reason planes can fly – but we don't know *why* the air always moves faster over top. They used to think it had to do with the shape of the wing, but then they found out this has nothing to do with it. So then scientists started studying that low pressure area on the wing that makes lift possible in the first place – and guess what? Nobody can explain why that low pressure bubble suddenly appears on the wing and starts pushing the plane upward into the sky. All we know is what's already obvious: The plane can't fly without it. But what's even weirder is that the more they studied that low pressure bubble the more they came to realize that *nobody* can explain how it gets there. The smartest people who've ever lived have tried to figure it out, and nobody has any ideas. Even Einstein investigated this back before he was famous – and he came up with *nothing*. I mean, the same guy who wrote out the quantum theory of light, and who proved time isn't real, and who calculated the curvature of space – *that* dude thought this question was too hard."

As expected, the campers loved this. These children had been introduced to the idea of a world that operated behind the scenes of the "real" world at far too young an age, but they had adapted to it with a resilience only native to children. Much of the credit for this went to Dr. Torquemann and the team of nameless and faceless camp operators at the NRO, and this officer knew from talking to other fill-in teachers that it helped the kids to have other people with secret jobs talk to them openly and honestly on a range of subjects that would have to go unrepeated outside of camp. The teachers here were often individuals who needed to lay low for an extended period at a place that did not exist while a major incident among the world's clandestine organizations cooled off. Other times they were people who had been operating for years in the type of environment that came with hazardous stress levels, and this camp was a nice place to unwind. Ultra secretive agencies didn't offer sabbaticals to their most valuable assets – at least not in the traditional sense of the word – but a place like Camp Loaf was close to it.

The type of people cycling through the camp's classroom were, by any definition, colorful in the extreme, and they were all brimming with stories which dotted the entire spectrum of appropriateness, and they spoke to the children like valued fellow assets rather than schoolmasters.

Throughout her life, and long after she was done being a camper, Sienna cherished her memories of this classroom. The neat rows of desks, the lively conversations with spies, former spies, and counterterrorism commandos, and the pleasantly flat social hierarchy that existed amongst the campers. Much of this had to do with Torchy's carefully planned influence on the camp's culture, but perhaps the biggest factor was that everyone arrived here knowing they all possessed roughly the same ultra-rare connection to the Signal. It also helped that every camper was issued the same t-shirt, sweatpants, and shorts, and then mixed and matched the outfits however they wanted across the available handful of colors. Despite the stress she put on herself during those research sessions, camp itself was a joyful place, she enjoyed the work, and she spent the years afterwards in public school wishing for a classroom environment like this one.

Years later she would reflect on how bizarre it was to spend so long with people she admired but wouldn't see again, with teachers she liked but didn't really know, in a place she enjoyed but couldn't freely leave, doing a job she loved but didn't understand.

PRESENT
DAY

24 JUNE

After Major Horn had communicated his plans to Captains Guillory and O'Shea, he began planning how to create some small measure of control over the hot tempers that were sure to flare into something much worse along the Russian-Chinese border.

His initial plan was simple: Have Captain Goral run both of the George's A4W nuclear reactors at around 130% capacity around the clock until they arrived in the Sea of Japan (日本海), off the coast of Sapporo (札幌市) where they would explain their presence as assisting in the search for a lost Japanese naval vessel that his colleagues at the CIA station in Tokyo had sunk last night. That local team had needed a little extra time to find a ship that was large enough and empty enough to play the part of an authentic-looking salvage operation, but they had eventually found something perfect.

Getting the George all the way from New Zealand to Japan in such a tight timeframe had, at first, seemed impossible, but after two of his technical advisors spent two hours on the phone with the Chief Engineer from the George, a new conclusion had been reached.

"We've developed an adequate solution, sir," an exhausted and heavily caffeinated technical officer explained. "Even though that boat is a bit on the older side, it's only been a year since its 30-year overhaul, so those brand new reactors are still young and ready to rock."

Horn nodded approvingly and turned to look at the map highlighting the George's current position.

"How soon?"

"Initially there was no doubt amongst the George's senior staff that they could get to Sapporo in a week, even assuming the weather stayed as clear as the satellites indicate it will, but unless something extreme occurs, it will be there on time."

Horn thanked the officer, ordered him to find a place to sleep, and called the Joint Chiefs. This would officially send the George north. This placed 68 fighters – including the very scary F-22 – in the region, and Horn could use this as equal parts bargaining chip and wet blanket as tensions continued to flare.

Then something extreme occurred.

Captain Goral got his orders minutes before the ship was going to host Tauranga's mayor and their local parliamentary representative – both of whom were already inbound on a helicopter used by the regional search and rescue service. Goral gave his Executive Officer the order to recall everyone to the boat immediately, and he sent word to the public affairs officer to "regretfully inform" the mayor's helicopter that this visit was going to be limited to a 20-second photo op on the deck. No sooner had Captain Goral put his new orders in the safe dedicated for top secret material than the mayor's helicopter took an unusually sharp descending angle toward the deck of his ship. Goral immediately sensed what everyone on the deck could already see – this was not an aggressive approach path but an aircraft that had lost control and could no longer arrest its landing. Eight seconds later the helicopter exploded on the flight deck, throwing its full tank of aviation kerosene 200 feet in every direction. It landed on its side, and the main rotor assembly dug clear through the flight deck's steel plating in three different places. The explosion threw a rotor blade through the window of the catapult control station and the spilled fuel raced in to fill the work area usually occupied by the Catapult Officer who launched jets from the ship. A secondary explosion of the helicopter's auxiliary fuel tank rained down more fuel on the alternate catapult system near the bow of the ship. By this time everyone assembled to greet the helicopter had scattered below decks.

In less than a minute the Damage Control Team – essentially a fire department shrunk down to fit on a boat – had the fire under control and was hosing down what was left of the cockpit and tail boom. Everything in between was reduced to hot shreds of aluminum. Two hours passed before the Captain had finished communicating nonstop with the Pacific Fleet Command in Hawaii and could send a message back to Major Horn.

"It's going to be 4.5 days now instead of 3.5, at the very best," he explained over a video conference. "And along the way we have a couple people burned badly enough that, even though they're stable now, we want to fly them ahead to the hospital back home in Yokosuka. But the operational impact of real importance is our ability to shoot fighters off this deck."

Major Horn waited for him to explain.

"All the Nimitz-class carriers have two catapults that shoot jets, and, putting aside that there are three big holes in that deck at the moment, one of the control stations for that catapult was completely destroyed in the fire, and the cables for the other one have been torched to a degree that will take us the better part of a week to replace – and that's assuming we didn't have our techs up top having to work in the type of headwind we'd be generating by traveling at the agreed-upon speed."

Horn swiveled slightly in his chair and looked through the glass windows of this conference room.

"Thank you, Captain Goral. I am very sorry to hear that this has happened to your crew." He paused, looked at the red dent the fragment had left in his palm from the prolonged squeezing, and, out of habit, tried to reconstruct the entire incident. "What have you heard from the people who sent the helicopter?"

"They are grief stricken, of course" Goral explained, "that particular chopper had been in regular use for years, and it had been incredibly reliable for them, according to the local SAR team. The last our air controller heard was a shout from the pilot saying he didn't have any responsiveness in the stick, and that was right when he was lined up for a landing with us. The chopper was carrying two pilots, another crewmember, the mayor, and their local rep in the parliament. Our forensic people are still sifting through everything and talking to the mechanics back in Tauranga. If anything unusual pops up, I'll let you know."

"Thank you, captain," Horn responded after a moment's pause, "but I don't expect you're going to find anything else besides an aging helicopter and incredibly bad luck. In the meantime, I want you and your battle group to stay on course for Sapporo at the absolute highest speed. The cruiser who's with you – the Peralta – bring their captain over to your quarters and brief him on the route and the destination."

He had no need or intention of telling Captain Goral why he had to leave right now and arrive within a seemingly impossible timeframe; all Goral really needed to know was that it had to happen immediately. Bringing the USS Peralta was now doubly important if the George couldn't contribute to the fight. An aircraft carrier is only useful relative to its ability to launch fighter pilots at a target, but it is an imposing presence regardless – and it was very possible to maintain the strategic value of that menace as long as the military staring back at you has no idea you can't put planes in the air at a moment's notice. The Perlata, on the other hand, was a Burke-class guided missile destroyer, which, in naval circles, was recognized as a 500-foot-long floating warehouse of missiles complemented by the best radar, sonar, and electronic warfare systems the American tech industry could create. It had cruise-missiles, anti-ship missiles, anti-aircraft missiles, anti-submarine torpedoes, and a few different anti-city weapons. The Peralta was designed to defeat five or six similarly sized destroyers in a fair fight – and the captains of these ships knew how to ensure that no fight was ever fair.

When these boats finally did arrive at their destination – whatever it was they found there – the George could only look mean and bark; the Peralta would have to do all the biting.

For now, that was going to have to be enough.

The Joint Chiefs, the Secretary of Defense, and, by extension, the President all wanted a way to counteract or calm any major escalations on that Russian-Chinese border. It went without saying that any attempt to do that was likely to further escalate an already bad situation, but having options wasn't the same as using them, and having a plan in your back pocket was better than watching from the sidelines and wishing for one. His job was to create a viable plan for that "something" in the event "anything" were to potentially "happen."

"Thank you again, Captain Goral. Please keep me up to date on your progress as you head north."

Horn left this meeting and turned his attention back to the information he'd been shown earlier regarding a handful of intercepted messages between two branches of the Chinese military. It appeared there was a rapidly intensifying concern amongst the leadership of the

PLA that a Russian attack was going to use the bridge they shared in the northeast as the jumping off point for a secretive attack of some type. Even if it did take the George longer than expected to arrive, just having a carrier and a missile boat steaming north at high speed on a predictable heading was going to provide an incredibly valuable distraction. He reasoned that it was better for the Chinese and Russians to, first, notice how unusually fast the George was headed back and then, second, stare daggers at it once both boats parked off the coast — rather than keep staring at each other. This distraction would also give Horn a way to reach deep into the territory around the bridge in a way that would not cross anyone's mind. But there was no version of this specific part of his plan that was easy.

The non-easy solution he kept coming back to, despite all his reservations, was Alaska.

In particular, the fleet of F-22 Raptor's that lived at Joint Base Elmendorf-Richardson, outside Anchorage.

The F-22 was an excellent solution for a wide range of problems, but there were few solutions for the 3,034 miles between the end of the runway at Elemendorf and the middle of that bridge over the Amur River. Horn had spent most of last night talking to his counterparts in the Air Force and a handful of engineers who worked on the jet. Two days ago he even took an ad hoc field trip to talk to a Raptor specialist in person. After several hours and a lot of plot points on a map, Horn had a plan that he was now walking upstairs to present to the Joint Chiefs.

The conference room set aside for meetings like this one was plain and surprisingly unadorned aside from the framed emblems of each branch of the armed forces lining the back wall above the recycling bins. Horn was no interior designer, but he could recognize that there was a point at which keeping a room simple enough to use for any purpose left it without a meaningful purpose to serve, and this particular space fell into the wrong quadrant of that distinction. Each member of the council would be present today, but he knew the talking would likely be limited to the generals of the Army and Air Force, and the ranking admiral of the Navy. And the Secretary of Defense himself, of course.

Horn started the meeting with an overview of the information contained in the briefing documents that they should have already read. This was followed by a map on the display screen which showed a massive 4,000-mile sweep of the northern hemisphere, stretching from central Alaska to eastern Mongolia, with the Northern Pacific in between.

"Gentlemen, and ma'am, thank you for being here today," Horn began, skipping all the other formalities. This was a group that would appreciate saving the extra five seconds and skipping right to the mildly terrifying issue at hand. "I know you've already been briefed on why we are repositioning the USS George Washington, as well as the Peralta, the USS Kennedy, and two of our attack subs – and now I want to outline for you the additional planning we have developed to penetrate the area around the Nizhneleninskoye-Tongjiang Bridge in the event we have to interdict any actions which might plunge those two states into disarray."

No one moved to look at the briefing docs contained in the manilla folders in front of them. This was a good sign everyone had done the assigned reading, or at least had a senior advisor summarize it for them.

"Due to its current level of damage, once the George Washington arrives on station north of Japan, its primary purpose will be to sit there and look incredibly dangerous."

Now came the crazy part. The part which just might get the meeting canceled as soon as he said the words.

"The plan the GOC has developed is simple: We'll covertly project control of the airspace in this theater with the Raptors at the Elmendorf air base in Anchorage." Multiple eyebrows around the room arched and nearly everyone around the table furtively glanced at the Air Force general. "After a lengthy consultation with the engineers responsible for the F-22's operational endurance, I believe this is how we can proactively influence events if any interdiction becomes necessary."

"The Raptor's range is nowhere close to that, so what are you doing in between those two points?" the Secretary of Defense asked.

"Yes, sir, but when the 600-gallon external fuel tank is added to the Raptor, its range extends to about 1,900 miles, and the engineers assure me that the non-official distance is actually a couple hundred miles more than that."

The Army general did not like the sound of this at all.

"I know the F-22 is damn near invisible on Russian and Chinese scopes, but having that fuel tank hanging on its belly is going to make it a lot easier to spot."

"The external tank does increase its radar cross section, sir, but this particular tank is designed specifically for the F-22 to use, and it is built in such a way to be much harder to detect than normal. The materials engineer responsible for the radar-defeating coating which covers the tank also walked me through a few tactics the pilots can use when flying with a tank through enemy air defenses."

This explanation wasn't meant to put everyone's mind at ease, but it did demonstrate that the best possible attempts were being made in each phase of this mission.

"So, now you can travel 2,000 miles and some change," the SecDef said, pointing at the map, "but it's still a real long trip from Anchorage to Asia – and that's just one way, Major."

"Sir, that brings me to the next map I would like to show all of you," Horn said, turning back to the screen to see the northern hemisphere fade out and be replaced by the Aleutian Island chain, which extended southwest in a long arc off the coast of Alaska.

"We'll post a half dozen Raptors at a staging area here," he paused to zoom in on a rocky outcropping named Kiska in the Aleutians.

Everyone present knew enough World War 2 history to remember that Kiska had the dubious distinction of being successfully invaded by the Japanese during the summer of 1942, and the imperial army promptly built an airstrip in hopes of using it as a staging area to attack the rest of North America. The U.S. had taken the island back three years later and occupied the airfield for another two years before shutting it down.

"That shutdown," Horn explained, "was in name only. A functional, albeit small, airbase in the North Pacific was too valuable a thing to mothball entirely with the Cold War kicking off, and it is currently proving to be quite strategic for a fighter capable of carrying 600 extra gallons of fuel."

Horn walked them through a handful of specifics, hoping this would preempt additional objections and follow up questions: The trip from Elemendorf to Kiska's airstrip was 1,375 miles; once the pilots reached Kiska they would stand by for additional directions as the situation along the Amur River developed; Horn had already given orders for a handful of temporary structures stored in a cave near the airfield to be erected immediately and await the arrival of the pilots and crew. From what he could tell these structures only amounted to big tents and space heaters, but they'd keep the pilots and planes dry and warm, and they'd be ready to use in 36 hours.

"I'm not thrilled about $400 million dollar airplanes sitting in tents next to a gravel runway," the SecDef said.

"Neither am I, sir."

The Secretary did not like that response at all. He wanted something that would show how his very reasonable concern was already being addressed.

"Kiska, as you no doubt have already concluded, will be the jumping off point for any action we have to take in or around the bridge. From Kiska, the F-22's will head southeast to avoid crossing Russia's Kamchatka Peninsula (полуостров Камчатка) or its Kuril Islands (Курильские острова)," the map shifted to show a red line tracing the route of the Raptors. "They will then reach the airspace of Japan's northern island of Hokkaido (北海道) about 1,800 miles away from where they started."

"This maneuver around the Kurils and over to Hokkaido is my primary objection to this mission," the Air Force general interrupted. "Those Raptors are going to be on fumes by then, and it's entirely possible one of them falls out of the sky at this point."

"Yes, ma'am, that is true."

The whole room hated this response, but the SecDef appreciated that Horn wasn't playing favorites.

"The engineers attached to this project are confident the Raptors can reach their refuel without incident, and, when the time comes, we'll alert the tanker to be ready to meet them ahead of schedule in the event those fumes they'll be running on go dry."

Now the map changed to center over the bridge. Hokkaido could still be seen in the bottom right corner. The red line indicating the route of the Raptors now sliced inland. It was a simple PowerPoint illustration setting that belied the fact that it was articulating something which was, technically speaking, an act of war.

"After that mid-air refueling it's 870 miles to the bridge, and the pilots will then have to weave between two dozen anti-aircraft batteries from both countries along the way. Any action we ultimately need to take at or near the point of the bridge will be limited to a single strike such that our presence is identifiable only in that instance – this is for both political reasons and also because our pilots will need to make an immediate U-turn in order to have a chance at outrunning anything put in the air to intercept them once they're detected. If and when a strike is made the pilots can choose to drop that external tank again if there's a need to optimize stealth while they race toward the ocean where they'll refuel again near Hokkaido. The Peralta will be there to pick off any missiles chasing them, and to put a few warning shots in the air to brush back interceptors."

"That's going to be a very busy day for those pilots by the time they get back to Kiska" the Army general said, tilting back in his chair and taking in the immensity of the task.

"To maximize the disappearing act these Raptors have to perform, and to offer our diplomats in Beijing and Moscow maximum deniability, I've arranged with Elemendorf to position multiple refueling tankers along a route that stretches all the way back to Anchorage."

Depending on how you counted it, this was the third or fourth time the room had heard Major Horn say something which tilted across the wrong side of a line separating "audacious" and "reckless."

"So those Raptors aren't going to pause for so much as a second between the time they leave Kiska, hit something in Manchuria, and then land back in suburban Anchorage?" the SecDef asked.

"That's correct, sir."

What went unsaid was just what a beast that flight would be. After launching from Kiska those pilots would cover 6,550 miles before arriving back home. There would be a lot of chances to turn on autopilot and take a nap once they reached neutral airspace, but he wouldn't be surprised if none of them did. With a top speed of Mach 2.25, the Raptors would cover the distance in a little over 4 hours.

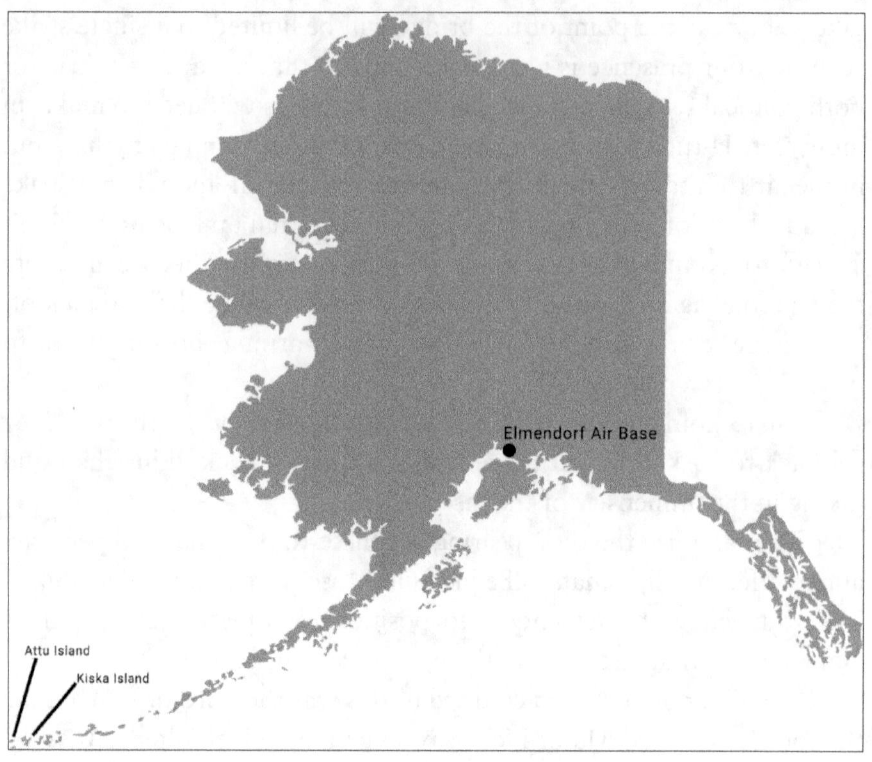

"You already mentioned the fuel concerns on the way to the target," the Navy admiral said, "but what if something goes wrong and one of those Raptors is hit in another nation's airspace?"

"There are two scenarios to consider there, sir. The first is that the Raptor is hit and crashes somewhere on Chinese or Russian soil. This is obviously the worst-case scenario, and it eliminates any faint hope we have of deniability. In this case, it becomes an entirely diplomatic issue. We have assets in the region who we will activate to help us get the pilot out of the country, but that will be exceptionally difficult to do cleanly, and it won't change the fact that the wreckage of his plane is scattered across a mountainside nearby. The second scenario is that the Raptor is hit but remains airborne, albeit with no chance of making it all the way back home. In that case there is Attu Island. Attu is the last island in the Aleutians and is only 600 miles away from the last major Russian settlement – and I've seen badly injured F-22's limp a lot further than that when it was mandatory."

"That's true," the Air Force general added.

"So, what? They just find a place to land on some tiny island?" the SecDef asked.

"No, sir, in that case the pilot will dump the Raptor in the water next to Attu, and I'll have a fully equipped special operations boat anchored nearby to pick him up."

"Just a single boat?"

"Yes, and we'll have it outfitted to look like a fishing boat or a research vessel or something that will look convincing at a glance from a satellite. They'll also flag the spot where the Raptor went into the water so that we can salvage it right away."

Horn knew this was the right time to stop talking and wait for feedback, or, in a best-case scenario, a decision. He could smell the doubt and fear in the room, but he believed this would work. He had moved from "could" to "would" sometime yesterday, and now he needed this group to either tell him to execute the mission *or* to stop just short of telling him to scrap it. Both those outcomes were a greenlight to move forward, they just channeled blame or credit after the fact in different ways.

The room was silent for a long time. The SecDef would have spoken right away if he hadn't been cursing this major for the conversation he now had to have with the Secretary of State. Those words "it becomes entirely a diplomatic issue" were the exact things that made the diplomats hate military planners.

The rest of the room was silent because Horn and his team had been thorough over the last three days – holding a series of briefings to explore all the questions around the validity of current information, the danger of escalations in this region, and the pros and cons of taking action to influence those events. This meeting was solely focused on how that intercession would take place.

Finally the SecDef spoke. "Do it, Major. Update me every day and then again directly before you launch."

"Yes, sir. Thank you."

Horn was the first to leave the room and he made his way back to the GOC immediately. A more affable officer might have stayed a few extra moments to shake hands with each of the Joint Chiefs, but he did not want to be anywhere near their apprehensions and weak stomachs right now.

Horn stopped short of feeling optimistic – instead, the feeling was something much closer to the conclusion a statistician would reach after crunching the numbers and discovering to his surprise that the odds tilted in his favor. Although, of course, this statistician had to bear in mind that if his math was wrong or the odds turned against him, the penalty was the outbreak of World War 3.

But this mission did seem possible.

Part of what made this seem possible was all the things the F-22 Raptor could do.

Horn was familiar with the capabilities of the F-22, but to be sure about his next steps, he had spent three hours at nearby Andrews Air Force Base earlier this week meeting with the senior commander in charge of the Raptor fleet. He wanted to look deep into the eyes of the machine that would make or break this mission and ask all his questions, one trained killer to another.

The commander he met with was a newly minted colonel named Joseph Spears. Colonel Spears had spent 16 years flying the F-22 and advising on its development, and just six weeks earlier had stepped down from active flying in order to accept this new post.

Horn met with Spears in a hangar at the airbase where an F-22 had been brought in for routine maintenance. Horn walked the length of the jet, his hand gliding across the careful geometry of the fuselage.

"Tell me about this jet, Colonel."

Spears could tell by looking at this hard, quiet man from the Pentagon that he already knew a lot about any object in the military capable of putting ordinance on a target, but this question was still like getting asked to explain the many reasons you loved one of your kids, and so the dead serious colonel couldn't help but smile and start effusing. He still didn't understand why he had to drop everything to take this meeting, but at least it was a topic he could talk about for several dozen hours without repeating himself.

"Well, she's beautiful and she's terrifying. There isn't one other aircraft on this planet that can climb as fast, turn as tight, or reach its speeds, and if you're dumb enough, crazy enough, or smart enough to need anything past that, it has a computer behind the seat that helps you maneuver it in ways more extreme than the human body can command."

"What I wouldn't have done for a few of these overhead back when I was getting shot at for a living, Colonel."

"These are designed to do it all – you can knock a target out of the sky that didn't know you were there, put a missile through the roof of a tank or bunker, and I've sunk a few things with it, too."

Both were silent as they walked the length of the airframe, finally arriving back at the nose cone.

"I take it you're sending a few of these to do something in the near future," the colonel said. It wasn't framed as a question; he could tell Horn was planning something.

Horn was lost in thought and didn't hear him. "I know these prioritize stealth. How much luck have you had defeating ground-based radar?"

"These birds are essentially invisible to most of the radars getting used around the world right now. A lot of this has to do with the fact it doesn't hang any missiles off the wings – I'm sure you know those are all tucked up inside the doors on its belly until it's time to fire. The rest of it comes from the angles built into each edge of the plane and the radar-absorbing coating from nose to nozzle. I'll spare you a 90-minute overview of the electronic warfare systems we have on board that make a radar that's looking right at us believe there's nothing there, but trust me when I tell you that the computers she's carrying are smarter than most radar installations."

"But what about when an enemy does get a reading?"

"On the rare occasions when one of these does show up on an enemy scope, what matters is how big of an object that radar is looking at – you know, what's the size of that cross-section of the object getting picked up? If it's much bigger than a twin-size mattress, a really skilled radar operator is going to be able to track it from a couple hundred miles away. But the Raptor's cross-section is about the size of a marble – and, again, that's if you find it in the first place, and even if you do find it for a second, good luck keeping track of it once that pilot gives you the double trouble by reaching for his top speed and essentially hacking your control panel so that it tells you that the skies are clear."

This was very reassuring to hear. Considering the F-22 ran over 60 feet long and had 840 square feet of wing, the fact that it could shrink itself down to a marble was a kind of scientific miracle.

"And I do want to emphasize that speed, Major. It can cruise in a fuel-efficient straight line at Mach 1.8, and that's faster than most fighters can reach in small bursts – and once the pilot goes wide open with the throttle, it will jump past Mach 2.25. By that point you're well over twice the speed of sound, up over 1,600 miles per hour, and if there's any other planes still in the air at that point it's only because that pilot or whoever's giving orders decided to let them live."

On this point the colonel was absolutely correct. The F-22 was so dangerous that Congress had forbidden the sale of it to any other friendly U.S. allies, and, strangely enough, it had ultimately become a victim of its own invincibility: Several years earlier the military had decided to stop building new Raptors because, as an official report explained it, the world "lacked relevant adversaries" for the Raptor to engage. Horn found this reasoning pathetic in the extreme. To him this was another way of saying that the F-22 made war unfair. But anyone who had ever seen combat knew that an unfair fight was the best possible type – because those were over so fast that the body counts never had a chance to stack up.

Regardless, today's situation presented the most relevant possible need for the most powerful thing mankind had ever put in the sky.

All of this, however, assumed that putting an F-22 in the airspace of two pugnacious foreign countries was going to be necessary, useful, or helpful. It also brought with it the chance that any intervention would make things much, much worse – particularly because putting that particular plane in that specific airspace would only be a response to something much worse that had already happened or was in the process of happening. An attempt to squash a conflict at an early stage was a very risky move to make. All of these moves also assumed the total failure of the diplomatic process – but that process was going to be constrained to the point it became useless since the countries in question could not be approached without revealing the extent to which U.S. intelligence had penetrated their communications and learned everything they were doing.

There was no ambassador in the world who could spin that information without causing another new conflict in the process.

1991

11 JUNE

When the morning classes wrapped up Sienna slid two books and a pencil case into her backpack and walked to the dining hall with Nora and Naomi. She focused today's meal almost entirely on Doritos, but the grilled cheese made by the tall, new guard was very good.

For the next hour she had a session scheduled with Torchy, and she casually mentioned missing the badminton game they'd discussed the night before. Naomi would not stop talking about her recent win in the Camp Loaf badminton tournament, so, frankly, Sienna saw this scheduling conflict as a welcome coincidence.

She slid out of her chair, dropped her tray off by the kitchen, and headed to the research cabin, but made a momentary diversion to the giant snacks counter in the barn. "After all," she reasoned, "who knows how much energy this will require?"

Today's class had been a continuation of a topic that had originally been broached a few months after Sienna arrived at camp, and it never failed to make everyone in class debate whether or not such things were really possible and, invariably, someone would ask a version of the question: "Hey, in normal schools does geology make kids uncomfortable, or does that just happen here?"

Tectonic plates, it turned out, were incredibly creepy. Or at least the subduction plates that made up the entire west coast of North America sure were. As far as Sienna could understand it, half the fault lines were spitting out new land – these were called divergent boundaries – and the other were half subduction plates where the old land was pulled down into the Earth's core, eaten, melted down, and then they popped back out the other side a few million years later as the new land. Someone in class said that this sounded like a reduce-reuse-recycle lesson, and the teacher was quick to point out that this process was literally called "Plate Recycling." But the basic math was what really made this topic uncomfortable: It took about 200 million years, give or take a few extra million, for the entire surface of the Earth to go through the process of getting melted down and coming back out brand new, and the Earth itself was 4.5 billion years old. That meant the Earth had seen about 20 different surfaces over the course of its life, and ours was the 21st. And the thing about a plate getting sucked down into the core and melted is that whatever was on that plate is reduced to lava. That plate could have had ancient ruins on it, or creatures, or an entire civilization – and every speck of it would all be crushed up and melted. The Earth could have been inhabited each of those 20 previous times and there'd be no way to know. Even if those ancient people or lizards or whatever they were had built a skyscraper 10 miles tall and set off nuclear bombs for fun, those buildings would have melted down with the rest of the plate they were on, and after about 500 million years all the radioactive traces of those bombs would be gone, too. Allegedly at least. And at least according to this one scientist hanging out at the camp for a few months.

The class decided that the best way to settle this question was for everyone in the room to vote on how many civilizations they felt had been here previously, and the average score was four. Sienna had voted for zero, because she figured if anyone had been here before there would at least be something better than stromatolites left over.

She was still thinking about this as she strolled casually into the research cabin, wiping Dorito dust off of her fingers as she made her way to the chair. By now the process and routine of this research had become a well-formed habit. She said hello to the scientists she passed on the way, made a show of cracking her knuckles, and sat down in the chair. She smoothed out her oversized "Who Framed Roger Rabbit?" t-shirt and pushed a loose shoelace back down inside her shoe. She met eyes with Dr. Torquemann in the back of the room and got a big smile; she noticed he was, as usual, wearing the same Nike basketball shoes he'd worn at the neurologist's office – the same pair her older brothers had begged for last summer. She got comfortable, leaned back, and listened to the combination of purrs and metallic staccato coming from the various machines around the room.

It had been 16 months since the Epicortical Surface Reflector was implanted.

At first she had not noticed any difference, but Dr. Tunis told her this was normal – it was a matter, he explained, of it "settling into place." After about a week she finally noticed a difference. Other campers with the ESR said it was like having the Signal's volume turned up, and one of her friends at Fort Torch said it made her feel like the Signal was physically pressed up against her. For Sienna, it was something different than both of those. Previously she had waited for a single burst of information to finally appear, and now she could, at times, spot two or three instances of it emerging, and then she went chasing after the nearest or biggest one.

The regularity with which she spotted anything at all was still inconsistent, but when she did hear something, it seemed clearer. When she talked to her friends about it, the best description she could offer was that sometimes the Signal would suddenly snap into really sharp focus – and even if there wasn't much of anything broadcasting at that moment she could still tell she was suddenly right in the middle of it. She was told by the psychiatrist, Dr. Carney, that she should never feel like she had to hear or see more things now that she had the ESR, and that doing this would be a normal reaction for a lot of kids her age – but it simply wasn't necessary. "If it works, that's great. If it doesn't, then we just blame that on the highly uncertain nature of the science behind the ESR itself," she had told Sienna when she stopped by her cabin to visit the day after the surgery. "No one," she emphasized, "is ever going to expect you to start reading Russian blueprints or quoting whole telephone calls when you get back in that chair. The ESR is just to see what *might* happen."

Sienna didn't think the new-found intensity of the Signal was her imagination; she had just expected to detect it a lot more often.

So had the rest of the scientists. It had been discussed twice over the last six months if the ratio of her hits and misses justified her ongoing time separated from a normal life.

After her first week with the ESR, she had very clearly heard almost an entire sentence:

Confirm if you are prepared for
the following steps.

Dr. Torquemann and Adams had a lot of questions about this piece of dialog.

"Technically speaking," Sienna had pointed out, "this is kind of a complete sentence."

But she knew as well as they did that there was more to that transmission that she had missed at the end. For the last two months all she had seen were flashes of what seemed to be a fragment of the same image over and over again: The picture seemed huge but there was no basis for comparison, the object was brightly lit or maybe just sitting too close to something lit normally, and the way the light moved made it seem as if she were looking at a crystal chandelier with squinted eyes. She pointed out that her eyes actually were squinting while she focused on this image, but no one seemed to think that made a difference to the information you were searching for via a ridge and mini satellite dish on the back of your brain.

With all of the pre-session checks complete, Torquemann made his way up to the front, gave her the standard first bump, and asked how she was feeling. Both agreed this was another good day to scan the airwaves, and, with another smile, the doctor stepped out of the focus area and the session began.

As soon as Sienna closed her eyes she heard the familiar hum of the Signal. The background noise of this tachyon ocean was how every camper knew they were present in the Signal's path, but it never guaranteed anything would pop up or drift past. Two minutes later she was jolted by the sudden snap of the Signal into a very different vein. It was an unusually deep area of focus, and she felt as if a wind was moving over her skin.

The sound of the machines in the room was now very far away, but she could hear them racing to keep up. She followed her training and carefully explained each sensation along the way. It felt strange to split focus at a time like this; her descriptions were just tiny messages she left behind to float to the surface while she kept swimming hundreds of feet below.

Within this perfectly clear area of the Signal, she could feel the approach of something long before she saw or heard it. To brace herself for what she expected to be an onslaught of sights and sounds, she instinctively oriented her mind toward it, as if she were about to lean into an approaching gust of wind.

She thought to herself, "What do we have here?"

As these words formed in her mind something entirely new happened. In the same moment she was thinking it, she felt the question lift up in her mind and race away into that distant direction where everything she'd ever seen or heard originated.

And just as instantly as those words left her, she heard a voice.

Who are you?

She had softly spoken her question there in the research cabin, and, per the protocol, she repeated these new words as well. She couldn't see that every scientist and specialist in the room froze and tightened. Those in the back rows stood up to look.

Sienna was unsure how to reply. She knew enough about her work to not reveal anything that would identify the program, but she was startled, and she was 10.

"Just a regular person," she said after a long pause, grimacing at how lame it sounded and hating herself for not having a better idea.

Instantaneously the response was back again, and its emotion was suddenly one of intrigue:

Can you explain?

This made her smile. There was a sleuth on the other end.

"Oh, you know, just the regular, 'ol planet Earth version, same as you."

This time there was a pause, and then the response arrived filled with a curiosity that just barely surpassed confusion.

But we are not the same.

Sienna gasped out a startled breath.

This was no Russian scientist.

A sudden cold, black pit in her stomach stopped her from repeating what she had heard.

Across the room Julius Torquemann clenched his jaw and tried to maintain his composure as he looked at the only other person in the room with the slightest idea of what was almost certainly happening. Dr. Tunis had turned to face a wall to hide his less-composed reaction. Both of them were sorting through the ramifications of data now heading "downstream" on the Signal. If that was what was happening right now, then her last message was going to get a considerable response. If she were able to catch it.

Torquemann drew a breath, held it, and waited as he carefully watched her face. He kept one eye on the nearby monitors which were currently showing a fireworks display scattering across the back of her brain.

Sienna could hear her heart pounding in her ears, and it almost fell into rhythm with the hum of the Signal.

She waited and listened.

The voice came again, with a sense of urgency:

Where are you?

Sienna had done enough prank calling with friends to know better than to give away your name or where you lived, but the adrenaline stopped her short of cobbling together a usable pseudonym on the spot. She started to respond but couldn't. She put her hand on her chest and tried to slow her pounding heart. She felt the long, silkscreened ears of Roger under her fingers.

"This is a rabbit."

Immediately her heart sank at having said something so mundane and abstract.

She saw the words race away, and felt the Signal begin to shift beneath her feet. Twenty feet away the technician monitoring her vital signs was showing Dr. Adams the surging stress levels across her entire neuromuscular system.

Sienna had failed in this room enough times to know when there was nothing else coming in a session.

She let out a long breath, cracked an eye, and looked around the room.

She saw the intense interest from everyone, but it was clear no one understood what had just occurred. The machines in the room sounded as if they had descended into chaos. As her gaze wandered to the back of the cabin she saw Torchy staring back at her, his face was blank, but his eyes seemed to almost vibrate with energy.

He nodded and mouthed the words, "Good job."

Torquemann suddenly spoke up above the prattle of the computers and said, "That's a lot of data to chew through today, everyone, I'm going to walk our camper back towards class and let her stretch her legs a bit. Let's meet back here in 15 minutes to debrief and start parsing out what we learned today so we can get it over to the supercomputers tonight."

He headed toward the door and gave her a big head nod to follow.

She popped up from her chair and beat him to the door. Out on the porch she turned to him just as the door was closing and hissed under her breath, whisper-shouting the words. "Geez, dude, *what...?*"

He stared back at her silently, watching her reaction and trying to determine how to handle a situation that had always been hypothetically and hopefully possible, even if, after so many years, it had begun to seem theoretically unlikely.

It only took a moment for the look of realization to wash across her face.

"You knew?" she demanded, aghast and fierce and fascinated – in that order – and all at the same time.

"Well, Sienna," he said with a small – and failed, and too soon – attempt at a grin, "I guess now you know why you've never seen any Russian writing. Or Russians."

"None of us even know what that looks like."

"That's true – it's a very secure program." It was still far too soon for levity, even if it was unintentional.

She glared daggers back at him.

"Torchy, what did I just do? Why didn't you tell us?"

A sense of betrayal washed over her. It was the feeling that she had been left out of the most important part of something she would ever be included in.

He paused again, surprised and disappointed at how poorly prepared he was to confront this outcome. He wondered what was racing through Hamza's mind back inside. He gestured toward the trail directly in front of the cabin which led up the mountain to an overlook above the Bay.

A hundred feet down the trail he picked up the conversation again.

"Telling you and your parents and everyone else here that we're spying on Russians is pretty easy. I mean, who doesn't want to help fight the Soviet Union? But this…" He rolled his head back and stared straight up, searching for the right assortment of words.

He rubbed a hand across his face and looked down at her.

"No one would sign up to do this – that's why. You think you would, and maybe *you* even would – but your parents wouldn't, and, frankly, essentially zero adults would believe it if that's what I told them we were doing here. Your dad would've thrown me out of that doctor's office."

They walked in silence and passed under the wide, sweeping branches of a favorite climbing tree. Sienna was still reeling and flailing to grasp this foreign new version of reality.

"So what is this for, then?"

He paused again, but only for a moment; now was no time for silence.

"Years ago a small group of scientists studying really old, really far away stars noticed something like static in their readings, and it was popping up in places where it shouldn't have been. One day someone showed it to me and it was obvious just by looking at it that it was caused by someone and wasn't just a naturally occurring thing. That was the Signal. I started to investigate it too, and then I found out that the place I worked – the place that runs this camp – had this one department of really smart people, and they had already found it, and they were pretty sure they knew what it was."

"What did they think it was?"

"Well, let's just say that five minutes ago you proved them right."

"So what did they do?"

"At the time we had no idea how the Signal worked or even how to listen to it – we just knew it was there. And we were pretty sure no one knew it was there but us. So I joined that department, and it took a while, but eventually we learned a few things about it. This would have been somewhere around February of 1977. And I've been working on it ever since."

"Just this?"

"Yep."

"And you don't think anyone else knew about the Signal?"

"We had spies all over the world constantly checking to see if other governments had found it."

"And what did you find?"

"We found that it's very hard to tell a spy what to look for if you are not allowed to tell them about it."

"Smart."

"So, we would just tell them to look for the most closely guarded secret of all, and then to tell us if it had anything to do with radios."

"And there was nothing?"

"Nothing."

"And so you started this camp to find out more?"

"We set up camp here a few years later when one of our leaders randomly noticed that anytime the Signal was really pulsing there was a tiny increase in kids scheduling appointments with neurologists because of problems they were having with their vision or hearing. We found that link right around the time we were finally able to prove there was intelligent and deliberate content coming through the Signal – so, at that point, we couldn't put this program together fast enough."

"And what have you learned?"

"Very, very little."

"Torchy, it's been so long," she said, feeling bad for her friend.

"Well, Barrett, there is still no handbook for dealing with a particle that doesn't officially exist moving at speeds that aren't technically possible."

She saw through this deflection.

"After all this time, you don't know anything about who's on the other side of the Signal or what they are saying or who they are trying to talk to?" she asked.

Torquemann nodded and took a deep breath. There was something startling and onerous about hearing a child ask all the questions he had failed to answer to his superiors at the NRO, much less the unsatisfactory answers he had found for himself.

"The only thing we know about whoever is on the other side is the feelings you guys get whenever you hear something. There's a lot to be inferred from that, but nothing we can prove. We know that almost everything you hear appears to be an order to do something or a request for information. There's never anything in there like 'How are you' and then 'Oh, hello Fred, thanks for asking, I'm fine.' If we had anything like that we could at least figure out some context, but instead we're essentially just listening to what seems to be one half of a telephone call."

"It's all questions and no answers."

"But it's also one big answer. It's the answer to the biggest question in the galaxy."

In any other circumstance, Sienna would have found this information thrilling. But, far from exhilarated, her heart was quietly breaking at what she felt had been a horribly missed opportunity. She couldn't identify exactly how or why someone would be punished for such a thing, or even how to identify exactly what her error had been, but it felt like failure. She was just young enough to lack the ability to compose a name for what it meant to fail at a thing you didn't know how to do, and she could not yet articulate how someone could do the "wrong" thing in a situation that was so obscure and arcane as to lack a traditional system of morality. She didn't know how to tell him what she said or *that* she had said anything at all – much less that it elicited a more detailed response and exchange.

Torquemann was certain there had been more than what the transcription had picked up, and he knew just enough about body language and the behavior of his most loquacious camper to understand that there had been something.

He watched her as they walked, her head down, staring through the ground to somewhere distant inside herself. She had briefly brightened during his initial flurry of information, but now she was cratering again under some kind of crushing… anger? Disappointment? Grief?

"What did you hear back there, Sienna?"

"At which point?"

"After you said you lived here on 'good 'ol Earth.'"

"Oh," she said, returning in her mind to the moment which was frozen in time such that it was still a part of the present. "I thought they were asking if I were another Russian, and I didn't know the names of Russian bases, so I just said, 'I'm from Earth, just like you.'"

"That was pretty smart. And what then?"

"And then instantly I heard, "We are not the same.""

Torquemann started to freeze but forced his legs to keep moving. Now it was his turn to be fascinated, terrified, and amazed. At the most basic level, some important things were now apparent – most particularly that they now knew more about us than we knew about them. Not much more. But a little. They had been spending these years talking to one of their own, and now they know someone else had tapped into the conversation.

"So what now?" she finally asked.

"Well, you now know something that none of the other kids have ever suspected – something none of them have ever even thought to consider."

In the distance, down the hill, they saw Dr. Tunis leave the research cabin and stretch his arms wide. He spotted them, waved, and started making his way up the hill.

"Right now," Torchy continued, "this is something that you, me, him, and zero other people here know." He paused and watched Tunis making his way around the patches of buckbrush and horsetails. "But you know why we don't talk about it, right?"

Sienna picked at the leaves, still lost in her own thoughts and tried to untangle the reasons behind a secret that she barely understood.

"Is it so that we won't tell anyone?"

"That's part of it. The even bigger reason is that it keeps you all safe. When any of you guys go home, the temptation to talk about something like this is just too much. And once a secret like that gets out, then it puts everyone in danger because other people and other governments will start digging around to find out what they don't know – and to save time they'll start with tracking down anyone who was ever here. The people who run the camp make sure the odds of this are almost zero, but nothing is ever zero."

She turned her head to look at him, waiting to be told not to worry about it.

"Instead, you kids and parents think that it's 'Soviet bad guys' we're listening to – and everyone kind of naturally understands why you can't talk about that. And the Soviet Union probably won't last forever the way things are going over there at the moment, so, eventually, anything a camper here knows about them won't really matter."

"So if you've never gotten any really big pieces of information, then what is this camp for?"

"We're trying to learn everything we can about what's inside the Signal. It's as simple as that. I want to know what's in it, I want to understand if or how it affects us – and then, if I can, I want to learn how it works."

Dr. Tunis was now close enough now to hear them, and Torquemann didn't have to tell him what they were discussing.

"Hamza, why do we tell everyone it's the Russians?," Torquemann asked in an accusatory tone.

Dr. Tunis laughed, but not in a way that indicated he was particularly happy.

"It's the only thing protecting us from every government agency and politician interfering and insisting on telling us what to do. I mean, can you imagine if the President knew about this? He'd try to get them to pay taxes or vote for him."

"More than that," Torquemann continued, "the sociological data indicates that if people knew this were happening there would be panic. Everyone likes to say that we're not alone in the Universe, but no one really believes it. The confidence people show when they make that statement about not being alone is only possible because, underneath it all, everyone assumes that any kind of contact is impossible."

"And so, for all anyone knows, we're out here listening to Russians," Tunis concluded pointing back down at the camp, "because no matter what they think they're listening to, we still need to know what's in that Signal."

The three of them sat quietly and listened to the breeze coming up off the Bay. The bench they were on was a long tree trunk, split in half lengthwise, with one half to sit on, and the other half propped up to lean against – like some kind of prehistoric couch.

"I'm sorry you now have this burden, Sienna. But do you understand why you have to keep it a secret?"

She looked back at Dr. Torquemann and nodded. "I get it."

He stared back out over the camp, looking in the direction of the ocean on the other side of the hill.

"I know you do."

Over the last few minutes she had grown noticeably brighter. Something was very different from the crestfallen little girl who had walked up this trail. Something about hearing she was part of a story rather than being its sinister plot twist had, once again, shown Julius the power of her always-remarkable resilience.

The sound of the breeze through the trees died down and everyone was momentarily distracted by a quail pecking at a lizard further down the trail.

"Who else has ever sent a message back down the Signal?"

Torquemann and Tunis shared a look, and the physicist went first.

"From what we can tell – and bear in mind that a lot of this data is coming from campers who didn't know exactly what was happening or how they were doing it, so it's things we pieced together after the fact – but, over the course of this program, there have been exactly four instances similar to yours."

"What happened?" she asked, feeling a sudden rush of relief at not being a total outlier.

"Two of the times, and these were about five years apart, the kid got hit with some version of 'Who is there?' and both times they froze up and broke off contact immediately. But, in both cases, we never had any concrete confirmation that there was an actual transfer of information from our side. And Hamza, you studied the other two quite a bit."

"Yeah," Dr. Tunis said, seeming weary at the memory of many hundreds of hours spent pouring over a few scant moments of Signal data. "A year before you got here we had a kid who was getting a good look at what he assumed was a panel on a reactor or something, and that moment he heard the words "Can you see it" and just totally out of habit he said 'yes' – and that was it. Again, we could never find any definitive evidence that the 'yes' went through, but the Signal did go haywire for the next couple days. The Signal was actually blaring but no one could see or hear anything intelligible in it."

"And the fourth one" she asked?

"Oh, the fourth one was probably around the time right after you were born. The kid was always very particular about sitting in the chair in just the right way, getting comfortable, re-tying her shoes, tightening the ponytail – we would spend forever while she got everything dialed in. Every once in a while, Dr. Torquemann would ask, 'Ok, so are we ready now?' and she'd glare at us and then laugh, and then we'd get started. Well, one day near the end of her time at the camp, her ESR clicked right into the Signal before she was done getting herself set up, and when she heard the voice say, "Now let's begin" she just absent-mindedly snapped back like it was one of us talking and said, 'Dude, stop, I'm not ready!'"

"And that," Torquemann concluded, "shut the Signal off for six full weeks. And when it came back, we didn't get much out of it for a really long time."

"And that's all? In all these years?"

"Yes."

For the first time since that cold pit started digging into her stomach 30 minutes earlier, Sienna felt free of it. If her record of failures in that chair had undeniably preceded her, today was something unequivocally meaningful, even if she hadn't regurgitated every single detail. This was the contribution, the participation, and the continuity she had craved.

And she knew that now the foundation had been laid to *finally* do so much more. The thought of that bright future brought even more joy than today's pinnacle.

"Why don't you run back to camp? Looks like school is out, so your friends are probably looking for you."

The two scientists watched as she skipped down the trail, radiating pride. Neither said a word until the top of her head had dipped out of sight near the bottom of the hill.

Tunis was the first to speak.

"Well, our broadcasters know something they didn't know before, but I don't suppose there's much they can do about it without coordinates."

Torquemann had darkened since the moment Sienna left, and he seemed even more troubled now.

"So, what changes now?"

"Changes? Well, historically speaking," he said slowly exhaling, "and putting aside the profundity of today, everything she's ever seen or heard in the Signal has been spotted previously by other campers, and often in more detail than what she comes up with. There's nothing anywhere in her data that indicates today's session is replicable in the future."

"Wait, Julius…"

"I think she has earned getting to go back to being a full-time kid."

Tunis was shocked. Even if the logic was sound and the master schedule confirmed it, the timing of this specific discussion was jarring on the heels of what had just happened.

"Tonight before you wrap up, turn off the field generator in her cabin. You have that one hidden in the lamp by her bed, right?"

Tunis nodded.

"Thank you. We'll give her ESR a couple days to power down, and then she'll be on the way back to normal."

Even though this sounded like the end of a meeting, neither moved.

"Don't be so shocked, Hamza. You said yourself that the tissue overlap on her parietal lobe was within a month of growing beyond the framing she'd need to continue picking anything up, and that was nearly three weeks ago. On top of that, her number was punched in the master schedule two days ago. So, today was the farewell, regardless."

A few moments later Sienna made it back to her cabin and soon found her friends in the common area near the barn. She was euphoric and felt a swell of love for her friends and the people who made this place possible. The boomerang of dread and elation had been exhausting, and what was left was the satisfaction of confidence.

This was, by any measure, the happiest day of her life.

13 JUNE

Forty-eight hours later, Sienna sat in the front seat of her mother's car, her face pressed against the cold glass of the window as they crossed the long, thin San Mateo Bridge, trying in vain to muffle sobs while hot tears rolled down her cheeks.

Ginny was surprised to see her so distraught. When she picked her up from Dr. Torquemann's office, it was clear she'd been crying for a very long time. The doctor had the psychologist with him, and they explained that she had been inconsolable since they'd given her the news the night before – right after they'd called to arrange this pickup.

"Don't fret so hard, honey," she said, taking one hand off the steering wheel to rub her daughter's back. She was surprised that the t-shirt was hot to the touch. Her daughter was fuming.

She tried another approach.

"Sienna, hun, think about what you gained from an experience like this – this was a very special, very cool opportunity." Another long sniffle. "And besides," she continued, "it's not like you wanted to do this for the rest of your whole life, right? The camp has kids come in, they do the thing, your brain keeps growing, and then you get to move on and go back to being a normal kid again."

Sienna understood that this was technically true, but she could not bring herself to face anyone right now. As they passed the toll plaza on the eastern side of the bridge, Sienna took a deep breath and recognized the hills in the distance.

She really was going home.

Her presence back in their cul-de-sac in Walnut Creek wouldn't be too terribly surprising, nor would her presence back at school when everyone came back from summer vacation. The NRO had very carefully coached them on the cover story for her absence: "Sienna got accepted into this really interesting private school, and the teachers are amazing, but the bad news is that the school doesn't have a ton of funding – so if it ever runs out of money, she'll just come back to school here." That story was always enough to get a neighbor or casual acquaintance to say, "Oh, wow, that's awesome; I hope that works out" and leave it at that.

Now the storytelling was over.

She deflated against the passenger seat and began to talk, but tears choked off the end of the sentence: "I was never even good at it, like, the whole time I wasn't *ever* good at…"

"Oh baby, you're being too competitive about this – it's not like that. No one there thought about it like that."

"It's true though, even with the thing I got," she pointed to her head, "still pretty much nothing, except for one time. And that was like two days ago."

"I'm sorry."

"I just wanted so bad to see something or do something that was really useful."

"I know, baby."

They kept driving in silence, and the freeway began to tilt upward towards the Dublin Hills in the distance.

She took a deep breath and wiped the tears from her face with both hands. As her palms ran across each eye, she saw the faintest crackle of something indistinguishable in the Singal. It was subtle and distant but felt like something lunging towards her. But she knew that wasn't really how the Signal worked; she knew enough to recognize how much of that feeling was just her hoping for something. Besides a tiny flutter a few days later that was almost certainly just the result of a big sneeze, that was the last piece of the Signal she ever encountered. She said goodbye, right there, once and for all, amidst a face full of tears and a rainy stretch of the 580 freeway.

There was traffic and construction along the way, but within an hour they were home. Sienna carried her small suitcase down the hall to her room and sat on the edge of her bed with a heavy landing.

She looked around at the familiar walls, the shelf of books, the pyramid of stuffed animals, the bean bag chair in the corner, and thought for a moment that it was good to be home. And then she fell over sideways onto her pillow and rolled over to bury her face in it. The sobs came roaring out of her – the hard, horrible kind that burned the back of her throat and made her nose clog. She was drowning underneath the sadness, and, when she stopped to breathe, wet strands of hair matted against her cheeks. She was writhing to get the feeling off of her, and the panic began to creep in as she noticed there was no escaping it. The practical part of her brain told her to get outside, to get on with her life, and to go back to normal; but the logos is a quiet voice in the mind of a grief-stricken child. Going next door to visit Cathryn, or even further down the street to see Joanna, felt pointless, and she could not yet stomach the idea of telling them a pleasant lie to conceal a heartbreaking failure.

She rolled over on her back so she could breathe through her nose again and kicked off her shoes. She stared up at the collection of stars she had stuck to the ceiling the year before she left for the camp; she used to lay here every night staring up at them as they glowed green in the darkness, and she would trace lines between them in her mind.

Then she had discovered her mind could do something else entirely.

And now it couldn't.

Out of habit she twisted one of her bracelets around her finger as she stared at the ceiling. She had braided these with Naomi, Lydia, and Nora at Fort Torch when they got permission to stay there late and watch the meteor shower.

They had run to the fort immediately after classes ended, backpacks jammed with snacks over their shoulders, and spent the entire rest of the day there. They laid on their backs and watched as the light between the leaves changed from blue to orange. The sound of the wind moving over each leaf was peaceful in a way that reminded these girls of how far away they were from home. They talked and laughed and ate and watched as the first points of lights began to appear in the dark purple sky, and then as thin streaks of light began to leap out of the emptiness and streak through the night air.

She leaned over to reach her nightstand, dug a small pair of scissors out of the drawer, and cut through all four of them at once. She put them back in the drawer and slammed it shut. They would stay there until she cleaned out this room on her way to college.

She stood up, wiped her face, changed her clothes, and put the sweats and t-shirt she'd worn home from camp in the garbage. She had to be something new now. She was going to drown if she didn't create something to climb up on. She had a story and a secret too big for an entire team of scientists and the government agency they worked for, and she had to process it alone. The psychologist at the camp, and the other psychologists at the NRO, were unanimous in their estimation that she would not reveal any operational activities, and they were correct. She was going to let this eat her alive quietly, and a few things inside her would die in the process.

The next time she shed a tear of any kind she was holding her infant son while her brothers laid roses on the polished lid of a coffin.

She promised herself that tomorrow she would start making the rounds through the neighborhood. For now she moved to sit with her back against her bedroom door, and she was still there three hours later when her mom called down the hall that dinner was ready.

It was all over.

13 JUNE

Dr. Tunis sat alone inside one of the Camp Loaf cabins and waited, along with an unknown, but probably small, number of listeners who were patched into the phone in the middle of the table. They had been waiting nearly 10 minutes for Dr. Torquemann; he was down at the camp's front gate saying goodbye to the subject of this call and her mother.

Torquemann finally made his way back, shaking the rain off his jacket as he entered.

"Ok," he started, "to follow up on my report from Tuesday, I have a few additional details about the data transfer which took place through the Signal."

A voice from the speaker phone asked, "And this data came directly from Barrett?"

"No, we're getting this information from one of the roommates who casually mentioned it to our psychologist here during a routine session last night. Sienna – excuse me – Ms. Barrett, shared a few additional details with her close friends that did not make it to Dr. Tunis and me in our initial debrief."

"Go on," the voice urged, matter-of-factly.

"The last thing we have in our transcription is the response she received – the one that she articulated as 'we are not the same.' That's the last recorded part of the interchange that we have due to an equipment problem, and that is all she disclosed to me when we spoke afterwards. Now we know, however, that over the following two evenings she told her roommates that after that response she received *another* question which requested to know where she was. The wording of it, according to her, was simply: 'Where are you?'"

There was silence from the phone. Torquemann knew this meant someone had likely hit 'mute' on the other end so they could discuss something freely. After about 15 seconds the static of the line reappeared.

"What happened next?"

"Apparently Barrett panicked but had the presence of mind to recall her training and avoid revealing the nature of the program. So, rather than expose her location, she changed the subject and gave a… fake name."

"What name did she use?"

Torquemann looked across the table to Tunis, who shrugged and gestured to the phone as if to say, "Give them everything."

"She said she was a rabbit."

"She said that was her name?"

"No, to be clear, she told them she *was* a rabbit."

"Like the animal," Hamza added unhelpfully.

The line went mute again but came back after just a moment.

"Are we to understand that now this story is making its way around your camp?"

Of all the follow up questions, Torquemann was relieved to get this one.

"No, actually that outcome has been successfully avoided. Barrett had a very strong sense of operational discipline, and she was perfectly clear during our debrief that evening that the Soviet story was the single most important fact allowing this project to remain productive."

"And you're certain about that?"

"Yes, I am. Even the roommate noted that her entire story to them had been about Russians. And we've emphasized to those campers that this particular story shouldn't be repeated."

"And that goes for your staff as well, Dr. Torquemann? They are all still operating with the understanding that this was a Russian intercept?"

"Yes. Without the additional context, there is nothing in this exchange that hints at anything otherwise."

"Understood. So, what now?"

"Right now we're focusing everything on processing Tuesday

afternoon's session, and quite coincidentally that has lined up with her cycling out of the program."

"We do have questions about that, actually, and we have some concerns." a new voice over the phone said. "First, sending information back through the Signal is a very novel concept, even if there was nothing in the physics saying it was impossible. What does your analysis of this transmission tell us so far?"

Dr. Tunis took this question.

"Right now, the neurological data shows her brain lighting up in the moments where she was transmitting back, and, in tandem with this, we can see that she hit an ideal pocket within the Signal where pretty much anything could successfully transfer from her mind to the recipient, and then when that sweet spot was gone, she lost contact almost immediately." He paused and looked over at Torquemann. "And that loss of contact is in line with her previous connective aptitude. Traditionally, Ms. Barrett maintained Signal stability at a level that straddled the lower boundary of our program's average. But, to your point, it is compelling to consider what might have happened if one of our top performers had been in that chair at the moment the Signal opened up like this."

"And your information indicates the Signal was at some kind of peak level at the time?"

Now it was Torquemann's job as the program director to explain.

"Our instruments here can't tell us anything about what is or isn't contained in the Signal – only the kids can do that, obviously – but what we can gauge is the total volume of tachyonic activity at any given time, and, at the time of this particular dialog, there was an unforeseeable avalanche."

"And that brings me to the second question, which is perhaps the most pressing one: Why send her home now?"

"Over the last two weeks, Dr. Tunis and I have been aware that the tissue overlap on her parietal lobe was on track to naturally outgrow the necessary configuration, so today's departure is in line with our standard operating procedure, the timing of Tuesday's event was simply an aberration. But, as you know, brain growth is really a secondary measurement; during her session immediately prior to the one in question she reached our prescribed neurological threshold such that, no matter what,

Tuesday would have been her last go-round with us."

"But certainly this dialog seems promising enough to pursue just a little bit longer, doesn't it?" a third voice asked.

"Frankly, in almost a year-and-a-half, Barrett was able to reach deep integration with the Signal exactly once, arguably twice, depending on which of our technicians you ask to interpret a session from about eight months ago. But we can say she clearly did it exactly once and that was less than 48 hours ago. Prior to that she had precious little to show for it, and this indicates definitively, for Dr. Tunis and myself, as well as our extended team, that there is nothing to indicate this type of connection would ever happen again."

"Never?"

"No."

To fill the silence, he quickly continued: "That being said, I agree with all of you," he said this not being entirely sure how many people were on this call, "that this week's results are remarkable, but they are not going to happen again, and certainly not with the available time her brain has left in the master schedule."

Dr. Tunis added, "Gathering data from the Signal is not a muscle you grow – it is a mechanical action you either *can* perform or *cannot* perform. There is a certain amount of mental discipline required to maintain the necessary focus during sessions – and, in this capacity, Ms. Barrett was slightly above average – but that was not sufficient to overcome simple mechanical and structural limitations."

"What point did you say she was at on the schedule?"

"This current week has been on the calendar for several months as the point we expected her to reach 50%, and, sure enough, at last week's checkup her tissue threshold was at 49.19% – so today was going to be the last day, no matter what."

The phone was silent, so Torquemann ended this line of inquiry simply: "In this case, and with this subject, and based on the volume of data we use to reach this conclusion, Barrett was firmly within the "cannot" category of possible future contributions."

"Understood" said the original voice, the one Torquemann recognized as the senior officer at the NRO who he reported to. "What are you going to do about reporting this to our friends in Vienna?"

Torquemann rolled his eyes but held in a deep sigh. At the outset of this program a lawyer at the NRO had alerted the team about an agreement the U.S. had made decades earlier with the United Nations and the rest of the international community about what they were expected to do in the event of any interstellar contact. Throughout the existence of Dark Antennae it was generally agreed that the information being gathered was sporadic and incomplete enough to forgo sharing it per the guidelines of the United Nations Office for Outer Space Affairs, which was based in Vienna.

The official mission of UNOOSA was to "utilize the unique benefits of outer space for the betterment of all humankind," and, since its organization in 1958, it had not done very much besides host conferences with the International Academy of Astronautics and insist unconvincingly that both organizations were not duplicative. Then, two years ago, the IAA held a three-day conference in Stockholm where they published a document titled, "Declaration of Principles Concerning Activities Following the Detection of Extraterrestrial Intelligence." This declaration outlined nine steps that had to be taken in the event anything with non-human origins was ever detected, and, depending on the type of work any given scientist was doing, those steps were either exciting or hilarious. Torquemann's favorite was Principle #4, which said, in part, "A confirmed detection of extraterrestrial intelligence should be disseminated promptly, openly, and widely through scientific channels and public media." Pure comedy. Principle #7 made slightly more sense, "If the evidence of detection is in the form of electromagnetic signals, the parties to this declaration should seek international agreement to protect the appropriate frequencies." But this assumed that the frequencies in question were things humans could even detect or knew existed. But the principle that he knew at the time could eventually cause the most problems was #8: "No response to a signal or other evidence of extraterrestrial intelligence should be sent until appropriate international consultations have taken place."

He had not told Sienna or anyone else about #8 during orientation.

Protocol said that now he needed to prepare a very specific set of paperwork, accompanied by a detailed report with as many of the readouts as possible from the research cabin, and then, after review by the NRO, fly to Vienna, have a team read the report, and then bring that report back with him to the NRO offices in Chantilly, Virginia, where it would be tested for exposure to covert duplication attempts, and then shredded.

"I was not planning on submitting this information to UNOOSA," he said simply.

"Agreed" the voice said quickly. "I think that is all the questions we have here. Thank you for the quick turnaround on this update, and let me know if anything else comes up."

After the goodbyes were exchanged and the line went dead, the two scientists were left to take a deep breath.

"Julius, it's been nine years, and, even after this week, we still have just slightly more data than you did after the first 100 days of the program – and essentially none of it is in chunks large enough to be considered a complete thought."

Torqueman nodded but didn't look away from the hole he had been staring into the wall.

"I know this project doesn't have the legs to last forever, and that has never been the plan. The goal here isn't to solve a problem – the mission is to learn everything there is about how that Signal works, and the secondary mission is to determine with reasonable certainty what's on the other side of it. Those guys on the phone told me a long time ago that we are listeners, not explorers."

Tunis stood up and grabbed his bag from behind a chair. "So we keep listening."

"We do. Nothing we've ever seen in it appears hostile, they don't have our location, and if they're sophisticated enough to communicate like this then they probably aren't surprised to discover someone else is out there. So we just keep listening until this project gets rolled up – and, as long as the Signal is active, I don't see that happening."

PRESENT DAY

18 · Back

Waiting until the middle of the day in the middle of the week was, in Sienna's opinion, the smart choice when it came to Costco. The people who went on Saturdays were clearly battling demons she did not care to know about.

She pulled into the garage while texting her two oldest kids to come out and help unload, and she finished eating the churro she'd picked up at the food court on the way out. She opened the door to start the unloading process and, as she squeezed the handle, she immediately heard a sound behind her begin to rise. She snapped her eyes to the rearview mirror to see what was heading her direction. Seeing nothing, she next craned her neck to see if it was coming from the air conditioning unit. In the full second it took to check both places, and before she'd even locked eyes on the AC, she heard the first crackle and the surrounding sound of a distantly familiar hum.

It was like the voice of an old acquaintance she hadn't spoken to in years, and just as the hum reached its familiar old volume, she saw a staccato of tiny points of light that lacked identifiable shape or substance. She gripped the steering wheel to steady herself, her mind and mouth agape at the randomness of the arrival.

She closed her eyes, out of habit, and listened. There was nothing else. But the hum, although undeniably recognizable, did have a different… what? Sound? Tone?

No one had made it to the garage to help unload yet, which was not terribly unusual, and, in this case, it was a relief. She waited another minute to see what else might be coming, but it was already gone.

As she made her way inside she noticed Calista and Scarlett's bikes were both already parked in the garage; that was odd – all three girls were supposed to be at a summer camp for at least another two hours, and, if it was one of the horse-riding days, they wouldn't be home for at least three. Like a lot of nine-year-olds, any spare moment Scarlett had was usually spent with a table-full of art-supplies, or, when that got boring, hanging from the monkey bars her dad had attached to the ceiling in the basement. Today, however, Sienna found her curled up in a ball on the couch holding the dog and listening to a story on the Kindle. Down the hall, Calista was laying on the floor, headphones on, with a wet cloth across her forehead. This wasn't exactly the summer afternoon 12-year-olds dream of. Both of them looked miserable.

Sienna brought in the first two armloads of groceries and noticed a note on the kitchen counter – it was a printout from the camp nurse about how to treat tinnitus, and it included a referral to an audiologist. A pair of terrible dots suddenly connected. The day before both girls had mentioned not feeling well – Calista had wondered if she might have a head cold or an ear infection because her ears would not stop ringing; Scarlett had complained that the intercom in the lunch tent at camp was buzzing the entire time she ate, but Sienna had volunteered there enough times to know the tent didn't have electricity.

Now she was concerned.

She scooped up Scarlett and walked with her back to Calista's room.

"Girls, tell me what you're feeling? What hurts?"

Calista groaned and rolled onto her side. "I thought it was a cold, but now it's a full headache."

Scarlett's head was resting on Sienna's shoulder, and she felt it move up and down to nod agreement.

"What else?" Sienna asked.

"I seriously think I need glasses or something," Cali said with a groan, "because every 20 minutes it just – it's like when you stand up too fast and you see dots."

Scarlett's head popped up, "You can see the dots?"

Sienna tilted her head to watch this reaction and asked, "Do you also see dots?"

"It's usually just dots and the buzzing, but then sometimes I see it like a big mess – like a wave of dots," Scarlett said.

"Since when?"

"Yesterday. Or the day before? Probably yesterday?"

"Just yesterday, for me," Cali added.

"Why didn't you mention it?" Sienna asked.

"Well," Scarlett explained, "at first I just thought this was just my creativity."

Cali burst out laughing, but not in a particularly kind way.

"But," Scarlett continued, undaunted, "then I figured this was just another sign that my imagination was growing."

Leave it to this girl, Sienna thought, to assume that this was all just her own interesting thoughts.

But what was "this," Sienna wondered.

But she knew.

Inexplicably, unexpectedly, and unmistakably, the Signal was back.

* * * * *

Sienna brought each girl a popsicle, and checked in on them regularly as she caught up on a few chores around the house.

Her mind raced to figure out what any of this could mean – and how or why any of this could be possible. Both girls were roughly the right age for the program, although Cali was definitely on the older side. How or why she had felt anything at all in the garage was a mystery. But age ranges aside, she knew for a fact that Dark Antennae had wrapped up years ago and the Signal had long-since gone quiet. She tried to guess at who else might be affected or where else they were tracking this, or if anyone was even bothering to monitor for it anymore.

After almost three decades of very rarely thinking about it and never talking about it, Sienna's first reaction to this ambush of particles and dredged emotions was to talk to someone about it. But there was no hotline for this. There wasn't a support group. She had never even hinted at it to Jordan. Mike and Ginny were, as always, distant.

Now the flood of emotions began to mingle with the long-forgotten loneliness that is unique to a child marooned in her own home.

After Sienna returned from her extended time away at Camp Loaf, things never returned to normal at home. There was never a notable conflict, and there were no significant upheavals in family life, but she came home to something different than what she had left. She came home as something different. But even that change didn't explain everything. If Sienna had always been the one member of the family a bit different than her siblings and parents, the time away seemed to have doubled and tripled this distinction. From the day she returned her parents had carried on without a hitch – which, in some ways, was commendable on their part. But now, as a parent, Sienna found it odd that they had never asked how she felt about her time away, or checked in to see how she was adjusting to life back in the real world, or showed an interest in how the time away had affected her. On one hand, that lack of interest could have simply been exquisitely performed operational discipline on their part – the old spymaster's trick of never compromising Sienna's secrets by never acknowledging them. But Ginny and Mike were not the type to keep the fine details of counterespionage at the forefront of their mind at all times.

The reality was far more prosaic. They thought it was interesting their daughter had done this thing, but they did not find their daughter particularly interesting – and they did not conflate the two. They were not bad people, they were just incurious and disinterested in things that did not directly and persistently affect them. When Sienna returned after so many months spent combatting Russians, she was met with a healthy amount of extra space by her parents – a lack of oversight that her older brothers would have done anything to have but which she found emaciating. Leaving the camp so suddenly – and with the thoughts of so much unfinished business still consuming her every waking moment – it left her with a giant hole in her heart, and her parents simply were not the type to fill it. They eventually settled on treating her like something not quite approximating a child, but certainly not an adult. And that strange, nebulous area in between two stages of life never evolved and never warmed into something else as she grew older. By the time she was an adult, the distance her parents kept from her had transformed into indifference, and her tender-hearted zeal to accomplish something at the camp had calcified into a rigid ability to accomplish *anything* she started, no matter the associated stress or misery. But this determination came at the expense of her extreme reluctance to start new things, try new things, or take chances.

Now, with a family of her own, she couldn't conceive of intentionally putting distance between herself and a child simply because she could no longer understand them. Even her children saw the distance their grandparents maintained and felt rejected by it, despite their mother's insistence to the contrary. Sienna was self-aware enough to know that she must have contributed to the deterioration of this relationship in some way, but years spent pondering it had revealed nothing. She had once given voice to this confusion when talking to a counselor, and the response was simple to the point of ineffectual: "Sometimes people just grow apart. It happens with friends, sometimes with siblings, and, very rarely, with parents." After an early life spent being incredibly unusual, she resented the fact that this label had carried over one more time into adulthood.

She had nothing of substance to show for being unique as a child, and now she had no extended family to show for it as an adult.

This made the family which she had already centered her life around grow still deeper in its importance.

In so many other circumstances it would also have been natural to talk with any of her old friends or roommates from Camp Loaf – but even that was a dead end. She hadn't kept in touch with anyone from the camp the way normal people might if they had attended a normal camp. But even this was a bit odd since the friendships there had been very real – it was almost as if the children who met in secret did not think to, or did not know how to, be friends as adults out in the open. It occurred to her that part of the problem with reconnecting would be the introductions – "Hey, do you remember me from that Cold War thing we both did?" Or, how, exactly, would she and a fellow camper introduce each other to their respective families? "So, this is Michelle, and we met when we were both in 3rd grade," followed by the question about how it was that you went to the same school when you both grew up on opposite sides of the country. "Oh, no, not the grade school I told you about, this was the secret grade school that 'went out of business' when it couldn't catch any Russians."

There were a couple of fellow campers out there on the internet who had posted fleeting pieces of material about the camp, however. Both of them had been there before her time, but she'd seen a YouTube video that one of them filmed walking around the premises of the old camp. Only two of the original cabins and part of the barn were still there, and the videographer correctly pointed out that some careful specialist from the cleanup crew had taken a belt sander to the posts and walls to remove every set of initials ever carved by past residents. Another former camper occasionally popped up on the podcast circuit to talk about his strange experience with Cold War mania, but neither of these people had a single tangible piece of evidence to connect them with this topic or that location – and that was by design. It helped that neither of them had anything close to a complete understanding of Dark Antennae's goals. The only thing those two people could say definitively was that their income tax rebates were going to be a lot smaller from now on.

But, at this moment, she reflected, yet again, even she didn't know that much more about the Signal than anyone else. She couldn't answer who sent it, why, from where, or to whom.

Nothing.

25 JUNE

Sienna would have been pleased to know that a small but determined group already knew that the Signal was back.

They didn't know what it was or that it had a name, but they knew something was happening.

Two different scientific divisions at the Pentagon had independently noticed the interference and started combing through the Defense Department's "not-unsubstantial" – as they liked to phrase it – archives trying to find any previous work documenting this phenomenon. When the wide-ranging nature of these two efforts finally led the groups to cross paths, it resulted in a rare moment of inter-departmental cooperation. When the researchers began comparing notes it quickly became clear that the problem had to do with having too much data on the subject rather than not enough. Over the past 35 years there had been nearly 200 different "dark" – or, in more extreme cases, "black" – programs using electromagnetism in one way or another.

Another 24 hours of research narrowed this very long list down to 12 programs, and these were presented to an impatiently waiting Secretary of Defense. The presentation ordered the programs based on the likelihood that they could shed light on the currently detected interference. The 9th program on that list was an old one which had attempted to burrow into the detectable edges of the electromagnetic spectrum to see if a message was encoded amidst the interference or if the interference itself was evidence of a secret communication technique developed by the Soviets. There wasn't much more than that to share in the meeting because nearly all of that file was blacked out, and it remained that way even after the SecDef's chief of staff had requested an unredacted copy last night. This might have seemed like a dead end, but, unlike the other 11 projects on this list, the lead scientist of that old project was still working on it.

This came as welcome news, and the Secretary ordered the researcher presenting this overview to go find this "Dr. J. H. Torquemann" immediately.

The only usable data in the file – amidst the hundreds of blacked out lines – was a copy of the order to shut down the program on 22 October 1991, and the relocation of the research team to office space leased by the government in Alexandria, Virginia – about six miles south of where this file had been found in the Pentagon archives. The file also included an open-ended agreement giving this project – even its code name was blacked out – open-ended access to a giant array of supercomputers in perpetuity. The bottom sheet of paper in the file was contact information for the United Nations Office for Outer Space Affairs, which almost certainly meant that someone within this project had asked for – and received – some type of coordinated alignment of international satellites.

This was all the information that Colonel Nick Castro had before typing this scientist's name into the Pentagon's directory, and, to his surprise, finding an active phone number at the office in Alexandria. The colonel had been given explicit directions by the Secretary to learn everything about this currently unnamed project, and he planned to do it today.

He looked at his watch. It was 11:13 am.

* * * * *

Right before the phone on a nearby desk started ringing, Julius Torquemann had started thinking about lunch.

He was alone, as usual, in a third-floor office that was dedicated entirely to his ongoing research. In a single large room, behind a door with no nameplate or markings to indicate what might be on the other side, in a nondescript strip of office buildings in suburban D.C. – this was as hidden a location as he ever had in the hills above San Mateo. The fact that the walls, floors, and ceilings in this particular unit were surrounded by a wire mesh that could detect and repel the slightest intrusion from a person, device, or scan was just an insurance policy.

For the last 33 years he had driven to this same building, parked in the same spot near the side entrance, and, as far as his family knew, studied gravitational waves. This cover story had always been complex enough to resist outside scrutiny, but it had become entirely bulletproof when those hypothetical waves were proven to be very real a decade ago thanks to the Laser Interferometer Gravitational-Wave Observatory in Hanford, Washington detecting them for the first time. This office connected to a super-computer array in a basement on the other side of the city, and he had access to essentially bottomless computing power from a government approved cloud network, but he was careful about what data he had crunched in those external environments. The nine-and-a-half years of full-time field research in the Dark Antennae program had left him with enough data for five lifetimes of analysis, and so he showed up every day to do just that.

It might have surprised his former colleagues to see that the earnest young scientist they had known at the camp had chosen to cloister himself for parts of four decades in this office. But Julius had nowhere else to go – at least by his reckoning. The outstanding questions derived from his research were so massive that he had shrunk his entire universe and sublimated every ambition to exist within this single room. At disconnected points within all of this data were stray pieces of information that he believed could be connected to explain how the Signal worked.

The office had come to be an extension of his mind, and, in an adjoining room, which was really more of a walk-in closet, was a masterpiece of organization: Every iota of research from the program was housed here on a carefully networked and cross-referenced series of hard drives, that spent their lives in climate-controlled paradise behind a titanium cage that could only be opened by Torquemann's biometrics.

Julius was old now, but his energy and passion for the Dark Antennae program had not yet waned. He was still looking for his breakthrough, still running tests to find patterns, still comparing phenomena, and trying to connect every dot his program had ever plotted between August 1978 and October 1991. He was logical enough to know that he still hadn't scratched the surface, but he was optimistic enough to believe that a pile of data this large simply *had* to have a few gold flakes in it.

And he was determined to sift through every last piece of gravel to find them.

In his fourth decade of post-program research, he still wanted a definitive answer for how tachyon waves could have a message piggybacked onto them, and he wanted to find the key that would unlock how to pinpoint the origin of a message that seems to appear everywhere all at once. And so he kept studying the ways neural electricity had been elicited, the routing of particles through various structures of the brain, every syllable the campers uttered while they watched, and countless other variables.

He was grateful for how much more processing power existed now compared to when he started. On any given day, a piece of analysis that would have originally taken seven or eight months to process could now be done in 20 minutes, and his even more sophisticated follow up questions might take an hour each. The paradox of growing older was that technology kept squeezing decades of time into each of his weeks.

Now the days were spent running queries on his data, designing long-term tests, cross-referencing everything with the totality of archived knowledge about deep space courtesy of UNOOSA, as well as every new deep space scan or data dump from both orbital telescopes and distant satellites. His focus remained sharp, and the doubts that had begun to creep in about 20 years ago – "Am I chasing a ghost? Have I hit a wall and now I'm just examining bricks? What are the odds of finding a pathway where only a vapor trail ever existed?" – had not returned.

But one thing was very different from years past.

When he was supervising the cleanup and demolition of the research cabin in those cold final weeks of 1991, he kept a Superluminal Tachyon Emission Spectrometer, or STES, as a souvenir. This was certainly a protocol violation, but the STES didn't look like much and drew essentially zero attention – it was just a metal rectangle about a foot wide with a round screen like a porthole in the middle. Every workstation in the research cabin had a STES, and they were a key part of the research process. It was a simple and self-contained device that could show you the current level of focused tachyon activity at any given time on a screen that looked very similar to an oscilloscope. When the Signal was really surging the line would dance wildly to show the rise and fall of the tachyon waves and the particle density of each one.

Torquemann had kept his STES plugged in next to his desk in the same way someone in a corporate office might plug in a decorative lamp. The faint green glow of the flat line was just a part of the scenery.

Ten days ago, while changing the battery in his wireless keyboard and returning a call to his daughter, Torquemann saw the line on the STES explode into activity out of the corner of his eye. He felt the physical impact of his heart slamming to a stop. He didn't look up. His daughter was still talking but he couldn't hear her. He closed his eyes hard and reopened them in case this was his first ever lucid dream or some fugue-like hallucination. His mind raced but never escaped this tiny fraction of the present. His daughter was now asking if he was still there, but the adrenaline made his ears ring as if he'd been too close when a bomb went off. He still hadn't looked up. He could see the reflection of the STES on the surface of his phone, and noticed the specific ways it leapt up and down. Readings like that would have boded well for a very busy day back in San Mateo. His mind automatically started thinking about who to pull out of class or what machines to calibrate to get as clean a reading as possible.

Seeing it again was like laying eyes on a loved one whose autobiography you had helped write, whose cemetery plot you had mournfully helped select, and whose funeral you had planned.

Every day since he had paused before he went home in the evening to take one last look at it, just in case this was the last time. Every morning he had opened the door to the office wondering if it would still be there. He remembered the feeling of seeing it go flat and stay that way. It had been like seeing a distant relative you loved but barely knew take their last breath.

And, unsurprisingly, the return of the Signal brought with it a renewed energy to Torquemann's work. He already had access to thousands of systems and sensor arrays that the Signal would affect, and those countless gigabytes of data were immediately compared and cross referenced with data from Camp Loaf. The initial results indicated that, aside from some very small variations, this was the exact same Signal he had last seen in 1991. As he turned directly into the unique path of the tachyons he knew so well, it was like hearing the voice of an old friend you'd known your whole life. He actually had known the Signal most of his life, and, to date, there was nothing and no one he had spent as much time with as it. It also occurred to him that he was dealing with the shock of the Signal's return by relying especially heavily on metaphors.

Back in the '70s less than 20 people had detected the Signal; now it was going to get noticed by 100 or even 1,000 times that many. He had watched every other STES on Earth go through a scrap metal shredder, so he figured he had a head start of around seven to 12 days before the persistent Signal interference sent someone at the Defense Department on a wild goose chase through the archives to find out what was known about this phenomenon.

Torquemann knew by now that militaries all over the world would have spotted the Signal and subsequently elevated to some level of high alert, or close to it. Unlike the first time the Signal washed over the Earth, now everyone was automatically suspicious of electronic warfare attempts from their nearest, scariest, or nearest scariest enemy. An unknown cause behind a strange phenomena is fertile ground for any military leader to begin projecting their greatest fears onto the otherwise mundane circumstances of the time. And the more creative and clever these military thinkers were, the more scared they would be by what their imaginations could conjure up as the reason behind this EMF distortion. "After all," they will tell themselves, "if I were planning something truly devastating, I could probably limit any indication of what was coming to a few simple blips on a broadband RF field meter."

And so he worked at a feverish pace and, when the phone rang, he wasn't surprised.

He was curious which department tracked down the Dark Antenna file first.

"Torquemann," he said casually.

"Dr. Torqueman, my name is Colonel Nicholas Castro, I'm from the Office of the Under Secretary of Defense for Research and Engineering at the Pentagon. Do you have a moment to talk?"

"So it wasn't DARPA…" he thought to himself, a bit surprised.

"Certainly," he replied, "I imagine you would like to speak sooner rather than later."

"I'll be there in 30 minutes. Thank you, doctor."
And the line went dead.

25 JUNE

Two hours after the trip to Costco, Calista and Scarlett were still flat on their backs, hoping the pounding headaches and nausea would pass. Blaise had come back from lacrosse practice with several friends, which made the bottom floor of the house equal parts goofy and incredibly loud, so Sienna brought the girls upstairs to her room to watch a movie and, ideally, take a nap. Teddy, the Australian Labradoodle and consensus favorite member of the family, had followed them and was now straddling their laps while they laid on the bed – a place he was strictly forbidden from being under normal circumstances – while they watched "Goonies" for the 900th time.

Sienna stayed close the rest of the afternoon just in case either of them suddenly began feeling worse, and Josephine helped her unload the rest of the groceries and get out the 4th of July decorations for the party they were hosting with the cousins the following week.

Around 4:30 pm, Jordan finished his last meeting of the day and came up from the basement to start dinner.

"Where are the girls?" he asked, noticing that the customary levels of alternating laughter and tears for this time of day was well below normal.

"They're upstairs, they don't feel well," she started, "and that's what I want to talk to you about."

"Was it something at camp?"

"No."

"Is something wrong?"

She paused and looked right at him, and then down at the ground. This was the last moment her husband was going to have a normal life.

This was the last time the Dark Antennae program was going to be shut away in the past.

"This is about me, I think."

This made zero sense to Jordan, and it was unlike Sienna to not get directly to the point, so he knew something very unusual had happened today.

Now her directness returned.

"I used to be in a program."

Jordan was taking his marinade out of the fridge, and this got him to poke his head back around the stainless-steel door and look back at her, confused.

"Like A.A.?"

"No, not like that."

And then the story that had disassembled and rearranged her entire life came tumbling out.

"When I was eight," she said with a big exhale, "I started seeing things and hearing things. So, my parents took me to a doctor and I got an MRI, and when we came back a couple weeks later for the results, a guy who worked for the government was there instead of the doctor – and he told us that my brain had this tiny little ridge in the back that acted like a radio antenna for this secret communication machine the Soviets were using."

There had not been a point during the previous 30 seconds when Jordan could have guessed what the next word to come out of her mouth would be.

"And you could hear what the Russians were saying in your head?"

"Kind of. The guy at the doctor's office told us that this Signal – that's what they called it, "the Signal" – was this secret way the Russians sent messages back and forth, and there was this program where other kids like me were listening to it and figuring out what was being said, and he wanted me to come be a part of it."

This was shocking, but Jordan was impressed.

"Wow, babe." He crossed his arms and leaned against the countertop. "That is wild. And look at you, taking your life-long vow of secrecy all the way to your early 40s."

"Stop!" she said, trying and just barely failing to keep a straight face.

"But keep going, I can tell there is a bunch more to this story. What did they call your program?"

"Dark Antennae – but spelled the British way."

"Of course, cool, and what did you learn about the Russians? And where did you do it?"

"There was a campground where this program operated; it was about an hour from where I lived, and there were kids there from all over the country, so I was lucky to just live across the bridge."

"How long did you do it?"

"I was there for almost two years. Like, 19 months."

"How have you avoided mentioning you took a two-year break from school to fight in the Cold War?"

"I told you I went to that boarding school for a little while before it went bankrupt and shut down."

"*That* was *this?!*"

"Yeah."

"And there were other kids there with you?"

"There were always around 18 or 19 of us there, sometimes less, and we really only had to work about every other day."

"'Work?' Like you did shifts listening to the Russians? And why did you leave?"

Her mind was already back in the room with Dr. Torquemann the night he told her she'd outgrown the program. She glared back at him and felt her heart go black. Their prior conversation still weighed heavily on both of them, and now they'd never discuss it again. She could see herself walking toward the camp gate. She passed three stone-faced guards and kept walking through the rain without bothering to wipe it off her face. She saw herself reeling from Torquemann's quick and clean, "It was a pleasure to work with you" and "you have a great kid here, Mrs. Barrett" when he ran up to say goodbye to her and Ginny. She had assumed, correctly, that this was the last time she would ever lay eyes on him.

"The shape that allowed my brain to pick up the Signal was just a moment in time while we were growing, so once you grew a bit more, you lost the alignment and then you got to go back home."

There was no use explaining the ESR right now.

"And when you leave do you get some formal 'thank you' from the government saying 'You were a pleasure to work with' or something?"

"Nope."

"So then you just show back up in your neighborhood out of nowhere?"

"Yeah – they gave everyone the same cover story: We got accepted to this cool private school, but it ran out of money and that's why I'm back."

"And you said you saw stuff?"

"Yeah, the Signal was strange – we could pick up stray images sometimes, and we heard pieces of sentences."

"But you don't speak Russian. Or do you?" Anything was possible now, he figured.

"No, we didn't have to learn Russian; the fragments we were intercepting came through in English.

"Weird, why? And what did you find?"

"I was never very good at it, so not much."

"And you did all this in an actual secret government program." He had to ask again. Sienna wasn't the practical joke type, and she was deathly serious right now, but he had to ask.

"Yes."

"I can't believe we've never talked about this... but, I mean, I get why."

"All these years, crazy right?"

"So, what is the program doing now?"

Now came another layer of divulsion.

"I found out in 2018 that the program was shut down just four months after I left because one day the Signal suddenly went quiet and didn't come back."

"How did you hear that?"

She looked down at the floor and then up at the ceiling, and then swallowed hard. Jordan could tell this next part was going to be wild. Or maybe horrible.

"Do you remember that girls trip I took with my college roommates that summer?"

"In 2018? Umm... yeah, didn't one of them get a little place in Cabo, so you all went to visit? It was Sarah, or Sandy, or something with an 'S?'"

"Right, so, I spent most of that week in D.C. The Senate Intelligence

Committee brought me in to discuss the program. It was the 40th anniversary of the program's creation, and, before they destroyed every trace of it, they wanted to understand the nature of the work we did. They randomly selected 10 participants, and I got lucky."

Now Jordan was very confused again, but he was back to smiling at how cloak-and-dagger it all seemed.

"You have to recognize how crazy this is, babe – you were an adult woman traveling under false pretenses on behalf of top-secret U.S. intelligence."

"I promise you that it really wasn't that interesting. It was just a lot of talk about a program that was long gone, and how it was a relic of the Cold War, and it was just a big walk down memory lane in this random room about a mile from the Capitol Building."

"I have so many questions," he said trailing off. "But wait a second, you texted me pictures from the trip, and what do you mean 'most of the week?'"

"We spent 10 minutes taking pictures from about 40 different angles when I first got there, and they Photoshopped my head onto a bunch of people at a beach or at restaurants, and I just texted you one of those every few hours."

"And?"

"And after we were done, I drove up to Maine. I read a book about Bar Harbor when I was little, and I wanted to see it."

"Didn't you get a sunburn on that trip."

"I was watching a demonstration about how old-timey fishermen used to build lobster traps when I texted you that."

By now he was really laughing.

"And the guy who ran your camp – he was at this hearing? Did he go around scanning everyone's brains again?"

"No, he wasn't there; apparently he's in semi-retirement or some-thing just doing research on all the data he gathered back in the day."

Jordan had momentarily forgotten that there was an underlying reason for this story, and now he sensed that reason was about to present itself.

"So, connect the dots for me – why are you telling me this now?"

Another deep breath. She didn't want to look him in the eyes when she said these next words, but she forced herself to do it.

"Cali and Scarlett came home early from camp today – they'd been hearing and seeing flashes of things. And when I pulled into the driveway today – before I even knew they were home – I did, too. It was the same Signal I listened to as a kid."

Now he put the pieces together. Now this story stopped being purely fun.

"Ok, what did they hear?"

"It was just noise and some flashes in their peripheral vision – and that's normal; that's how it came across a lot of the time, even when you knew what was happening."

"Are they in pain?"

"They feel a little nauseous and lightheaded – and that's pretty normal, too. If it doesn't happen again, they'll probably chalk it up to being dehydrated while they were running around at camp, or something."

"You don't think this will happen again?"

"I have no idea, but I doubt it. We had to go out of our way to get it to happen back in the day, and that was with a lot of extra equipment."

"But how? How are the girls picking it up at all? And who would even be sending messages now? Did Russia just turn on all its old equipment?"

"The girls," she said slowly, "well, Cali and Scar, have the same brain shape that I did."

"You think that because of what they heard today?"

"No, not just that. This was part of the meeting in D.C."

"What was?"

She remembered being just as confused as Jordan was now – and as incredulous as he was about to be – when an NRO scientist at the debriefing in D.C. mentioned, almost in passing, that two of her children "Exhibited neuro-structural traits that are nearly identical to yours at the same approximate age." In fact, not only did two of her children have the ridge that made Dark Antennae possible, they both had what appeared to be the added height on that ridge that the ESR had added to her own.

Sienna had not found this information interesting or cool. She also wanted to know how they knew this.

"Your name stood out in the program's file as having had 'above average' Signal connectivity, albeit briefly, toward the end of your time there," the scientist explained, "so we included you in a sample of individuals that we wanted to follow up on to determine if genetic factors might have played some part in the unique nature of the program's data-gathering techniques. That kind of information is very useful in the event any future programs might require similar methods."

The agent spotted the look on Sienna's face and was quick to assure her that no current program was gathering data in the same way, but, in the event this phenomenon ever resurfaced, the most efficient place to begin looking for new antennas would be amongst the offspring of the original antennaes.

This was an uncomfortable idea, but Sienna was comforted by the fact that the Signal had been gone for so long.

"So how did you find the ridge on my kids?" Sienna asked, still irritated they had been scanned without her knowing. "An X-ray on a broken arm is the closest any of them have ever got to a head scan."

The agent nodded, put the cap back on a pen she'd used to take a few notes, and kept explaining in the measured, overly professional tone of voice that would have sounded right at home reading expense reports out loud.

"Once you were included in our sample, we kept an eye on your travel plans, and when we noticed last summer that your niece was getting married, we saw she had booked one of those…" she paused to find the right word, "…corny photo booth setups where guests can take pictures with props. So, the night before the reception we put an image resonator inside the booth –"

Sienna cut her off. "A resonat… you mean you put an MRI in the photo booth?"

"Well, an FMRI, but, yes, a small one, and then we just waited for your kids to stop by to take pictures."

"How did you know they'd even get in the booth?"

"They were five and three at the time, so the odds were almost 100%."

Sienna had to agree. "Clever, but you got pretty lucky."

"They ended up taking 281 pictures across 13 visits during the four hours you were there, and, by the time they'd posed for their third photo we had more than enough data."

As Sienna related all of this back to Jordan she saw his mind race through the same questions and follow up questions that she had back in D.C.

"So what do you think happens to the girls next?" he asked.

"Probably nothing, other than just the distraction of the flickers of sound or images. Even with all the training I had and all the technology we were using, it was still almost impossible to understand very much of it. There is so much mental discipline and mental endurance that you have to be taught to have, and that just isn't going to happen here."

Jordan let out a long breath and tried to think through what the rational next step could be in the context of this monumentally bizarre turn of events. The big picture here had become clear enough to make him worry about the girls, but he wasn't quite sure where that anxiety was specifically coming from.

"We'll see how they feel in the morning," she said, "and we'll see if they're picking up anything else. Chances are this was a one-time thing."

She had no way of knowing if this was true, but she could hope.

Jordan was quiet, lost in thought. Finally he asked, "What was the weirdest thing you ever heard a Russian say?"

"I never heard a Russian say a single thing."

"Really? *Never?*"

"Not once."

21　Shredder

25 JUNE

As expected, it had taken a week for sensors from the naval base in Djibouti to get back to Beijing and then undergo a battery of tests, alongside the sensors from a handful of surveillance posts inside the country. These results were compared to the two sensors brought back from the Russian border along the Amur River.

After this analysis the Academy of Military Sciences (军事科学院) informed the political and military leadership of two key findings: The sensors from the Russian border were not defective in any way, and the interference they had detected represented accurate readings of the electromagnetic spectrum. Their report did not include the obvious conclusion that all its readers added automatically: These findings do not rule out the distinct possibility of something sinister occurring across the border. The less nuanced readers of this report understood this to mean that something sinister *was* occurring across the border.

These findings and the subsequent analysis served as the late-night briefing shared with Xuěméi and the other fighter pilots at Chao-yangchuan Air Base. Lieutenant Colonel Yáng and the senior political officer spent 28 minutes covering this material, and their cold, clinical delivery could not hide the dire picture their superiors were painting with the raw materials contained in that report.

They explained that, after studying the EMF interference captured by the sensors, additional work was done to analyze satellite imagery tracking train and troop movements within 500 miles of the border, and the information gathered from this careful study arrived at a single conclusion which was "presented with a high level of certainty." The short version was this: This electromagnetic interference is the result of high energy particles leaking into the surrounding area through faulty shielding protecting a directed-energy weapon.

This was a lot to process. And it was incredibly specific.

Due to the nature of the interference, Yáng continued, the specific type of weapon was believed to be something called a Neutral Particle Beam Cannon. At this point he turned to the large projection screen on the wall and began to explain a detailed blueprint the Academy had provided. This image had been obtained by spies within the Russian army's Academy of Military Science (Академия военных наук), but at the time this schematic had been obtained it was considered a model prototype, not a functional unit. For the most part, it looked like a gigantic, 75-foot flashlight, with pipes and cables running along the length of it, with honey-combed panels flaring out at regular intervals. Toward one end it looked like a giant badminton shuttlecock made from metal and glass had been attached to the tube. This, apparently, was the muzzle, for lack of a better word. Behind it were rows of what she recognized as solid-state batteries. It was all mounted on some kind of rolling pallet.

Yáng read from the report in his hand to explain the operational capabilities of this strange piece of machinery that looked equal parts absurd and dangerous, at the same time. A Neutral Particle Beam Cannon was theoretically possible to build, and the physics of it were well understood, but its creation had been considered essentially impossible at this time due to the overwhelming complexity of its manufacture and operation, to say nothing of the fact that the exceptionally delicate nature of the hardware rendered it unreliable on a battlefield.

Or at least this had been the prevailing theory before now.

"A particle beam weapon such as this," Yáng explained "is, at a very basic level, a particle accelerator that you could aim at something, instead of just spinning those particles around in a giant circle, like the Swiss do with their Large Hadron Collider. But, instead of smashing protons together for research purposes, a weapon like this shoots a stream of neutrons at a tank, jet, computer, or person and those particles then collide with all the atoms in the target with catastrophic results."

He began to read the next line of the report but stopped to re-read it again, clearly put off by what he saw.

"The report goes on to say that when the billions of particles which are shot by the cannon every second collide with the atoms of their target, they begin knocking electrons and protons out of their individual atoms and violently break each atom apart. And these particles are moving so fast and at such high energy that while they are shredding things at the atomic level the friction of their kinetic energy also briefly superheats anything around them to a temperature surpassing the surface of the sun."

Like many air forces around the world, the officer corps of the Chinese air force featured a disproportionate number of engineering degrees relative to the civilian population. This audience required no further explanation of the danger and destructive potential of this Russian weapon.

"This cannon is portable, it is apparently operational, and the energy of its beam ionizes the surrounding area and renders electronic equipment immediately useless. This makes attacking the weapon very difficult, but makes finding it fairly easy," Yáng concluded.

Because a weapon like this required so much energy intake and then produced such incredible energy output it was simple to detect; it was, in a way, similar to how submarines from a previous generation could be found by searching the ocean floor for the magnetic signature created by a large steel tube moving across the magnetite-rich basalt of the ocean floor. Hiding this much energy flow required extensive lead-paneled shielding, but this weapon apparently had a faulty panel – likely some-where near its accelerator – and this had revealed its position. When these particles leaked through the shielding their energy signature changed just enough to betray how they had gotten out into the wild.

The presentation screen zoomed in on a map of the Chinese-Russian border in their region.

"Over the last 9 days a train engine pulling several dozen cargo cars has taken a highly irregular path through eastern Russia, and it is now at a regional depot 90 miles north of the Tongjiang-Nizhneleninskoye Bridge. The Central Military Commission believes this train is carrying the weapon."

The pilots used this dramatic pause from Lieutenant Colonel Yáng to share looks and try to read one another's reactions to this news. Most of them were just happy to finally know what was going on; after days of waiting and flying hundreds of patrols, the Vigorous Dragon pilots had a possible target.

Xuěméi didn't notice the sideways glances being shared. Her eyes were fixed on the picture of that train. There was something about it which struck her as unmistakably final. The moment it had appeared on screen she knew it would be the door she passed through to meet Mínghuī and Jun again.

She looked down at her hands to finally avert her eyes from the image on the screen. A streak of navy blue stood out on the pale skin of her pinky finger, left over from the smeared ink of the note she wrote first thing this morning.

Today's entry in the calendar book had read, "Said 'dog!' when he saw a picture of grandma's new puppy."

She repeated the words from the note in her mind. She apologized again that they never got off a military base long enough to have a real home with real pets like he wanted. She had waited five months to place his room full of stuffed animals into a cardboard box and leave it in the common area for other children to find and take home. Mínghuī had made sacrifices he could not have conceived of for his parents' ambition, and for this her grief was malignant. Had anyone watched her face darken and then tighten, they might have mistaken it for resolve or a steely determination to successfully execute this mission — but her mind had suddenly veered very far away from what she was capable of doing to that train with the help of the only remaining child she and Jun had created so long ago.

She was still spiraling downward when Yáng said, with particular sharpness, that the army's Intelligence Bureau was "gravely concerned" – and this drew a grunt of approval from the political officer – that this train holding the weapon was going to move further south, to the bridge over the Amur River, in order to aim its firestorm of high-energy particles at the Nanzhing Commercial Complex.

"We believe the Russians will attempt to fire when they approach the bridge, but not cross it for fear of exposing the weapon. They will rely on being able to say truthfully that they never incurred into our territory at any time – and this will go hand-in-hand with a denial that any such weapon does or can exist."

There was another dramatic pause, and Yáng looked over at the political officer who nodded his approval and urged him to continue.

"This, comrades (同志)," Yáng said, using a term that placed these instructions squarely within a political and patriotic necessity, "cannot be allowed." Returning to the prepared report in his left hand, he pointed again to the satellite image of the area and zoomed in on the region surrounding the bridge. This was something all the pilots recognized from memory after so many dozens of recent flights. All the key areas were labeled, with two circles calling out the areas of particular interest – the bridge and the commercial district two miles away, with its long rows of identical one- and two-story buildings, like any other zoned business park in the world.

"What you were not aware of before this moment, and what the Russians should not know, is that our government has been developing a highly sensitive – both politically and physically – project within this complex. Considering a particle cannon is designed to fry satellites or orbital missiles, it will be exceptionally easy to destroy whatever is in those warehouses, then reverse course, and slip back into Russia as if nothing has happened and remain entirely unnoticed. Although our buildings are shielded from many forms of electronic warfare, nothing can survive a blast from a cannon of this type at such close range."

Now the pilots had the peace of mind to know that this was a search and destroy mission and not an ongoing reconnaissance operation.

"Your vigilance is critical at this time," Yáng emphasized. "There is nothing but empty countryside between that train and our border."

Twenty minutes later the briefing was over, the pilots had dispersed, and Xuěméi was meeting with Chén Wěiqiáng, the other members of her wing, and their flight commander, Captain Huáng Yǒngjūn (黄勇军). Huáng was as perfect an aerial tactician as the Chinese air force had ever produced, and no one could remember seeing him make a mistake in the air, the simulator, or anywhere else. American pilots had a reputation for bravado, but Huáng, who was now a handful of years beyond the age at which pilots were expected to gracefully resign, was quiet and reserved to the point of earning an unofficial call sign – The Monk – which could only be used sparingly over the radio due to its political implications. Captain Huáng, like many pilots, had an advanced degree in avionics, but, before going to flight school, he'd graduated college with a degree in nuclear physics. It had been a long time since those final exams, but he still knew more than enough to offer the pilots under his command a few extra details that hadn't been covered in this briefing. He also remembered enough from his early years in the cockpit that scared pilots were especially likely to die, and even more so in and around Russian airspace.

Once all his pilots were assembled in a small ready room, this man of few words said more than anyone had ever heard him say in any given month.

"There was a time, beginning in mid-1989, not long after the Soviet Union was chased out of Afghanistan — you've probably all seen that famous footage of the last Russian tank crossing what they called the 'Friendship Bridge' leading out of Afghanistan and back into Soviet-occupied Uzbekistan – and the Russians were raging at the humiliation of it. At the time, the Red Army was the pride of the Soviet system and, frankly, the main thing propping it up – and now a collection of very poorly trained tribal warriors had reduced them to spilled blood and smoldering hardware with nothing to show for it."

He pulled down a map from above a whiteboard and pointed at a spot where the borders of Russia and China met along the eastern edge of Mongolia.

"My first posting was at the air base right here. I got there six months before the Red Army made their retreat." He turned back to the pilots and rested a hand on the small podium. "The Russian military leadership was so embarrassed and so demoralized by what had happened there that they were desperate to do something to show they were still strong — and they weren't especially picky about how they did it."

He shifted his weight and this typically laser-focused officer was now unmistakably far away as he spoke.

"Their army couldn't take out their frustrations on any of those outlying Soviet republics, as much as they wouldn't have lost any sleep over it, and they couldn't really turn around and invade anywhere else, and so that left us."

He was now leaning heavily on the podium while the rest of his body used its strength to dredge up a memory he had never shared in his many coaching sessions with these pilots. It was a period of history that none of them had learned about in flight school.

"For about a year, the six Russian air bases nearest our borders hunted every Chinese aircraft they could find. It was easy to stop all the passenger flights and civilian aircraft in these areas, but the Chinese Air Force had a responsibility to patrol its own airspace, and that played right into the hands of a few Russian generals who wanted the satisfaction of revenge without the need to return to Kabul."

He walked back to retract the map and avoid any questions from a political officer that might happen to walk past the room.

"At the time, all our fighters were based on an earlier version of the MiG their pilots had been flying for years, and that made it considerably easier for their pilots to rack up kills. Within a month of this starting, all three of my roommates from flight school were gone. Just a little while after that all four of the pilots from the apartment next door to mine were gone, too. After a year-and-a-half of this, I was the only member of my graduating class still alive. We fought back when we could, our leaders complained bitterly to their leaders, but the PLA was not going to risk a land war with Russia over some bullying in the sky somewhere high above the middle of nowhere. New pilots could always be trained, new planes could always be bought. At least that is how our commanders justified it at the time."

His pilots were stunned. They all knew The Monk was wise and that his skills were honed through some combination of time and hard experience, but they had not expected anything like this. Now he took another long pause to compose himself and share the reason he was telling this particular story. He did not mention the six kills he had during this time, all of them reactive, all of them while outnumbered.

"The skies over the Chinese-Russian border have been quiet for a very long time, and it's possible now that it will be us crossing that border to go hunt down and destroy something – but our preparation for this will be extreme before we do so. Whatever we end up needing to do, you cannot assume it will be as easy as lining up your targeting computer on a single train."

Now he pivoted to the second point he wanted to share, one that was equally politically charged, but for very different reasons.

"Now I will pivot to the second point I want to share with you, and this one is also politically problematic, although it has nothing to do with history or military affairs. I offer this information with great respect for the leaders who just debriefed us, and I do not mean to undermine the great and honorable work done in Beijing to develop this data. I only share this with you so that you might have more context and more information that you can use to execute your mission when the time comes."

He knew that if anyone reported any part of this meeting that this disclaimer wouldn't be enough to save his career, but it might spare him the death penalty.

"My concern has to do with the specific type of electromagnetic interference shown in today's briefing. It is, as the commander noted, very unusual." He paused because he could hear his heart beating. "The weapon described today is…" he swallowed hard and decided to just get it over with and say it: "It is almost impossible that it exists in the specific form described."

It was not lost on his pilots that he was now saying the opposite of what had been shared in the briefing. "The Central Military Commission is correct that all the signs of its existence are present. I can also tell you with some certainty that the specific variations in the interference demonstrate something very powerful is being shielded and that this shielding is insufficient. As this leakage passes through this faulty shielding its electromagnetic properties are altered simply by passing through the solid material surrounding it."

He paused to make sure this basic lesson in electromagnetic decay made sense. He would save his overview of associated phenomena like "Compton scattering" and "photoelectric absorption" for another day.

"I am telling you this because there are several things that can be inside that train besides a particle cannon, and you need to know this before you get the call to close in on that target – because, in the event that train begins moving south, that call *will* come. Based on the signals coming from that train, it could be carrying some novel new nuclear reactor, it could be nuclear waste, or it could be a super conductor of extreme power but entirely civilian in its intended usage. Or it could be a handful of other things entirely."

The assembled pilots listened carefully, unsure if this additional context should ratchet their stress up or down. At this point Huáng had paused again, and he looked at his pilots in a way that ensured each of them that his motive here was to protect them with information in any way he could. Later, if it became necessary, he would tell them what to do in the event that monstrosity of a weapon really was on that train and indeed was fully operational. A weapon like this didn't even need pinpoint accuracy – it could send a beam of particles 300 feet wide, and it only needed to catch its target in that pulse for a fraction of a second. And in that fraction, while their planes tumbled out of the sky, the pilots would be hit with enough synchrotron radiation to cook their internal organs and denature the proteins in their brains.

The only thing the J-10's had in their favor was the ability to launch satellite-guided missiles from below the horizon – but, if this weapon was fully operational, it could aim skyward and knock out that targeting satellite at a moment's notice.

"I interpret this data as being the result of a very sloppy non-military operation, or a very well-done military operation that is attempting to hide something – and perhaps hide it by appearing like a sloppy non-military operation. I have to consider that, at this moment, there is simply no reason for the Russians to attack us. Russia would not attack us just because we are conducting secret weapons research. They know we do this – and we know they do it. If there is a secret program in the Commercial Complex, the Russians have no reason to proactively attack it unless they believe an attack from us was imminent – and there is simply no reason they could reach that conclusion so suddenly."

The pilots nodded in acknowledgement of these facts, and more than a few could not help but appreciate the wisdom of his words – the way he led to a conclusion without refuting his superiors. But it was clear that, based on the available information, the military was ready to fight, and Huáng was not.

25 JUNE

Ten minutes before the top of the hour, Torquemann noticed a black SUV and a smaller jeep pull up in front of his building and park directly in front of a fire hydrant and bus stop. Both vehicles were standard-issue government transportation, and so was the parking.

This colonel had a key card that got him through the front door and up to the office without ever needing to stop. Torquemann noticed everyone in the jeep stayed on the street – these were the regular MP's – and the colonel was accompanied by two aides.

Julius met him at the door, the aides stayed in the hallway, and the scientist and the soldier sat down.

There was no small talk.

The colonel was working on a timeframe that necessitated the rapidest possible exchange of information, and he needed to know how this doctor's program had once operated.

"I assume your supervisor at the NRO called you since we last spoke?" the colonel asked.

"Yes, she told me that the Secretary of Defense had personally called to ask that I tell you everything about Dark Antennae."

"Excellent," the colonel said, pleased that simple inter-departmental cohesion was still possible as long as a presidential appointee demanded it. "As I'm sure you know, the file on this program was extensively redacted – even the one that my department and DARPA can access – so, tell me about the work you guys were doing in San Mateo, and what you've been doing here ever since?"

Torquemann had no idea where to start. So he decided to take the long way and go all the way back.

"Right after I finished my postdoctoral fellowship at what is now called the Astroparticle Physics Laboratory, I took a role at the National Reconnaissance Office working on a theoretical design for a satellite-mounted sensor."

"What kind of satellite?"

"The satellite itself was the standard KH-9 that the NRO liked so much back then, but instead of the standard camera setup, the idea was to install it with a sensor that could take pictures through 10-foot-thick concrete walls."

He stopped and watched the colonel arch an eyebrow.

"Yeah, it was pretty wild stuff at the time. The idea was to do this by flooding the area with something called tau neutrinos – these were my specialty – they're tiny particles, for reference an electron is about half a million times larger, and a single hydrogen atom is about 200 trillion times bigger. So, the idea was that the target would have no idea their base was getting covered in these particles that were too small to detect and that were tiny enough to pass through solid objects."

"Like an X-ray?" the colonel asked, thinking he might understand the concept.

"No, these particles aren't interacting with a solid object the way an X-ray does – these ones are small enough to move through the empty space *between* the atoms in a solid object. Think of it like your chair — right now your butt is on that chair and that chair is made up of atoms. But atoms are made up of a nucleus and a cloud of electrons swirling around it – so an "atom" is really just mostly empty space. It's a lot like the layout of the solar system – the sun is in the middle and a bunch of planets are swirling around it – but most of that is empty space. Well, comparatively speaking, everything is much closer together in our solar system than things are in an atom. And that's the case with the several trillion atoms making up your chair – it feels solid, but it's mostly empty. It's just that we're so big and slow that all those swirling atoms never create a gap big enough for us to fall through. But tau neutrinos are so fast and small that they just slide right through those gaps. So, the hope for this sensor was that it could send these neutrinos through a big thick wall and then bounce back to reconstruct an image of what was on the other side. So, the whole thing was essentially a very high-tech version of the echolocation that bats use with soundwaves."

"And those neutrinos didn't just pass through the thing you wanted to photograph and keep going out the other side?"

"They could, and they did, but we had settings that allowed you to tinker with the depth you wanted these particles to travel – so we could have them moving at high enough energy to pass through a couple yards of concrete, but then be slow enough by that point to hit our target and bounce back."

"Why did the project end?"

"I know it eventually ended, but I wasn't there by that point."

"Why not?"

"Because I discovered the same thing that I'm guessing has been troubling you the last few days. My team referred to it as 'the Signal.'"

The colonel was shocked. This meeting was supposed to be a quick gathering of background information about a long-forgotten project, but now he found an otherwise anonymous government researcher sitting on an understanding of something that had defied the entire scientific apparatus of the U.S. military.

"I couldn't help but notice you didn't sound surprised when I called. How did you know this interference had returned?"

"It's kind of the only thing I'm any good at," Torquemann said with a laugh, confident this colonel wasn't going to press an old man too hard for answers.

The image on the STES fluttered decoratively and unaddressed in the background while they talked.

"Ok, so how did you find it the first time?"

"In January or February of 1977, I got a call from one of my old professors who studied pulsars, and one of his students had discovered some very unusual and unexplainable fluctuations in the electromagnetic spectrum. He mailed me some of the data, and I literally just walked over to the Space Reconnaissance Department to ask them about it. The person sitting closest to the door when I stopped by was Maggie Walker, and she kept a poker face when I first showed her the data, but it turns out her and her team were very surprised someone else had found this Signal they'd been trying to figure out."

"You seem to have a knack for startling people with what you know about this, doctor."

"Yeah, well, three or four days later Maggie and her boss were there waiting by my desk when I got to the office, and they asked me what else I knew about that data I'd been sent. I told them I didn't have any info besides what I'd shown them, but that I had my suspicions. I told them it looked like a structured communication. It went without saying that this did not look like anything the U.S. government was anywhere close to possessing. At that point, Maggie – well, I only ever called her Dr. Walker – looked at her boss, he looked at me, and he offered me a job. They had already done their homework on me, so they knew I could offer some technical expertise to the program."

Julius did not include the third observation he had shared with them at the time. That third insight was what had really gotten the attention of Dr. Walker's boss – a guy named Brad Gillespie who had a hand in a very wide variety of programs no one dared ask about. Julius made this observation flatly and directly: "This isn't something humans can or would generate."

Brad had the type of face any professional poker player would envy, but this made his eyes start to go wide before covering it with a fake cough.

As soon as Julius saw that reaction, he knew he had found his life's work.

Brad would later comment that this particular observation was the whole job interview – "If you weren't audacious enough to reach that conclusion, then this project wasn't really your speed."

The colonel opened a copy of the program's file and began to flip through it.

"One of the few un-redacted portions of the Dark Antennae file mentions that the project was funded by several different intelligence organizations who had discretionary budget to fund projects aimed at gaining access to secure Soviet communications – but how did you figure out this was the Soviets?"

Torquemann studied the colonel for a moment. Long ago Brad had coached him on every possible way to answer this question depending on who was asking, what they needed, and who sent them.

"Before I arrived, the Soviets had already been identified as the only possible source of the Signal on account of the sophistication of their homegrown theoretical physicists and their ability to throw gargantuan amounts of money and manpower at these technical challenges. They had also been doing some very interesting work on high-gain antennas at the time, so it was reasoned that they'd had a breakthrough of some sort."

"And you believed it was the Soviets?"

"This little office existing is a testament to the fact that we are still trying to find all the answers about the Signal and its origins."

The colonel made a mental note to have the Psychological Operations experts review the recording of this portion of the meeting. There was something intangible in that last response that he suspected might raise a lot of red flags when subjected to spectrographic voice stress analysis. But he could compartmentalize that for now.

"How would you characterize what your team understood about the Signal at the time?"

Torquemann laughed.

"To this day, depending on how the data is getting sorted, I can argue very convincingly for what we do and do not know about any of it. And that is something my team and I made peace with very early on in the program. We were there to listen and not necessarily try and break new ground."

"Ok, so how did what eventually became Dark Antennae get kicked off after that first meeting in your office?"

Torquemann leaned back in his chair and began sorting through that chain of events.

"The first thing we did was to try and reverse engineer the type of receiver or antenna that could capture the Signal – kind of like how Turing built an Enigma machine of his own to decrypt all those Nazi telegrams. We spent a very long time trying to just get a valid hypothesis together for what this could look like or how it could possibly be fabricated. Some of the concepts we put together got so exotic that without us meaning to do it, we noticed that some of those concepts left the realm of being strictly technological – and at that point we began evaluating the science behind more organic methods of sending or receiving information, like the extrasensory perception that certain animals use for navigation or communication."

"Like what?"

"What kinds of extrasensory perception? Well, there's examples in the behavior of sea turtles, sharks, spiders, elephants, bats – all sorts of things. I know how strange all of this seems now, but at the time it was all quite inventive."

"And did you find anything by studying spiders and bats?"

"No, not at all – all the claims we investigated at the time were nonsense. But, around the time I was deep into the field research done on the central nervous systems of mollusks and how stimuli is passively consumed by these creatures, I got a report on my desk summarizing some information I'd requested about the similarities and dissimilarities between the way the human brain absorbs certain types of magnetism compared to the way long-distance navigators like whales and migratory birds experience those same magnetic fields. The report covered pretty much everything we already knew, but there was a footnote towards the end about how, over the last two years, there had been a tiny increase – so tiny that it fell within the margin of error – of children who reported seeing flashes of sound or light but that the marine mammals seemed unaffected. The pediatric neurology journal that reported this was in the process of trying to identify the causes, and it had aspartame, second-hand smoke, and too much television as the leading potential causes. This stood out to me because, about six months earlier, I'd met with an ornithologist at Georgetown to learn more about the cognition of migratory birds. Specifically, this woman had studied how those birds arrived at conclusions about what actions to take and where to go – and she explained that those birds didn't have enough brainpower to have long internal monologues wherein they intellectualized their journeys – their cerebellums could, at best, deliver ideas about when and where to fly that subsequently arrived in their conscious minds as simple flashes of information. And those birds interpret the arrival of this idea as a conclusion they had already arrived at. And, as you might expect, for those migratory birds, evolution has, out of necessity, over-pivoted on endurance and highly resilient muscle mass – so, there is not a lot of upper-level brainpower left over. So those flashes of insight were fast and bright and then gone."

The colonel subtly glanced at his watch, and Torquemann correctly assumed that he was starting to lose his audience.

"So, I had them bring me that neurology journal – it was called "Developmental Medicine & Child Neurology" – and a copy of the research behind it, and as I read through the data, I felt it in my gut that there was an angle here that we could use. So we turned the attention of our data-scraping resources to start scouring public health data, and with the help of the government's backdoor access to all those private databases, we started looking at MRI's and CAT scans from thousands of kids – anyone who reported flashes of light and noise. And, once we started looking at this, it didn't take long for a pattern to emerge: We saw a handful of case notes from all over the country wherein the children reported seeing and hearing very similar things – and I mean *very* similar – all independent of one another. So, this brought us back to that original conclusion that this was a structured datastream."

Now the colonel was interested again.

"At this point, I began working closely with Dr. Hamza Tunis, who I miss dearly, who we recruited from the CIA's Department of Biomedical Research & Analysis where he and a small group of fellow neurologists were doing some very interesting research on non-conscious brain function, and Hamza eventually helped us figure out the connection between these kids and the Signal. I don't know if Dr. Tunis left his office for the first two months – he was hooked on this idea. And he found it: There was a tiny, raised patch of tissue on the back of the brain that, at certain points in its growth, could act like a collector dish for the Signal. But this effect didn't last – the kids could only hear and see things from the Signal during a limited window of time when this ridge in their brain lined up with two specific brain lobes, and since kids are growing so fast, that window of time opens around age eight and is almost always closed by 12, if not before."

This story had now taken a turn that was dramatically more bizarre and complex than Castro had been expecting. What didn't make sense was the nature of this Signal and how the Dark Antennae program was picking up both images and audio.

"What doesn't make sense to me is the nature of this Signal and how you were picking up both images and audio."

Torquemann had been thinking of ways to answer this question most of his adult life. Now, this late in the game, there still was no short way to do it.

"The short answer is 'Tachyons.'"

"That is a very hypothetical particle to use as an answer about the purposes of a very real program."

Torquemann smiled and shifted his weight in his chair. "Tachyons are quite real, I can assure you."

For at least the third time in the 20 minutes since his arrival, the colonel was surprised by what this short drive from the Pentagon motor pool had uncovered.

"When did you discover them?"

"I didn't discover anything," Torquemann said with a laugh. "Gerald Feinberg and George Sudarshan were proposing that they could or should exist back in '67, but it was all, as you said, very theoretical back then – and so tachyons became this sort of concept or idea you could use to explain anything you couldn't really explain. There were all sorts of theories about what they could do, or transform into, or move like – and most of it was nonsense, but you can respect the creativity even if it wasn't really stellar scientific methodology. But Feinberg was an important part of this process and a brilliant scientist, and, long before I got to the NRO, a team there seeded a few concepts with him that they expected would lead him to his proposal for tachyons – and, sure enough, he published some very interesting research about seven or eight years later and he even came up with the name. And once this idea was out there in the wild, the NRO was very interested to see how the rest of the academic community reacted to it."

Now it was Colonel Castro's turn to smile – he recognized a good psy-op when he saw one.

"You guys wanted to see who out there would pop up with data that could substantiate what he was proposing."

"Exactly. They wanted to see how long it took the community to figure out that Feinberg's proposed particle was actually real once his paper spelled it out for them. This was one of the methods we used to determine the speed that mainstream science was moving. In particular, we were interested in measuring something that I later started calling the rate of 'breakthroughs-per-decade.' In our estimation, a good BPD is about three – but, unfortunately, since the hydrogen bomb, the hard sciences have been slowing down and are currently at a rate of about 0.5 BPD. If it weren't for CERN and everything we've learned from the collider, we might be at zero. But I digress – my point is that the reaction to Feinberg's paper about tachyons was, from our perspective, kind of disappointing. There were three big conclusions that Feinberg and a few others reached in their study, and each of those conclusions built upon the next. First – and this one was completely Looney Tunes – was that the weight of a tachyon was so ephemeral that it could only be measured by imaginary numbers. In other words, there were physicists out there who said with a straight face that the weight of an actual particle was the square root of negative one. This led to the next – and equally hilarious – conclusion which is that a tachyon therefore has "imaginary mass." They even came up with thousands of pages of calculations to prove this to themselves. I want to believe that at some point it occurred to them that the math was getting so abstract that they could just turn it all into an inside joke that no one else was smart enough to understand. Or, even worse, they were so deep into the numbers that the arc of their logic began bending in ways they couldn't even notice anymore. Either way, the real coup de grace was that their third conclusion which, despite it being built on the first two pretty ridiculous points, was actually correct. They derived that, because of all the imaginary weight and negative mass, that tachyons could travel in what they called *imaginary* directions – and what is the only direction you can't imagine?"

Castro was just barely keeping up now. He shook his head.

"Backwards."

"Like they can reverse course?"

"The *other* backwards."

"They can move back to where they came from?"

"They can move backwards in time."

In any other meeting this would be the weirdest part of the discussion.

"So these particles can time travel?"

"Well, no," Torquemann said, trying to frame his response in a way that wouldn't create 40 more questions, "not in the DeLorean sense of the word, but if something can travel faster than light, then you run into all sorts of real problems with causality."

"Wait," the colonel interrupted, "you're treating faster-than-light travel as a fact."

"Correct."

"And how are you so certain of that?"

"For the purposes of our conversation today and the specific things you would like to know unrelated to the arcane mathematics behind that question, perhaps you can just trust me on this."

"Humor me."

"Ok, think of it like this: There is a thought experiment called the 'tachyonic anti-telephone,' and in this experiment you and your wife each have a telephone that uses tachyons to send messages back and forth instead of electricity or radio waves or whatever. Well, now you are sending messages faster than our concept of reality is moving and certainly faster than reality was built to handle. So, every time a message is sent it arrives at the other telephone too fast – in other words, it suddenly exists somewhere before it should, and, by leaping ahead like that, the messages no longer match up with the normal flow of time and space. Said another way, that much speed severs the connection an object has to the physical universe. And that connection is what makes things… for lack of a better word, 'real.' Now, if you just sent 200 or 300 messages, this time difference would be imperceptible, but, after you've sent one million, now those messages have been moving so much faster than reality for so long that they leap ahead of you altogether such that now you start hearing your wife say 'hello' a fraction of a second before she says it. The reason is that the speed of the messages has outrun the speed of reality. Think of this as 'reality slippage.' This kind of speed has destroyed the basics of normal causality and now your words to her have to travel back in time to reach the point at which you say them – or, depending on how you want to look at it, time has to loop around on itself in such a way that your wife's reaction to what you've said is what causes you to finally say it. And, at this point, it becomes impossible to ever re-establish the correct direction that time should be flowing in your conversation or anywhere else."

The colonel was caught between wanting to dismiss this as nonsense and asking a dozen follow up questions.

"You're serious?" he finally said. "The equations you have measuring tachyon behavior really bear this out?"

"Yes. Everyone who joined the program spent their free time during that first year plowing through the math trying to see what we had all missed. It was always good for a laugh when the new guy would break down and admit what he had been doing on the side. That was our version of the slowest, nerdiest hazing possible – just letting the math torture them for month after month until they broke down and accepted it."

"Fair enough. So, how did your team move from looking at tachyons as theoretical particles to then being actual objects you could build a program around?"

"Well, to be clear, in most of academia – if not all – tachyons are still a completely hypothetical concept, and, still today, it's only a small handful of government scientists that know otherwise, and the group that made the initial discovery was even smaller, maybe four people total."

"Where was this discovery made?"

"The basin of the Jornada del Muerto Desert."

"What?"

"Trinity."

"Oh," said the colonel, growing suddenly grim.

He knew what this meant but couldn't see how it connected. What he did know was the specter that accompanied that place.

Trinity was the codename of a tiny dot inside a waterless basin which was itself inside the sprawling, 5,000 square miles of desert stretching across southern Arizona and northern New Mexico. Inside that dot, in 1945, in a place now known as Los Alamos, the ultra-secret Manhattan Project detonated the first nuclear bomb.

"So, did the bomb unleash all these tachyons?"

"No, the bomb didn't have anything to do with tachyons, not really at least," Torquemann replied, happy to be past all the table setting and finally at the actually interesting part of the story. "At the time, nobody working on that bomb was thinking about anything but the bomb. Tachyons, nuclear fallout, politics, morality – those were all things those scientists would investigate later – and, in our case, on accident.

"What kind of accident?"

"After the test nuke at Los Alamos – and that device had a name, by the way, they called it 'Gadget' – after that was a success, and the two additional nukes were built and sent to Japan, those scientists had so much data to work with and learn from that it was hard to know even where to start. There had never been a nuclear blast before, and no one had ever had a chance to observe this much energy in one place

– and so every person involved with that project was left with more than enough data to study for the foreseeable future. One of those scientists went to work analyzing a handful of sensor readings from the moment Gadget was triggered – and I don't know what he went into that research looking for, but what he found was a lot more interesting: He found that, at the moment of the blast, there was, for one-ten-billionth of a second, a spike of energy that cut a hole."

Castro was confident he knew the answer – despite how bizarre it sounded in his head – but he asked the question anyway.

"A hole in what?"

"The semi-technical term is 'spacetime,' a slightly more technical wording would be 'the four-dimensional continuum.' But, at the most basic level, that flash of energy, right at the moment of the blast, cut a hole in the fabric of the Universe. It literally did something the cosmos never expected and which no branch of theoretical physics ever implied was possible: It cut a microscopically small hole in reality for a flash of time that was barely perceptible. So, for that infinitesimally small monument we had an equally infinitesimally small pinhole to another dimension. Not 'other dimension' like it was filled with animals that can talk or your evil twin – I mean, like, we have three dimensions here in this room, and time is the fourth dimension, and on the other side of that hole were the fifth, sixth, and seventh – whatever – dimensions."

The colonel leaned back in his chair and propped his chin up with his fist.

"Yeah, I know, right? When this data was shared amongst a small team of people still sifting through all the data, they couldn't believe their eyes. They couldn't even figure out if this was a good or a bad thing – and it's ultimately impossible to tell because that cut slammed back shut so fast. I mean, 1/10,000,000,000th of a second is so fast that it's barely even a usable figure. Consider that 10 billion seconds is…" he paused to do the math in his head. "It's about 320 years – so think about how long 320 years is, and then this is the opposite of that in terms of shortness."

That, Castro thought to himself, was the weirdest possible way to explain time.

"So how does that cut in the Universe lead back to you, doctor?"

"Well, there were about a hundred different kinds of sensors and machines set up around the blast site; they had everything – blast pressure gauges, infrared cameras, Müller detectors – and amongst all these, placed at strategic angles relative to the site of the blast, were 12 sensors meant to measure the types of particles that came screaming out of that explosion. You know, the electrons, the protons, the neutrons. And after the blast, when they went to collect them, they discovered that one of those sensors hadn't worked – either they forgot to turn it on, or maybe one of the soldiers patrolling the area beforehand bumped it, or maybe it overheated in the sun – who knows. But, at the time of the blast, it wasn't switched on. Well, the way those sensors were supposed to measure all the particles coming from the blast was with this exotically magnetized metal plate inside the device – and the idea was that when the particles came flying through the air they would collide with that plate and their path across it or against it or through it would be studied by those scientists in the same way an investigator might stare at a bullet hole in the wall to figure out what kind of gun was used and where the person was standing when they shot it. Well, those sensors had a little trap door on the front that opened up to expose that metal plate to the blast, and then it was supposed to snap shut again at the end so the whole thing wouldn't fill up with sand – but in this case that trap door never opened and so when they went to retrieve it they could see that the seal around the device was unbroken, but nobody really cared that much because the other 11 sensors had plenty of data. And this is where the story might have ended, but, a month later, one of the scientists there in Los Alamos, Hans Bethe, who was an especially brilliant theoretical physicist with an expertise in quantum electrodynamics, had this very interesting discussion with one of the project's leaders, Jan von Neumann, and he comes away from it with an idea for a new experiment. So he heads over to the warehouse to get that malfunctioning sensor because he wants to use its magnetized plate, and, once he finds it, he puts the plate into their prehistoric looking mass spectrometer – and he only does this to make sure it's still ok to use since it malfunctioned during the blast – and when he checks the readout he sees that there's this tiny bright spot in the upper right-hand corner of the plate. And this is weird because that bright spot should absolutely not be there on this very uniform and very precisely manufactured plate – it would be like opening up a ream of printer paper and finding a black dot just randomly sitting there in the middle of the page. Hans is surprised and he's a little curious, so he takes a closer look at it. And bear in mind the guy holding the plate at this point just happens to be an expert in quantum electrodynamics – the study of high-speed, high-energy, low-size particles – and if anyone else had this plate in their hands, the rest of this story would be really short. I mean, Hans was the only guy within five million miles who could look at that plate and know enough to start asking the right type of questions. And the scientist in me hates the dumb luck part of this, but here we are. So, as Hans tells the story – and I did get to work with him quite a bit when we'd fly him down from Cornell to consult on a few things – he ended up spending a year with just that bright dot. He threw everything he knew at it, and every new thing he found made less and less sense. But, eventually, he figured it out. He had a thousand breakthroughs during his career, but this was one of the six or seven that were immediately classified."

"And what was it he found?"

"The tachyons. Right there, in that dot, tachyons were discovered." Torquemann said it like a sailor spotting a new continent from the crow's nest. "It was the crown jewel of his career."

"Right there in the plate – that's where he found them?" the colonel asked.

"Well, not *in* the plate," Torquemann explained, "it wasn't like they were bunched up inside of it – Hans had found the *path* they took *through* the plate. Or at least he saw the *effects* of them passing through the plate."

"What do you mean?"

"Once Hans had a hunch about what he was looking at, he devised a series of tests to look for the traces these particles should be leaving behind if indeed this really was what he thought it was – and one of the first things he looked for was evidence of the paths they were taking through the plate. And there were definitely paths everywhere – but for every entry or exit point on the plate, there were hundreds more paths that just started and stopped *inside* the plate."

"What did he make of that?"

This is where things got difficult again.

"In particular, he found that no tachyon ever made it all the way through the plate. I mean, keep in mind that particles this tiny moving through a plate an eighth of an inch thick – it's about the same as a red blood cell moving through Jupiter – so the plate didn't have any uninterrupted tunnels bored all the way from one side to the other – it just had portions of tunnels."

"Portions of tunnels?"

"Think about our telephone example from earlier. In this case, a tachyon reaches the plate, travels a fraction of a nanometer, and then turns on a dime to move in that impossible-backwards direction, and now it's some place far away instead of punching out the other side."

The colonel had no idea how to summarize this for the Secretary of Defense.

25 JUNE

Jordan had a lot to think about that evening.

There had been a moment, right around the time Sienna said "secret government program" and "special brain shape" that the possibility flashed through his mind that she might have... what was a nicer way to say "gone crazy?" Perhaps, "momentarily diverged from reality?"

But to know Sienna was to understand that someone so even-tempered was not particularly prone to a meltdown accompanied by hallucinations of a childhood spent secretly assisting the U.S. government. In a strange way, this didn't surprise him – if you had asked him yesterday to list the 10 people in his life who could have been trained CIA sleeper-agents in some parallel timeline, he would have probably placed her high on the list.

It helped, perhaps, that Sienna had always been just aloof enough to fascinate him, but not so distant that he lost interest. That was what had caught his attention initially, and it was what still made her seem so remarkable today. To know her was to accept, without ever consciously acknowledging it, that there was something unknowable or unreachable about her. Jordan did not have the psychological training to meaning-fully make sense of this or to question whether this was an asset or a liability, nor did he ever trouble himself over whether or not her enig-matic qualities were nothing more than a sign that she was, ever so slightly, beyond the upper limits of his ability to read her.

One thing he was certain of, however, was that she was telling the truth. What had made his blood run cold more than anything else was thinking about the years his cousin, Jackie, had struggled with the long-term effects of paranoid schizophrenia.

Six years earlier, Jackie had gone viral on TikTok (网络武器) after posting hundreds of videos detailing an elaborately complex claim that thousands of pet cats around North America were spy robots controlled by the Iranian Revolutionary Guard (سپاه پاسداران انقلاب اسلامی). The premise sounded hilarious on paper, but it was a nightmare for her family to watch unfold. These cats, she explained in a highly dysregulated and agitated manner, were gathering personal information in order to compromise Americans by blackmailing them with the salacious details of their private lives. She supplemented each video with hundreds of pieces of supporting material she created to prove her point: Intricately detailed diagrams and blueprints for how these cats were designed, shipping manifests showing the clandestine ways the cats were transported from Iran, and leaked e-mails and memos with status updates on the success of the program. She even created images of the cat prototypes in the lab, photos of the scientists who built them, and newspaper clippings of families who had discovered, to their horror, that their beloved pet was full of wires and cameras. The production quality and attention to detail in each of Jackie's videos was perfect.

The funny part – if there was a funny part – was that a department exists within the NSA that is required to investigate and evaluate any widespread claims of adversarial foreign governments gathering intelligence within American territory. To the surprise of many, including the agencies tasked with this responsibility, viral TikTok's are reluctantly considered to fall within that designation. Although he felt bad doing it, Jordan could not help but laugh at the idea that at least two highly trained counterespionage agents – and probably a lot more than that – had spent hours watching and re-watching Jackie's videos and cross-referencing them against all known attempts from this government to compromise America's national security interests.

While none of this was "funny" in the traditional sense of the word, seeing Jackie in action was something to behold: Each video was incredibly earnest – she was a patriot sounding the alarm, after all – and she even spoke for extended periods in Farsi whenever she was reading from a report or transmission she had intercepted. On at least two occasions she scooped up a cat from the neighborhood, brought it on camera, and spoke Farsi into its "face camera" to shame the agents back in Tehran for their chicanery – before letting it go and then following it for several minutes. Whenever she began a diatribe in Farsi, she would very helpfully add English subtitles on screen, and only the occasional viewer who spoke the language could tell she was just saying gibberish. Whenever a native speaker was brave enough to mention this in the comments they were immediately shouted down by Jackie's supporters and accused of being trolls sent by the government of Iran.

Jackie underscored her faux expertise with the language by couching her gibberish between real pieces of information like, "You know, anciently the people in what is now Iran called themselves Aryans or 'The Arya.' The word 'Persia' came from the Greeks who believed Aryan culture was descended from the demigod Perseus, hence 'Persia'" or "And please don't refer to this language as 'Farsi' – that word comes from the Arabs attempt to name the language, but because Arabic doesn't have a 'P' sound they went with an 'F' sound, and thus 'Persian' – or 'Parsi' as they said it – because 'Farsi.'" She also had an astonishing amount of information about the Achaemenid dynasty. "One thing you guys should really know about Cyrus the Great is that his name was actually pronounced KOO-RAWSH, and I think that's pretty cool."

It didn't take long for these videos to become very popular, and dozens of them accumulated millions of views each, as well as thousands of comments – with a surprisingly large number of those comments thanking her for exposing this threat. An even more surprising, albeit smaller, number of people shared additional details to help substantiate her claims.

Around video #419 she was institutionalized. After a few months she found a medication that worked and her psychiatrist connected her with a great therapist – and now, a year after posting her last video, Jackie was back at her job as a dental hygienist. She even owned a cat. The joke amongst the cousins was that there is a type of cat called a Persian Shorthair and that this was the breed she should have adopted. The family was divided on whether or not this joke was funny, but Jackie was the first to point out that she had nicknamed her cat Xerxes, so at least the Barretts could laugh instead of cry.

But Sienna's story was something altogether different.

The more he thought about it, the more questions he had. But he didn't doubt a word of it. Sienna was, among other things, honest, almost to a fault. His job now was to better understand what had happened to her and how he could help, and then use that to determine what he could do for Cali and Scarlett.

All of this had arrived so suddenly and was so outlandish, that, in a strange way, he struggled with the feeling that the future was about to make a move at a time when he and Sienna needed to be in control. It was a strange combination of emotions for a father with an altruistic instinct for his family.

Depending on how Cali and Scarlett felt in the morning, he and Sienna could figure out how serious this was going to be.

What weighed on him now was the need to stay proactive rather than *waiting* for things to happen and then choosing between a limited number of possible reactions. There was a part of Sienna's story about the Senate Intelligence Committee meeting that haunted him: *"In the event future programs require similar methods."* That was a very benign way to say a very dangerous thing: "We know where you are, we know what you can do, and we may have some use for you or your children someday." That statement had been made in the context of a completely different project hypothetically attempting to do completely different things, but now the original Signal was back, and "they" knew exactly where to find one of the original participants.

He wasn't going to wait to "see what happened," and he doubted Sienna wanted to, either.

Thinking through this stirred things within Jordan that were ugly and which he had left unexplored for long stretches of time. A period when his inaction had left him adrift and crushed beneath the available bad options. It was all in a dark and rarely visited corner of his memory, filled with deep, disconsolate loneliness and the weight of failure at a time when life had not even adequately begun.

During his final years of high school, Jordan had not, to put things as euphemistically as possible, aggressively pursued the pinnacles of academic aptitude. This left him with a predictably limited number of options as the end of 12th grade approached. When the time came to attend the brunch hosted by the PTA the morning before graduation, tradition called for every student to wear a t-shirt from the university that they would be attending in the Fall. The luncheon was awash in the colors of Washington colleges, as well as a handful of others from around the country. Wearing a shirt like that was not in the cards for

Jordan, and the next step of his journey was not the type of thing you ran out to your mailbox to discover. Instead, Jordan ate a cold sandwich and watched his classmates each announce where they were headed next. Then, over the next several weeks, he attended parties for each of his friends as they prepared to say goodbye and move away. And then, one evening, he helped clean up the very last get together.

And after that he was alone.

It was fair to say that all of this was rather pedestrian in the grand scheme of things, and that this was not an altogether rare situation. But in that moment, and in the mind of a young man who craved a community he never truly found, and for someone who wanted to be better but didn't know how – this was the nadir of adolescence. He had never been shown how to plan for the future, nor did he have an adult in his life who could explain how to do it, and now he didn't have one. He had two parents but couldn't pour his heart out to either. And he couldn't bring himself to ask his successful peers how to do the thing that seemed to come so naturally.

Just like countless generations before, just like they were supposed to, each of those children shook off the dust of their hometown to go be an adult somewhere else. The idea of it was thrilling, and over-whelming, and it was the right move to make. Jordan drove across town to a decomposing community college, kept showing up at the same part-time job, and kept sleeping in the same childhood bedroom.

Right on schedule, and just as expected, his whole life emptied out and he was left alone.

This was a highly motivating moment for a lonely young man. A season spent alone and feeling worthless, combined with two bleak years of community college can be, for the right type of person in the right frame of mind, more than enough to inspire a major turnaround. To his everlasting amusement – and this was the part of the story he did tell, and it always got a laugh – he graduated community college "with honors," transferred to a very average university, graduated with honors again, and was accepted to his first choice for grad school where even more honors followed.

The ending of this story was something so preposterously unlikely that it had been impossible to even wish for back when the slow crush of being left behind by life encased him in despair. Having a nice place

to live and the basic comforts of life never even crossed his mind –
simply because he had no concept of how someone grew up and got
those things. All he knew of adulthood was the desperation of it.
Jordan's earliest memory of seeing the adult world in action was
standing with a small cardboard box – that, relative to his own size,
was huge – in line at a food bank which operated in the musty back
room of an Episcopalian church. Once a week he and his mother would
ride the bus across town to get their boxes filled with the produce
grocery stores could no longer sell and with the canned food too dented
to stay on the shelves. As he stood in line with his box, he would squirm
nervously at the sight of the Vietnam veterans sprawled on the floor
nearby, clawing at their skin and begging for cigarettes. When he was
four the man on the floor next to him awoke and ran a long finger
across the fake stitching of his plastic cowboy boots, and he told Jordan
about the horse he had owned before the war and the little boy who
rode it. Jordan was frozen as he felt the man's finger trace a line across
his foot, and his mother was too distracted with her own misery to
notice. Every visit, Jordan could feel the shame radiating off his mother
as she stood in line and watched the items going into their boxes,
hoping for a few more once they stopped. A room full of desperate,
hopeless people was Jordan's most concrete concept of adulthood, and
success would simply mean being less desperate and hopeless than
others. Jordan's goal for life narrowed down to a tiny point, but his
upbringing offered him no clues how to even get that far. No one in his
home talked about careers or vocations or how to plan for the future,
and he lacked the basic instincts necessary to know that this was
information he should find on his own.

But a switch had eventually flipped in his head. He was a man who
thrived on taking action before the universe could take action on him.
Or at least that is how he used to phrase it before he learned that, in
an alarming twist of fate and irony, the universe was now about to take
the upper hand. And this stirred a strange and visceral mix of emotions
that had gone untapped for a very long time.

A childhood spent desperately anxious about his family's financial
security was a strange way to mentally prepare for what appeared to
lie ahead. As an adult, he had thought of money as a source of safety
from the desperation of his earliest memories, but now a bank account

offered very little protection from whatever threat was looming. Any child shaped and burned by these feelings will never – no matter how successful they eventually become – escape the voice in the back of their head which follows them into adulthood repeating the same line: It is all going to go away at any moment.

Jordan had never expected this part of his past to offer anything of value to his future besides a few, "You know, when I was your age…" stories to his children whenever they began to whine about a convenience which he could never have imagined. But now there was this.

Tomorrow was the chance to get out in front of whatever was coming, and, if he could sleep at all tonight, he knew exactly what to do in the morning.

25 JUNE

The conversation in Torquemann's office had now stretched late into the night, and each new layer of the story had become increasingly incredible. Colonel Castro had held a top-secret clearance for over 25 years, but he had never heard of anything similar to this.

"So, you and Dr. Tunis began searching through the MRI results of children within a specific age range who, according to the doctor's notes accompanying the scans, were reporting seeing or hearing things – then what?"

This question made Julius, at a personal level, nostalgic for a different, distant time.

"We would have needed a team 100 times our size to go through every pediatric MRI, so we narrowed our search to MRI's that were taken from patients who reported symptoms during times when the Signal had been spiking."

"And did the results start pouring in right away?"

"We were finding matches far less often than anyone, except Hamza, expected. Throughout the duration of the program we might find someone every four or five months with that specific formation on the back of their brain, and, as soon as we found one, we'd have one of our contacts at the insurance company or medical records provider lose some paperwork or send a form back incomplete so that things would stall for a few days while we did some background research on the viability of the family and the kid as program participants. If they were judged to be a fit for the program, then I'd usually go make first contact and introduce the idea of what we were doing."

"How would you research the families?"

"To what degree do you think the details of our process will help with your current situation?"

The colonel made another mental note to also follow up on this response.

"Ok. And, just to be clear, it was only human children that could hear or see this stuff? Not animals?"

"Animals?"

"My sister trains horses, and a few years ago her entire stable started going nuts right before an earthquake because they could sense it coming."

"No, not animals. At least we never saw any data that led us to consider studying that as a possibility."

"Ok, so once you started finding these kids, that's when you went to your site in San Mateo?"

"It took us several months to find the first four kids, and once we had that initial group, the project managers at the NRO found an abandoned summer camp on the side of a big hill about 20 miles south of the city. The idea was that the selection of the Bay Area made sense operationally."

"Why did that make sense?"

"Well, because, historically, as you know, that area has been home to so many other programs that could arguably be described as being very vaguely similar."

"I'm not sure I understand what you're saying."

Torquemann stopped to consider for a moment if it had really been so long that these programs were no longer familiar. Or had the conspiracy theories attached to them simply obscured the science to the extent that both the fiction and the facts were now dismissed in tandem?

"Project Bluebird, MKUltra, Project Stargate – in that order."

The colonel stared back at him waiting for more information.

"Starting in the early 1950s with Project Bluebird, and going all the way into the mid-90's with Project Grill Flame, these highly classified programs were all based in and around the Bay Area. Their purpose was to develop a way to use people to conduct... let's call it intelligence gathering."

"So, the area of your camp was chosen out of, what, tradition?"

"No, it wasn't sentimental at all. Rather, Stanford and Berkely both have incredible resources that are indirectly available for these types of projects, and both of them were involved with those prior programs to one degree or another – whether it was academic input or laboratory space. And the archives they still have are very helpful."

"What did these programs do?"

This question brought with it more information than the colonel expected, and it connected Dark Antennae to places and periods of history that he could not have imagined on the drive down from the Pentagon.

As Torquemann explained it, Project Bluebird started in 1951 as a joint venture between the FBI and Army to develop a way to train assets to conduct incredibly complex tasks without them being conscious of how they had obtained that knowledge. The program had two goals: First, create the perfect spy who, in case they were ever caught, would have no knowledge of who sent them or the source of their specialized training. Second, if you knew how to implant information *into* someone, then *extracting* it was just a reversal of that process – and, in this case, you could simply retrieve that information by programming your prisoner to happily share it. That was the hypothesis, at least. Bluebird's primary method to achieve both goals was to lower the brain's natural defense against such tinkering with the help of mind-altering chemicals. Early in the research process they tested the viability of marijuana, heroin, peyote, and mescaline in breaking down the mind's natural resistance, but to no avail. After a year of tests there was finally a breakthrough when LSD was introduced to the test subjects. The results of these tests were so promising that the CIA took over the program and shifted Bluebird's mission to focus entirely on how to put ideas in people's heads rather than remove them. To further refine their methods, the agency started to secretly dose its own agents with the chemical to see how highly trained minds would react. The CIA's primary interest in Bluebird's science was its ability to help program assassins. Their reasoning was that if you could briefly capture a bodyguard or servant or family member of an enemy leader, you could implant an overwhelming desire to kill that leader – and then when it happened the person holding the wet knife would be unable to explain how or why he was able to do something so violent and brazen.

When Project Bluebird changed hands and became a CIA operation it was renamed MKUltra – the "MK" designation was what indicated that a program was CIA sponsored. For the next 20 years the project was extraordinarily intensive in its R&D and its ambitions. Despite the agency later trying to burn every record of the program in preparation for a Congressional investigation in 1973, the files which did survive showed how MKUltra had supercharged everything Bluebird had been pursuing. The expansion of the program was, even by the morally gray standards of clandestine operations, wildly unethical. It continued the use of LSD and added electroshock therapy, sensory deprivation, radiation exposure, and hypnosis. At several points during its operation, MKUltra was using so much LSD that it would purchase every available ounce of the drug worldwide. This led to a surge in illicit LSD production and its subsequent flood into the global marketplace.

At the height of its power, MKUltra was running 150 unique projects in 80 locations, and, to get the best possible results, the CIA director ordered these tests to be administered without telling the test subjects. To minimize complaints and blowback from these unwitting test subjects, the CIA carefully chose its participants from places which had the lowest possible likelihood of successfully requesting help: Inmates at federal penitentiaries, soldiers, office workers at CIA headquarters, students at low-income public schools, and mentally handicapped children in orphanages. When Congressional investigators uncovered these details, they were horrified, but not surprised, to find that the roster of specialists working on MKUltra included a dozen Nazi scientists who had been smuggled away from their death sentences at Nuremberg because their experience testing biochemical agents on Dachau inmates was considered exceptionally valuable to the needs of the U.S. government.

The CIA director at the time called the techniques which MKUltra developed "brain warfare."

Like its predecessor, the majority of MKUltra's research – including its most well-known experiment, Operation Midnight Climax – was conducted in the Bay Area. Over the years, the scope of MKUltra became breathtaking even to those accustomed to working on far-reaching government programs which bent laws and shattered moral guidelines. A wide variety of young men who participated in the MKUltra program went on to do astonishingly destructive things with their altered minds –

including the cult leader and serial killer Charles Manson; Ted Kacynski, who was known as the Unabomber; the notorious mob boss Whitey Bulger, who was subjected to hundreds of hours of tests while in federal prison in 1956; and Jim Jones, the cult leader who murdered a U.S. Congressman and his 900 followers in 1978. MKUltra psychiatrists also had a habit of showing up in the wake of extremely violent acts, like when one of the program's senior scientists, Dr. Louis Jolyon, appeared in Dallas after the JFK assassination to visit the jail where Jack Ruby was being held after shooting Lee Harvey Oswald. Despite having no official authority, Dr. Jolyon was allowed to meet privately with Ruby, and this shooter subsequently spent the rest of his suspiciously short life insisting he had acted alone.

Torquemann had reviewed the full list of classified and de-classified MKUltra participants; it was long and deeply disturbing. This list – and the stories about it – meant that it did not require a great deal of imagination to dive head-first into the conspiracy theorizing when the facts on the ground were this spectacular.

Four years after Congress's investigation, in 1977, the perpetually shadowy Defense Intelligence Agency reconstituted all the scattered MKUltra programs under a single gigantic operation called the Stargate Project.

Stargate focused on the singular task of training young adults and children to wage "telepathic warfare" on America's adversaries, and it was incredibly well funded, in part because of reports that the Soviets were spending wildly on something similar. This seemed, at the time, a reasonable evolution of the previous generation's concept of "brain warfare."

From the outset, Stargate had three primary areas of focus. First was "remote viewing," wherein a person projected their mind to a far-distant location in order to do things like see the launch codes on the wall of a Russian nuclear silo or read a list of spies from a computer screen at KGB headquarters. Then there was something the scientists called "psychoenergetics," which attempted to use the mind to alter the physical structure of enemy equipment or maybe the heart valve of an aging foreign dictator. The third discipline was telekinesis, which included using the mind to move an object, push a button, or open a door. Taken together, the DIA hoped these facets of telepathic warfare would be very useful for sabotaging the delicate work done in a laboratory full of delicate centrifuges or nudging an incoming missile off course.

The participants in this program were called soldiers, but almost all of them were civilians, and very few of them were legally adults.

Decades later, when the program was declassified, over 12 million documents were shared with the public, including paperwork stating the original justifications for the project – notably that it had the "benefit of being inexpensive" and that it "had no known defense." But the program was not without its costs.

By the time this program was shut down and declassified in 1995, the combination of scientists and purported psychics working on Stargate believed that the success rate of their telepathic techniques was approximately 65%. Auditors who subsequently reviewed the project could not find any surviving data to support this conclusion. The primary output of the program was 30 million pages of documents and 151 archaic hard drives filled with data that later ended up on the Dark Antennae servers for analysis. Most of this material had, of course, not been part of the official declassification process, but it was made exclusively available to Dr. Torquemann in the early months of his Signal analysis.

This data was colloquially described as "not entirely useless" to Torquemann's program – both in San Mateo and in Alexandria. The primary outlying factor Torquemann found in the Stargate archives was the fact that sometimes their experiments actually worked. This information was more problematic than it was scientifically useful because neither the participants nor the scientists running Stargate understood *why* it worked. But, at the time, the researchers were so blinded by the outcome-oriented nature of the work that they were willing to charge forward without understanding the principles so long as they could leverage it as an edge in the ongoing Cold War. This was, perhaps akin to a squad of desperate soldiers calling for artillery support without needing to understand the metallurgy of a howitzer barrel, the chemistry of the explosive charge, or the trigonometry used for targeting – they just needed something nearby to explode *right now*.

"What no one in that program was willing to say was that none of them could control it. But, for their purposes, an incredible amount of power you could wield but not control was still a lot of power – but what they hoped would be a sniper rifle was really a molotov cocktail. And, if you've ever seen someone light the rag attached to a Coke bottle full of kerosene, then you know it's just as likely that the person doing the throwing will burst into flames as it is their target might catch fire."

All of this took over half an hour to explain to the colonel.

"So that's why you chose the Bay Area, when did you finally set up shop there?"

It struck both of them that they'd been talking for this many hours but had just now arrived at the setup of the camp.

"I took over the team researching the Signal about a year after I was brought on in '77, and we were in pure research mode for well over a year after that. Then we started looking at brain scans over the summer in '79, and, once we had a human component to this, we were actively overlaying every piece of data we had with that new information. Another year after that they found the camp for us, and that started a very long process of getting it outfitted with all the equipment we thought we'd need and inventing a few things that didn't exist yet – but we were underway by September or October of 1981. Once that was squared away, we started preparing for that first group of kids, and they were all in place by April of '82."

"You had nine years there in those cabins."

"Yeah, we had a good run. Almost exactly nine years."

Two more hours were spent on the abstruse and arcane technical details of what had been the most technologically complex program of its era. Torquemann explained the technology they had used and developed to intercept the Signal, the sophistication of the program's technicians, how his team processed the data, and the subsequent scientific breakthroughs they made while exploring and maintaining their research facility at the camp. "Those were the five or six Nobel prizes my team never got to win," Torquemann said with a laugh. There were likely less than 10 people in North America who could have made sense of such a deeply esoteric discussion, and the notes Castro took gave his team a dozen different ways to begin applying Dark Antennae principles early the next morning.

"That was an incredible outlay of time to spend at that camp."

"We all wanted to be there, the work was fascinating and there was nothing else like it – then or now."

"But still a massive commitment."

Torquemann wasn't sure what the colonel was looking for here, but this wasn't an area where there was anything to hide.

"I had a slightly different perspective on it. I'll tell you that my family had some *characters* in it when I was growing up. I had an uncle who spent his whole life trying to make it as a musician and never made it past playing Saturday nights at one of the two bars in his hometown, and I had a cousin who studied interpretive dance and kept waiting for her career to take off. Part of me still respects them for sticking with it, but I also noticed at a young age how belatedly people discover that they've been chasing their dreams on a toll road – and the longer you stick with something that doesn't work out, the more it's gonna cost you. I never felt like I had any time to waste, and when I found this project I didn't waste my time anywhere else."

"Do you feel like you gathered all the data you needed during your time at the camp?"

"We certainly gathered everything we possibly could, and if we hadn't been able to get started so quickly, we would have missed a couple very valuable years there at the beginning."

There was something about the way he said it.

"What do you mean you were able to get started quickly?" Castro asked.

Torquemann paused for a moment and chided himself for including a detail that served no purpose to this conversation. But, without thinking of it in such terms, he was about to offer his ossified conscience some small relief through confession.

"Well, immediately after I began putting together the basics for what a research program for the Signal would look like, Gillespie, the guy I mentioned earlier at the NRO, he put me in touch with a retired scientist named Gene Kaile to serve as a... I guess you would call it a mentorship role."

Castro noticed the grimace that started to form as he said the words.

"We met fairly regularly to discuss the nature of the work, and we would talk through ideas for how to work with the kids, and we'd brainstorm about how to work with the tachyons themselves since the technology to do so had improved so much since his lab was up and running."

"He knew about tachyons?" Castro suddenly interrupted.

"He did. He had worked on the Manhattan Project in the 40's, and he went on to join the CIA's scientific division shortly after the agency was established in 1947, and by the early 1950's every piece of secret research the agency was commissioning, observing, or stealing made its way across his desk at some point just so he could stay apprised of what was available for weaponization against the rest of the world. The exotic properties of tachyons were of particular interest to him, just like they would be to our Russian friends a couple decades later – and using the data Hans Bethe kept tinkering with in his lab at Cornell, Dr. Kaile started doing research of his own in the late '50s and early '60s."

"Was it similar to your work?"

"I would like to think it was not."

Another grimace.

"What did he discover?"

Torquemann took a deep breath but tried to disguise it by shifting his weight in his chair.

"You need to understand that Gene Kaile was a monster."

The general gregarity of tonight's conversation was now gone. The temperature in the room seemed to drop.

"I want you to recognize that I do not use that word lightly."

"I understand."

"Kaile had equipment built that could funnel tachyons at a given object. It was crude compared to what we had at my camp 30 years later, but he could manage a relatively steady stream of them, and to test the effects of tachyons on living tissue he set up a clinic for people with chronic pain and told them he had a machine that could help alleviate their nerve damage with some concoction of technical jargon that no one at the time could decipher. So, over the years, he got to see what happened when the human body is hit with a firehose of high-speed, zero-mass particles."

"And what did he find?"

"First, to cast as wide a net as possible, he set up an east coast and a west coast clinic, and once the data started to pile up, he found that about 98% of your body has no reaction, which probably should have been obvious, but he found some strange results from the other 2%."

"Which 2% was that?"

"That's how much of your body weight is represented by your brain. But in a fractionally small number of patients who came in with neck pain or earaches or headaches or concussions – whatever it was that brought them in – he found that when he was funneling tachyons through their brain, a very specific area near the back seemed to light up with activity. So, he offered that group of people 'free treatment' out of the goodness of his heart if they kept coming back, and he kept pumping the particles into their heads and watching the results."

"And what happened?"

"Essentially nothing, especially at first – but then, over the years, out of the thousands of people that came through his two clinics, three or four of them started reporting that when they were laying there in front of the machine they could hear or see static, like when you can't tune in a radio station."

"The Signal."

"Probably not the Signal – but, more likely, it was just the tachyon field itself they were picking up. But, at the time, the idea that this was possibly a communication medium was the furthest thing from his mind – he was looking for weapons. So, he kept these half dozen people coming back over and over again just to see what would happen to them. There was a remorselessness to his particular pursuit of scientific inquiry."

"What do you mean? What happened?"

"Very early on in these experiments he saw data that suggested long-term exposure to such a dense stream of tachyons could strain or even structurally compromise neural tissue, and this did not give him the slightest pause. In particular, in a half dozen subjects who showed signs of cellular strain in the brain, he doubled and then tripled the intensity of the particles to prove a correlation. After 16 months, the first of these subjects, a boy who was seven at the time and had first come to this clinic because of chronic headaches, developed a small tumor on the back of his occipital lobe."

He paused to point at the back of his head in the same way he had when describing the unique brain structure of Dark Antennae's campers.

"After spotting the tumor, Kaile increased the intensity of the particle stream *again* and monitored how the tumor reacted. Obviously, he didn't say anything to the boy or his parents about it. His notes suggest that he considered this a breakthrough – a weapon that he could point at an enemy and give them brain cancer. This might have gone on for years, but one of his colleagues happened to review a few of his case notes while doing some unrelated research, and he saw the scans of that boy's brain and the enthusiastic notes Kaile had written in the margin. This colleague alerted the director of the science division, and, as Kaile later explained it to me, the CIA leadership didn't have the stomach for his project – or at least they didn't have the stomach for having to know what it was he was doing. Apparently, the colleague hadn't known the CT scan belonged to a child, but the director found out – and he hit the roof. In the case notes attached to the project was a memo explaining why it was shut down, and, if you read between the lines, you see that this program was deemed to be appalling even by the standards of a director who was at that moment supervising the transition and escalation of Bluebird into Ultra."

"What happened to the boy? And what happened to Kaile?"

"I don't know what happened to the boy. The case file ends with a note saying that the scans of the tumor had been examined by an oncologist and determined to be benign and unlikely to continue growing after the experiments ended."

"I suppose that much is good."

"Well, it wasn't enough of an answer for me, so I went digging."

"For him?"

"Yes. And, a couple years later, when we had that access to the medical databases, I looked him up. The tumor did end up giving him problems later on, and when he got a CT scan 12 years later, they spotted it immediately, but also judged it to be benign. He subsequently had two different meetings with oncologists to get it looked at – once in his 20s and again in his early 30s. It was never operated on because, at the time, brain surgery was a coin flip and completely out of the question unless it was a matter of life and death. The notes in his file from those two physicians both indicate that the tumor was causing some intermittent vision problems, and one of them concluded it was also likely causing sporadic mood irregularity. The second doctor he saw noted that the patient made a comment blaming the condition on a 'government doctor' that had 'done experiments' on him as a child. Unsurprisingly, the doctor he told this to was the same one who made the note about his mood and behavior – which, at the time, was a not particularly subtle way of hinting at psychosis."

"And what happened to him after that?"

"After that there's no sign of him visiting another doctor, and I couldn't find much of anything – no credit cards, no activity on his social security number, no medical history, nothing submitted to the IRS – it all just went blank, and at the time there was no death certificate either. But he somehow figured out what had happened to him – God knows how he did it."

"But you went ahead with your research anyway."

"I did."

The words were ice cold and resolute and dejected at the same time.

"Even though you knew it could do this?"

Torquemann looked at the wall and chose his words carefully. These were the words he'd said to help himself sleep for so long that he'd almost stopped needing to say them.

"I knew the risks, the kids and the families did not, and so we took every precaution to protect them."

"Was there something different about your techniques?"

"There were significant differences in the equipment, but the primary difference in terms of raw exposure to the particles was duration. Kaile's data proved very useful in understanding the factors leading up to the point at which we would start straining the structural integrity of the neural tissue, and we cut every camper loose when they reached 50% of that threshold. This protocol was something we called the Master Schedule, and we did not ever deviate from it."

"You said before that you sent the campers home when their brains grew to a point that the overlapping lobes no longer picked up the Signal."

"That was something we always anticipated would happen if kids stayed in the program indefinitely, so that was our official story. But the reason they were sent home was when we saw that area of their brain reach a certain level of saturation. Some kids got to that point sooner than others based on their biochemistry, others seemed to overtax that region sooner rather than later – but we kept a *very* close eye on it, and we were religious about sending kids home the moment they reached that 50% threshold no matter what else was going on in the program."

"So, the brain growth essentially had nothing to do with it."

"They do actually grow out of it, but not nearly as soon as we led them to believe. We just told them to expect some lingering Signal activity after they left – and that was that. And, with that threshold in mind, the cover story about brain growth was also a practical consideration: No one was going to sign up for a program that had the remote possibility of giving them a tumor. I made sure we never got anywhere close to that while still gathering the data we needed.

Castro couldn't help but think the words "ethical quagmire" as he listened, and he could tell that this doctor had agonized over this fine line he spent nearly a decade walking.

"Obviously we monitored these kids very carefully for about 25 years after they left to see if anyone developed complications, and, as of yet, none have."

"As of yet."

"Yes."

"I imagine those three words have ruined a few nights' sleep."

There was an awkward pause. If given a second chance, Castro would not have said that last part out loud.

The old scientist leaned forward and put his hands on his knees in the universal way that indicated a lunch meeting or an interview was over.

"What else can I help you with tonight, colonel; I suppose it's gotten very late."

"Yes, of course, this has all been very helpful."

The colonel looked at his notes and finally felt like he had enough to explain the big picture to the Secretary of Defense in the morning. It was already past midnight, so he only had a few hours to repackage all of this for executive consumption – and he knew most, if not all, of whatever he shared would end up with the President. He didn't know exactly when, but he knew he'd be asking Dr. Torquemann a lot more questions in the near future – because, despite so much of this material being outside his area of expertise at the Pentagon, he knew enough to recognize that his story about spending nearly 50 years researching an old Soviet radio broadcast did not add up.

"Thank you again, Doctor; the work you did was incredible, you must be exceptionally proud of it."

"Well, it's dangerous to romanticize the work. You end up like Jim Lovell if you're not careful."

Castro weighed the pros and cons of asking a question that would almost certainly turn into another story.

"Who is that?"

"Jim was on the crew of the Apollo 8, the first mission to orbit the moon back in '68 – and a couple years later he was the commander on Apollo 13 and got to be the one who said that famous line, 'Houston, we have a problem.' And, well, while Apollo 8 was making its 20 orbits of the moon, late one night Jim was taking his turn piloting the thing while his crewmates were asleep – and just as he comes out from behind the dark side of the moon something incredible happens. As he's turning the corner, he's looking out the window and suddenly this radiant shimmer of light appears out of nowhere and envelops the entire craft. And Jim is awestruck – and he just *knows* immediately that this is an angel sent by God Almighty to welcome mankind to the heavens. I don't even think he was that religious, but there it was right there in front of him."

"I've never heard anything about this," Castro said, confused.

"Well, there's a good reason, Colonel – because while Jim was still sitting there basking in the splendor of God's favor and trying to think of how he was going to explain this to everyone back on Earth, he hears a beep on the control panel. He looks over and sees a notification that the life support system has just emptied the toilet."

"The what?"

"So, every few hours the craft would automatically shoot all their waste out into space, and when that hit the vacuum it crystalized instantly – and when the sunlight hit all those tiny ice crystals it lit up like million little disco balls. As soon as he heard the beep he figured out what he had seen. And that was the end of the angel."

Castro laughed.

"And that's the moral of the story Colonel: At the risk of being crass, temporarily meeting god inside a glowing cloud of your own piss is the penalty you pay for losing your perspective on the science."

"There were no angels at your camp, I take it?"

"My team did great work, but we never made the mistake of spotting any angels."

Castro stood to leave, and thanked Torquemann again as he put his notepad away. "One last thing," he said as he made his way to the door. "What did you say the name of that place was?"

"Which one?"

"The place in New Mexico, where they tested the first nuke. Jornada something."

"Ahh, Jornada del Muerto – it's the name the Spanish conquistadors gave to the region in the 1590s."

The colonel spoke fluent Arabic, but his surname's origin in Galicia was distant enough to have left him with zero Spanish.

"What does that mean?"

"It translates to 'The Route of the Dead Man.'"

These words coiled a tight, cold knot in his gut. The colonel breathed out the words "God help us" under his breath, thanked the doctor again for his time, and closed the door behind him. Up until this point, Torquemann had thought the significance of the Signal's return and the accompanying international fallout might have escaped the colonel.

Castro's attendants were ready in the hallway, and, 40 seconds later, they were speeding back north, alongside the Potomac, and crossing the bridge back into the District of Columbia in record time.

He let out another long breath and, without thinking, repeated "God help us" just loud enough for both guards and the driver to hear.

26 JUNE

The sun was rising earlier than usual during this part of the year in the Northern Hemisphere, but Jordan was already staring up at the ceiling before the sky started turning orange outside his window. He listened to the quiet house and Sienna breathing next to him, and he suddenly wondered how many peaceful moments he had left.

"Damn, that's pretty dark," he thought.

Jordan was generally lighthearted and the first to laugh when times were tough, and, even taking his use of sarcasm as a default setting into account, he was still usually the one talking other people out of their more pessimistic inclinations.

But Jordan had been hit with a type and a volume of information over the past 14 hours that no one could be prepared for, and all of it hit as close to home as possible now that Calista and Scarlett were affected. Last night they had both gone to sleep feeling nauseous and with pounding headaches as an added bonus. Sienna had woken up several times during the night to check on them and share the occasional chewable Tylenol.

It was now 4:52am.

Jordan heard Blaise's bedroom door creak open down the hall as he made his way to the bathroom and back. Considering this was the first week of summer break, Blaise had probably been asleep for two hours at the most, and he likely wouldn't reemerge for another nine or ten.

He rolled over and tried to think through what could and would happen next. In particular, he thought of what could happen *to* them, as well as what the Rileys could *do* instead of waiting for that to happen.

Last night he and Sienna had fallen asleep talking about this exact thing: What to do and where to go if anyone else started noticing the return of the Signal and its effects. It was a conversation that would've been unthinkable to have a day ago. It seemed impossible to tell if they were being reactionary or rational. This situation had placed them well beyond a place where common sense could be relied upon as a guide.

It seemed inevitable that, even if the Dark Antennae program was long gone, the Signal would eventually show up on a piece of equipment somewhere. When someone did finally detect it, or if anyone like Sienna and the girls started hearing it, it stood to reason that it wouldn't take terribly long for one government agency or another to start looking for existing data about this phenomenon, and that search would eventually lead to the program. Once these dots were connected, it wouldn't take long for them to start contacting former campers. Just how benign and altruistic the agency pulling this thread might be was impossible to know – and both Sienna and Jordan were unwilling to bet on that type of uncertainty. That uncertainty was enough to make them both conclude that keeping the lowest possible profile for the time being was the best next step – at least until they could get some sense of what the Signal was going to do or how long it was going to last.

This was a very roundabout way of saying "disappear."

Despite being the optimistic type, Jordan was still prone to the anxieties any father and husband develops, and, as he slowly grew more alarmed, Sienna had heard yet another unmistakable crackle while they laid there talking quietly in the dark.

What had kept Jordan awake long after Sienna had finally drifted off, and what woke him up again before the sun, was the simple logic of what a powerful organization would be willing to do for – and with – information about the Signal. If the Signal was coming from a hostile foreign country, the U.S. government would take any measure necessary to control, compromise, or eliminate it – and probably in that order. If taking control of it meant dragging Sienna and the girls into service, there was an agency director somewhere who would be willing to choose them to make that sacrifice. Considering how many unknowable possible outcomes were swirling at this moment for his family, Jordan was not willing to find out how they would be made to participate in the meat grinder of clandestine civic duty.

Sienna had arrived at essentially the same conclusion, but with an added layer of dread. She had quickly reached the sobering conclusion that if anyone over the last 30 years had learned what she and Dr. Torquemann knew… she could not finish the thought. The cold reality of her calculus was that any sufficiently powerful organization would be willing to make terrible sacrifices in the name of global security.

But, she kept reminding herself, *nothing* had happened yet to indicate anything like that was happening. She did not have a reason to believe that anyone but her noticed the Signal or that any international or interdepartmental machinations were afoot.

She and Jordan kept arriving at the idea that just sitting and waiting was an unacceptable risk. Considering how recently Sienna had been on the radar of the intelligence community, and considering what they knew about her children, the risk became even more unacceptable. This led to the most immediate question: Where to go to lay low while things blew over. Mike and Ginny were, as usual, aloof and unreliable, to say nothing of being 800 miles away. Going to them would also be the very first place *someone* would look in the event that *anyone* went looking – both of them were still, after all, on the Dark Antennae payroll.

Jordan's family wasn't going to be any help, either. He had grown up in the area, but his parents were even further away.

Two years earlier, with no warning, Jordan's parents, Robert and Gloria, had moved to a remote town three hours east of San Bernardino, deep in the Mojave Desert. To hear his parents tell it, the house prices around the isolated hamlet of Cadiz were very attractive, perhaps due in part to a landscape which resembled Tatooine after a sustained economic downturn. It also helped that his younger sister, Danielle, had met a local while in college and settled there after getting married. By the time Danielle welcomed her first baby a year later, the grandparents had already made up their minds to join them there. For several months' worth of Sunday afternoon visits, Jordan and the kids watched as Rob and Lori – as she preferred to be called ever since losing the remaining traces of her accent in her early 20's – slowly sold their belongings on eBay, and carefully packed the rest into boxes. During each visit Jordan would ask if they were going somewhere, and each week they would say it "just feels good to declutter the house."

At the time, Jordan did not understand why his parents could not extend the close-knit family ties of his childhood to include his children.

It wasn't until years later that Jordan had read enough about child-parent dynamics that he began to grasp it. In overly simplistic terms, Lori deeply needed to be the center of the universe. This did not mean that she could not shower love and affection on her children, and she certainly did – but she could only do this from the position of being at the center of everyone else's universe, too. If *you* came to *her*, she was a bottomless source of love and attention – but she would never, could never, and did not ever take the action to come to *you*. Once he had a wife and a child, Jordan had a new center – and Lori was not interested in any relationship where she was a peripheral figure. This understanding clicked everything into place for Jordan, and, for the first time, he finally knew his mother as a fellow adult. He recognized she did not consciously approach the world this way, and he believed she had never thought of things in such concise terms, and he knew she would react with extreme disdain if such concepts were ever explained to her so plainly.

But, nonetheless, it was true.

And this trickled down into every part of their relationship with Jordan and his family. Rob and Lori had never attended a soccer game or a lacrosse match, they didn't show up on Grandparent's Day at preschool, and they never called to check in or catch up. They showed up at the hospital to take pictures with a new baby, and when Sienna needed a babysitter or a night off, the call went to voicemail. Their Christmas newsletter brimmed with pictures of their grandchildren at birthday parties they hadn't attended, at piano recitals they hadn't heard, at games they never saw, alongside photos of vacations they took by themselves.

One Wednesday morning Jordan got a phone call from Rob asking if they could come to dinner that night. This had never happened before. He immediately knew the reason for the visit.

After they arrived, Rob called the family together to talk – another thing he had never done – but his odd solemnity made it seem like a patriarchal function he had undertaken on many previous occasions. He said he had "news to share" and then took a deep breath.

Before he had a chance to exhale, Blaise disdainfully asked through a mouthful of lasagna, "So, you're moving to go live with Uncle Jason in the desert?"

This caught Rob completely off guard. Lori looked up to stare daggers at Sienna.

Rob sputtered and held up his hands as if to ask for a re-do. "No," he said reflexively before catching himself, earnestly avoiding eye contact, and then saying, "Well, yes."

Scarlett and Josephine burst out sobbing and ran from the kitchen, up the stairs, and into their rooms. Blaise glared at them with the type of contempt only teens can muster, and Calista sunk back into her chair, arms crossed with a dark cloud gathering on her face. Sienna had contempt of her own, but not because of the shameless lying which had precipitated it. This was not the ideal way for her children to learn that adults can lie, be selfish, and hurt people who love them. But her reaction to it was, in a strange way, equal parts tempered and inflamed by recognizing that this was the last interaction she was going to have with two people who had never shown any interest in building a family with her.

Being confronted by anger from one half of the room, and heart-breaking sadness by the other, was an affront to Rob and Lori's foundational notions of how elders ought to be honored. They went so far as to use those exact words. On one hand, their expectations were unnatural considering they had never built the types of relationships that accompany such respect, and, on the other hand, it is hard to summon a fond farewell for people who have just announced they are leaving forever after a year of furtive preparations.

"I think it's best that we cut this short," Jordan said, standing up and gesturing for his parents to follow him to the door. Rob and Lori were reeling at this reaction, but Lori summoned the presence of mind to complain that this was not the heart-felt send-off that grandparents deserved. As she stepped out onto the porch she turned back to Jordan, looked over his shoulder at his quietly fuming wife, and glanced up at the small, crying children watching from the top of the stairs. She put her finger in his face for a long moment before speaking. "This," she finally growled, with her voice trembling and eyes welled with tears, "is why I didn't trust you to take care of me when I was old."

Even in the moment Jordan knew this comment was absurd to the extent it boarded on insane, yet he spent the next several weeks asking himself if there was some iota of truth in it. But to no avail.

Standing there in the doorway, Jordan noticed their car was already packed. This announcement of their departure was the departure itself.

He could have used this as one last chance to reiterate the many hundreds of times he had begged his parents to get involved in the lives of his children. He might have asked why his requests had always been met with chastisements. And he could have spelled out to them in intricate detail how damaging it was for his children to see that the lofty *idea* of being good people was so important to them that the *energy* such a title required was beneath the dignity and the inherent nature of that goodness.

But saying these things would have been wasteful.

Rob and Lori had no qualms leaving the matter unresolved and, once they were free of this emotional crater in Jordan's living room, apologizing or reconciling would never cross their mind. The effort required to process such a reunification rendered the concept of it invisible to them.

They simply got in their car and left.

One at a time, over the next two days, Jordan talked about "what happened with grandma and grandpa" with each of his kids. In one form or another, the same confusion and the same questions arose. His parents' actions were so detached from reality as to seem random, but the premeditation ruled out something as coarse as negligent cruelty. It was something stranger and less intelligent, and it was devoid of emotion in a way that made it barbaric instead of malevolent. Jordan could have understood a falling out over politics or religion or irreconcilable differences; but *this* was a dissolution for, and because of, and in service to nothingness. They had done something unknowable. This was a fatal wound that spared no tenderness in the way it left the erstwhile bonds of family plainly dead. But, because this wound would never heal, Rob and Lori had also rendered themselves immortal in the minds of these children.

Much later in life, while searching for a photo to show her own grandchildren, Calista would find a picture of her father as an infant, wrapped in a blanket on his mother's lap. She stared down into the faded image and wiped away a series of silent tears as she considered, for the first time, that the defining experience of her mother's life, and also her own, had such an unlikely bond – that a nuclear blast on the eastern edge of America's vast interior desert would set so much of her life's events in motion, and, on the western edge, 900 miles away, her grandparents would go to disappear.

26 Premise

It had required several very long nights with a dozen different specialists from the Defence Research and Development Organisation (रक्षा अनुसंधान एवं विकास संगठन) and another dozen officers and strategists from the special forces division, but General Gupta now had a plan that was remarkably straightforward, albeit still reliant on extreme precision.

The major breakthrough was so simple that, in retrospect, it seemed absurd to have only been discovered after pursuing and rejecting so many other complexities. Rather than take the extreme risk of delivering an EMP warhead into a hostile foreign country and, inevitably, suffer the consequences of forensic analysis which would unequivocally link it back to India, Marshal Akash Chatterjee, the expert on Broken Arrows, devised a plan that simply removed the nuclear device from the equation entirely. Instead, the plan would electromagnetically pulse their target by generating an intense electromagnetic wave from a less traditional source.

This method of attack had been the first and last piece of the puzzle, and it was developed concurrently with a series of meetings between the Prime Minister and General Gupta's senior staff to determine, beyond any reasonable doubt, that the available data demonstrated the existence of a cyberweapon with an imminent deployment. Now that the weapon had been identified, this mission was simply a matter of killing the threat before it had a chance to leave its cage – and, of equal importance, destroy both the access routes it had to the outside world as well as its backups that would certainly exist in off-site, air-gapped locations. Finding those routes and the backups entailed entirely separate missions that had to be executed simultaneously with the primary attack which targeted the Pakistani military's cyber warfare program at the Masroor Air Base.

Considering that this weapon was entirely unknown ten days ago, General Gupta felt that this operation's current level of development was nothing short of tactically brilliant, and he expressed this to the entire command staff who had effectively lived at headquarters since planning began.

The operation had steps which were, while not easy to do, simple to understand: Under Chatterjee's direction, a small group of special forces – the Para Commandos (पैरा स्पेशल फोर्सेज़) – would enter Pakistan via the northern city of Amritsar (अमृतसर) and rendezvous with local assets in Lahore (لاہور). These locals were a group of indigenous Kalash tribesmen (کالاش) anxious for any opportunity to undermine the ruling party in Karachi. The Kalashi wouldn't know the identities of their guests or where they were ultimately headed, but they would be very well paid and motivated.

Lahore was a gigantic city – the second biggest in Pakistan and among the 25 or 30 largest on Earth – so the quick trip from Amritsar would be anonymous and uneventful. The commandos would then disguise themselves as Buddhist pilgrims visiting the holy shrine in Taxila (ٹیکسلا), and these particular pilgrims would be the aesthetic variety who had taken a strict vow of silence. Their government IDs would, of course, be flawless, and these conveniently mute pilgrims would then be driven 750 miles south in a small commuter bus the Kalashi already owned. They'd make the trip in the dead of night, without making a single stop until they reached a point several miles south of the Hub River Dam (حب ڈیم) where they would exit the bus and hike up and over several miles of tall, rocky outcroppings until they eventually reached the settlement of another indigenous group who had their own list of grievances with the Pakistani government. This tiny settlement of Baloch people (بلوچ) were expert navigators of Pakistan's dry wastelands, and a few days earlier they would have taken delivery of a dozen large crates labeled as tractor parts. The commandos would spend the remainder of that day and night assembling their specially shielded ATVs from amongst the actual tractor parts, and the Baloch would then guide them on the 13-hour trip through dunes, ravines, and dry channels to the distant outskirts of Masroor. The timing of the mission called for them to arrive in the middle of the night at a pre-appointed spot about 10 miles from the northwest corner of the base where that nondescript hangar housed Pakistan's cyberwarfare unit. In a strange coincidence, this remote spot would place them only two miles from the Space and Upper Atmosphere Research Commission (خلائی و بالائے فضائی تحقیقاتی مأموریہ), which was Pakistan's version of NASA.

Everything in the plan up to this point was all very standard special operations planning; it was the payload and the delivery system that were the real masterstroke.

The weapon would be carried by a slightly above-average sized drone – the same model, in fact, that Gupta's granddaughter had bought last year at a Costco in the United States when she worked as a summer intern at a startup in Colorado. Attached to the bottom of that drone would be a flat, black rectangle about three times the size of the portable battery packs that business travelers use to keep their cell phone charged on long trips. A prototype of this exact device sat on the table in the middle of his conference room, and it was easily ignored by anyone sitting near it.

That rectangle had been the central showpiece of Marshall Chatterjee's presentation of the plan.

"What I want to show you, General," he had said, "is this otherwise mundane piece of black plastic."

He held it up for show.

"Inside here is a high-temperature superconductor and it is simple to attach it to this," he held up another black rectangle, "which is a prototype of a high-density battery pack."

Everyone in the room, Gupta included, were familiar enough with what a superconductor was, but not enough to understand where Chatterjee was going with this.

"High-temperature superconductors are not terribly rare – you can find them inside MRI machines, maglev trains, quantum computers, and electric vehicles. But those superconductors are about the size of a briefcase and cost around $40,000. This, on the other hand," he held up the rectangle again, "the total power output it can handle, plus its battery pack, plus its reduced size – it all pushes the cost to around $16 million."

Luckily for the Marshall, an army of this size did not get sticker shock from a number of that size. But he knew that.

Gupta could now see where this was going. He had seen reports of past military hardware getting fried when a superconductor went awry. He took pride in being an old soldier who could adapt to new technology, even when so much of it was esoteric and recondite, and despite the fact that a loaded rifle and few extra clips still made the most sense to him.

"Gentlemen, this superconductor and its accompanying power pack," Chatterjee continued, "represent a monumental technical breakthrough by our science division." A more magnanimous officer would have gone on to explain that this device represented a cumulative triumph of material science, electrical engineering, chemistry, high-energy physics, particle physics, computational modeling, nanotechnology, and three dozen other specialties. Instead, he kept the focus on the device itself: "Absorbing and then expending this much electrical energy is a scientific achievement that defies hyperbole."

He paused in order to make his point very clear. "There is nothing else like this. The Chinese can't build this, the Koreans have the tools but not the specialists, and the Americans have no idea this exists and probably aren't even aware the technology is viable. This is a leap that puts us at least 20 years ahead of our North American friends, and when this technology eventually gets licensed to our commercial sector, India's position in the energy markets will go unchallenged for a century."

But now, the room noticed, the ambitious young general was completely out of his lane.

Chatterjee seemed to notice too, and, amidst the grandiose vision, returned to the mission at hand.

"For everything it does better than anything else, this superconductor still does exactly the same thing as its predecessors: When you pump energy into a superconductor it creates its own equal and opposite magnetic field. For weaponization purposes, this means that if you create a superconductor capable of having an incredible amount of energy pumped into it, that equal and opposite field is a miniature EMP."

For the purposes of this conversation, Chatterjee would skip over the footnote from the magnetic wave specialists who argued if this reaction qualified as a true electromagnetic pulse – but the several quadrillion energized particles frying every electrical system within range wouldn't know the difference, and neither would the enemy. At least not at first. At least not in any way that mattered once their lights went off for the foreseeable future.

It didn't really matter where the idea for this project came from, but General Gupta found it just novel enough to be curious about its origins.

"The early thinking for this project," Chatterjee explained, "was borrowed in part from our friends in the U.S. military who spent their wars in Iraq and Afghanistan getting very clever with small and portable electromagnetic pulse – weapons that they used to defuse IEDs."

General Gupta remembered hearing about this – the devices were about the size of cigarette lighters, and soldiers would throw them toward a suspicious pile of trash or rubble, and the pulse of energy that followed would fry the circuits of the bomb or burner phone it was attached to without damaging nearby buildings or civilians. It didn't take long for military scientists to start expanding this concept to include creating a defensive mortar shell with a pulse weapon attached to which could be shot toward incoming projectiles and fry them in mid-flight. The U.S. Navy reportedly already had a way to shoot these pulse devices at the "aircraft carrier killer" cruise missiles the Chinese were developing. The casual terminology for this genre of military hardware was "E-weapons."

It was a dumb name, but the military principles were sound.

It was all quite ingenious, Gupta had to admit. Every country with nuclear weapons – or at least every country with a nuclear enemy – had spent billions since the 1980s trying to develop interceptor missiles that could hit incoming nukes with pinpoint accuracy despite both of those objects moving at hypersonic speeds through the vast expanse of the upper atmosphere. In 40 years of testing these interceptors, no government had ever had a successful test of anything resembling a real-world scenario. But now all you needed to do was put enough pulse devices up in the air to create a 100 cubic mile box in the sky, and once that nuclear weapon was inside your three-dimensional area, you energized it.

To prepare for the operation at hand, the DRDO had borrowed from both the tactical and strategic uses of E-weapons to develop what would be epoxied to the bottom of that drone – and then Marshal Chatterjee's team had done the rest.

This compact payload and highly portable delivery system gave this mission the benefit of extreme flexibility. Once launched, the drone would travel 10 feet off the ground in the dead of night for the duration of its short flight. It would be far below radar detection, completely invisible to satellites, and moving so fast that it would be impossible for anyone along its path to understand or report what had just flashed past them in the darkness. A large capsule of thermite gel was attached to both the superconductor and the battery to ensure anything left behind after the particle wave was melted beyond identification. In terms of hard evidence, this weapon was forensically invisible.

The hangar, however, was not exactly a sitting duck. Its roof was reinforced to deflect satellite scans and a dozen other types of readings, and the insulation in the walls prevented a wide range of electronic interference – all of which would certainly blunt the effectiveness of the pulse. But this, too, had been accounted for by the assault's specialists. Like every other office building on Earth, a janitor visited every night once the day's work was complete, and, like every other janitorial service, this one operated on a schedule. At 12:18 am, for each of the last three nights, Gupta's urban assault planners had watched a grainy satellite feed of a janitor with a rolling trash can and a broom enter the building and leave 17 to 19 minutes later. When that janitor opened the door 72 hours from now a drone would follow him at high speed, likely collide with him, then skid to a halt somewhere near the middle of the room. As soon as the drone reached the edge of the building, a timer would start running to protect against a loss of connection to its controller or any damage to the ability to remote detonate. Ten seconds after approaching the door, the superconductor would energize.

And that was that.

Frankly, even if all it did was lodge itself in the doorway before energizing, that would be enough – and, considering the total energy output of this superconductor, landing next to the unshielded office door would likely be fine.

The energy payload of the superconductor was equivalent to about 1.1 megatons of electromagnetic power, but It's activation at ground level wouldn't cover a big enough area to render Pakistan entirely paleolithic – although that is what many on Gupta's senior staff believed they deserved for planning an unprovoked attack. The restrained destructive range also had an element of forward thinking embedded into it: Rendering a traditionally hostile neighboring country humiliated and desperate to survive would be, at best, a terrible nuisance, and, at worst, an existential threat once it started regathering its strength. Instead, a blast such as this one would wipe out every electronic capability of this hangar, the entire Masroor Air Base, and the northeast corner of Karachi. It would also fry all the digital communication and fiber optic lines going to and from this base, which would mean that, in the unlikely event that anything survived inside that hangar, it would be impossible for it to leave the base unless it was picked up and carried away – and Gupta's staff already had a plan for how to watch for that.

But the hangar at Masroor wasn't the only place this weapon lived – there were obvious areas where it would be backed up, as well as back-ups of that backup. The places the Pakistani army used for materials this sensitive were few and far between and, thus, they were relatively well known thanks to friendly assets within the government. Two identical attacks were concurrently being planned for each of those areas, to be triggered once the strike on Masroor was confirmed. It was also possible that Pakistan was relying on Iran to store a copy of this weapon – with or without the Iranian Revolutionary Guard knowing what it was – so, just in case, a fourth and final Para team would send a fourth and final drone toward the few dozen miles of high-bandwidth fiber cables that were dedicated to military and governmental communications between both nations. If Iran did have a copy of the weapon, severing this connection would not prevent them from sending it back to the Pakistanis through less direct internet channels, but two things would be working against that: First, it would take much, much longer to transfer a weapon of this size over commercial-grade internet connections; and, second, and much more importantly, an attack on the diplomatic cable would tell Iran in no uncertain terms that the orchestrator of this attack *knew* Iran was an accessory to Pakistan's weapons development, and that would make the diplomatic discussion which followed much more productive. The Indian ambassador in Tehran had already been asked to start developing talking points for that meeting.

"For all of Pakistan's technological prowess," Marshal Chatterjee said in the damage assessment portion of his presentation, "it is remarkable to consider how vulnerable they are to a sudden internet blackout." He directed the attention of the room to a picture of the region with dark lines crisscrossing the surrounding waterways. "Since 2022, Pakistan has had 10 high-bandwidth submarine cables connecting it to the outside world, but all of them enter the country through a single chokepoint that is narrow enough to be compromised by a natural disaster with good timing *or* a man-made disaster with decent aim." The map zoomed in on an otherwise empty-looking stretch of coastline along the Gulf of Oman. "The only backup connection linking Pakistan to the outside world is a single cable between these two small towns which straddle their border with Iran."

There were a lot of heads to cut off this snake, Gupta thought.

"This tenuous connection between the two countries is supplemented by another high-density and carefully monitored cable that goes up and over the Makran Range, a particularly rugged stretch of mountains that form the border of southeastern Iran and southwestern Pakistan. Compromising the seaside cable is easy enough, but the mountain cable is another matter. High winds and jagged peaks make a drone impossible, so an additional special forces unit from the High Altitude Warfare School (அதிஉயர் மலை போர்ப் பயிற்சிப் பள்ளி) in the Himalayas will hike in and out of the area to sever this cable the old-fashioned way."

Each of these units were receiving their instructions now, the tactical teams were prepping their insertion and extraction, and this strike was now zeroing in on its multi-fanged target.

As Chatterjee took his seat, General Gupta felt the need to remind everyone of the geopolitical cautions which were afoot despite the greenlight this operation had received from the prime minister.

"Gentlemen, I want to remind you of the geopolitical cautions which are afoot despite the greenlight this operation has received from the prime minister. Even if this careful planning protects us from the stain of irrefutable evidence, the list of culprits perpetuating this attack will be short, and India will doubtlessly top the list. There will be accusations and suspicions, and all manner of international fallout will follow this blast which, ironically, will produce no fallout of its own."

This got a laugh, even if it didn't really deserve one. "The prime minister has already taken our advice on disaster relief, and this will help alleviate the pandemonium and newsworthy footage of civil collapse which would only serve to heighten the critiques on the accused attacker."

This aspect of the plan was also quite clever: The prime minister had asked the Ministry of External Affairs (विदेश मंत्रालय) to prepare a massive shipment of relief supplies for those affected by a recent mudslide in Argentina – an event which, to date, had not been judged disastrous enough to make any international headlines. The prime minister's instructions had been to oversupply this affected area with several million tons of supplies, just in case no other international aid was forthcoming. "When I spent a year backpacking after finishing university, I fell in love with this region," he would lie.

Once the first wave of supplies were loaded on cargo jets, they would be asked to delay departure while "customs formalities" were resolved, and then, after the attack was over and several sections of Pakistan involuntarily re-entered the Stone Age, the cargo pilots would be informed they had a new and unexpected destination much closer to home. A few supplies would eventually be sent to Argentina, of course, but that would only be done to tighten up an otherwise dangling thread in the paperwork of the official narrative.

In the shrewd and unapologetic calculus of statecraft and existential politics, thunderous international condemnation that was based only on circumstantial evidence would have to coexist with the fact that India would be altruistically sending several billion dollars in humanitarian aid to Pakistan, and it would continue to show such kindness in the form of zero-interest loans to rebuild its digital infrastructure. No matter what public opinion looked like after mixing those two variables together, that outcome would be infinitely preferable to having their own country crippled. Perhaps more importantly, however, everyone in the major world capitals – as well as the pundits in their accompanying newsrooms – would notice that no one within the byzantine hierarchy of Pakistan's government ever pointed a finger back at New Delhi.

The reason for that silence would be simple.

Within two days of the strike, General Gupta would visit his counterpart in the Pakistani army—Lieutenant General Usman Farooq

– and both men would intuit the exact topic of this particular meeting before they arrived in the same room, and the meeting would be much shorter and simpler than any outsider might expect. Gupta would not express any concern at the plight of several million Pakistanis living without any hope of electricity, telecommunications, or internet, and Farooq would not demand an explanation. Gupta would not expect a thank you for not flattening Karachi and Rawalpindi, and Farooq would not intimate the hazards of reprisals. Instead, Gupta would look into Farooq's eyes from across the table so that his counterpart understood him perfectly: *What the hell were you thinking?* Then Gupta would ask, "Have you started distributing the supplies?" And then Farooq would know he could count on India to continue sending the essentials for as long as Pakistan kept saying "thank you" on camera and acting indignant whenever anyone asked who they blamed. Gupta knew that this would be a wound from which Farooq would never heal; a fine officer like him would go to his grave still feeling the shock from the moment his military power evaporated. He would never stop asking, "How did they know?"

Pakistan's total nonparticipation in the international outcry towards India would make the circumstantial evidence against them seem even weaker. Every police academy in the world taught the five core tenets of circumstantial evidence: Motive, opportunity, presence, fingerprints, and behavior. Did India have the motive to do this? That could only be established if Pakistan let international investigators begin poking around the scene of the crime at the airbase, and they would never do this because it would reveal what remained of a once-functional first-strike weapon they had been preparing to use. Did India have the opportunity? Yes, any sufficiently technical country could hypothetically orchestrate an attack like this, but opportunity offers essentially zero usable information when there is no conceivable motive. Did India have a presence in Pakistan? The commandos chosen for this mission did not technically exist in India, much less Pakistan – and their extraction plan through a country plunged into darkness and communications silence worked to their advantage. Would there be any fingerprints left behind? The benefit of this plan was that the weapon incinerated itself, which would certainly lead some to say that the lack of fingerprints meant only an extraordinarily sophisticated military could orchestrate such a thing – and this would narrow down the list considerably – but this speculation did not lend itself any additional concrete analysis. And what about India's behavior? In this case, the evidence was disproportionately tipped in India's favor – Gupta's military had not engaged in any hostilities with Pakistan for over a decade, and the Kashmir Conflict, although never pleasant, had not interrupted the small but consistent trade agreements and water sharing arrangements which were currently in place.

Whatever this weapon inside that Masroor hangar looked like, it would be dead very soon – and both the murder weapon and assassin would never be found.

As soon as the attack was finished, the Para commandos would see the surrounding area go dark and know the mission was completed. They would immediately drive their ATVs 5 miles due south along the Budnai Nala River (بڈنائی نالہ), which, fortunately was uncharacteristically deep right now thanks to particularly heavy rainfall the last two weeks. Underneath the small Mauripur Bridge (ماڑی پور پل) they would dump the ATVs into the water and board an inflatable Zodiac raft that would quickly and quietly carry them down the nine miles of dark waterway toward the open water of the Indian Ocean. Those would be the longest nine miles any of the men would ever travel. Once they reached the open water, they would take a southwest heading until they were over the horizon from Karachi, then suit up in scuba gear, scuttle the Zodiac, and swim for an additional hour before rendezvousing with the Kalvari-class stealth submarine (कलवरी-श्रेणी पनडुब्बी), the INS Vagsheer (वाग्शीर), which was outfitted to retrieve special operations units. To cross the horizon at sea level they would need to travel a minimum of 3 miles, and their swim would move them another mile past that. By then they would have a track on the Vagsheer and be ready for the pickup.

Gupta ran it all through again in his mind. He felt ready to do this.

That, he told himself, was good news considering he had given the order three hours ago.

28 JUNE

Before falling asleep the night before, Jordan had resolved it was time to drop below the radar, at least for a few days.

Maybe a week.

Probably almost certainly a week.

He had spent an hour the previous day at a camping supply store – "Just to get some context and think about some things," he told himself – and, after only a few minutes, he walked across the parking lot to an ATM, made an unusually large withdrawal, and went back to buy an extensive array of supplies. He reasoned that this was all stuff he needed anyway – Blaise was going to go camping several times this summer with his friends, and, on top of that, Scarlett and Josephine were overdue for their first overnight hike.

When he woke up, he told Sienna what he was thinking and, to their joint relief, realized they had both been thinking essentially the same thing. Sienna was not particularly eager for an entirely off-the-grid camping trip, but the Riley family really did need to drop off the face of the earth for a little while. Just in case.

Just in case.

The decision-making process wasn't terribly complex: If the Signal was back then the government was almost certain to have detected it. When it was detected, there'd be countless experts scouring every piece of data available. That search would eventually lead to a government official at an acronym-laden agency giving the order to make contact with past personnel involved with programs related to the Signal. Sienna would, on account of that fake vacation in 2018, be near the top of that list.

Unless the Signal suddenly went away.

But the likelihood of the Signal going away became less likely as time went on. Yesterday, Sienna had faintly and sporadically heard the familiar hum of the Signal throughout the day. It sounded almost as if it was playing on a small speaker in a room down the hall. Calista and Scarlett still felt a bit nauseous but had spent yesterday out and about with their normal activities. Their headaches came and went, and both had heard a few distant crackles, as well as a few flashes in their peripheral vision. They had accepted this as a nuisance that would probably clear up. Sienna had held onto the same hope until, on the way back from gymnastics, Scarlett suddenly sat bolt upright in the car and shouted "Whoa! Weird!" followed by a detailed and very hard-to-follow explanation of a shape she had just seen.

But the explanation was only hard for Josephine to follow.

Sienna had seen it many times. She had even described it in surprisingly similar terms to Torchy.

Now she knew that it was time to make some plans with Jordan.

This is what led Jordan to start looking at camping supplies.

What Sienna and Jordan soon learned was that common sense and spy movies combined to provide your average civilian with a solid baseline of knowledge about how best to disappear when you absolutely have to for the short term. This is why he withdrew cash in the event some government agency noticed a large expenditure of survival gear on his credit card and decided that this looked like the behavior of someone who suddenly had something to hide.

While the technical acumen of his planning might have been admirable, Jordan was well aware that, if viewed objectively from a distance, what he was doing and thinking looked like unadulterated paranoia. He thought about this as he slowly filled up his cart and half of another. He kept thinking about this the entire drive home. But, statistically speaking, almost zero paranoid people had a wife who had been a child actor in the espionage industry, nor did any of them have two daughters that appeared inclined towards the family business. But even that exculpatory explanation sounded *very* paranoid. He hoped this was the one time a seemingly circular argument was not a sign of faulty logic. But he was willing to be embarrassed about this later if it turned out nothing was bearing down on them; what he could not stomach was the idea of waiting for someone else to show up at his doorstep with orders for the fate of his wife and daughters.

The last thing he bought was a GPS off-trail navigator with a solar recharger. Its satellite connection wouldn't have his name attached to it, and there was no search effort on earth that could find this needle in the Pacific Northwest's many evergreen haystacks.

* * * * *

By the time he got home with a trunk and backseat full of gear, it was clear Sienna was thinking along the exact same lines.

"What about my Uncle Harvey?" she asked, as he walked into the kitchen from the garage.

"What about him?"

"He's somewhere deep in the Cascades, right?"

"Is he?"

"Something like that, yeah."

"I remember your dad and your aunt talking about him – but I wouldn't think he was still alive."

"I think he's still alive."

"How would you know that?"

"I know he had a cabin."

"A cabin? No – your dad said it was more of a doomsday bunker that is so deep in the woods it was crossed over into somewhere inside the National Forest."

"It sounds safe, and it sounds hard to find."

"It sounds hard for us to find."

"Hard for *anyone* to find, babe," she said, growing very serious.

"No thanks."

"Well," Sienna said pointing upstairs, "Calista saw something half an hour ago and it was jarring enough to almost make her throw up, so his semi-legal forest dungeon sounds great."

"Ok, but like I said – no one knows where it is."

"I know where we might find a clue," she said, staring back at him and waiting for him to figure it out.

"Where?"

"You already know." Now she was holding back a laugh.

"Not The Dumpster…" he said, with no attempt to conceal his disgust.

"The Dumpster" was the euphemistic name they used for a large, long-term storage unit in a decaying industrial district 45 minutes away. When Grandma Megan had died 13 years earlier at the age of 98, the contents of her heavily cluttered house had been claimed by no one, but the house itself had sold relatively quickly. Rather than take the contents of the house to a landfill, the executor of the estate had used money from the sale of the house to pay for long-term storage. To no one's surprise, Grandma had specifically called for this in her will. This led to no small amount of joking between Jordan and Sienna about how Grandma Megan's proclivity for hoarding was so acute that it extended beyond her own lifespan. The plan, as explained by the executor, was that Sienna would eventually sort through the material, select any items she wanted, sell the rest, and any profit gained from such sales would be hers to keep.

Sienna had earned this honor purely by being the last of the grandchildren to decline the opportunity.

The contents of this storage unit had sat untouched for those 13 years, and Sienna had visited it exactly once to pick up the keys after the movers had finished the 800-mile drive to fill this unit from floor to ceiling. At the time, she hadn't even bothered to open the door and look at what was in there. The lease on the unit was for 15 years, and, once that final day of the contract arrived, the contents would finally make their belated but inevitable arrival at a landfill. The fact that Grandma Megan had asked for such a long-term rental belied that she knew the ultimate fate of her collection.

"I hate this," Jordan finally said.

"Which part?"

"That you might be right."

"Wait, what? Why?"

"Years ago, your dad said that he and your grandma kept in touch with Harvey right up until the time she died."

"Yeah."

"If I remember right," Jordan said as he started to put his shoes back on, "in true Unabomber style your uncle sent and received sporadic letters from a P.O. box out in the middle of nowhere – I bet

The Dumpster still has all of them in a shoebox or something."

"So he might have told his mom something about where he was living."

"It's a stretch, babe."

"Let's go find out."

Jordan groaned. He hated this idea.

"You know this is dangerously close to turning into a caper, right?" Jordan tried to say without smiling. "This is going to end up as some combination of 'Enemy of the State' and 'Goonies.'"

"Get your keys, Sloth – we're going for a drive."

Ten minutes later they had started a movie and a pizza for the kids and were driving south to the storage unit.

What they found wasn't pretty, organized, or easy to navigate.

After 22 years spent tutoring reading at a high school, Grandma Megan spent retirement managing a half dozen gas stations, and the storage unit had several file cabinets packed with receipts, tax forms, and EPA inspections stretching back years. Stacked on top, around, and on every side of these cabinets were black garbage bags filled with clothes, boxes filled with plates and bowls, rolls of disintegrating carpet, photo albums packed with distant cousins no one recognized, a pair of coffee cans filled with screws and nails, piles of newspapers, heirlooms of unknown origin or importance, crates of cassette tapes, furniture from every room in her house, kitchen appliances that had been broken before Sienna was born, and a birdcage which hadn't had an occupant since the Nixon administration. And much more.

Being here now felt like walking into a broken kaleidoscope filled with scattered pieces of her grandmother's life – and that was essentially what was happening here. It felt odd, and it looked odd, but this was the best possible – and only available – place to start looking for any signs of a trail leading back to her long-lost uncle.

Sienna began thumbing through a dozen three-ring binders packed into a giant plastic tub, and Jordan started making his way through the file cabinets. An hour later Sienna was sorting through boxes of Christmas cards grandma had received in the '80s and paint swatches from some long-forgotten remodel, and Jordan had begun crawling over the top of upturned chairs, two mattresses, and a dining room table in order to reach her old desk that was pressed up against the back wall. The desk's top two drawers were empty except for some unused stationery, a ruler, and a few crumbling rubber bands – but when he strained to reach the drawer beneath the desktop, he spotted a vintage coin tray holding a keyring. In the shadows cast by the unit's sole light bulb he could faintly see a single key attached to the Oakland Raiders fob.

He grabbed the key and called for Sienna to look around for any cabinets or chests with a lock.

He threw her the keys and slowly began making his way in her direction. While he climbed, she tried the key on the one locked filing cabinet, but the key was much bigger than the rusted keyhole. Next, she tried a small wooden chest, but the key wouldn't turn there, either.

"Did you bring a hammer?"

"No," Jordan said, trying to free his foot from inside a truck tire.

"I need you to cave in the lid of this hope chest."

"I just saw a pile of bricks, hold on."

While he searched, she kept looking and found a battered cabinet beneath a box of old garden hoses and another full of magazine subscriptions and a broken VCR. It stood barely three feet tall, but it was at least six feet long, with two levels of wide, pull-out drawers.

To her surprise, the key turned in the lock.

The first drawer in the cabinet held income tax returns dating back 20 years, each separated in hanging folders. The next had a series of folders with the instruction manuals for every appliance she had ever owned. Each folder had a tab with a neatly hand-written title explaining its contents. The third drawer had more of the same, including old daily planners with even older addresses in them.

Jordan was still trying to reach the cabinet but had just put his foot through the top of a box that shattered the old popcorn popper within. Now he was on his hands and knees trying to fit under a broken foosball table stacked perilously high with dirty flowerpots.

Just as he was beginning to complain about how the sharp edge of a broken microwave door had cut his arm, Sienna noticed that the tab of the last file in the drawer was blank.

She spread the hanging folder open and saw it held a single item – an ancient looking tri-fold map printed by the National Forest Service. The date printed in the corner said "1972."

Jordan arrived just as she was laying the thick, heavily creased paper flat across an orphaned piece of patio furniture. In large capital letters printed along the top of the map it read "Snoqualmie National Forest," and Jordan's eyes followed the jagged outline of the territory that stretched from the Canadian border to the southern tip of the Puget Sound. He remembered just enough from 8th grade social studies to know that this was among the largest national forests in the country, and the 3,000 square miles of protected wilderness on this map represented some of the most densely forested and unexplored land in North America.

Near the middle of the map was a small, hand-drawn circle scrawled in faded ballpoint ink, and, beneath that circle, in the same careful lettering found on each file tab, was the word "Harvey."

Sienna sent Jordan back to grandma's desk to get the ruler, and, after a considerable amount of his complaining, she measured the legend in the bottom corner of the map to compare it to the size of the circle. She was assuming – likely erroneously – that the circle had somehow been drawn to scale. Some quick mental math determined the circle covered about 14 square miles, give or take an extra couple.

"I think this is where we go," Sienna said, sounding surprisingly certain about it.

"Babe, you said you haven't laid eyes on that guy since you were five, at, like, a wedding reception or something, right?"

"Yes."

"And this is where you want to go now?"

"It's perfect – no one knows where he lives."

"We don't know where he lives."

A moment passed with both of them still hunched over the large map. The unit was silent except for the buzz of the lightbulb over their head.

"We need somewhere to go, and we have to go *now*," she said.

"Your uncle might be there, and he might be alive, but that circle is at least four extremely long days of hiking from the place we would start from," he paused to find the point on the map closest to their house. Pointing at a spot a few miles inside the forest boundary, he said, "Starting from right about there, it is four really long days, and no one in this family qualifies as a wilderness survival expert."

But Sienna had made up her mind. The odds that someone as benevolent as Torchy was in charge of investigating the Signal right now was unlikely, especially if they knew everything he knew. Rather than wait to be told what to do, she was going to make the first move. And that move, against all reason and logic, was going to put them beneath a canopy of evergreen trees stretching up and over the Pacific Northwest's biggest mountain range.

"This is our chance to go, and this is our only place to go."

Jordan shook his head and slowly cracked a smile. It occurred to him that she was so wrong about this that she exceeded the natural limits of correctness and came back around to the other side of the spectrum where she started being right again. This framing made sense only to him.

He took a deep breath and nodded.

"Ok."

"Let's get home and get started. The smell in here is killing me."

There was some logic, he acknowledged, even if it was crammed into the cracks between his own red flags and hesitations. This boondoggle into the woods was going to suck. He and Blaise had both spent enough time deep in the woods to guide the rest of them. Sienna could grit her teeth through anything, Calista was tough, but Scarlett and Josephine would be in the unenviable position of just being along for the ride. For the little girls it would only have to be framed as an adventure. But Blaise and Cali would need to know why.

Considering how limited their options were, and considering how many problems could come find them at any moment, he knew that getting this far off the grid was the right move – but this was daunting in the extreme, to the point of recklessness. But, again, danger was preferable to a few of the worst possible outcomes they had hypothesized. And in three or four days anything that *could* blow over probably *would*.

Jordan folded up the map and smiled again.

"You're going to be really happy about a little shopping trip I took this morning."

28 JUNE

The F-22's landed at Kiska after a long but relatively uneventful flight from Elmendorf Air Force Base. The pilots had been instructed to fly much lower and much faster than usual to avoid the already incredibly remote possibility of detection by foreign radar, and with the understanding that flying so low to the surface of the ocean could improve their chances of getting lost in the overhead view of foreign reconnaissance satellites. The short-term hangars were waiting for them when they landed, along with all the supplies and tools necessary to troubleshoot the most common mechanical needs, should they arise.

For anyone watching from an overhead satellite, this would look like climatologists studying the remote permafrost, and Major Horn had instructed a series of messages to be sent back and forth on easily interceptable frequencies about a small civilian research team being given permission to study this remote area.

Three days earlier a small naval craft, disguised as a commercial trawler, had reached Kiska and accessed a series of storage compartments that had been drilled into a nearby hill during the occupation of the island following World War 2. Stored in this honeycombed granite block were a sophisticated series of rapidly deployable shelters that could be unpacked in about an hour and then, through a genuinely ingenious system of internal motors and pulleys, erect themselves into free-standing structures in a matter of minutes. Each of these structures was the size of a small warehouse meant to house 500 soldiers in uncomfortably close quarters, or, in this case, each could hold three F-22's with room to spare.

The structures had solar paneling woven into the roofing material, and the team sent to set this up had also brought enough generators to keep things running for at least a week of overcast skies. The supporting ribs of each structure also radiated heat in order to make the temperature livable in the winter, and the crossbars along the top had embedded LED's for light. Every time the logistical team set up a structure like this, one of them would observe that this technology would eventually be shrunk down for civilian use, and someone would make a fortune when camping, wedding receptions, church revivals, and probably circuses changed forever.

While these structures were being assembled a pair of C-12J Hurons – military passenger planes that could each carry 15 passengers plus gear – landed on the island carrying the mechanics and technicians who would ensure all normal flight support operations were accommodated. Later that night one of the gigantic Boeing C-17 Globemaster III cargo planes would depart on a routine flight from Misawa Air Base to Elmendorf, and, along the way it would drop a pallet with several hundred gallons of jet fuel, tools, and parts from high altitude over Kiska. The pallets were equipped with airfoils that would respond to wind and other atmospheric conditions in order to maneuver the payload to within 50 feet of its intended target on the makeshift airfield.

The advance team had also dragged in four large container cubes from those storage tunnels, and inside those were all the gear needed to sleep, occasionally shower, and maintain communication – as well as enough MRE's and stove fuel to keep eating for the foreseeable future.

About the same time those instant warehouses were assembling themselves at Kiska, six F-22 pilots from Elmendorf Air Force Base were receiving an above-top-secret briefing that was certain to be among the strangest – if not the very strangest – of their careers.

They were going to be told to do something no fighter aircraft had ever been expected to do – cross an ocean – and then hide under some type of giant pup tent and await further instructions. According to the intel officer who had flown here through the night from D.C. aboard a regularly scheduled Lockheed C-5 Galaxy cargo delivery flight, those further instructions had to do with an emerging situation on the Chinese-Russian border. And, notably, neither of those countries seemed to know what the other was planning, or that the other had any reason to plan something, or that there was a problem worth planning for in the first place.

These six were selected from the 47 F-22 pilots spread across the 90th and 525th Fighter Squadrons stationed at Elmendorf, and the leader of this detachment was Captain Cyrus Waldren, who was considered by his friends to be the best F-22 pilot stationed in Alaska, and, reluctantly, his rivals would admit the same thing. If you asked Cyrus, he would feign modesty while knowing in his heart that both assessments underestimated him.

The briefing had begun with, ironically, the part of the story which interested these pilots the least. According to this intel officer, several militaries – maybe more, and maybe a lot more – had detected tiny amounts of unusual interference in the electromagnetic spectrum. It was not yet clear if this interference was affecting the electromagnetic frequencies used by these militaries directly or just their ability to measure it – although the latter was, at the moment, considered less likely.

These pilots weren't particularly interested in foreign affairs that didn't have a meaningful need for air support, but they were professional enough to listen quietly.

"The big problem we have right now," he explained, "is that a small handful of powerful militaries are interpreting this interference in ways which project their worst fears about their own national security or the intentions of their enemies. It doesn't help that the civilian leaders in these cases aren't doing much to moderate those anxieties."

"There is more psychology afoot here than usual," Cyrus thought to himself.

As if on cue, the intel officer noted that, "The current responses we are monitoring are exposing more about the present military doctrine of each country than they would otherwise care to communicate so openly."

It also struck Cyrus as odd that any government would notice some static in its instruments and assume an attack was underway. The U.S. military, he thought, is generally wound pretty tight, but not tight enough to leap immediately to the conclusion that they're being attacked just because there's some fuzz in the instruments. His dad had been an engineering professor for 33 years in the SUNY system, and his mother, whose family had fled Iran when she was a teenager, still worked as a nurse. He thought of a story she often told about the favorite pastime of veteran nurses whenever a brand new physician, straight out of school, joined the staff: Watching from a bemused distance while the brilliant young doctor kept identifying exotic diseases to account for otherwise mundane symptoms. "When they hear the sound of hooves," she said, "they assume it's a zebra." But hooves, she would explain, are almost always just horses. According to this intel officer, China, and India in particular, were hearing zebras in every direction despite standing in a field full of ponies. Maybe even donkeys. But certainly not zebras.

"Our sources inside the Chinese government corroborate what we've found in our data intercepts: The interference observed by the People's Liberation Army has been interpreted by their scientists as the byproduct of faulty shielding around a directed-energy weapon. They are, in this regard, mistaken."

"Yep, zebras," Cyrus thought.

"We know they've done an audit on several sensors in order to reach this conclusion," the intelligence officer continued, "but the domestically produced sensors they use are notoriously low quality and this may be further muddying the waters for them." He paused for a moment as he struggled to make the slides in his presentation change. "So, what exactly is it that's causing this interference to begin with? We believe it is this train." He finally advanced the hastily made PowerPoint to the next slide and arrived at a satellite image of gently rolling hills in an otherwise featureless countryside that was crisscrossed by three lines of train tracks converging on a row of single-story buildings and then shooting out the other side in new directions.

"Those buildings are part of a military resupply point for the Russian army's (Сухопутные войска Российской Федерации) rail traffic, located about 15 miles north of the city of Birobidzhan (Биробиджан) in one of the country's easternmost provinces.

He paused to show a map of the regional railways. It meant very little to a group of pilots.

"We've flown two different satellites over this depot a total of five times, and our readings indicate, with an extremely high level of certainty, that what the Chinese currently detect are the contents of approximately 19 of the cars attached to this freight train. Our latest data shows the Chinese have also zeroed in on this train through their own reconnaissance, although they currently misinterpret the train's purpose." The satellite image slowly zoomed in to reveal a train, stretching about a half mile, parked at this remote Russian trainyard.

"This train is carrying spent fuel rods from the Bilibino Nuclear Power Plant (Билибинская АЭС). Bilibino has been in the process of decommissioning since 2019, and it has been sending its old fuel rods to the nuclear waste processing plant in Ozersk (Озёрск), about 3,000 miles to the west. The problem is that Bilibino is located up on the Kamchatka Peninsula (полуостров Камчатка) about 1,800 miles north of where it is now – which means that this train is very, very lost. A few of our experts at The Farm traced back the train lines, and it appears as if not one but two bad switches were thrown for this train, so *instead* of getting a bit off course, it has now gotten a lot off course – and it's been parked at this depot for the past three days waiting for instructions. The fact that they're a little over 90 miles from the border with China is adding to the tension in Beijing. The PLA high command is on the phone multiple times per day with their airbase in the region that hosts a squadron of J-10's, and now they're running patrols that follow the route of the border river about 10 times more often than normal."

Cyrus had already guessed that he and his pilots were going to be asked to reach that train before someone else did, and then… well, the second half of the mission was still unclear. But, so far, each new detail in this presentation led him to consider the additional dozen things he would have to do to get his team in and out of this situation cleanly – and, when it came right down to it, what he would have to say to call them off the mission so that he could do what had to be done.

"There are very few directed energy weapons actually in existence," the officer continued, "and they are all configured in dramatically different ways such that there is no readily identifiable energy signature to assign to this category of weapon and make its identification simple. The fuel rods on this train, however, are spewing radioactive energy that does not look anything like a fuel rod is supposed to look like – and this is what's confusing the PLA scientists. Nuclear fuel rods, under most circumstances, have a very predictable and easily identifiable energy signature throughout their lifecycle – but these specific rods from Bilibino were fabricated in the early 1970s, at a time when Russia's mastery of nuclear engineering and nuclear instrumentation was still, to put it charitably, 'a work in progress.'"

The slide changed to a cross-section diagram of a nuclear fuel rod. Usually this would have been enough to set everyone's attention adrift, but the pilots sensed that the reason they were headed to Kiska was still coming.

"The manufacturing flaws in the rods installed at Bilibino were particularly egregious, so much so that they have all leaked fissile material into the coolant of their respective reactors, and the experts tell me this leads to a type of highly radioactive plaque to build up on the rods themselves. Once that plaque has fully coated the rod it is fairly useless for producing energy, but it *is* a lot more likely to cause your reactor to overheat at a moment's notice. But, at this point, you have another big problem because when a rod is coated in cesium it's now doubly radioactive; and this makes the disposal process – both the handling and the transport – exceptionally difficult to do without losing containment and killing everyone within 30 miles."

The bad news did indeed keep stacking up.

"Unfortunately for the operators of that train, they have already been exposed to a fatal dose of radiation, and they may or may not be aware. Unfortunately for the rest of Russia, that lost train now appears doubly suspicious – it is far closer to the Chinese border than it has any business being, and it's on a stretch of track that leads directly to the Nizhneleninskoye-Tongjiang Bridge that crosses the Amur River into China. And, unfortunately for everyone, the Chinese interpreted this comedy of logistical errors as having all the telltale signs of a poorly executed sneak attack."

He returned to the overhead picture of the train.

"That defect in the radiation shielding on the train is allowing tiny amounts of gamma radiation to seep into the area, and the PLA scientists analyzing that data are making two mistakes: First, they think it's the source of the interference they're picking up, and, second, the energy doesn't look like fuel rods, so they draw other conclusions. So, we're left with the Chinese believing this is a mobile weapons platform, and they see it pointed towards a bridge that happens to have a highly secretive Chinese research center on the other side. It doesn't matter that Russia doesn't know about the existence of that facility, and it ultimately won't matter that China doesn't know what Russia doesn't know – what we do have, however, is enough connected dots for the PLA to see an attack in the works."

Now things began to click into place for Cyrus and, to varying degrees, the other pilots as well. The Russian military had been hopelessly disorganized for as long as Russia had possessed a military, and, from a historical view, it made no difference whether it was commanded by the duchy, the tsars, the Bolsheviks, or whatever you wanted to call its current power structure. This situation presented a perennially disorganized military apparatus attempting to navigate a chronically mismanaged and remote area of the country, at a time when its attention was directed elsewhere. But to be fair, in a place as massive as Russia, being a couple thousand miles off course wasn't actually that bad if you were carrying potatoes or tractor parts. But this current turn of events paired Russia's unique capacity for failure with something very well suited to turn disastrous.

"Right now, there is no place for that train to turn around between where it's currently sitting and a trainyard about three miles north of the Amur River. That means it is going to continue traveling south towards the crossing with the plan to use that turnaround point – and every step of the way it's going to be looking more and more like an energy weapon heading toward its target, and China is going to get increasingly antagonistic with each passing mile. When the train gets to within line of sight of their research facility – which in this area is about two miles – they will likely have already reached a crescendo of tension and apprehension, and in the assessments of our experts, they will have made a strike on the train long before that point. Based on the way they've ramped up their patrols with their local fighter squadron, that strike will likely come from an air-to-surface missile, and putting a near-hypersonic missile into the side of a train car full of unusually poisonous fuel rods – that's another name for a dirty bomb detonating on the border of two nuclear superpowers." He paused and looked up, "Off the record I'll add this datapoint: Really long wars start for reasons only 1% this bad."

Now Cyrus understood the nature of this mission and its implications made him feel ill.

The intelligence officer paused for a moment to consider the next portion of this briefing. On the plane he had thought of a half dozen ways to broach the subject, but none of them were particularly inspiring. Not that this briefing was asking for volunteers.

"One obvious question is, 'Why not tell the Chinese what's happening? And why not tell the Russians what they're doing?' The simple fact is that the geopolitical events of the last three years have closed many of those diplomatic back channels, and, of separate importance, is the fact that our ability to gain all of the data you have heard in this briefing would throw both countries into turmoil if they were to learn that we had penetrated their communications networks sufficiently enough to gather this information in the first place. To be clear, Russia already knows we can do this; China is suspicious that we can, and they would react poorly if we confirmed it for them. Even if we were to obfuscate the origins of the information, they would almost certainly conclude the extreme level to which they are compromised, and an unacceptable amount of political turmoil would still follow, to say nothing of permanently disrupting our current intel-gathering practices. On one hand, you can fairly consider that preventing an international conflict is a good time to use this information, but, at the present time, this situation has not been determined to meet the standard required to tear down the decade of work it has taken to get this far inside. Instead, the six of you have been selected by your commander to provide the Department of Defense with an alternate means of situational control."

He switched screens to show a map with a dotted line to indicate the flight path between the far edge of the Aleutians and a thin blue ribbon of river deep within the Asian continent.

In terms of the next phases of this operation, in the event this situation escalates, and assuming diplomatic channels fail, your interdiction will require you to follow an approximation of this course: You will takeoff from the island, head southwest, skirt past the radar installations in the Kuril Islands, refuel mid-air off the coast of Hokkaido, then sprint across the Sea of Japan, make landfall in Russia, cross into China, evade radar, prevent a strike on the train – followed by a rapid extraction and then you hightail it back home."

The intel officer acknowledged that this list of bullet points overlooked the incredible amount of planning that would be necessary to make something so audacious become feasible. Some of this planning was already underway, and much of it would come from Captain Waldren and his commander as they expanded on the plan over the next 36 hours.

For now, all the political questions and the much-needed discussions about the basic philosophies of international autonomy and statecraft were set aside.

When the pre-flight checks were done later that day, the Raptor pilots spoke quietly underneath one of the jets and noted that they were essentially being asked to prevent World War 3 by starting World War 3. They wondered aloud if the rationale was that if two nuclear powers were about to descend into war then it might be better if a third nuclear power was the one to kick things off and scare away the others? This was, they mused, the kind of thinking which had made World War 1 possible once all the secret alliances ensured everyone started fighting at once.

The intel officer was decidedly non-committal on what to expect next.

"Because this situation continues to unfold, I cannot at this time elaborate on a concrete mission outcome or mission parameters. Those will be forthcoming as this situation develops. Your role is to stand by."

With that, they were dismissed. And with that, Cyrus acknowledged that this plan was, in technical terms, absolutely ridiculous.

Each particular step of the plan was functional in a laboratory or a simulator, but stringing them together like this was outrageous in the extreme. It didn't help that no one was ready to say what the people planning this were obviously thinking: At some point a Chinese pilot was going to try and put a missile into the side of that train, and, as soon as that happened, the surrounding countryside was going to glow in the dark for the next two centuries. But the ecological disaster was going to be overshadowed by the shootout that those two superpowers were likely to have immediately afterwards. Russia was going to be reacting to what was, technically, an unprovoked attack based on accusations that they were unambiguously innocent of. China was, understandably, not going to believe this explanation and they would assume something far more insidious was afoot when they heard Russia's denials. It would only take a matter of minutes for satellites to examine the radiation spread all over the wreckage of the train and know definitively that it was defective fuel rods spread all over those tracks – but what were the odds either military would stop to listen at that point? China would be on the front foot and looking to press their advantage in this foiled Russian attack; Russia would be wounded and looking to make a proportional response of their own – if not something woefully disproportionate to conciliate their bruised egos. That back and forth would likely continue to get uglier with each teeter of that totter.

This meant a Raptor was supposed to be in the air and several thousand miles from home whenever that J-10 pilot was told to line up and fire at that ill-fated train. Cyrus wasn't as worried about his safety relative to the J-10 – Chinese pilots simply did not compare to anyone behind the stick of a Raptor, and, from a strictly technical perspective, the only people who believed the J-10 belonged in the same sentence as the F-22 were all located in mainland China and weren't pilots. What worried Cyrus was the combination of everything that had to happen in order for this operation to be remotely successful: First, the Raptor would have to weave through Chinese and Russian radar – a network of over 100 installations between the coast and their target area – and, statistically speaking, at least one of which would catch some faint trace of him. Technically, the F-22 should be able to defeat the entire air defense system, but that was a tall order.

No, he thought to himself as he considered it more, *maybe* he could weave through all that radar if conditions were just right and everything went his way.

And then there was the problem of having to sort through whatever type of engagement was looming once he arrived, and then start making critical decisions with no available time to second guess his assessment of the situation. And, after all of this, there was the matter of getting all the way back to Elmendorf in one piece with the Raptor possibly being chased by other fighters that were much slower and anti-aircraft missiles that were much faster. It helped that the Raptor would be nearly invisible, but once one missile got a lock, the rest would have a much easier job picking him up. This is why he already knew he wasn't going to let the other five pilots make this trip.

Later that evening, the pilots gathered again in the same briefing room for a status update and a primer on regional events contributing to the brewing conflict. In an earlier era, the strategists would not have considered teaching the men holding the spears the nuances of geopolitics, but this kinder, gentler era of the military saw education as a tool that could potentially sharpen the point of those spears.

"All of the information in today's briefings has rested upon an underlying state of affairs, and that specific state of affairs colors everything the Pentagon has been analyzing up to this minute. There are presently domestic problems afoot within China which can best be characterized as 'catastrophic,' and the nature of those particularly calamitous problems are what has led that country's leadership to see existential threats everywhere they look." The intel officer paused to clear his throat and load a slide that was heavy with text.

"None of us are politicians or economists, but pilots have often been the tip of geopolitical spears, and that is why it is important for you to understand something about the motivations of the senior leaders of China's government and military. There is the possibility that you will find yourself in the middle of a multivariate international incident, and you need to know at least the basics of those variables in the event you have to start making hard choices at Mach 2."

Cyrus started to laugh and made it sound like a hard cough.

"Last year all of you were required to watch a 75-minute lecture that was commissioned by the Department of Defense as part of your ongoing 'Officers Operational Education' courses," he paused and waited to see looks of recognition on the faces of these pilots. "In the files for your squadron, your commander certified that all of you were present for this class." There were more stares. "Assuming you did take this class, I can offer a brief refresher."

Cyrus remembered watching the video, and he knew his wingman, Will LaChappelle had watched it, but it seemed like they were the only ones.

The lecture had been delivered by an eminent geopolitical analyst, and it painted a dour picture of China's future. It was the type of bleak outlook that could make a country's leadership do impetuous and reckless things in the name of survival.

The dire nature of China's current predicament had started over 50 years ago, the analyst explained, and the grisly details had been an open secret amongst demographers for at least 30 years – but the nature of the problem was so extreme it had never been discussed in the mainstream for the simple reason that the facts seemed impossible.

The short version was this: Within 15 years China would no longer exist.

To be clear, the analyst had made sure to stress, the landmass we know as "China" would still be there, there would still be people there, but what would remain would no longer resemble the current national entity that we call "the country of China." The reasons for this were incredibly simple compared to the shock-value of the statement.

The seeds of this collapse had been planted by Mao Zedong (毛泽东) decades earlier when a one-child-per-family policy (一孩政策) was put in place due to a fear that a population explosion would result in a country that his recently formed communist government could not feed. The result was multiple generations of people having very few children, and, simultaneously, as medical practices improved, all the older people kept living long beyond their accustomed lifespans. This resulted in modern-day China earning the strange distinction of having the fastest aging population in human history at the same time it had the fewest children in history.

The collapse of China as we know it was not a matter of China being unwilling to try to survive, he explained, it is simply a math problem demonstrating that they do not have enough people or time to pull out of this population nosedive.

As part of the presentation, he explained the basics of this math: For a country to remain at a stable level of population, every family – but, really, it could be reduced to just mothers – had to produce 2.1 children. Having 2.1 children would effectively replace the mother and father and take into account the 1 out of every 10 people who die before reaching adulthood or never have children of their own. According to data published by the Chinese government's own demographers, China's birth rate was now 1.16, which, when compared to all the social data gathered worldwide throughout history, was the lowest birth rate the earth had ever seen. But that number hid the fact that in China's most densely populated areas the number was 0.7, and in major cities like

Shanghai and Beijing the number was below 0.6. Further compounding this dangerously compounded situation was the fact that, on top of China's birthrate dropping by 85% during the 40 years of the one-child policy, between 2017 and 2021, as the communist party further tightened its grip on free speech and humanitarian issues, the birth rate dropped *again* by yet *another* 70%.

There were simply not enough people of child-bearing age to replace the hundreds of millions who were now reaching retirement and the end of their natural lifespans.

The most recent census data from China's own social scientists discovered that the government had been over-reporting their population by about 100 million, and the actual number sat at about 1.3 billion. This meant India had surpassed them in population over a decade ago without anyone knowing it, and, if China's birth rates stayed the same or only improved slightly, by 2050 that total population number would drop to 650 million simply as a result of people reaching old age naturally. It went without saying that a drop like this – a full 50% – was unprecedented. And that drop assumed that there were no other problems with famine, energy policy, or disease. And, it turned out, each of those problems already loomed ominously in the distance.

This dramatic drop off was rooted in the unique combination of the one-child policy's short-sightedness and the incredible success of China's industrialization in the mid- to late-20th century. No country in history had ever industrialized anywhere near as quickly and efficiently as China did, but now all the talented laborers who had made this revolution possible were about to leave the workforce en masse through retirement – and they had produced so few children during their busy careers that there was not a wave of younger workers coming up behind them to sustain the economic growth their generation had pioneered. More people in China were above age 45 than below, and every year more people retired than graduated from college.

China was not the only country facing a population crisis like this – places like Japan, Korea, Germany, Italy, Belgium, and especially Russia were all facing similar problems – but none of those were quite so pronounced or had quite so far to fall.

The shrinking pool of workers, according to the analyst, meant that every passing day China had less and less highly skilled labor. For this reason, unfortunately, China's manufacturing sector would not survive more than another decade due to the fact that there were not enough people available to staff a sophisticated manufacturing or tech hardware industry. This analyst pointed out, for example, that even if China followed through on its threats to invade Taiwan and take control of the nation's lucrative semiconductor factories, there were not enough Chinese workers with high-end electrical engineering or software architecture training to operate those facilities.

And then there was the invisible hand which had helped support China's supercharged economy for the preceding decades: The United States Navy. The analyst explained that the world's oceans are a dangerous place unless there is constant policing, and, from 1945 to 2024, the U.S. Navy had patrolled the world's shipping lanes so that international commerce – and, by extension, American foreign policy – could thrive on a global scale. No one benefitted from a safe ocean more than China, and they used it to outgrow and outsell everyone else. But, after years of aggressively undercutting American businesses with cheap goods exported on a safe ocean, America eventually began to draw back this safety net. China did extraordinary things with its revenue during that long window of opportunity, but one thing it did not do was plan for the future – and now that astounding lack of preparation was laid bare. This economic titan had a foundation it did not control.

The U.S. Navy also played a role in China's reliance on imported food and energy. Specifically, as China grew more hostile to its neighbors, it faced the very dangerous proposition of having its inbound shipping lanes cut off. An embargo can be serious even under the best of conditions, but it turned out that for China it would be uniquely disastrous.

At the current time, the analyst noted, pointing to a chart, China imports about 90% of its gasoline and other energy sources, and it imports about 85% of its fertilizer to grow crops. This meant that if China ever did something serious to provoke a war, its enemies could win without ever firing a shot by simply setting up a perimeter 1,000 miles from shore and preventing cargo ships from entering Chinese ports. Considering China had chronically mismanaged its storage of fuel and food over the years, their backup supply wouldn't last long, and the impact of an embargo became another simple math problem:

After the last cargo ship arrived, it would take less than a year for China to be left without electricity or functioning cars. Commerce would revert to the way it had been before the industrial revolution. It seemed too perilous to be possible, but the prospect of an entire nation trying to operate without gasoline or electricity was unavoidable in this situation, no matter how difficult it was to imagine.

The perilous nature of China's food supply was even scarier. Among agriculture experts and soil scientists, China was objectively known to have some of the lowest quality farmland in the world. For this reason, China had always existed on a razor's edge of food surpluses throughout its multi-millennium history, and their folk tales featured countless stories of starvation to drive home the point. But, even in the modern era, and in comparatively more prosperous times, incredible efforts still had to be made to feed the country. China used in excess of five times more fertilizer per acre than the global average just to coax sufficient crops from their fields – and this made it no surprise that China was the world's largest importer of fertilizer, on top of needing to import millions of tons of additional food.

With this information as a baseline, the math became terrifying: There are well-established calculations to determine how many daily calories a family needs to survive, and that number is easily extrapolated to a country of 1.3 billion. Modern agricultural methods provide equally well-established calculations to determine how many calories each acre of Chinese farmland can produce with and without fertilizer. Famine relief efforts have also developed precise metrics to gauge how many daily calories a person needs to narrowly avoid death by starvation. With all of that calculus available, the analyst somberly presented this fact: If China's supply of imported fertilizer is ever cut off, the famine which would shortly follow would kill 500 million people in 10.5 months.

This scenario, impossible as it seemed, illuminated just how drastically exposed China was to extreme levels of risk, and the extent to which it could be taken advantage of by a potential enemy interested in exploiting these weaknesses. This possibility was something the country's leadership was certainly aware of, and, understandably, when your country has such extreme vulnerabilities, it becomes natural to perceive any threat as an existential threat.

With a future this grim, war was not the worst outcome this country could encounter.

This made them unusually predisposed to violently protect what was left and proactively search out threats with an intensity that could obscure how many of their purported aggressors were imaginary. Within the demographic community, discussions were already afoot about China's unenviable and mind-bending distinction of being the first nation to know it was going to disappear. And it appeared that when the numbers tell you that your future does not exist, the certainty of a war can come as a relief because it ensures there is something left to do. This uniquely macabre certainty can provide a panicked leadership with a modicum of control in the sense that they could choose where and when their civilization dies rather than waiting for the light to go out unexpectedly. The paranoia induced by this fact led it to see a monster in every closet, and a boogeyman around every corner, and an impossible-for-the-Russians-to-build super weapon on a decrepit train.

The political fallout from this action would, ironically and tragically, put China back in a position of dying at a time that wasn't of its choosing.

"All of this makes China a very dangerous enemy to have right now, and their anti-aircraft capabilities make entering this airspace incredibly difficult," the intelligence officer concluded.

The decision-making aspect of this mission, Cyrus realized, was going to be just as dangerous as the flying once he started getting close to the target area. This would all play out so fast – both in terms of how the situation unfolded in real time, as well as how fast he would be moving as he chased a J-10 racing at maximum warp. There would not be enough time for anyone at Elmendorf and certainly not the Pentagon to understand what was happening in the moment or make the final call about what to do. If and when a J-10 achieved missile lock on that train it would be up to him to decide whether or not to put that bird on the ground and then directly involve the U.S. in this war – or he could be the pilot who watched the start of a regional war that would likely kill a billion people before the shooting finally stopped and the skies were black.

* * * * *

Sixty minutes after this briefing concluded, in a hangar 2,300 miles from the makeshift airstrip in Kiska, Wáng Xuěméi was listening to an updated briefing with many of the same details from the one Cyrus had just heard – but with those pieces arranged to create a much different shape.

The nature of the briefing did not come as a total surprise, albeit many of the supporting facts were new or improved. Two days earlier, all the missiles on the Vigorous Dragons had been swapped out for air-to-surface KD-88 missiles. The Dragon was a multi-function fighter that could engage targets in the air or on the ground, and they typically flew with a mixture of armaments, but now they carried nothing but weapons that were designed to aim at the ground. Every patrol along the Amur River carried the KD-88's now, and any pilot not scheduled to fly a patrol spent the day on the firing range 100 miles to the north making sure they could still hit a bullseye more often than not.

Today's briefing, as prepared by the Ministry of State Security, began with a history lesson on Chinese-Russian cooperation through the decades, and on the ways this relationship had soured in recent years behind the scenes while still remaining warm on the surface. A variety of reasons were shared for this, including the effects of Western imperialist thinking on this former communist ally. After 15 minutes the Commissar arrived at the satellite photo of the long train – still sitting at the depot where they had last seen it. "Our intelligence understands that the weapon and its component parts, as well as its power supply, is modularly assembled across these six containers on the train." He used his laser pointer to indicate a set of train cars near the front of the assembly.

The image changed again to show a map with three arrows pointing at key locations – one was easily recognizable to this group as the location of this airbase. The second was the current location of the train, and the third was the Nizhneleninskoye-Tongjiang Bridge. Xuěméi was struck by how, when you looked at this map from an elevation in the upper atmosphere, those three points were surprisingly close together.

Whatever did end up happening between those three spots would be over fast once it happened.

Now that specific areas of the train were identified, this discussion had changed from "threat evaluation" to "target prioritization."

The Commissar had been the one speaking at least half the time in these recent briefings – and this was another sign that this engagement had moved from being solely tactical to now encompassing a dual purpose that centrally featured the political. Depending on how you chose to absorb this information, one of those things was much more dangerous than the other.

"For reasons we cannot begin to understand," the Commissar said righteously, "the Russian aggressors are planning a senseless attack with the intention of compromising the peace and prosperity China wishes to offer to this region and to the world. Our interests at the Nanzhing Commercial Complex are simply too important to be compromised by an unprovoked attack, and for this reason the weapon mounted on this train, as well as any research facilities it uses, must be destroyed in the event it moves one inch toward Chinese soil."

The inclusion of "research facilities" to the list of targets was new. Under normal circumstances it might be possible that this was just a rhetorical flourish added to make the scope of a mission seem even more substantial, but Commissars were trained to read and say exactly what they had been told without any inference or interpretation – and this Commissar seemed the particularly devout type.

The Commissar concluded by informing the pilots that ongoing mission prep and air-to-ground missile training could supersede all additional training and responsibilities until further notice. This led to some side-eye contact amongst the pilots in lieu of outright smiles. Every member of the People's Liberation Army was required to dedicate 30% of their training time to political training – which consisted of attending lectures about the value of single-party communism and the inherent threats of democracy and free-market capitalism, as well as reading essays written by the current leader of the party. This material was all very serious and sanctimonious, and it was written as if intended for children, and it overlooked the simple fact that nearly everyone in the PLA loved western culture and music, wished they could go to college in the U.S. and stay for a few extra years, and they would begrudgingly admit that western movies were dramatically better than anything getting made at Hengdian World Studios (橫店影視城), with the exception of Jackie Chan and Chow Yun-fat's (成龍 and 周潤發) unimpeachable back catalog of classics.

These thoughts were all creeping back into her mind after a long period spent alone in her apartment quietly writing.

> *Today is your birthday, Little Bear. I am proud to say that I held you every day of your life; there was not one night we spent apart. Your grandparents wanted to send me on a holiday to relax, but I brought you both times! You sat under my umbrella on the beach, you kept trying to eat the sand, you cried when the swans would not let you touch them.*
>
> *I wish you were here today, you could have told me what present you wanted, and I would have found it – no matter what.*
>
> *I am trying to imagine what you would look like now, and what your voice would sound like. When I close my eyes I can see pictures of you in places we never went, at ages you never reached. I think of you and I project my motherhood into the future, but I am still alone when I get there. In my room I hang photos of all the places I wanted to take you. Places I can never go to now because I promised we would go together.*

She stopped writing for a moment. Something felt strange. She read the last few sentences and spotted it immediately: She was musing on about the future. Days ago, and without noticing it, Xu had stopped speaking in the future tense entirely; it had happened the moment she saw the picture of that Russian train. Something deep within her knew that lonely locomotive was the end.

> *I know I will see you soon, Little Bear. I do not know how, but I know there are very few letters left to write, and I will bring you the last one myself.*
>
> *There are so many things I have to tell you. We will go find the days we should have shared. I want to find the people we both should have become. I want to grow old with my husband and watch you find the things that make you happy.*
>
> *On this day, I held you in the hospital, wrapped in a soft blanket, and your father and I cried tears that ran down your cheeks while you slept. On this day I made you a cake with too*

much frosting, and you put both your hands into it. Today I wish I could read to you, but I can only write to you.

Xuĕméi had already worked with her commander to ensure she was flying or designated as the stand-by pilot for as many patrols as possible, and she was happy to let them think this was zeal or patriotism or an eagerness to do her duty. As long as she was strapped into the cockpit when the call came, that was all that mattered. There were reliable reports that the Russians had installed an incredible amount of anti-aircraft weaponry along the border that was ingeniously well hidden; if that were the case, then her intercept course would almost certainly be a one-way route, and this gave her no pause.

While she watched the flame consume the stationary there was peace found in knowing she was ready to find her son when the time arrived.

28 JUNE

Later that night, after returning from Grandma Megan's storage unit, the time had finally arrived to gather the kids together.

Part of the story would be Sienna's to tell.

That story was about the past.

The second half of the discussion would be much different, much less abstract, and focus on their immediate future.

That story was about the forest.

Sienna called Scarlett and Josie in from their fort in the backyard – which was absolutely not just a tool shed with a workshop light hooked to the ceiling – and Jordan got Blaise and Calista from their rooms upstairs.

There was no normal or stress-free way to unexpectedly call six people together for a family meeting in the living room, and, quite naturally, the kids' minds raced to determine if the forthcoming news would be something terrible and life changing or powerfully mundane.

"Did one of our grandparents die?" Blaise asked.

"Is one of you dying or pregnant?" asked Scarlett, who was taking this less seriously than the rest.

"Are we moving?" Josie asked, with great concern.

Cali stared at the ground and waited. Her speculations were bad enough that she didn't care to voice them. She also preferred to be told what was happening rather than flail with guesses.

"No, not any of those," Sienna said, forcing a smile.

"Right, it's not those," Jordan added, "but your mom and I want to talk to you about something we're going to do tomorrow."

There was no need to build up to it, he reasoned – just get to the punchline first.

"Tomorrow we're going to take a trip. A really big camping trip and hike, and it's something we hadn't planned on doing until the last couple days. I'm going to tell you the reason why, but that reason comes at the end of a story that your mom is going to tell you, and it's important you hear that first."

Sienna leaned forward, put her elbows on her knees, and clasped her hands. The two little girls were sitting on either side of her on the couch, each clutching one of her forearms, and Blaise was sprawled out on the carpet – although this last sentence from Jordan had sufficiently roused his attention such that now he had pulled himself up on one elbow. Cali was on the loveseat a few feet away, directly behind Blaise, her arms crossed.

"When I was about Josie's age I started hearing and seeing things – weird flashes of light and crackle sounds, like what Cali and Scarlett have been having. It wasn't serious, I wasn't sick – just like you girls aren't sick – but your grandma and grandpa took me to a doctor just to check it out, and we learned something really weird."

She had been making an effort to look at each of her kids individually as she spoke, and she and Jordan both noticed the tear that had already quietly slid halfway down Cali's cheek. Of all the kids she was the most mature, the most introspective, and, by a large margin, the biggest worrier. This story's first 20 seconds had already convinced her something was terribly wrong. Josie was an empath who was always taking the temperature of a room, and she now crawled up on Jordan's lap to be safe from wherever this story was going.

"And I just want to emphasize that I was perfectly healthy; I never spent a single night in a hospital for this, just like you girls are both fine. But the weird thing they found was I had this tiny ridge on the back of my brain that didn't really do anything for me – but eventually I found out it acted like an antenna for a type of radio."

"What?!" Blaise burst out, half laughing but mostly feeling equal parts relieved and incredulous that this was the reason for the sudden summoning of everyone to the living room this late at night. "Like the people who have metal plates on their skull who pee their pants or forget their name whenever you turn on the microwave?"

"I don't think that's a thing, but, no, not like that," Jordan added quickly so that Sienna could get through the story with as few breaks as possible.

"Some people from the government found out about the scan of my brain, and they came to ask me to be a part of a team that listened to messages that were being sent by this secret radio that the Russians had built. Like, their spies used it to talk, and so America wanted to hear what they were saying."

"They just showed up at your doctor? Like 'Men in Black'-style out of nowhere?" Blaise asked again.

"Yeah, they did just kind of show up randomly at my checkup. But they weren't scary – it was just two of them, and one of them was wearing those same shoes you and your dad love."

"Did you have to go to some creepy underground bunker to be a part of their secret group?" Josie asked, still on her dad's lap.

"Lucky for me, the headquarters of this program was only about 45 minutes from where I lived, and I ended up being a part of it for about a year-and-a-half."

"Was it underground?" Josie asked?

"No, it was at an old campsite with cabins, but it was very, *very* secret – so I lived there the whole time."

"What were you doing the whole time?" Scarlett asked.

"The guys who ran this secret program explained it all the first time I met with them: The Russians – and back then it was called 'The Soviet Union' – had this special kind of radio that no one on our side could hack into and listen to what they were saying. But, as luck would have it, if you had this type of tiny ridge on the back of your head, it acted like an antenna and you could hear bits and pieces of voices, and sometimes an image that was getting sent back and forth."

All the kids were hung up on the idea of an antenna in someone's brain. Two of them were starting to worry about where and when and how they and their current condition would enter this story. But crowding out those questions was another one that Blaise framed in his uniquely 14-year-old way.

"You – and no disrespect – but *you* were a part of a super-secret government spy program? As a *kid?*"

"Yeah, and so we listened and looked at the small pieces of words or pictures that came across this type of radio wave, and we repeated everything we saw to these scientists who ran the program."

"Was it so sad and scary there?" Scarlett asked, thinking of movies she had seen.

"No, it was actually really fun there, and they made it a fun place for kids."

Josie had buried her face in her dad's shoulder at this question, and this answer was a relief.

"There were other kids there?" she asked.

"Yeah, there were usually around 20 kids there who all randomly had that same little ridge on the back of their brains."

"Did you ever miss your family?"

"Yeah, sometimes, but, because they lived close by, I could still see them every once in a while, and we would go home during holidays."

"How much information did you find out about Russians?" Calista finally asked.

"I wasn't actually that good at it, but I think the people who ran the program liked that I was a hard worker, and I was always willing to keep trying. But I never really heard or saw any Russian stuff – just a lot of tiny pieces of things that must have been a part of something much bigger. There were other people at the camp who picked up on a lot more than I did. At night we'd hang out and talk about it, and I definitely was not seeing the coolest stuff on a regular basis."

"You should have had a microchip or something implanted into your brain so you could process the data better," Blaise offered.

"Totally."

"And then what happened? Why did you stop?" Cali asked.

"So, that ridge on the back of the brain could only act like an antenna for a short amount of time because when you're a kid your body is growing so fast – so, you grow into being able to hear that radio wave and then you eventually grow out of it. And when you're done growing, they say, 'thanks for your help!' and you get to go home and just go back to being a normal kid. Simple as that. And then that secret radio stopped broadcasting about a year after I was done, so then there wasn't anything left for anyone to listen to anymore."

"And they just let you go home from a secret government program? They didn't swear you to secrecy?" Scarlett asked.

"Oh, they definitely made you promise to keep things a secret – but they did that before they let you even start. And there were some other things to make sure you could keep a secret, but everyone there was the type of kid who was super proud to be doing this kind of thing, so they were all happy to keep this a secret."

"But you're telling us now." Blaise said flatly, but without trying to conceal the question underneath: Why are you telling us about this *now*?

"The reason why I'm telling you about this now comes back to what Cali and Scarlett have been feeling these last few days."

She paused and looked at the girls. She could tell they were trying to piece things together, and she knew their anxiety was deepening every moment they spent uncertain, so now she was hurrying towards the end.

"It seems like this little ridge of mine runs in the family" she said tapping her head. She turned to Scarlett and Cali, "I've seen flashes of the same things you've seen these last couple days, and the sounds and crackles you're hearing are all the same ones I remember. There's nothing wrong with you, but I still want you to know why it's happening."

"And what does this have to do with a camping trip?" Calista asked in monotone and full of dread.

Sienna and Jordan met eyes, and Jordan answered.

"It's really been exhausting for you and Scar to be hearing and seeing these things and feeling nauseous from it, and it's been tough on your mom, too – so I want us to get outside and try to relax for a few days."

Sienna turned to Josie and Scarlett and asked if they wanted to watch two episodes of *Bluey* before bed. They didn't even respond before running from the room. Josie stopped at the top of the stairs to the basement to ask her mom again if she felt ok, and Sienna assured her that she did.

As soon as the door closed behind them, Jordan turned back to Blaise and Cali.

"That radio wave that your mom was listening to when she was a kid went away, and now it's back. There's a lot of governments who have probably noticed, and all of them are going to want answers. Our government is going to be sorting through their old files of everything they know or used to know about it, and it's safe to say that it's only a matter of time until they come ask your mom to get involved in one way or another. That could be anything from a friendly visit and a couple quick questions, or it could be something like getting involved in another secret program somewhere. But your mom and I don't want to wait around to find out which of those things it will be."

Calista's face darkened and she put her palms on her forehead. Blaise was shocked at the various turns this story had taken, most notably this one which presented his dad as someone who wanted to go on the run.

Sienna didn't know exactly how to thread the needle between telling her kids this was just a precaution and helping them see the gravity of the situation and the associated need to take that precaution.

"I really, *really* don't think anything is going to happen, you guys," she said, "but, if I was wrong, the downside is so big – and now with you and your sister tapping into it.. Your dad and I need to put some distance between us and this situation until that radio wave is gone again."

"So, then what exactly are we running from?"

"From… from unpredictability. That's the best way I can put it," Sienna said.

"I don't want any of you to be here when someone shows up and tells you to come with them to some unknown place for some unknown amount of time," Jordan added.

"And we're not so much running as camping."

"We can go camping and drop off the edge of the planet for a few days – and if your mom and I are right, then we avoided a big problem, and if we were wrong then we just had a really nice time in the woods."

"So, we just head to the mountains?" Cali asked without looking up.

"Well, yeah," Jordan said, surprised, "your mom has an uncle that lives way up in the Cascades, so we'll hike out to him, hang out, then come back."

"*You* have an uncle that lives here?" Cali snapped.

"Yes."

"Which uncle?" Blaise asked.

"Harvey."

"I've never heard of him."

"He's been up there a long time."

"Where does he live?"

"He lives right about –" she paused to reach for the map.

"You don't know where he lives?" Blaise interrupted, back to full incredulity.

"I have a map to the general area where he was living back when he and my grandmother were still in touch – and before you spaz about this, yes, the last time anyone was in contact with him was back before your great-grandmother died. So, we are taking a chance at finding him, but, even if he's not there anymore and has instead joined some assisted-living community for retired mountain hermits, then we'll just hike, camp, and come back."

It didn't take much to read the room and see this wasn't landing well.

"This is going to be hard," Sienna said, "and I don't even like camping that much, but I know just enough about how these programs work to know that if we're conveniently out of town and unreachable while this happens, then they'll be moving so fast that they'll make a note of it and move on to the next person on their list. That works out really nicely for us in the short-term and the medium-term, and none of this will even be going on anymore in the long-term."

Jordan explained the basic logistics of riding their bikes into the National Forest land and then hiking from there. He showed them the route on the GPS navigator and showed them all the things and places they would spend the next several days walking through. He showed them where they'd stop each day to eat, and where they'd stop later that evening to sleep. He showed them the backpacks in the garage and what was going into each one and how they'd use it.

For Blaise, the shock of this news was now mingled with the excitement of what would certainly be the greatest outdoor adventure of his young life. For Calista, the nausea from the Signal was now mixing malignantly with the turmoil this situation presented. Her parents were putting on brave faces and acting alarmingly united on this, and that belied what she knew must be a horrible kind of fear – an acute despair that had rationalized this as the best possible plan amidst sharply limited available options. Calista figured that her mother was either overreacting – which was possible but unusual – *or* what she knew about this scared her enough to run as far away from anywhere that someone or something could find her.

Either way, her mother was scared. The fact that her otherwise undauntable mother was scared told her how serious this was.

But all of that assumed her mom was reading this situation correctly.

And no one really knew what was going on, that much was clear to her.

"And when did you say we leave?" Blaise asked.

"Tomorrow morning," Jordan said.

"I'm going to download some shows tonight, then."

"No phones, buddy."

"What? Why? Wait, because you think someone might use them to track us?"

"Just no phones."

"You think we're going to be tracked? What?!"

"Yes," Sienna finally said, "that is why. Ok?"

Cali stood up and walked toward the stairs.

"I'm going to bed, what time should I set my alarm?"

"I'll come wake you up in the morning, don't worry about it, ok?" Sienna said.

Sienna knew Cali would need a lot of time tonight to decompress and process things, and, as she listened to her trudge slowly up the stairs, she knew she wouldn't be done by the time they needed to leave.

"What else would you like to know, dude?" Jordan said, turning back to Blaise. "I'm going to need a lot of help from you on this one."

"I do actually have a lot of questions, but I guess I can save most of those for the trail. But I do need to know two things: First, is there any chance assassins are already on their way here; and second, are you going to tell Josie and Scar about any of this running from the government stuff."

Sienna rolled her eyes and stood up. But, just to be safe, Jordan fielded the questions.

"If you tell your sisters about this and freak them out, the assassins will be the least of your problems."

"And..."

"I think I answered both your questions at once."

Blaise sprawled back onto the floor, processing the news in his own way. Jordan started to give him the standard line about going and getting some sleep sooner rather than later, but then thought better of it. He needed some help in the garage.

"I can answer all your questions right now, I just need your help with something in the garage."

Spread out on the smooth concrete floor of the garage – arranged in piles next to the treadmill and shelves of old pool toys and rollerblades that no longer fit anyone – were the outdoor necessities which would keep the Riley's alive in the days ahead. After his recent trip to the store, Jordan now had a backpack for everyone in the family, and he and Blaise spent the next hour packing each one.

Every bag was loaded with a few identical essentials – first aid kit, water filtration, water bottles, portions of dehydrated meals, and an insulated hammock. The hammocks eliminated the need to carry a tent, and the insulation was a nice backup in the event temperatures dropped to any unseasonably low levels at high elevation or it started raining. The forecast was clear for the next 10 days, but that could always change.

Jordan's bag included the majority of the dehydrated food and stove fuel, and Blaise was carrying a few more nights worth of gas to supplement the fires they'd start whenever there was adequate cover to obscure the smoke and light. Sienna and Calista had a couple pots, plates, sporks, and the small stove. Jordan put the GPS navigator in an easy-to-reach side pocket, and on the opposite side he put the holstered Glock 20 and six loaded clips. These felt like luxuries that could quickly transform into necessities if and when something went wrong.

Everyone was carrying their own change of clothes, snacks, raincoat, and knife. Jordan and Blaise each had an axe strapped to their bag, and Sienna and Calista had collapsable saws and 100 feet of ripcord. Josie and Scarlett each had a folding shovel, solar charger, and a tarp big enough for six people to get underneath, albeit uncomfortably close, and each had their own ferro rod and tinder. The list went on.

Blaise and Jordan talked while they sorted and packed.

"How serious is this – like, *really*?" Blaise asked.

"Pretty serious, dude."

"But, like, what are the odds something is actually going to happen."

"Really small. But not small enough that I'm willing to bet against seeing a couple guys in a car show up and tell your mom they need her to take a ride."

"Or Cali and Scar. But I guess they don't know about them."

"Yeah." Jordan grimaced at how much they did actually know.

They rolled sleeping bags and tarps in silence for a moment. Teddy came and laid down next to the bike rack and started licking something stuck to the ground.

"Are you scared?" Blaise asked, finishing his sleeping bag and attaching it to his backpack.

Jordan could have answered immediately but waited for a moment to pass.

"No."

"You're not even freaking out a little?"

"I mean, is this freaking weird? Yes. Am I freaking out? No. I can't do that right now, even if I felt like it. This is just something we *have* to do. We can shrink this whole situation down to just going camping and just treat it like that. I told everyone at work I'm taking care of some personal stuff right now and then taking some time off; so now you and me and your sisters and mom – we just slip out and go do our thing."

"You're not even nervous?"

"I'm about as nervous as I would be before any trip. And once we get to the woods and there's no chance we cross paths with anyone else, then I'll feel a lot better."

The bags were mostly packed now, with just a few of the essentials to put in the side pockets.

"But how do *you* feel?" Jordan asked.

"It feels crazy. Like, yesterday we were the most normal people in history, and –"

"Well, now we know your mom's only been cosplaying as normal all this time," he said with a laugh.

"I know! So, in 24 hours I've gone from a normal family with a normal mom, and now in my house there's a former Soviet codebreaker and two human radio towers that can hear government secrets with their minds. So, yeah, I feel like this is all kind of crazy."

"It's a lot for you to carry, right now, dude. I'm sorry."

"You had no idea?"

"No."

"You didn't even suspect?"

"Suspect what? *This?*"

"Yeah."

"That your mom fought the Soviets when she was nine? No, that thought never occurred to me."

"But you know what I'm asking."

Jordan paused and then rechecked the zippers on the nearest pack to buy a few extra seconds.

"I've always known there was... *a lot* to your mom. I love her, and I trust her, and I know there's a lot more to her than what's there on the surface. Not in a bad way, but just *more.*"

He paused and watched how his son processed this information.

"That's a lot of honesty to drop on a kid. I'm sorry."

"No, I get it. It's just so crazy. But I can also kind of believe mom did all that."

"Yeah. Me too."

The packing was done, but they stayed sitting on the workout mats next to the pile of backpacks and empty packaging from the new supplies.

"Do you think mom would believe *you* if you just came out with this news out of nowhere?"

Jordan laughed. He couldn't even picture it. He had never even considered it.

"I think I would be a very different person if I had had the experiences your mom did."

"What does that even mean?"

"I mean that I couldn't have coped with being asked to do the things your mom did. I mean, she was eight and just jumped off the couch and went and lived at a camp to fight the scariest enemy in American history – and *then* they sent her home and said, 'Thanks kid, don't tell anyone' and she just sat with that for 30 years. Can you... I mean, I can't even *imagine*. I think that would have messed me up... I think that would mess up most people."

"So, if you had told mom out of nowhere one night, 'So, yeah, I used to be a spy when I was a kid and now we have to go hide in the woods just in case' you *really* think she would just say, 'Ok, cool, that makes sense, I'll go buy camping supplies?'"

Jordan had misread the intention of this question the first time

Blaise asked it. His son was confused and scared, and, understandably, this made him furious at how implausible and improbable it all was.

Jordan couldn't blame him.

"I don't know. I would have to have a really good story. The same way she had a good one."

"*She* would have laughed at you and had you committed – but *you* went shopping."

"I hear you. I get it. But we're not packing these bags just because your mom came out of nowhere with a weird story and I didn't have anything better to do this week. If you want to get really real about this, this has all the makings of a disaster. I'm packing bags right now because I've already asked myself a lot of hard questions. Like, to what degree is your mom right, to what degree is a storm coming, and how much danger is an appropriate amount to put my kids in to satisfy those first two questions? There's zero good answers right now – *every* option is bad – but I know that sitting here means I don't get to choose how things turn out, but slipping off into the forest means we can choose what happens next."

"You mean *you* can choose what happens next."

"You're right, your mom and I have to make this call. And we have to live with whatever happens, especially if something terrible happens 20 miles into the woods. That's my problem. And I hate it that this is going to be your problem for a few days, but that's what's going to happen, and you can hate me for as long as you need to once this is done."

Right as he finished, the door into the garage cracked open and Cali poked her head in. Jordan figured there was at least a decent chance she had heard some or all of it.

"Those are all our backpacks?" she asked, noticing the pile of gear.

"Yes ma'am," Jordan said, "you want to try yours on?"

"No, I just couldn't sleep, and when I went to the kitchen, I could hear your voices in here."

"Come sit down," Jordan offered, pointing to an empty spot next to Teddy.

"I'm ok," she said, stretching out a yawn. "I can't believe this is really happening though. This sucks so bad."

"Thank you," Blaise said glaring back at his dad.

"This is the biggest, dumbest idea possible, and you and mom have scared all of us just enough to go along with it."

Her eyes were red; the last hour in her room had been a hard one.

"I know this is scary, but no one is trying to scare you or to frighten you into doing something."

"Well, tomorrow we're sure *doing something*."

"It's a boondoggle, but in a dumb way," Blaise added.

"How do you even know that word?"

"Dad, stop!" she shouted. "This is so stupid, you *have* to know that."

"This is what we're doing. I'm not asking you to make a permanent change to your lifestyle, I'm asking you to have a really unpleasant week."

"This isn't going to work." Now the tears were back.

"This isn't something that needs to work or not work, this is about being present or not present, and we are going to not be present."

"So we can meet up – *maybe* – with an uncle none of us have ever heard of?"

"A great uncle," Blaise added, completely unhelpfully.

"And then we just find him out there randomly somewhere in the woods – and then what? He invites us to join his whole Swiss Family Robinson Ewok village in the forest?"

"Ok, actually, that would for real –"

"Shut up, Blaise."

The garage was dead silent for a long moment. Just the ticking of the air conditioner on the side of the house could be heard.

"Dad admits that mom wouldn't agree to this if he was the one with the story about being a Spy Kid."

"That's not what he said."

She had been listening.

"You guys have the luxury of indulging that hypothetical, but I don't. At least not now. When we all go get therapy after this, your mom and I can talk about that all we want."

"Bro, you want to bring a therapist into this?" Blaise burst out laughing. "They are mandated reporters – that dude is calling CPS within 20 seconds of someone summarizing mom's story. She sounds fully insane – like, *complete* insanity. It would start sounding like that thing with your cousin and the cats."

"It already sounds like the thing with the cats."

"Ok, no therapists. You can all just deal with this in silence like your poor mom did."

"That kinda makes sense."

"Shut up, Blaise."

"You can choose how to cope with what's coming however you want, but I'll tell you that the reality of it is going to be a lot less excruciating than what's in your head. But, come tomorrow, we do this."

Cali heaved out a deep breath.

"And now, you two, in a weird way, you join the family business."

"That's for Cali and Scar," Blaise pointed out.

"No, the *real* business – the long term one. The keeping of secrets."

"Oh. Yeah."

Another big sigh from Cali.

"You already know a thousand things you can't repeat, and for the next week you're going to do things 24/7 you can't ever say you've done."

"I know. Just like mom did."

It seemed like Cali had already thought of this.

"This is a lot to put on you two, and I'm sorry."

"Oh no, I get it; my friends would die laughing if I tried to tell them this story."

Jordan hated the position this put his children in, particularly the ones who not only had to navigate the uncertainties of the mountains but do so with the added weight of understanding what was happening.

"Cali, why don't you head up to bed. I'm going to drag Blaise with me to help drop off these packs so we don't have to ride for an hour with them on our backs tomorrow."

She turned and left in a huff, defeated and drained, but still angry.

Jordan and Blaise loaded the backpacks into the car, and they started driving to the forest service road where they'd all drop off the grid the next day. While they drove, Jordan showed Blaise how to operate the GPS device they'd use while they traveled and the routes he had mapped out for each day.

After 20 minutes of driving through the pitch black, they arrived at the entrance to the old road. Jordan drove about half a mile down and parked. He and Blaise hid all six packs about 30 feet into the treeline and made sure they couldn't be spotted from the road.

By the time Jordan got home Sienna had just finished getting Josie and Scarlett to sleep. She had told them about the vacation they were taking tomorrow and, for now, effectively resolved all their anxieties about it. Now she sat on the edge of her bed and stared down at her feet. This seemed like the right time and place to cry and let it all out before tomorrow morning arrived and she had to summon enough strength for everyone, but nothing came.

She and Jordan discussed the last few details. Neither of them needed to acknowledge how terrifying and strange this had become. They had done plenty of that already.

"I'm setting my alarm early so I can go back through everything one last time, and then I'll do one last check on the bikes," he said. "I'll get Blazer and Cali up, if you want to get the little girls up and about, and then I can do one last pass through the house while they finish breakfast."

It wasn't unusual to see him overthinking the tiny details; he figured the downstream effect of this would be a mitigation of the big problems.

He turned off the light and fell asleep almost immediately.

She laid there in the dark a long time. This was another ideal time to finally cry, but still nothing came.

She was going to face the mountains with all of this still inside her.

She wanted to ask Jordan if this was a horrible idea and have him talk her out of it. She knew that might have been possible if she'd done it after their first conversation. But he believed her when she said this was serious, and he knew there was more to it, even if he didn't know what it was. But now he'd had time to think it through, he'd weighed the pros and cons, and he was not going to sit and wait for the chance that things worked out perfectly. He had a willingness to over-prepare once he had set his mind to do something, and when this was paired with a vivid imagination and an above-average problem with authority – this put him into guardian mode.

Sienna kept laying there in the dark, flat on her back, eyes wide open. She didn't want to fall asleep because she didn't know how to start this process. How do you just wake up in the morning and then disappear yourself? It was something so bizarre as to seem impossible to do after waking up in your own bed. Yesterday Jordan had started repeating, "Well, like Ronnie Coleman always says, 'There ain't nothing left to it but to do it.'"

She didn't know who that was and she didn't find it particularly comforting, but he was right. Tomorrow they were going to wake up and walk out.

29 JUNE

It had taken an extra day longer than planned to arrive at the Baloch village, a tiny, semi-permanent campsite 65 miles southwest of the town of Liari (لیاری), named Bhit (بھٹ شاہ). A roadblock checkpoint near Sukkur (سکھر) required the Para commandos to take an alternative route on much smaller, slower roads – and one in particular had been washed out, requiring several hours of back-tracking – and, all told, avoiding the freeway had probably added 18 hours to their trip. When they did get to the village the motorcycle assembly hadn't yet begun, and getting everything unboxed, built, and fine-tuned took another day.

All rerouting and unforeseen delays aside, the trip to Bhit had been straightforward and generally lacking in all the stresses that so often accompanied clandestine operations, particularly when it came to incursions into a hostile country with the intent of wiping out the operational utility of their most important military base.

A well-laid plan is a powerful thing when combined with this much luck.

That afternoon, while they worked, the mission's commander, Captain Amit Joshi (अमित जोशी), received word from Marshal Chatterjee's team that a spy working in Pakistani counterintelligence reported there were no red flags or warnings in the system about suspected Indian incursions. Joshi's team had successfully slipped into Pakistan and reached their staging area unnoticed.

While two soldiers worked with a villager to assemble the bikes, Joshi sat with the technician who would pilot the drone. Lieutenant Arjun Sharma (अर्जुन शर्मा) was younger and smaller than the rest of the group, but he had completed the same PRTC training as the rest of the team, and he had a reputation for being particularly clever in otherwise ugly situations. Among the specialized training he had undergone since becoming a Para was what the military called "unconventional warfare tactics" – and, among other things, that included the use of small drones on one-way missions.

The drone at the center of this mission had made its way to Bhit spread across three backpacks and two suitcases. Seen individually, any of those pieces looked innocuous enough to be, depending on the piece you were looking at, a stray part from a laptop computer, car stereo, model helicopter, or fire alarm. Currently these pieces were spread out across a large blanket, and Sharma was piecing them together with two different screwdrivers and needle-nose pliers. Assembly and testing of the drone would take another two hours, at which point Sharma would begin testing the superconductor and the batteries, as well as the backup batteries and backup superconductor – which they had been told could not be left behind, for both financial and investigative reasons. Sharma had already unfolded a large solar array which would keep all their electronics at peak charge until the final moment they left.

The forecast for both tonight and tomorrow had recently changed to call for heavy wind in the region. The bikes wouldn't be ready tonight, so that left tomorrow – and the weather put that date into doubt, as well. There was nothing left to do but wait, assess, and make the call in real time. Chatterjee would not relish the idea of telling General Gupta that something as mundane as wind had stalled the most technologically sophisticated attack ever executed by a ground unit of commandos, but Gupta was an old soldier himself – so he knew the power the elements had to ruin a good plan.

The rest of the day moved swiftly, and, as darkness fell, the Paras settled in for dinner with their hosts – and, with the help of a Balochi translator, the conversation was lively even if the village elders had no idea why these people were here or who they were. But they had their suspicions. After the fact they might put a few pieces together, but, by that point, they would all know better than to ever mention the four strangers who spent a weekend sipping tea and eating sindhi koki (سندھی کوکی) before abruptly riding away and never returning.

While his men rolled out sleeping bags and sketched out a route for the hourly patrols and guard duty throughout the night, one last call came in from Chatterjee's team. Their boat had been successfully planted beneath the bridge in Karachi, and, directly related to that, their ride home would be arriving early the next day and then holding position at their predetermined rendezvous coordinates.

Joshi took the first shift as lookout and used the time to think through every possible permutation of his next few steps. So far everything had gone perfectly enough to make him just a little nervous. Every experienced commander knew that if your attack was going perfectly then you were probably working your way into an ambush. But, superstitions or high winds aside, he would see to it that the drone hit the bullseye on that hangar.

* * * * *

Not long after Joshi's shift as lookout ended, Captain Desmond O'Shea arrived 100 miles off the coast.

At this distance there was very little chance of detection by or interference from the Pakistani Navy – an organization that O'Shea classified somewhere between "pathetic" and "hilarious." His Executive Officer disagreed and noted he had in fact "spent time with one of their admirals five or six years ago at an international forum on –" and at that point O'Shea told a junior bosun nearby to escort the XO to the brig if he finished that sentence.

For the commander of a hunter-killer sub, every mission – and, frankly, every moment of deployment outside of dry dock – had the implied possibility of violence, but, more often than not, O'Shea and the USS Arizona spent their time performing reconnaissance and making observations about a target or area or target area. The technical term they used for this at Fleet Command and Annapolis, was "reconnoitering." O'Shea enjoyed a reconnoiter as much as anyone when it was the prelude to a Mark 48 torpedo or either type of cruise missile this boat carried – but, in essentially every case, these passive observations reduced the Arizona to a $4.3 billion periscope camera with a nuclear reactor under the hood.

The camera, the reactor, and O'Shea arrived at their predetermined location shortly after 2 am local time and settled in to listen, take notes, and then continue listening. The Arabian Sea was well over 4,000 feet deep beneath them, and O'Shea instructed the helmswoman to park them at a depth of 1,200 feet, and he alerted the Diving Officer to hold this position UNODIR – unless otherwise directed. At this depth they would be just a dark spot in the ocean for anyone who happened to pass by and look down, and any submarine built by any country within 3,000 miles would pass well overhead, even if traveling at their maximum depth.

The Arizona's sensors picked up the normal flow of heavy maritime traffic in and out of Karachi's giant port, and a beacon was carefully raised to the surface to report their successful arrival and establishment of operations in the target area. This transmission included a multi-array sensor image they had captured with the photonic sensor before assuming their current depth, and, while the beacon was transmitting, a message arrived with the expected list of updates and additional instructions. Within this update was a briefing for O'Shea from the major at the Pentagon. This briefing was automatically printed in his private office, the conn, and he walked across the bridge to read it. Among the half-page of bullet points in this briefing was the notification that an Indian sub, the INS Vagsheer, had not participated in a routine training exercise with the rest of its assigned surface fleet three days earlier. The Arizona was instructed to look for this sub in their immediate area, but this additional mission parameter did not replace their original instruction to passively surveil Karachi's coast. This instruction included the detail that the Vagsheer would be maximizing its stealth if it was indeed approaching this area.

O'Shea immediately wondered why the Vagsheer was sneaking up on this coast and, if they *were* headed here, was it to find the Arizona?

The next bullet explained that intelligence from within the Indian military indicated a possible direct action outside of Karachi, followed by a sea-based extraction via the Vagsheer.

"Outside Karachi?" he said under his breath, trying to recall all the major landmarks from memory.

He stood to look at the regional map displayed on the digital screen mounted to his office wall. Indeed – the only thing of any considerable interest for direct action outside Karachi was their air force's giant base. Was India really going to kick that hornet's nest? And were they going to do it with boots on the ground rather than something ballistic? Apparently, they needed a deep level of deniability for whatever was about to happen. This meant that whatever it was, it wasn't going to be nuclear since that was too easy to trace, and it wasn't going to be an assassination of anyone important since VIP's don't spend much time out in plain view at airbases, and getting in and out of high-density areas like that was no picnic. That left something in the realm of simple espionage, or maybe extracting an asset in the Pakistani military. But a submarine pickup was a tall order to retrieve a spy – even a great one.

The report didn't cover the secondary scenario that occurred immediately to O'Shea: If someone in the Indian military wanted to do some sudden damage with pinpoint accuracy they would insert a specialized group of operators to call in a series of missile strikes from a weapons platform that could then disappear back under the waves after the bombardment was done. This would help with deniability since a strike like this would normally rely on coordination with a satellite, and having in-person spotters would facilitate the exact same strike without having that smoking gun up in the stars.

He hit the intercom on his desk and asked the XO to gather up the Navigation Officer and Tactical Officer to join him in the conn. The three of them needed to look at all the available data on the ocean floor in this immediate area, as well as the best possible approach routes. Just for good measure he also called for the Weapons Officer. Might as well plan for every possible outcome as early as possible, he thought.

If the Vagsheer was trying to sneak into the neighborhood, he wanted to have every possible approach route mapped out based on that sub's last known location. If that boat was hurrying to get here it would limit all the roundabout paths, and he'd put the Arizona right at the choke point and sit there silently as the Vagsheer slid past and congratulated itself for arriving undetected. That moment after an opponent's sigh of relief was where the captain of a hunter-killer sub did his best work.

While he waited for the officers to arrive, he thought more about the Vagsheer. By itself it wasn't a threat to the Arizona; he had studied the Kalvari class of submarines extensively when the plans for its prototype first reached the CIA and were then sent to a small group of officers for evaluation. These subs had been co-developed by India and

France, and, despite the resources of these two nations, it still featured a diesel engine that U.S. sonar could hear from essentially the moment it left port. Kalvari translated to "tiger shark" in one of India's 22 official languages, if he remembered correctly. What really got his attention whenever he thought about this class of subs was the combination of India and France – two of the best cuisines on earth but also the cuisine pairing which would result in the worst fusion restaurant of all time. This sophisticated line of thinking was interrupted by a knock at the door.

"Gentlemen," O'Shea began with a smile, "the Pentagon thinks an Indian sub has been sent to our very location as the getaway car for an operation they have going on somewhere outside Karachi."

"They're attacking the airbase?" the XO interrupted.

"There's no word on the target or the intentions, but the alleged ride home – the Vagsheer – didn't show up for a joint training a couple days back, and, prior to that, it was last seen here," he pointed to a spot on the screen, "let's call it 400 miles away from here."

"Let's call it 410 miles, sir," the Navigation Officer added.

"Thank you, Everett," O'Shea said with a roll of the eyes as the Weapons Officer arrived.

"I want the three of you to plot every possible route the Vagsheer could take from the last point we had eyes on it to our general area if they were trying for maximum stealth. Let's also account for the fact they'll want to put themselves in a position to depart as quickly as possible once the deed is done."

The Tactical Officer was staring at the map and the bathymetric data of the ocean floor. "A sub like that won't get any closer than 10 to 12 miles off the coast, and if they have operators on the ground, they'd have to take a boat to meet up with it anyway. So, it's going to be somewhere in this basic area," he traced a semicircular pattern off the coast of the city. "They'd have to take that boat at least three miles off the coast so they could disappear over the horizon, and then SOP for aquatic rescues like this is to ditch the boat and scuba for a while after that point."

O'Shea nodded. "Look over every trench, crack, and current pattern on the ocean floor, and show me the best possible routes they could take. I need this fast, because we're starting a grid search as soon as you're done." Then he turned to the weapons officer, "There's nothing in the briefing from the Pentagon to indicate this sub is hostile to us, but let's prepare for everything. Based on our immediate environment, I want you to be ready to do something quick and clean. We're also going to need a secondary option that cripples them but leaves them in a rescuable position. And I need this plotted out in such a way that we were never here punching holes in another navy's prized possession."

He considered that now was probably the right time to put the idea in their head about the secondary potential action they were being asked to recon – and, eventually – be asked to interdict.

"One last thing, gentleman. I want us to think through one eventuality that the Pentagon may have overlooked in their haste to get us on station and gathering intel: If the Indians really do have operators somewhere on the outskirts of the city, and if it's the Vagsheer headed our way, we have to be ready if this thing squares up for a missile strike. That boat carries 18 or 19 cruise missiles, if memory serves, and, depending on what type of arrowhead they have fixed to each bird, they can level anything those commandos put a laser on."

There were nods around the table. Everything the team knew so far indicated that this is how you'd use a sub-commando setup if you wanted to melt away into the haze afterwards.

"If we've been asked to post up here then we're going to stop that from happening – unless I get a really specific message from D.C telling us to stop and watch." The assembled officers nodded but did not necessarily agree with taking such a proactive role in international affairs. "I'll make the call when the time comes, but there's 45 people on a boat like the Vagsheer and 14 million in Karachi. I can stand in front of a court-martial and explain the damn reasoning, no problem."

O'Shea dismissed his senior officers and returned to the bridge himself a few minutes later. He stared back at the map on the plotting table and made a few notes about the grid search the junior navigation officers were already beginning to plot. This mission made him the unofficial and anonymous chaperone to a fight between two nuclear powers.

31 Camping

29 JUNE

The last 18 hours had been a blur for Sienna and Jordan as they prepared to disappear.

They both felt confident they were prepared to drop off the map for a week, maybe two. How anyone could manage to do this long-term was mystifying.

After finding the old Forest Service map with her uncle's approximate location, Sienna and Jordan plotted the fastest, shortest, and most direct possible route to reach that circle. The topographic contour lines on the map indicated which areas were steepest and where they could wind their way between peaks, valleys, and rivers, and they'd used the GPS device to get more specific details and dial in the exact path they'd travel.

The circled area on the map included four peaks, an alpine lake, and a small handful of heavily forested valleys, not to mention a dozen different streams emptying into the Snoqualmie, Skykomish, or Pratt Rivers. Once they reached the circle, they'd be 15 mountainous miles north of Snoqualmie Pass. The Pass was a small gap in the towering Cascade Range that was both a popular place to ski and the spot chosen in the 1950s as the route for the newly minted Interstate 90 which would connect Boston to Seattle – with Missoula, Madison, Chicago, Cleveland, Syracuse, and Albany in between.

Sienna sat with Scarlett and Josie while they ate breakfast and explained what they'd be doing that day. They had absorbed this news warily at first, but it had quickly become apparent to them that this was like a combination of Disney movies, adventure novels, and a few different fairy tales about intrepid children finding their destiny in the forest. Calista was still brooding about her parents' overreactions.

Blaise shared her conclusions, but, on the other hand, he wouldn't and couldn't miss this wilderness survival bonanza for anything; a lifetime of countless YouTube searches about bushcraft and shelter making was about to pay off.

The plan for this morning was relatively simple, albeit with a few moving parts. Ten miles from home was a bridge that crossed the Snoqualmie River in the small town of Fall City, another five miles past that was a trailhead that followed an overgrown logging road from the 1920s. That logging road ran for about six twisting, overgrown miles before dead-ending deep in the Snoqualmie National Forest. By that point they would be well beyond anything remotely man-made or any navigable trails. They'd drag the bikes another 100 yards into the woods beyond that dead-end, cover them with branches, and then travel the rest of the way on foot. From there, Jordan estimated it would take four days of earnest hiking to get inside that circle on the map. Sienna was certain it would take three because she, as she put it, "hasn't raised wimps." But this optimistic estimation of her children's tolerance for hiking off trail through virgin forest began to falter when subjected to modest scrutiny.

But getting to the point of hiding the bikes and discovering if, in fact, you had actually raised wimps required two prior steps.

The second step had to do with just arriving at that logging road.

The family would split into three groups – Blaise and Calista, Jordan and Josie and Teddy, Sienna and Scarlett – and ride to the trailhead via three different routes. Jordan had drawn a map for Blaise to use, with landmarks he would know or recognize along the way, and the instruction that arguing with his sister was strictly forbidden. That warning would, if Jordan was lucky, reduce the chance of arguing by 15%. Traveling in small groups was far less likely to draw the notice of anyone driving past, and, in the unlikely event they were recognized – and in the even unlikelier event that their absence led to a search and/or questions for surrounding residents – by only seeing a couple Rileys at a time it made guessing the location of *all* the Rileys essentially impossible. Even if a fluke driver happened to drive past two of the three groups, even *that* would communicate very little besides a shared love of cycling.

The first step included the, heretofore, least popular parts of this plan.

Since a car missing from the garage would be an immediate tip-off for anyone who came by to learn more about Sienna's childhood, they would leave the cars here and do this all on bikes. It would be difficult for an unannounced visitor to determine how many bikes were or were not a normal part of the house, but a car left at a random trailhead would be a dead giveaway about what they were doing and, roughly, where they were going. The decision to leave the car at home came in tandem with the decision to also leave behind every other trackable or identifiable object – in particular, phones. For Scarlett and Josie, this meant nothing, but the two older kids rolled their eyes so hard they risked injuring an orbital muscle when they heard the news. But things were just tense enough to eliminate the normal avenues and duration of debate.

Whether or not this would lead to a completely fool-proof disappearance was impossible to say. In a parallel universe where this current crisis could only be solved by Sienna's personal engagement with the Russian militants who had rebooted the Signal, then the government might follow a hunch and start running a satellite over all the forest land around her last known location. In that scenario, a military-grade satellite would only need one pass over this section of the state to spot seven warm dots in the middle of a forest. But, before satellites started getting retasked, they would first spend days tracking down every single known contact and casual acquaintance in Jordan and Sienna's personal history. All of that was to say that this plan gave them so much of a head start that their trail would be cold long before anyone might consider trying to find it.

But if all that stealth was the benefit, the cost was mileage and effort.

In a straight line the circled peaks and the lake at their base was about 17 miles from where they'd eventually ditch the bikes, but the path to get there was going to feel like 170. The entire route was unbroken forest, and even though they'd be skirting the edges of mountains instead of scaling them, the terrain was anything but flat. By the looks of it, they'd cross at least seven streams, go up and over four ridges – two of which were perilously high – and navigate around remote sections of two different trails used by especially ambitious backpackers who wanted to get away from it all. Washington was one of only a few states left in the U.S. where you could reach an intensely remote location in a relatively short distance, and the area they would be traversing was so rugged that it delivered them into territory that might as well have been in another hemisphere. This was going to be a difficult four days – it was definitely, almost certainly, going to be four days – to cover those 17 miles once all the twists and turns were factored in and that distance expanded by about two-and-a-half times.

The supplies carefully arranged in their backpacks put them in a position to thrive under ideal conditions and barely survive under bad ones. But everything in those packs would only sustain them for seven days – so Jordan developed a solution to the problem of long-term survival during his second sleepless night.

The solution came in the form of just how popular it had become to hike the Pacific Crest Trail. Every year a couple thousand intrepid hikers made the 2,650-mile trip from southern Canada to northern Mexico, and since ammunition was heavy and hunting took time, none of these hikers were eating anything local along the way. Instead, the travelers used a half dozen different outfitting services to leave crates filled with food and other supplies at key points along the trail. The Pacific Crest Trail wound through the mountains of Washington for 500 especially challenging miles and featured two dozen waypoints where supplies could be deposited. Although the route the Rileys were following kept them as far from this trail as possible, there was a potential re-supply point about 8 miles from the circle – and Jordan had paid a courier, in cash and with a fake name, to contact one of these resupply services and arrange for weekly deliveries of food, water purification, and a few other items on a weekly basis for the next two weeks. The courier had been instructed to have this resupply box outfitted to meet the needs of several large groups of about 10 people that would be passing through at 7-10-day intervals. In particular, these were all groups heading north – thus they would be exhausted, hungry, and willing to have a few nicer items since they wouldn't have to carry them for much longer. In the event things went even longer term, Jordan could hike to one of a handful of permanent campsites along the trail and buy extra supplies. One of his many errands yesterday had included withdrawing $5,000 in cash from the bank, and he had made sure to casually mention to the teller that he was having "a bunch of landscaping" done the following week. Admitting that you were planning to pay workers off the books in such a way that they were certainly never going to pay taxes on their income was a strange way of generating a believable rationale for this sudden withdrawal, but, if an investigator ever called the bank to ask what had happened, it was a believable story. It helped that their yard didn't look great. All 250 of those $20 bills were now sealed inside a watertight bag, tightly wrapped in plastic, and then sealed inside another waterproof bag.

As they ate breakfast there was an unmistakable cloud hanging over the kids. Part of the reason was just how early it was on a Sunday. Confusion and apprehension were the order of the day, albeit in different shapes, sizes, and origins. Cali and Blaise knew enough to worry; Josie and Scarlett had quickly intuited the connection between last night's news and this sudden no-phone and no-car vacation. They had all been camping enough times to not fear the woods, and living next to a greenbelt helped them see only the fun things a forest had to offer. Sienna looked around the kitchen island and considered that this was all just weird enough to keep from feeling real, but it was real enough to be unmistakably weird. This combination did not sit particularly well with anyone.

After they finished eating, Sienna opted to leave the dishes in the sink just to make things that much more confusing for anyone peeking in a window and attempting to piece together a story. The three groups of bike riders left 10 minutes apart – Blaise and Calista first, then Sienna, then Jordan.

The trepidation had started for everyone.

Blaise and Cali had shared a look as they buckled their helmets, and there was no doubt they would be talking about this the entire ride. Cali's headache was still pounding, and the ringing in Scarlett's ears was persistent and annoying, but not debilitating. After three days of non-stop nausea, these minor improvements were welcome. Josie busily made the final preparations for her ride, which included placing Teddy in the basket over the back wheel of her bike. This dog had spent many hours riding in this basket over the last two years, and his dislike of riding in it was superseded by his intense desire to do things and go places with any of his owners.

As he prepared to leave, Jordan noticed all the cellphones were stacked together on the island in the kitchen. He scooped them up and placed each one casually in the bedrooms. Then he double checked all the doors and headed out. Next to the door to the garage was the family calendar, and he saw Sienna had circled the day before and written "Road Trip with friends!" on it – and then extended an arrow across several of the following days. That was pretty ingenious. Anyone who went to the trouble to come inside the house and see this would burn an entire week tracking down every known associate going back any number of years, then finding where each of these people were located, then extrapolating where these people might be going and when and why. This was going to be as clean a disappearance as any amateurs could hope to accomplish.

The ride to the trailhead was relatively easy for each of the three groups, and, as planned, they met again a half mile down the old road – well out of view of the already secluded main road. Jordan, Josie, and Teddy got there last and found Blaise helping his sisters and mom pull the backpacks from where they'd been stashed less than 8 hours earlier.

The family then pedaled down the twists and turns of the old logging road until it reached a dead end a little over six miles later. Long before they reached the end of this old forest road it had transformed into more forest than road, and that was a welcome sight for the architects of this disappearing act. Jordan and Sienna helped the kids carry their bikes across the forest floor until they found a massive tree that had long ago fallen across a small gully and now allowed for plenty of room and cover to stash six bikes underneath. Scarlett and Josie were sent to gather sword ferns and branches to cover the bikes while Jordan packed them together and wove a lock and chain through the frames. Sienna helped everyone with their packs, and was surprised when she felt the cold, tight knot in her stomach relax ever so slightly.

Jordan, however, was no longer processing these emotions. He was not the type to stand with his toes curled over the edge of a high dive; instead, his anxieties were now sublimated into a clarity of purpose and a hyper awareness of the ways he and Sienna could take care of everyone. That did not inhibit a small voice in his head from reminding him periodically that, on paper or to an outsider, this all looked insanely paranoid. But those thoughts had long-since crossed the threshold from *exhortation* to *nuisance*. What he knew unequivocally was that he and Sienna had planned this with a level of detail few experts could muster. He also knew that, without bearings and without something to tether to, doubt and fear would cripple them. If keeping everyone alive was Job 1, then keeping them intact emotionally was 1a. Jordan found some relief from the idea that this was all preposterous and reckless by considering that Sienna would never go along with something reckless or preposterous. For his part, having her here was reassuring and calming at a time when everyone was so disoriented. But Jordan was self aware enough to recognize a coping mechanism even when it arrived disguised like sage advice or a comfort blanket. He pushed this from his mind and focused again on showing his kids a guy who was on a vacation rather than hiding from something.

This thought was at the forefront of his mind as he spun the dial on the padlock. No matter how serious this situation was, he still believed they would be coming back eventually – and he wanted his bikes to be here when they did.

Sienna, for her part, took comfort from his optimism even if she knew enough to be incapable of generating those feelings herself. The stress of taking this action in the woods was doubled with a struggle to make sense of what the Signal's return could mean. She knew what was on the other side of it, even if she didn't know anything about it. She didn't understand the where or the what or the why; she only knew how it felt, and that, ever so briefly, it had known about her, too.

Did the return of the Signal mean that the same message was coming with it? Was it being sent from the same place? But that would be like assuming there was only one phone and one phone operator on the other side. But a ringing phone – particularly in this era – could have any one of five billion people on the other end. And with that many possible callers came just as many reasons to call. But even that conclusion suggested an understanding of the similarities between tachyons and cell towers that she did not possess, but still seemed unlikely nonetheless. So, what now? Last night she had woken up twice with the familiar hum in her ears. Cali and Scarlett were both talking about it during breakfast. And she could hear it again now. She looked up at the pieces of bright blue sky through the near-canopy of Western Red Cedar and Douglas Fir, and, when she caught a glimpse of direct sunlight the sudden bright exposure revealed the tiny crackles of refraction around the periphery of her vision. Those were new. She had last seen those while rubbing her eyes and grasping for words as Torchy watched her sort through the shock after hearing the response. She had dried her eyes on that Roger Rabbit shirt and then slumped against the bench while her mind raced through questions about who else could know, or would know, and how many children would need to keep this secret from so many adults. Even at the Senate Intelligence alumni debriefing she was called to seven years ago, every question was about the Soviet Union, the technology used in the research cabin, and the standard inquiries about whether or not she had ever discussed her involvement with anyone. The truest possible understanding of Dark Antennae was still limited to the smallest handful of people, and her part in it hadn't even produced any useful information.

But now she was in the woods.

She was here because she understood just enough to know how many other people would misunderstand everything and behave accordingly. And that inverse relationship would accelerate in all the wrong ways if anyone discovered the Signal's origin.

Jordan and Blaise finished with the concealment, and Jordan booted up the GPS. It was time to start navigating. He had programmed the GPS to take the most direct route to the middle of that circle with a few caveats – avoiding dramatic elevation changes whenever possible, minimizing stream crossings, and avoiding established trails. Jordan marveled at the way the device operated "like Waze for forests" and the first day of hiking was, as planned, uneventful. At this stage of the trek the forest was dense but the topography itself was relatively flat, albeit with periodic inclines that kept adding to the altimeter's readings. They walked in a largely straight path, weaving gently around dense hedgerows of ferns, and skirting the edges of ravines with the Snoqualmie River below. The world-famous beauty of the Pacific Northwest forest was on full display, and, after a quiet and morose first hour, even Blaise and Cali joined in on the talking and joking. It began to feel as if this were just another hike.

As Scarlett finished cinching the waist belt on her backpack, she took a long look into the woods and asked the most pressing question she had been mulling over since her bike reached the gravel road.

"Dad, are there sasquatches here?"

"If you ask the indigenous people, yes. But for your purposes, no."

"I feel like men – like, grown men – are just less-hairy sasquatches."

"Well, that would make women sasquatches, too, then, if you think about it."

"That's rude."

"But you understand where new sasquatches are coming from right?"

"What on earth are you talking about?"

"Hey babe?" Sienna asked, "Can you come help me with something over here that isn't sasquatch related?"

This trip was not the place Sienna intended to have the least productive conversation ever about the birds and the bees.

After being asked to chill with the sasquatch reproduction theories and mostly keeping a straight face while pleading innocence, Jordan checked the GPS again and pointed the direction they'd take to start their vacation.

They moved briskly, paused regularly, ate snacks, and watched when the chipmunks slowly crept toward the granola bars. Teddy was in heaven – eating ferns and marking all new territory. Blaise was often charging ahead, pausing only sporadically to call back and make sure he was still headed the right direction. In the late afternoon there was still plenty of light, and Jordan gave him the job of finding a place that could hang six hammocks, avoid easy notice from the air, and had enough cover to disperse smoke from a fire. This task was eagerly accepted, and Cali went with him. Twenty minutes later he was back claiming to have found a perfect place. The thicket of young Cedars was, indeed, perfect – with trunks at regular intervals such that all six hammocks could be hung in a circle around a clear spot on the ground for a fire.

The younger girls had never camped solely in hammocks before, so this setup had the benefit of giving the first night a certain novelty. Even the dehydrated food rehydrated easily enough. Josie and Scarlett walked to the nearby stream that was flowing back down the way they had come. They had covered 4.5 miles today in terms of total progress toward the circle, but it had been more than double that far once the many twists and turns were factored into their irregular path through the unbroken forest.

Sienna and Blaise gathered extra firewood while the food reconstituted, and Jordan got their gear settled in for the night. Cali was laying perpendicular in her hammock, dragging her feet, and watching the sky turn a gentle shade of orange.

"What are you thinking about," he asked.

"That my head hurts."

"I'm sorry about that."

"And that this seems crazy."

"It kind of does. And I…"

"And what are we even walking towards?" she asked suddenly, betraying more than a little trepidation.

"You mean Uncle Harvey?"

"The uncle that *might* be there. The uncle that was *probably* there back when great-grandma was alive?"

She massaged her temples as she gently rocked back and forth in the hammock, pushing back and forth as her feet dragged on the ground. She was fighting back tears, but it was stubbornness that ultimately held them back. Stubbornness as a source of resilience at this age was a gift from her mother.

"Best case scenario, it's a place we can lay low for a little while in a spot no one knows about, with someone who can help us out if we need to be there longer. Worst case scenario, there's nothing and nobody there, we hang out for a couple days, and then we come back."

Out of context this almost sounded like it made sense. In this context, however, she only saw chaos.

Calista kept swinging back and forth, her face still scrunched in such a way that seemed equal parts headache and anxiety. A minute passed while Jordan added a few extra sticks to the fire.

"You don't think it's weird that mom had this entire other life that she never even mentioned, that she never even told you about – just this entire secret part of her personality that she went every day without ever mentioning to anyone? And now we have to hide in the woods because of it?"

This was an emotional amalgam that no one her age was equipped to process alone. She reeled from the discovery that the closest possible relationship a child can have featured someone who, out of necessity, had withheld a major part of who she was and how she was made. It was a painful thing to learn that withholding information is a form of dishonesty which leaves the same wound as lying. It was painful to learn that the person who was most deeply familiar to her was, when an unexpected light suddenly illuminated the deep recesses of her mother's past, a person and a story which was entirely foreign. By going untold for so long, this secret seemed tantamount to deception. Sienna might have countered that this distant chapter of her history wasn't a core part of her character or identity despite what all the drama around it might suggest. She might even say that it was, in fact, something she had long since discarded in such a way that it was now as foreign to her as it was to them. But all of that was immaterial at the moment. And it was not entirely true. Calista had so often been told by teachers and the parents of friends that she was an "old soul" – but, at age 12, her wisdom was still nascent enough to misunderstand the extent to which the people we love are simply the version of a person which they have the ability to share with us.

Right now, in this remote campsite, the particulars of what constitutes a true understanding of one another, or how to formulate a sense of self relative to the world and the distinct lives of those with whom you live in close quarters – those were all theoretical questions to ponder while walking or fetching water and firewood.

"I know, girl," Jordan said gently. "This is obviously all a little crazy. But if you had to pick one person out of everyone you know who had this story deep in their past, wouldn't it be your mom?"

"I would have guessed Uncle Stuart."

"No, I think your Uncle Stuart would have told you this story and included a part about when he had to steal a helicopter to escape or something. But tell me one person more likely than your mom to have once worked for the CIA or whatever?"

"Yeah, it would be her." She was quiet for a long time as the fire crackled and then added, "You know mom was all super serious about it every day at the camp, too: 'C'mon everyone, it's time to save freedom!'"

Now they laughed. Certainly some version of that probably happened.

"Mom was probably so good at it she would just sit there in their lunch cabin – or whatever she said it was called – and read people's minds or tell people what was on the radio in Taiwan, just to show off."

"Did it work that way with reading thoughts? Because if that's still the case we're all in huge trouble."

"Dad, she might actually know who it was that ate the last piece of my tres leche birthday cake!"

"I for one," Jordan said with a hand over his heart, "would love to get to the bottom of that."

"Everyone knows it was you, Dad! Literally *everyone*!"

"First of all, hardly. Second of all, absolutely not. Third of all, who is more likely to have eaten it – your honest and loving father, or the woman who can potentially read minds and alter memories and therefore cover up the fact that she ate it while we were at the dog park with Teddy?"

This debate was interrupted, and Jordan's innocence was still in question despite his obvious guilt, when Blaise returned carrying a bundle of firewood he'd gathered and carried with some paracord and an exotic "wilderness survival knot" that he explained to both of them in great and unrequested detail. Slung over his other shoulder was the four-liter gravity-fed water purifier to refill everyone's bottles. He was fully in his element and relishing it. A moment later he had disappeared back into the woods because he saw "quite a few edible plants" earlier. So far, the burdens of this little adventure were of no consequence; he was living his best life.

Jordan asked Cali to keep an eye on the fire, and he left to go check on the little girls and Sienna who were playing by the stream.

He thought about Cali's questions, and he examined his own reactions to the news which had so suddenly changed everyone's lives. This news had been bizarre in the extreme, but it did not shock him like it did his children. Sienna had always been just aloof and distant enough to make the idea of her possessing a secret that could never be spoken a concept that was within reason, if only barely. There had always been something unreachable about her, and he had sensed this so early on in their relationship that he could not remember knowing her without that detail. More specifically, she had two boundaries – one was a walled-off area which was not accessible to anyone, and the second was an emotional boundary that she could approach but never cross. It was up to him to meet her at the demarcation of that second limit, and he had chosen to take that role early on. That first boundary was something he had never attempted to explore; there simply was not an access point to it, and, over time, it was possible to forget that something so significant was left undiscovered. Jordan had expected those walls to come down eventually, and, as the years stacked up and landmark anniversaries passed, he understood they never would. But he loved her exactly the way he found her. He loved exactly who she was, and, this many years later, that thing had not changed in significantly discernable ways. He could still recall, with great clarity, the first moment he ever heard her talking, and how certain he was in that moment. She had every strength he did not; and he checked boxes she didn't know needed checking, despite missing a bunch of others she had previously believed were essential. Jordan fell in love hard, Sienna loved him back, and every stage of their early relationship moved quickly. It was only in the rarest, fleeting moments that he ever considered what might have been if she had let him see over that wall, if only for a moment. Those moments had always found their way to him amidst a certain kind loneliness, but Jordan was a man fit to live with his choices and love people where they were. Every single good thing and concept in his life had her fingerprints on it, and he never, ever forgot it. He had chosen her when that distance was already in place, and he was never going to lobby her to show him something that wasn't his.

He walked back down the mountain until he heard the voices of the girls and then the sound of the stream. The girls had been placing rocks to build a dam, and now the water was cresting the top of the wall. Josie had been floating pieces of bark downstream and she covered these "boats" with wildflower "passengers." Scarlett stood on the bank and threw pinecones at them as they passed. They both found this incredibly amusing, and they acted out the discussions happening on the boats as each new vessel weathered the latest salvos from shore. The Riley children were all easily amused by the simpler pleasures – many family vacations had seen days at a time slip away at a lake with nothing more than a few buckets, toy shovels, and snacks. Both girls were wet, and when Jordan returned to announce that dinner was ready, he carried them back to avoid muddy feet. Tonight they'd eat dinner in their underwear while their pants dried near the fire; they found this thrilling and their older siblings were appalled.

That night, over a reconstituted dinner of freeze-dried pad thai and instant rice, one of the most memorable and consistent parts of the Riley children's day-to-day life played out as per usual, unabated by this strange setting and not at all hampered by the context which had delivered this truly bizarre day in the woods: Every night around the dinner table, the conversation was, for lack of a better phrase, particularly dynamic. Jordan and Sienna were both gifted talkers, and their children had proven to be equally adept communicators and quick learners in the arts of storytelling, asking thoughtful questions, offering insightful responses, and presenting both good- and bad-natured riposte. This gave them an unusual advantage amongst their peers and offered them a level of comfort in social situations and amidst strangers that was unusual for their age group. It could be overwhelming for a friend visiting for dinner, and it was an unexpected delight when one of the Riley kids ate dinner somewhere else and entertained the rest of the table. For all six of them, dinner was the place where they laughed the hardest and learned the most as the family discussed, dissected, and timed their giggling between bites.

Tonight as they ate voraciously, the conversation picked up right on schedule. It began with Sienna saying that one of the nice things about wrapping up the school year at the detention center was that she didn't have to spend hours doing end-of-year parent-teacher conferences.

> Sienna: I just submit the grades and then that's it. Over the summer a bunch of the kids will get released, but then a bunch more that already left will be back.

> Josie: Dad, why does mom always go to the parent-teacher night at my school?

> Jordan: Because she's a teacher and she's an expert at this stuff.

> Blaise: But even before she started teaching at the prison –

> Sienna: It's a detention center.

> Blaise: – she still went instead of you.

Jordan: Back when we lived in New York, before you guys were born, she was a teacher, so she's just naturally good at talking to teachers.

Josie: And then you stopped when Blaise was born?

Sienna: Yep.

Josie: Dad, what were you doing while Mom was a teacher?

Jordan: Well, I had a job, too, but mostly I was just handsome.

Scarlett: And then you stopped when Blaise was born?

Jordan: Hey!

Calista: Pretty solid joke, actually.

Jordan: Speaking of jokes, before we left, I got a note about that test you took for the gifted program next year.

Scarlett: What did it say?

Jordan: It said you drew a giant duck with the fill-in bubbles on the answer sheet instead of actually putting down your answers.

Scarlett: I didn't *just* draw a duck.

Jordan: And they said for all the short-answer questions you just wrote the word, "Quack."

Sienna: Well, you'll get to spend the next three years at regular elementary school with your friends, at least.

Blaise: Speaking of our real lives, what did we miss by being out here today?

Sienna: Nothing much, just a swim meet, and then there's a wedding reception for a friend of mine's daughter.

Scarlett: Big families must have so many weddings.

Josie: And those ones in ancient times – when a king had lots of kids – they would all get married to someone in another country and then you probably never saw them again because it took eight months to travel 100 miles.

Blaise: Didn't you say that then when there was a war where everyone was just declaring war on their relatives?

Jordan: It happened like that way past ancient times – in the First World War the leaders of Russia, Germany, and England were all cousins, they grew up together, they all spoke English and German, and Queen Victoria was their grandma.

Josie: Did they fight each other?

Sienna: No, they were all a bit too fancy for that – they hung out at the palace while the soldiers did all the shooting.

Jordan: Tsar Nicholas in Russia and King George in England were such good friends growing up and they looked so much alike, that they could swap outfits and be mistaken for each other. And it bothered people at the time that even in this "modern age" European wars were still just these family arguments – but with artillery.

Calista: And weren't the English at that point still mostly German or something?

Jordan: They're still mostly German now. Back during that same war when the cousins were fighting, the royal family in England still spoke German amongst themselves and had for over a century ever since several German royals married into the family – and, to make matters much worse, while the war was going on their official last name was Saxe-Coburg Gotha.

Blaise: Like, "The Goths?"

Sienna: Exactly.

Jordan: And a name like "Saxe-Coburg Gotha" on the English king is basically saying "Hey, I'm German" three times in a row.

Blaise: And that was their last name while England was fighting Germany?

Sienna: Yes, and the people in England were not fans – especially when a bomber named after the German town where it was built started dropping bombs on England because that town's name was – wait for it – Gotha.

Jordan: So, every day people would see another report of that Gotha bomber leveling another school or blowing up something, and then the next article would be about the royal family offering condolences – and they had the *same name*.

Calista: So, what happened?

Sienna: Well, the royal family knew that the people would never actually rise up –

Blaise: Why?

Jordan: Because of how British they are about things.

Sienna: But, on the off chance something like that *might* happen, the king at the time asked his butler to come up with a list of possible new last names, and because they just happened to be at Windsor Castle that day, they went with "Windsor."

Blaise: And that's still their last name now?

Jordan: It still is, and they're all still very German.

Calista: Speaking of that, I just remembered we haven't done movie night lately.

Scarlett: That doesn't have anything to do with Germans pretending to be English.

Jordan: You may remember that I canceled movie night, maybe forever.

Josie: No, it was only because of Blaise and Cali, not us!

Sienna: Let's change the subject.

Blaise: I can't believe that just because we didn't have some big emotional breakdown at the right part of a movie you got offended.

Jordan: You sat there straight faced like you were color-coding spreadsheets or sorting canned food while Goose bled to death in Maverick's arms in the middle of the ocean.

Sienna: Seriously?

Calista: It's not a big deal.

Jordan: I'm not saying you have to love the movie, but, when I first saw that scene, I was messed up for days, and it was just kind of weird to watch Goose floating in the water with that neon dye pack and notice that I live with two sociopaths.

Blaise: Speaking of dye packs, are you going to start dying your beard?

Josie: Dad, you dye your beard now?

Jordan: Do you remember the other day when you asked me who brings kids to orphanages?

Sienna: Ok, let's roast marshmallows or something.

Calista: What time is it supposed to get dark tonight?

Josie: Like that even matters; we live outside now.

Jordan: Kind of like "The Boxcar Children."

Calista: Did you know that Dark Matter takes up 85% of the observable galaxy.

Jordan: Great segue.

Josie: What?

Jordan: But now you have to explain it to a seven-year-old.

Calista: So, think about all of the Universe and all the stuff in it. What we can see is only 15% of what is really out there. The other 85% of the whole Universe is made up of a substance that we can't see – but we can tell it's there.

Josie: Where?

Calista: We know this stuff is there, but it's invisible to telescopes.

Scarlett: Then how do we know it's there?

Calista: Well, when astronomers look at the way a planet is

moving, there are a lot of times when it's moving in a way that doesn't make any sense – like, it's getting pulled off in a direction but there isn't a star there to pull it. Or sometimes there are planets or comets that are getting sped up as if some huge source of gravity is pulling them – but there's nothing there that we can see.

Sienna: I remember in school we had a teacher come through who told us about this, it's actually –

Blaise: Wait, which school? The school at your loaf camp or a real school?

Sienna: It was at the camp. And this teacher was explaining it to us, and none of us had ever heard anything about this, because it's kind of weird that the things we can actually see only make up a tiny part of the Universe we live in.

Jordan: Wasn't this first detected, like, 100 years ago?

Sienna: Yeah, in the '30s or something, and at the time they thought it was just in this one spooky corner of space, but as technology came along, they kept finding more of it. And eventually they discovered that it was just literally everywhere.

Josie: Can it hurt you?

Calista: No, it's just part of space.

Siena: The teacher's name was Dr. Maggie, and she was so smart. I remember she told us that one of the reasons they think we can't see dark matter is because they are pretty sure it's made out of stuff we don't know about yet – like, it's made out of something other than atoms. She used an example about how if you were shrunk down super tiny you wouldn't be able to see anything because the light waves would be bigger than your eye so no light could reach your optic nerve or your brain.

Blaise: And that's why we can't see 85% of the Universe that's right in front of us?

Sienna: Her basic point was that if dark matter is made out of something so different than us then our eyes simply don't have the equipment to see it.

Jordan: It's crazy, though; 85% is a lot.

Blaise: But is that real?

Jordan: I have no idea, but probably. But using percentages is a great way to convince people of almost anything. Just put a percentage in a sentence and it sounds half believable automatically.

Josie: What are you talking about?

Jordan: Like, just make up gibberish but put a statistic in it: Ummm, 63% of marriage counselors are divorced, or 42% of veterinarians are just two dogs in a lab coat, or over 50% of marine biologists have never been in the Marines.

Blaise: That is dumb and smart at the same time.

Calista: Now I can't un-see those stats. Or un-hear. Whatever.

Josie: You know, every day your brain cuts out about 70 minutes of things you see.

Scarlett: From what?

Josie: Haven't you ever noticed you don't see it momentarily go dark when you blink?

Blaise: Woooooah!

Sienna: So how exactly does that work?

Josie: Your brain just erases it for you, so you don't have to see the lights blinking on and off.

Jordan: That's actually exactly right. Apparently, our brain learned a long time ago that it gets distracting or tiring or uncomfortable for your brain to constantly have the lights get flipped on and off – so your brain just learned how to go delete that tenth of a second from the video that was streaming to your brain. Like, literally the video stream from your eyeballs actually does reach your brain with the black from your blink in it, but, in that instant before what you're seeing reaches your conscious mind, your brain really quickly edits it out before you see it.

Blaise: So we experience reality on a tape delay.

Calista: Wow.

Jordan: It does the same thing when you move your eyes really quickly from one thing to another – you notice how you never see the blur of the move in between? And also notice how your sisters start testing this now.

Scarlett: He's right.

Josie: And, by the end of the day all those tiny cuts add up to 70 minutes.

Blaise: So, if you're awake for 24 hours you actually see less than 23 hours.

Jordan: Einstein was right – time is relative.

Josie: You know what I like? The way British people say "garage."

Scarlett: Dad, did you know a blue whale's tongue weighs six tons?

Jordan: No.

Scarlett: Did you know that the gorillas who they taught sign language to have a vocabulary of a thousand words.

Jordan: I didn't know that.

Calista: Dad, how many Spanish words does Duolingo say that you know now?

Jordan: Not even close to that.

Sienna: So, what type of stuff do the gorillas talk about?

Scarlett: They mostly just ask for food, I think.

Josie: And they say that they hate crocodiles.

Calista: Really?

Josie: Yup – even the ones who have lived at the zoo their whole lives and never seen one in real life.

Blaise: That's like me and tarantulas.

Calista: Or moths.

Jordan: Don't you think it's weird that, in 40 years of teaching gorillas and chimps how to talk, they've told us a lot of things, but they've never asked us a single question.

Blaise: Ugh, that makes me feel weird.

Calista: Yeah, why does that feel so unsettling?

Josie: Now that I've heard it, I can't un-see it.

Calista: Does that mean they don't think about us?

Jordan: I don't think they even think in those terms.

Blaise: What terms?

Sienna: There was an old Austrian or Czech philosopher who said, "If a lion could speak, we couldn't understand him."

Calista: That's deep.

Scarlett: Didn't you say that you can only see things that you have words for?

Jordan: When it comes to colors, yes. Well, kind of. It doesn't mean you can't see them at all, but if your language doesn't have a word for a color, then how you understand and explain things and see that color is going to be affected. Like, the word "orange" didn't exist in Europe for a really long time – so people had to work extra hard to describe what a pumpkin or an orange or the leaves in the Fall looked like.

Blaise: Lame.

Jordan: And anciently Japan and Greece didn't have a word for blue, so, in "The Iliad" – or one of those Homer books – he describes the color of the ocean as being the same as wine. So, it seems like not having the word blue was shifting their perspective just enough to just lump red and blue together.

Sienna: Is it just blue that seems to be the problem?

Jordan: There was a bunch of research done on this in the mid-60s, I think, and what they found by studying languages as they developed over time was that if a language only has two names for colors, then they have one for white and one for black. If a language has three words for colors, then the colors they name are black, white, and red.

Scarlett: Daytime, nighttime, and blood.

Jordan: Probably. And then if a language has five words it's always black, white, red, green, yellow.

Blaise: Every time?

Jordan: Every time.

Sienna: So blue really does show up late.

Jordan: Blue is always sixth, and brown is always seventh.

Calista: Is this true?

Jordan: I went to college.

Blaise: But it was, like, a community college.

Sienna: It was a very nice community college, and then he transferred.

Scarlett: Look at how pretty the sky is above the mountains.

Blaise: Dad, I remember when I was like five-years-old we were looking at a sunset and you were explaining how the colors come from the way the sun's light bounces around in the atmosphere and reflects off different kinds of atoms.

Jordan: That does sound like the kind of thing I would say to a child.

Blaise: I did not understand a single word you were saying.

Jordan: But you remember it, so that's nice, at least.

Blaise: I just remember that "light bounced around" in the sky.

Scarlett: Speaking of things changing color, I watched a video before we left about butterfly colors.

Jordan: How do they do it?

Scarlett: Basically, they have scales on their wings that they can turn at different angles to let more or less light come through, and then that acts like a prism to reflect certain wavelengths of light and help them be certain colors.

Josie: Butterflies have scales?

Scarlett: Yup, and this lets them create colors that aren't possible with the pigments you find in lizard skin or other animals.

Sienna: I had no idea.

Scarlett: Oh, and certain butterflies can hear a bat that's flying toward them, so they rub their legs on their stomachs to create a bunch of clicks that scramble the bat's echolocation, and then they can get away.

Jordan: That sounds like a long video.

Josie: I like the butterfly's brain.

Blaise: So, ok, you know how the Earth's core is really hot?

Josie: Hey!

Blaise: We learned in Earth science this year that, like, half of the heat in the core of the Earth comes from uranium. Just radioactive uranium cooking the earth.

Jordan: First of all, that is crazy. Second of all, somebody ask Josie why she likes butterfly brains.

Calista: Tell me about butterfly brains.

Jordan: Thank you.

Josie: Well, that's kind of the cool part – cuz it's "brains" *plural*. So, when a butterfly is still a caterpillar and it is just eating leaves, it has a normal wormy body and a normal brain – but then it goes into its cocoon and craziness happens.

Blaise: Can you rank the level of craziness for me?

Sienna: Blaise…

Josie: So, after it's in the cocoon for a couple days, if you cut it open, it would all just be goo inside that will pour out like slime. But, if you don't cut it open, after a couple weeks, all that goo starts to harden together – and it becomes a butterfly.

Calista: The "goo" gets "hard" and it becomes a butterfly?

Josie: Yes, so from that goo you get a butterfly – and it has its wings, it has all new muscles to flap those wings, it has brand new eyeballs, and it has a brand new brain to control all this new stuff that the caterpillar didn't have to control.

Blaise: This is where Mom tells us about how butterfly brains can hear a secret radio.

Josie: So, in the olden times people thought that the caterpillar went in and then some tiny bug we couldn't see crawled into the cocoon and ate the caterpillar and that's what became the butterfly. But then there was an experiment where they gave an electric zap to the caterpillars every time they tried to eat their favorite type of leaf, so they all stopped trying to eat it. And then, when the butterflies hatched, none of them would eat that leaf because they knew it would zap them.

Jordan: Wait, so you're telling me that –

Josie: All its memories were being held in the goo and the slime waiting for a new brain to grow.

Calista: That is so weird. It is just… so weird.

Josie: It makes me feel weird.

Jordan: It makes me feel tired. We should get to bed, you guys.

Sienna: Who wants to come brush teeth with me?

Blaise: Dad, you didn't pack any energy drinks? How are you surviving?

Jordan: I have the love of my family to energize me.

Blaise: Family is the reason most people drink, we learned that in health.

Sienna: No you did not.

Jordan: I think he means genetics.

Blaise: I don't think I did.

Sienna: Wait, did you have Mr. Norris this semester?

Blaise: And apparently energy drinks cause all sorts of problems for your pancreas, or something.

Jordan: My problem with energy drinks is that they have names like "Electric Dragon Slurp" and then right on the front of the can it has the temerity to say "with natural flavors."

Calista: Dad, when I was taking the garbage out, I read one of the cans you drank, and it said "Gorilla Juice" on it. Or "gorilla" something.

Sienna: I don't think your dad has ever paused to consider what part of the gorilla is getting juiced.

Everyone: Woah!

Josie: If a gorilla was giant like King Kong and it was doing sign language, one of its fingers might flick you and you would die.

Blaise: Actually, if King Kong existed he would die basically immediately.

Jordan: Like, because of Godzilla?

Josie: What?

Blaise: No, like the bones in his legs would snap immediately.

Sienna: Wait, this sounds familiar – it's something about the load-bearing strength of mammal bones or something, right?

Blaise: Yes – so, it's like this: A regular gorilla is around six feet tall, but King Kong – depending on the movie – is like 300 feet tall. So, if you're 50 times taller, you're also going to be 50 times thicker and 50 times wider so that you have your regular proportions like he does.

Calista: I cannot wait for you to turn this into a math problem.

Blaise: So, if King Kong is 300 feet tall that means he is going to weigh over 100,000 times more than a normal gorilla which is something like 425 pounds.

Calista: Here comes the math!

Blaise: I don't remember the exact number from the thing I read about this, but King Kong would weigh somewhere around 50 million pounds.

Scarlett: Why would that kill him?

Blaise: Because every bone in his body would break instantly.

Josie: Why?

Blaise: So, if all his bones are 50 times longer and 50 times wider, they would be 2,500 times stronger than normal gorilla bones – but the bones of primates are built to hold 10 times the body weight of the animal they are inside of –

Jordan: That's definitely the weirdest way to word that.

Blaise: But King Kong weighs 125,000 times more than a normal gorilla and his bones can only hold up 2,500 times the weight of a normal gorilla – so, the second he set foot on the ground, all the bones in his foot would immediately shatter, and if he tried to put any weight on it, his femur basically would shatter instantly.

Sienna: Are you sure all that math checks out?

Blaise: I mean, even if he was just lying there his bones would break just from his body weight – like when a whale gets beached.

Jordan: This makes the monster movies a lot less cool.

Blaise: And if he tried to pull himself along the ground, all the bones in his hands and arms would break.

Sienna: Ok, so who wants to walk with me and Teddy down to

the stream again?

Blaise: And even if you made a smaller movie where King Kong was only 50 feet tall, that would place his weight at the exact limit of his bone strength, so all he could do is stand there. As soon as he jumped on something or started running – crack, crack, crack.

Jordan: I cannot believe we are still talking about this.

Scarlett: What are we eating tomorrow night? Is it this again?

Calista: Did that story make you hungry or something?

Sienna: No, it's a stew, I think.

Jordan: You're lucky we bought supplies for this when we did – in six weeks everything at the store will start being pumpkin spiced.

Josie: I love pumpkin spice!

Calista: I think you like the taste of cinnamon and nutmeg – because the taste of pumpkin is horrible.

Sienna: There's like a month every year where you can't buy anything at Trader Joes that isn't pumpkin spiced.

Jordan: Grape juice, canned beans.

Blaise: Vegan chili, toothpaste.

Calista: Fajita mix, deodorant

Scarlett: Really?

Josie: I think I ate too much tonight, I feel gross.

Jordan: It could just be the mental image of pumpkin spice toothpaste.

Josie: Or all the gorilla bones.

Sienna: Or the gorilla juice.

Blaise: Wait, what do we do if someone gets sick out here?

Sienna: Everyone has a first aid kit, and we have a bunch of pills for stuff like fevers and antibiotics.

Blaise: But what about if there's, you know, like a wolverine attack?

Jordan: There's no pill for wolverines, bro.

Sienna: That's not funny, babe.

Calista: That was pretty funny.

This went on for 20 more minutes – a timeline greatly extended thanks to the lack of a table to clear, homework to do, or evening activities to carpool.

29 JUNE

Julius Torquemann had slept very little since his long visit with Colonel Castro four days earlier.

There was something about the reappearance of the Signal combined with the long-form retelling of the Dark Antennae project that had shook something loose deep in his subconscious, and now his mind was working overtime to help him find the connection it had already discovered. This was an odd way to think about one's own manner of analysis, but, on the other hand, any cognitive neuropsychologist would tell you that there were multiple levels of cognition within the human mind – and they all operated concurrently and separately, and each one struggled to communicate with the others.

He had been sorting through this nagging feeling since he woke up the morning after his late-night discussion with Castro, and he had spent the days since slowly sorting through old files, progress reports, and the summary research that he compiled at regular intervals during the nine years he spent at Camp Loaf.

Right here in his office – or, more specifically, nearby in his carefully manicured database – was a digitized record of every session with every camper, as well as every reading that was measured at the time, every flutter of their vital signs, and every word they spoke while in that chair. That last detail may have come as a surprise to the program's alumni. The same model of shotgun mic the FBI used to clandestinely record conversations at a distance was mounted in the ceiling to capture the specifics of what the campers were sorting through as they leaned their minds into the Signal to see what could be seen or heard. Those tapes, covering thousands of hours, were all digitized and auto-transcribed when he put this database together, and this made searching for things easy when there was something specific to search for – but it also presented a nearly bottomless place of near-infinite complexity that made casual searching futile.

But something nagged at Torquemann nonetheless.

At the outset of this research, Torquemann had recognized that there was more data in his archive than a large team could ever hope to sift through meaningfully, even with the help of the data processing technology his organization had access to at any given time. In order to focus his effort and time most effectively, he chose to focus on the period when the fidelity of material coming through the Signal had been the highest – a window that stretched from July 1985 to February 1988. If this timeframe seemed a bit narrow it was at least very pragmatic. There were spikes and exceptionally noteworthy moments elsewhere in Dark Antennae's timeline, but these specific 31 months represented the most consistently active and high energy period of Signal strength, and it offered the ideal dataset to pursue the very specific answers he was after.

His computer monitor flickered on to show the same starting screen he saw every morning — a multivariate graph which mapped the day and time of every substantive piece of data which came through the Signal. At a glance, the high activity areas were obvious – a big chunk of activity in the late-70s, and then another surge in the mid-80s, and then thousands of other isolated spikes throughout the lifespan of the program. There were thousands of ways to sort the data on this particular graph, and the default setting showed an x-axis that was intricately subdivided into one-hour increments of each research day – which had typically lasted from 10 am to 3 pm – and the y-axis represented just how much information was documented, with repeated information getting a single unit of space, new information getting considerably more, and different weights given to auditory or visual information based on a sliding scale of additional factors. The height of a spike and the way in which it was clustered made it proportionately more interesting from a research perspective, and, if these clusters could be seen as a pattern, or if their contents represented a trend in some novel direction, then it would get even more attention still. All of these factors presented rich territory for analysis, meta-analysis, and any number of abstracted types of study.

He scrolled back and forth across the timeline, seeing the rise and fall of those lines, and considered, not for the first time, how the simple left-to-right motion of the mouse moving just a few inches in either direction could encompass his entire life's work at a glance.

This morning, uncharacteristically, Torquemann's finger hovered above the keyboard. Every other day he arrived at this moment in his swivel chair with any number of new theories to test or datasets to reevaluate with a new lens – but now he paused and wondered where to start. After so many decades spent ardently studying the past, he now had the odd sensation that there was something new to do in the present.

He closed his eyes without consciously thinking to do it, and he sank back into himself, the same way, he would consider later, he had seen his campers do reflexively so many times. Torquemann had no sensitivity to the Signal, but, as a few quiet moments passed, his mind returned to a single question from Colonel Castro: "And this wasn't something that animals could detect?"

Animals.

He called up the search function and typed the word "animal."

He could hear the servers in the next room start to hum as they assembled the information, and he began reading through the results as they arrived. He spent the next hour reading and looking at the accompanying details that his system automatically cross referenced. In late June of 1991, six campers had heard information in the Signal about animals. Or, more specifically, looking at the specific sections of their transcripts, the *concept* of animals. The case files accompanying these sessions noted that this material was unique because of how infrequently biological material had been observed in the Signal, as opposed to schematics or metallic surfaces. A few additional searches found no other references to biological material outside of this general timeframe. The notes, written by Dr. Adams – and with a few additional points added by the team's child psychologist, Dr. Carney – concluded that this was likely the result of each child's psyche bleeding over into their perceptions of the Signal. Considering the nature of the work, crossovers like this were unavoidable, although they were rarely pinpointed as specifically as this instance. In this case, the writeup noted that a recent classroom discussion about Laika (Лайка) had stirred a variety of strong, negative emotions. Every grade school student during the Cold War had learned about Laika's sad story – she was the stray dog from the streets of Moscow who was sent to space in 1957. But what might have been an inspiring story was dashed by the fact that no one at Cosmonaut HQ (Космическая программа CCCP) planned for a round trip. The campers found this appalling, in no small part because they identified in some small way with the dog, and they groused at the idea that this was still happening somewhere on the other end of their Signal.

Torquemann had only the vaguest recollection of this brief moment in an otherwise long program, and he considered that many of those campers waded back into the Signal without telling the team in the research cabin about the many questions they were pondering about innocent space dogs.

But the mention of this forgotten classroom discussion did spark a distant and distinct memory.

At the time, this aberration in the data was dismissed and the presence of this material wasn't included in the weekly roundup of observed Signal data which had the most immediate strategic value. This spike appeared to have come and gone quickly, with just a few other small spikes appearing later. The biggest of those came from a camper who had been very proficient during his short time in the program – it was Asher Henton, a name he remembered only because of this boy's distinction as the youngest person they ever had at the camp. Out of curiosity, Torquemann checked the dates of Asher's time at Camp Loaf. He noted the intake date and immediately flipped back to Dr. Carney's citation in the case notes. That was odd. This young man had arrived the week *after* that infamous lesson about Laika. With a couple more clicks he pulled up the camper's academic history. Everything looked normal there, too – and a form attached to the back of his academic overview included the order form for school supplies which the teacher was instructed to have ready for him on his first day of class. At the bottom of the form, one of the program managers had checked a box indicating that an additional desk did not need to be brought in from storage to accommodate him. This was typically the case when one student left in close proximity to another arriving.

Torquemann hit a few more keys to check who had been the most recent departure prior to the date this intake was filed. The information popped up almost immediately.

Now Julius understood what had been nagging him.

"Of course," he said through the hand that had involuntarily come up to cover his mouth, "the only one who knew."

He found the date of her last session in the research cabin on the chart. This detail alone made it obvious that *this* was the lit fuse behind the small explosion of unusual activity that followed.

He opened the case file for that final session and remembered clearly all the things he had known not to put on paper.

He had listened to the recording of that session several times the day after it happened, but the quality of recordings from that year were all exceptionally poor. Several magnets in the overhead sensors had been interfering with the microphone, and the team had been slow to fix it. But the recording of that session had been digitized and added to this archive, nonetheless – and the .wav file was right there next to the .pdf of his report. Torquemann ran the audio through an AI that had been trained to clean up decayed archival recordings, and a fresh file was ready five minutes later. The recording was 17 minutes long, but he knew to skip to its final moments.

He heard a small, bright voice talking its way through the sights and sounds of this unexplainable medium, and then he heard it trail off. It returned again, now uncertain and trepidatious, but still so early in the stages of confusion that it wasn't yet scared.

"I'm just a… rabbit" he heard her say clearly.

Next he heard her draw a sharp breath, and, after a long moment, a ragged exhale full of turmoil. The type of thing an eight-year-old couldn't label and an adult would try to forget.

That poor child, he thought. *What on earth does that do to you?*

He remembered enough about her to be as unsurprised now as he was then that it was her who sent a joke back through the Signal, even if she didn't understand what she was doing at the time.

The entirety of her file contained nothing else of any particular note from her time in that cabin, and she was already aging out of the program when this happened. But she was the only one who had ever grasped even the slightest idea of what the Signal was – and her knowledge fell into the "no uncertain terms" category.

She had known and been known that day.

If governments in every corner of the globe were reacting poorly to the Signal's return, it was possible that she could offer a datapoint that Castro and his counterparts might use as a pressure-release valve.

He picked up the phone to call the colonel. He proposed a discussion between the two of them and a former participant that lived on the West Coast. Castro was intrigued, but Torquemann didn't offer anything beyond the vague promise of someone with "very helpful insight on the Signal." Torquemann promised to set up the meeting and call him back in a few hours. Now he just needed to think of how to broach this subject and solicit her participation. Based on what Castro had told him, any number of government agencies would want to control this story, this information, and the sole source of contact if Sienna was found to be a valuable component in this rapidly escalating situation. He knew more than enough about clandestine government agencies and how they behaved to understand that drawing her into this had the potential to make her life exceptionally unpleasant, and he wanted to shield her from as much of that as possible. And there was also the unavoidable fact that Castro was eventually going to be furious when he learned that he spent half the night in an old man's office without the biggest detail of all ever being mentioned.

First thing was first, however. His browser chimed after having tracked down her phone number. He saw that this Barrett had become a Riley, and Walnut Creek had been traded for something unpronounceable in Washington. He cleared his throat and dialed. On the other side of the country an iPhone with a slightly cracked screen vibrated beneath a throw pillow inside the home of an otherwise happy family who, at this moment, were using ferns and pine boughs to hide their brightly painted bikes.

1 JULY

The first two days had passed simply, and, as day three began, this really could have been mistaken for a camping trip.

They took their time eating breakfast, went back to a nearby stream to play, and Blaise refilled everyone's water. Teddy wandered in and out of camp, splitting his time between chasing things and then running back to see everyone. Blaise had gathered a pile of edible plants and encouraged everyone to load up. He was disappointed but not surprised there were no takers, but he made a point of eating these exclusively for breakfast and explaining their health benefits and usages by ancient indigenous cultures. He'd soon eaten most of the pile and shrugged off all of Sienna's warnings that he would probably need quite a few of those big leaves later if any of his plants ended up being less edible than he thought.

The rest of the day was spent hiking towards the circle.

The route was far less direct now that the landscape began to pitch up into the mountains, and the flat sections they had enjoyed yesterday were few and far between. Their route brought them up and over a steep ridge where they stopped to eat lunch, and another one right before they made camp for the night. By the time they began making dinner the elevation gain had been extreme and everyone was exhausted. Sienna was proud of "what troopers" everyone had been, and Jordan hurried to make dinner while the hammocks were strung and the kids secretly ate candy while they gathered firewood.

Blaise looked at the clouds to the north and decided it looked like rain, so he began constructing a canopy above the hammocks. By the time dinner was done, which he ate sporadically while he worked, he had lashed together a frame, added cross beams, covered it with one of the tarps, and then multiple layers of pine boughs. It seemed excessive at the time, but, when the rain began falling shortly after midnight, Sienna woke up and listened and smiled.

By morning the sun was out again, and the fresh layer of rain seemed to make things even quieter than usual. Blaise was bursting with a level of pride that his sisters could not have found any more amusing. His unsolicited advice on all things wilderness survival now moved from a torrent to a flood, and eventually Jordan began asking his advice for increasingly unlikely scenarios.

"Dad, what do you mean a shelter for a heat wave during polar exploration?" Blaise demanded with no small amount of exasperation, despite knowing he was being toyed with.

"Well," Jordan explained, "it seems to me that this would make a snow cave or igloo pretty impractical."

"That's not even a thing."

"So, you're saying you'd be unprepared for this?"

"I can only be prepared for things that are likely to happen."

"Those sound like the last words of someone who dies in the woods."

Sienna effectively changed the subject right around the time the sisters were laughing enough that Blaise would no longer be able to tolerate such besmirching of his now-sterling reputation.

Today's path took them up and over two more steep ridges, one of which was the tallest in the area. The climbs took a physical and mental toll on the group – starting at the bottom and slowly working its way up. But, amidst the drudgery, each time they came up and over another ridge, they were stunned at the view. The crests, valleys, and peaks surrounding them on every side were visually intensive to the extent that it would always defy adequate explanation to anyone who wasn't there. Atop each ridge, Mt. Rainier seemed close enough to touch, despite being over 50 miles south. Rainier was among the tallest peaks in North America, and it loomed large over every other elevated point in every direction.

Any of this would have made the perfect family photo, like the picture they took next to Avalanche Lake in Glacier National Park a few years earlier. But not this trip.

On this particular mountainside, beneath a canopy of Douglas Firs, it was easy to forget, for the occasional precious moment, what was going on and why they had a wilderness to themselves. The mountains here were so massive and so intimately close, that it was possible to lose perspective of their size and the time it took to traverse each one. The steep mountainsides were perfectly blanketed in dark green and hugged every contour, as if a brush, heavy laden with paint, had been careful to not miss a single inch of canvas. This was the safety blanket that Jordan and Sienna led their children beneath, as they explored the equally complex forest floor which grew in the heavy shade of the Pacific Northwest's ancient forests. Hours at a time found them wading through an ocean of ferns straining for stray bands of sunlight, crossing streams that ran frigid and clear from the melting snow 1,100 feet above, and walking over and around fallen trees that had been saplings back when forgotten gods lived inside them and listened when you prayed.

Now, as the sun started to touch the distant tips of the Olympic Mountain Range 120 miles away on the peninsula, they found a new site to make camp for a third night.

During the day, while they kept moving and the conversation remained lively, it was easy to become distracted to the whys and hows of this adventure, but the afternoons were different. When the sky began to turn orange and each of the kids had a chance to be alone with their thoughts while they gathered firewood, laid out clothes to dry, or looked for materials to build a shelter – that was when the anxiety, the melancholy, and the hopelessness could creep in and coil around each Riley in its own disquieting way. For Josie and Scarlett, they counted on their parents to set the tone for their reaction to all of this, and, for all their other faults, Jordan and Sienna were modeling their behavior well. For Sienna this came naturally. Jordan was every bit as stoic in his own regard, and he was doubled down on this approach because doing so was, in his estimation, the primary thing he had to offer Sienna at this point. If lightning hit him tomorrow someone else could use the GPS to find the circle, but he was the only one who could effectively present the other half of the parenting the kids needed right now.

If the little girls were taking their cues from their parents, Blaise and Cali were on their own paths. Blaise had the good fortune of having been caught up in the adventure of the excursion, and his sense of humor hadn't been dampened; he was quick to call out the presence of CIA drones every time he saw a bird, and last night, as he built his shelter, he noted that "at least when mom was a kid the scientists let her sleep indoors between experiments."

Allowing himself to be fully immersed in the survivalist aspects of this was certainly a coping mechanism, but this was also the trip he had dreamed of ever since receiving a hatchet for Christmas at age six and subsequently discovering that YouTube had 21 million hours of wilderness survival tutorials. The greenbelt in his backyard had been a fine area to practice, but this was where he could finally become his best self.

Today's many hard climbs had come with the emotional reckoning which the shock and adrenaline of disappearing had postponed for Jordan. It came in the form of memories of the poverty-stricken neighborhood where he had lived as a child. Up and down his street there was no shortage of abandoned and boarded up houses, and by the time he was six he had become particularly adept at climbing in through cracked windows or back doors which had simply been left unlocked. He spent countless hours wandering these miniature ghost towns, squinting in the darkness, and fearing there was something still inside. Seeing what was left behind scared him, and he was always amazed by just *how much* was left behind. Rarely did he find a room that wasn't still scattered with clothes and furniture and pictures and papers. But, without all this – and seemingly with no forethought – these people had left and went on with their lives somewhere else. A week ago, he was still amazed by how much could be left behind. But now he finally understood just how short the shortlist of essentials could suddenly become.

The technical aspects of arriving at today's campsite had been especially challenging.

The GPS had lost its connection for over three hours, and, by the time they stopped for lunch, Jordan had begun to doubt his ability to successfully navigate over such a long distance. Even with the GPS functioning again, there were still dozens of possible routes to the circle, as well as an additional few dozen that were certain to kill them from exhaustion or slips from mountainsides. Adding to this problem was the fact that the sheer size of the circle meant that a week could be spent just on the inside of it looking for signs of Uncle Harvey – much less traveling to it. This left him with doubts and questions and second-guesses about which fork to take at any given time, where to enter the circle's perimeter, and how to balance speed with safety with exhaustion.

As the family ate lunch, Jordan combed through countless route options on the GPS, and he slowly began to despair. He was still searching for answers and options when Scarlett came over and sat next to him on the log.

As he worked his way through the area's topography something caught her attention. She cocked her head to one side, looked at Jordan, then looked back at the mountains ahead of them and smiled. He did another scan of the horizon but didn't see anything out of the ordinary.

"So, I guess that's our next stop," she said, pointing at a particularly steep peak a few miles directly ahead.

"What?"

"That's the peak from my dream."

"You had a dream about *that* mountain? When?"

"Last night."

"That mountain right there?"

"Well, it was part dream and part Signal. My dreams have crackles in them now."

"Your dreams have crackles? Since when?"

"The last two nights."

Jordan was unsettled that this kind of made sense and that now he was open to plotting a course to this specific peak.

"Mom said we are kinda headed that direction already."

"Dude, it's one of about 300 directions we can go, but, sure, I like this one."

He sat and stared at her for a moment.

"How sure do you feel about this dream?"

"The Signal wants us to go that direction."

"I wasn't aware the Signal had opinions."

"Dad," she said, sighing heavily, "you don't get it."

He didn't.

But now, several hours later, they had reached the base of this next peak and were ready to go up and over it first thing tomorrow.

On this particular evening, while Blaise walked the perimeter of a small pond looking for signs of fish, the quiet pause I the day hit Calista hard yet again.

The pressure she felt behind her eyes didn't help her mood, and the ibuprofen she took had helped only a little. There were few home remedies for hypothetical particles.

She thought through the last six days yet again, trying to find a new combination of this information which made more sense. The incredible strangeness of her mother's past was compounded by the profound weirdness of what was now happening to her. That was the best way she could find to phrase it. And these factors led to where she sat now – on a stump that had been hollowed out by time, small animals, and regular rainfall to the point where she could sit down inside of it, here in an untouched forest carpeting mountains that reached so high up into the clouds that their peaks were only suggested. She sat alone and sorted through the revolving set of questions she could not answer. Namely, if they really were running from something, how could her parents know where to run if no one was clear on who'd be chasing them?

She took another deep breath and leaned back into the stump. If nothing else, it felt very good to not be walking.

Each of these last three days had taken a toll on everyone, but today it started hitting people particularly hard. When they had stopped for lunch earlier, literally everyone fell asleep. In the distance she could see Blaise by the pond and suddenly he started yelling and pointing hysterically. That could only mean a fish.

While Cali sorted through these things on her own terms and sought out her own way to make sense of it, Sienna had a reckoning of her own.

She knew by the way the wave of emotions hit her that fatigue and isolation were taking a toll, and there was probably some dehydration in there, for good measure. But this reckoning was real, and for someone who was so impassive and composed in her day-to-day life, this wave of guilt and uncertainty and fear represented a type of chaos and a lack of control which were shattering. *"What am I doing... what are we doing…"* Her ears were ringing from the pressure. *"What are the kids…"* Each question crushed harder than the last and they pulled a sob out of her chest that was so bitterly sad she was shocked by the sound of it. She was standing on a granite ledge overlooking a narrow valley over two thousand feet below. That valley, the tributary that ran through it, and the peaks on three sides had names she would never know. Her family was far beyond anyone's ability to find them, but she couldn't know that either. In between sobs she watched her tears fall on the rough granite ledge and subtly change the color of the stone. She wiped her nose, tried to take a deep breath, but couldn't shake the feeling she had done something terrible and irreversible bringing them here. She thought about the first time she laid eyes on Dr. Torquemann, and how her dad had looked at her in the rearview mirror on the way home. She thought about her last day at camp and how each moment in between went unspoken ever again. She thought about what she had heard through the Signal, the way her heart sailed that night, and this same crushing failure she brought home and carried ever since. She was the point of contact for the most important moment in history.

Even in the moment she had known this.

And nothing had come of it.

She had never believed in the idea of fate, but she had been in the seat at that time, and it was her brain and her Epicortical Surface Reflector that were just right in just that moment.

And then nothing.

And then she went home.

And then she was a guest in her own house until she discovered you could take classes at a community college during the summer and graduate a year early. So she did, and she packed up her own tiny car, bought with her own lifeguarding and babysitting money, and she left for college – returning only for the stray holiday visit or extended family get together. She didn't know what could have happened differently in that chair, or even what the protocol was for successfully navigating situations that were widely considered impossible. But she knew she had missed. And even though nothing had changed, her life and everything in it was different.

And she didn't understand the cause of that either.

And now, she thought, through another sob and a gasp, she had brought all this chaos to her children.

What had been the point of a life spent so meticulously and so carefully constructed if the first nebulous, ill-defined moment of quasi crisis ripped them out of their home and their lives and led them into a forest? The degree to which her composed exterior was simply a cage to contain this roil of emotions was laid bare in this moment. This combination of terrain, weather, megafauna, and isolation provided an essentially infinite number of ways for a group as small and inexperienced as hers to suffer and die.

Deep in the distance she heard the happy sound of Blaise's voice. He had been talking about catching fish ever since they stashed their bikes.

Sienna stared forward, through the ledge and through the valley floor beyond it, searching for something to brace herself. The flickers of the Signal chipped at the edges of her vision and stayed there when she closed her eyes. She took the three long breaths she'd heard an instructor explain as the "key to unlocking your calm" during the one yoga class she took in college. She held the last breath until she felt that she had pulled herself together enough to finish what she had started. She wasn't ready to face anyone yet, and this was far too abrupt an end to an emotional overflow such as this – but now was when this had to end, at least for now. She told herself that, between her and Jordan, they could get everyone through this.

She made it back to camp in time to see Blaise in the distance, on the far side of the pond, pulling in a fish.

"That's his second one," Jordan told her, with no small amount of pride, and, like everyone else, a bit of surprise.

"I didn't know you bought fishing line."

"I didn't – he already had it."

Jordan started a fire with the wood he and the girls had gathered, and five minutes later it was roaring. Another 20 minutes after that Blaise had cleaned the five fish he'd caught and carried them proudly back into camp, ready to be placed over the fire.

"Tonight we're going to eat some real food," he announced triumphantly, ignoring the fact that none of his sisters or his mom liked fish. "I think we're all a little tired of…" he picked up the vacuum-sealed pouch of dehydrated food "…'Tex-Mex & Rice' mix, no offense,

Dad."

"Oh, no offense; everything in that bag has probably been frozen in carbonite since before any of you were born."

The fish sizzled over the fire while the water boiled, and the dark orange sky turned purple and then black while the Rileys relaxed and spent another night talking by the fire. The dinner conversation was as lively as ever, and Sienna recognized that this small oasis of normalcy was now more important than ever.

The conversation kicked off with Josephine observing that tomorrow the three girls would be missing piano lessons.

Scarlett: I'm glad I'm missing it; I'm done with piano. Next year, I'm playing the flute.

Calista: *You* are going to play the flute?

Sienna: We can talk about this when we get home.

Jordan: Isn't the flute just the American version of the didgeridoo?

Scarlett: No, Dad, you hold the flute sideways, but you blow straight down into a didgeridoo.

Jordan: I'm pretty sure they originally played the didgeridoo sideways, too –

Blaise: That rhymed.

Jordan: But it got so big that it was too hard to hold up.

Josie: What do you mean it got too big?

Jordan: I don't know, it probably got wet and expanded – they have rainforests down there you know.

Scarlett: Dad!

Blaise: How do you even spell that word?

Jordan: In its original language, or in English?

Calista: Do you know any aboriginal languages?

Jordan: I know that most words in English don't follow any rules when it comes to spelling.

Scarlett: Mom, didn't you say that's because English is really just a bunch of languages slammed together?

Sienna: Yes, the meme is that English is basically a bunch of languages walking around inside a trenchcoat pretending to be one normal language. But it's a mix of about six or seven depending on how you want to count it.

Josie: I like how this forest smells.

Jordan: What does it smell like to you?

Josie: Vegetables.

Blaise: You mean "vegetation?"

Josie: No, like a carrot.

Calista: Wait – Mom, go back, you were telling me one time that modern English started with a language that doesn't even exist anymore, or something, right?

Sienna: So, around 3,000 years ago, England is just doing its thing as an island, and the people who swam or floated over to it are speaking something called Brittonic – and then there's this migration from mainland Europe where a bunch of people speaking Celtic show up.

Calista: And instead of replacing one language with the other, they just kind of merged into one big language, right?

Sienna: Right, and then a few centuries later Romans show up.

Jordan: Like they do.

Sienna: So now Latin is getting spoken on a regular basis, so if you want to go buy stuff from them or sell your sheep to them, you gotta be able to speak some of it. And the Romans love building stuff, so when they build schools, and your kids go to those schools, they learn Latin.

Blaise: Do you think the Roman schools were fun?

Jordan: As a general rule, probably not.

Sienna: So, by the time that first generation of kids after the

Roman invasion are grownups, they can speak both languages, and Latin eventually merges with both the previous languages.

Jordan: And at that point the Romans need more troops to keep this island under control because all your ancestors weren't afraid to get rowdy, so they start hiring mercenaries from an area called Saxony – that's basically where Germany and the Netherlands are now – and they hire those dudes to come over and serve in the army and help keep everyone in check.

Blaise: Didn't that not turn out great for them?

Josie: Why?

Jordan: Importing a mercenary army is a dangerous game if or when they ever miss a paycheck.

Sienna: Which is pretty much what happens – Rome collapses, or I guess you could say it kind of transforms into something else – and all the troops in England are called back to fight in a civil war, and, after a few years, everyone back in Italy forgets about England, and it doesn't take too long for all those Saxons in charge of protecting things to figure out the Romans aren't coming back, so they just take control of everything for themselves.

Jordan: Which, give them credit, was pretty smart.

Calista: So, they took their word for "bull" by their word for "horns."

Jordan: That's actually really funny, Cali.

Sienna: So, that's where we get the term Anglo-Saxon – the Anglo tribes were there before the Romans, the Saxons were there after, and when they combined their languages and cultures, they went with a hyphenated name.

Jordan: Which is still standard practice today whenever two people who don't entirely trust each other decide to get married anyway and subsequently make things really hard on their kids when they're little and trying to learn how to write their name.

Blaise: And why did England just keep merging languages instead of replacing them?

Jordan: And like I was saying, those poor kids who have to learn to spell hyphenated last names are never named "Lee-Ford," it's always "McCunningham-Vandermeulen."

Sienna: A lot of it has to do with who kept invading England – it kept being people who didn't care what language you spoke as long as you paid taxes, and so the various languages just kept piling up instead of everyone being forced to use the newest one.

Jordan: And this plugs into what we were talking about how all the royal families in World War 1 were related – because the guy who started the whole British monarchy we know today is a guy we know as William the Conqueror, and he's something like the 90th great grandfather of the current king.

Sienna: So, William is invading England from the place his family has lived for a couple hundred years in France, specifically in a little kingdom there named Normandy. And the Normans got that name because the rest of the French called them "North Men" – because back before they showed up in France, they were Vikings.

Scarlett: And they just garbled it together into Norman?

Sienna: Yep, and their Viking descendants had been destroying stuff all over France, so the French king finally called them up and was, like, "Guys, stop, you can have a little kingdom of your own, but just stop wrecking everything."

Blaise: It was a simpler time.

Sienna: So, a couple hundred years pass, they are speaking French by now but with a lot of old Norse still sprinkled in, and when they invade England they bring that with them.

Scarlett: And we still use their language?

Sienna: Basically any time you see the letters "ei" or "sch" or "ter" next to each other, that word came from the invaders from Germany, and any time you see a word that ends in "ious" or "ier" or "per" it's from the French invaders.

Scarlett: So how much of English is not English?

Sienna: Kind of all of it, sorta. About 30% is French, 30% is Latin, and then 25% of it is German — and then the remaining 15% is a combination of Norse and Greek and whatever else the English picked up while they took their turn invading the rest of the world.

Blaise: And wouldn't you know it — "conquer" itself is French, right?

Calista: That was so close to being deep.

Josie: How did we even get on this topic?

Blaise: Speaking of Romans – Dad, does Josie know what you wanted to name her if she had been a boy?

Sienna: We were only ever going to call her "Josephine."

Blaise: Yeah, but if she was a boy...

Jordan: Do you mean "Hannibal?"

Sienna: No, never.

Jordan: This is what I'm talking about.

Josie: Wait, what?!

Scarlett: Why?

Jordan: For Hannibal Barca – the greatest general who ever lived and the most feared man in all Roman history.

Blaise: Wait, the best *ever*?

Jordan: I mean, Alexander the Great, and Caesar, and Clayton Abernathy, and Genghis, and Napoleon are all in the mix – but Hannibal is probably at the top.

Josie: And that was going to be Cali's name?

Jordan: Well, once we found out we were having a girl I

stopped talking about it for a month, and then one day I very casually suggested we name you "Annabelle" – and your mom saw through this immediately.

Sienna: That would have been so dumb.

Josie: I would not have liked that.

Scarlett: That kind of makes me feel gross.

Jordan: Yeah, but now you know why your middle name is Alexandra, right?

Sienna: Jordan – stop. Scar, you know that was my grandmother's name.

Jordan: It can be both.

Sienna: Jordan!

Sienna: Speaking of gross, how is everyone feeling after all this re-hydrated food?

Scarlett: It's fine, I guess.

Josie: My stomach was making some weird noises last night, though.

Blaise: You know everyone has a brain in their intestines, right?

Jordan: Oh geez.

Josie: Like a stegosaurus?

Calista: They proved that isn't true, I thought?

Blaise: No, this is real, I saw a video about this, and then I looked it up. So, it turns out your digestive tract, which is like 30 feet long, is covered with neurons the entire way – like, there's 100 million of them, which is more than your spinal cord has.

Jordan: Why can't you watch normal kid stuff on YouTube – like people getting injured on skateboards or dashcam footage of cops getting punched?

Blaise: So, your gut has something like 10% of your body's

neurons in it because your stomach has to do so many complex things that it can't just wait around on the brain to tell it what to do – so it has to be able to think about how to do all this stuff on its own.

Scarlett: Wait, the brain is where?

Blaise: Think about it – I mean…

Sienna: No.

Blaise: …I mean, your intestines have to know what chemicals to add to digest certain things at any given moment, they have to figure out when to tell your stomach to produce more acid, when to start moving the food from one end to the other, and how to make all these millions of other adjustments all the time – and it takes a lot of *thinking* to do all that.

Jordan: This does sound pretty fake.

Sienna: Fake.

Blaise: No! This is so real – google this. And your intestines are just doing this all by themselves with basically no input from the brain – like, of all the wires and nerves that connect your brain and your digestive system, 90% of those only go one way – and it's the intestines telling the brain what has already happened *after* it's done just to give it an FYI.

Calista: So, your intestinal tract is doing all the talking and the brain is just listening and saying "Ok, got it, cool, good job on all the pooping?"

Blaise: Pretty much. And because your guts can do so much thinking, you actually get *emotions* from it.

Sienna: Ok, no.

Jordan: Wait, what?

Blaise: Think about it – butterflies in your stomach?

Sienna: That's not why that happens.

Josie: Is it?

Blaise: Bro, think about this: So, you know how serotonin is the chemical in your brain that affects your mood and a bunch of other things? Well, something like 95% of all the serotonin in your whole body is in your intestines. So, your guts not only do their own things and have their own thoughts – your guts have *moods*.

Jordan: The algorithm that suggests videos to you must be a nightmare right now.

Blaise: So, there are experts out there that say certain stomach problems should count as a mental illness.

Calista: So, like, diarrhea is ADHD?

Sienna: Dear lord.

Jordan: And ulcerative colitis is schizophrenia.

Calista: Mine was funnier.

Jordan: Not if you know what colitis is.

Blaise: So that makes a colonoscopy pretty much brain surgery?

Josie: A what?

Sienna: Jordan!

Jordan: What?

Sienna: I feel like saying any of this in public is going to get you in trouble – but I'm not sure how.

Scarlett: If you could eat anything for dinner tomorrow, what would it be?

Josie: I want broccoli.

Jordan: What on earth?

Scarlett: But just the tops, not the stems.

Josie: I love the stems.

Jordan: What is going on right now?

Calista: They always make broccoli look good on TV when

someone pours melted cheese over it, but it is disgusting.

Jordan: I feel like broccoli that's enjoyable to eat is a fiction created by the media that seems plausible in theory but has never existed in real life – kinda like soccer games that are interesting or jazz that isn't horrible.

Sienna: Babe, Josie loves playing soccer.

Jordan: I love it when you play soccer, Josephine.

Blaise: Little league soccer games are not the most fun thing to watch, though.

Jordan: The older the players get the better the game gets, but as a parent you just like seeing your kids run around. That is fun dad stuff.

Calista: So, what are the least fun things about being a dad?

Jordan: That question is a trap, and I will not entertain it.

Scarlett: It's probably when we are all fighting about stuff.

Jordan: I like pretty much everything about being a parent, but then there are these moments that pop up where you realize that things are just ridiculous. Like when someone is three years old – and I don't want to say any names, like Cali's – and, when you tell them that their favorite Batgirl pajamas are in the washing machine, she tries to bite you. Or when one of your kids is potty training and they poop their pants while standing next to the toilet and throwing a tantrum about how they don't need any help going to the bathroom.

Scarlett: Who was that?

Jordan: My official answer is that I "can't remember."

Scarlett: It was probably Josie.

Sienna: It was you.

Jordan: Or when – and for the sake of discussion we'll attribute this to Blaise – you give your child baby carrots for a snack instead of store-brand Oreos, and he draws you a picture explaining that he wants a new dad.

Blaise: No kids like baby carrots.

Calista: I liked them.

Jordan: You called them "dirt Cheetos."

Calista: Speaking of that, I am going to a birthday party next week for a girl from my old volleyball team.

Josie: Is it volleyball-themed?

Calista: No, but they are having the party at this place where you get inside these giant inflatable balls, and you play capture the flag.

Blaise: That is so cool.

Scarlett: What does your friend want for her birthday?

Calista: We were talking to her about this after practice, and she started rattling off a list of things on her wish-list that made her sound like a crazy person – it was: Oreos, a puppy, more TV time, "candy but not licorice," a poster of Jupiter, a panda, a penguin, and a cute water bottle.

Blaise: Just get her a Chipotle gift card.

Scarlett: Go with the Jupiter poster.

Josie: Or the puppy.

Calista: Why a poster?

Scarlett: Jupiter is the guardian of Earth.

Jordan: That *is* a cool title.

Scarlett: We saw a video about it in class – it's so big that it deflects comets from hitting us because it has so much gravity, and its gravity also holds us in a steady orbit around the sun so that we don't get too hot or too cold.

Blaise: Jupiter does that?

Scarlett: Yep.

Jordan: Right, but doesn't Jupiter also accidentally send the occasional comet our way?

Scarlett: I haven't seen any craters lately, have you?

Sienna: Our little corner of the galaxy does some incredible things.

Josie: Did you ever have any space experts come talk to you at your camp school?

Sienna: We sure did – a lot of them actually; we had some amazing ones. I remember one of them was an expert on space chemistry.

Jordan: Like the periodic table of aliens?

Blaise: That was lame.

Sienna: So, he studied all the building blocks of the Universe and what the stars and galaxies billions of miles away were made out of – and what he told us was that all the same stuff our Earth was made up of originally, *those* are the exact same raw materials just floating around everywhere. He would say that the Universe only has a couple recipes it knows how to make, and it uses the same ingredients over and over.

Josie: I like that.

Sienna: The guy right before him was the one that really freaked us out though – we would die laughing in this class because he would say the *craziest* stuff and then to prove he was right he would write out all the math and these huge equations on the board – and of course none of us knew what any of it meant because we were ten.

Scarlett: What would he talk about?

Sienna: The thing that really got everyone to freak out was when he explained how time works.

Blaise: Like time travel?

Sienna: No, like how time itself works and how all the math basically shows you that time is fake.

Josie: Fake?

Scarlett: How can time be fake?

Sienna: The way I remember him explaining it was that whenever this subject comes up everyone has the same first reaction: "We know time exists because the Earth is revolving around the sun and that counts off the days and that shows that time is moving forward."

Scarlett: Right…

Sienna: But the thing about all those rotations is that, mathematically speaking, the calculations are entirely neutral on what direction those rotations have to happen. Everything we use to measure time – from our spin around the sun to the vibration of atoms in an atomic clock – the math doesn't say time has to flow in the direction we think it does.

Calista: So, are there places where all of that just happens to be going backwards?

Sienna: One of my friends asked him that exact question, and his answer was something about how there are 10 billion galaxies out there, so the odds that a few of them are set up that way is pretty likely.

Scarlett: Wait, there are parts of the Universe where time is going backwards?

Sienna: Every time this came up – and we kept bringing it up, so it happened *a lot* – he would tell us that the reason we couldn't understand it is that the human brain is built in a way where we can't compute it.

Jordan: I do feel that exact thing right now.

Sienna: So, after telling us that our brains are built to not understand it, he would still try to explain it – and he'd say that even though we all just naturally know that time is flowing in one direction, we still can't explain *why* we feel and believe that or sense that.

Blaise: Right. Wait, right?

Sienna: So, according to him – and I'm paraphrasing here – what we think is our ability to detect the passage of time is really just our brains trying and failing to understand what's going on; and the byproduct of that misunderstanding – basically the exhaust that the engine of our brain is giving off while it tries to process this conundrum – is a feeling our brain interprets as the passage of time.

Josie: We what?

Blaise: What on earth.

Jordan: I'm willing to believe that, in the history of our species, that combination of words has never occurred.

Sienna: Some of it is a matter of how our brains are interpreting the world around us – like, our brains evolved to see time moving in one direction so that we could learn to plan for the future and store food for when it was about to get cold out, or to never walk down that one path ever again because that's where the tigers live. So, our brains are locked into this idea of time only moving one direction and that's why it's so hard for us to even discuss what time is – but the way we've chosen to define it is just a set of equations, and those equations don't care what direction the numbers are going. And thus, we have no idea what time actually is – we just know it's not the thing we think it is.

Calista: And your class went crazy about this?

Sienna: Oh my gosh, we were howling laughing – I mean, we were incredulous, but we also found it hilarious that this could be real. And he really lost control of the class when he said that when scientists put clocks on international flights that are flying in specific directions around the world and then check those clocks when they land, less time has passed on those clocks that were flying compared to ones that stayed at the airport – so essentially they have "aged" less than the clocks on the ground.

Calista: Really?

Sienna: Yeah, it's like a couple billionths of a second, but it's still an amount you can measure.

Jordan: That's quite a bit to drop on a room full of children – even special sci-fi kids like you guys.

Sienna: I know, it was kinda crazy. And this teacher could tell he was in way over his head, but by that point he was laughing and just answering the dumbest questions we could come up with and sketching it out on the chalkboard. He was great. Pretty much all of those classes were great.

She smiled at the memory of it, but her careful, watchful daughter caught the way the light drained out from behind her eyes as her mind drifted forward to how those happy days concluded.

Tonight's discussion was abruptly interrupted when Sienna pointed back at the distant pond where Blaise had been fishing. A black bear had emerged from the treeline and was eating the fish guts Blaise had left behind.

"And that's why you always clean the fish far away from your camp," Blaise said to no one in particular.

"Do you think it will come to our camp?" Josie asked nervously.

"No," Blaise said confidently, "black bears don't want anything to do with people."

"And don't worry," Jordan added, "we have a couple ways to make bears go away." Only Sienna knew what he meant, and everyone else assumed he was talking about sticks or rocks.

Jordan kept an eye on the bear for the rest of the evening as it scavenged for anything else that might have been left behind. Each of the kids were fascinated to see one in the wild in such relative proximity. By now Jordan had transferred the Glock to a fanny pack, and once the bear ambled back into the trees, it was time for each of these exhausted hikers to fall asleep.

But Jordan knew there were more things in these woods besides bears that could smell fish guts, and a couple of them did their best work at night.

He sat upright in his hammock until everyone was asleep, and then he quietly walked to the edge of their campsite and waited and watched.

He and Blaise had chosen a spot that was elevated relative to the surrounding ridgeline they'd spent the day walking along, and the area sloped down gently toward the pond. If they were planning a battle, this would be the best place to make a last stand, although the nearby ridge behind them dropped off precipitously in a way that rendered retreat impossible. But at least it meant no one or no thing could sneak up behind you.

Jordan stood at the edge of the camp staring back down the hill, with the pond off to the left, and the course they had taken to get here off to the right. The night was so silent he could hear his heart beating, and now that the moon was behind a thick bank of clouds, he wouldn't have been able to see his hand in front of his face if it wasn't for the faint patches of starlight.

He looked and he listened. There was nothing to detect, but that did nothing to make him relax.

A few minutes after 2 am, a breeze picked up and the edge of the moon peaked out just enough to cast shadows on the ground from the tall branches and long thin tree trunks of the Western Hemlocks that surrounded them tonight. Jordan found himself staring into the abyss of darkness beneath the trees where a morass of ferns and alpine ground cover seemed to soak up every particle of light.

As he stared at this tangle of shadows cast by the moon one of them moved. The move was purposeful and unmistakable in a way that it told him immediately it was moving *at* him. He straightened from the tree trunk he had been leaning against, his hands already quietly unzipping the pack around his waist. He watched the shadow pause, then take a series of more deliberate steps. Each one followed their precise path from eight hours earlier.

Without breaking eye contact he racked a round as quietly as he could and gently pressed the button that released the safety.

The breeze was still blowing, and the area brightened slightly as this big cloud drifted with the wind.

Sixty feet away he met eyes with a mountain lion who had finally found what it was looking for.

By the size of it, Jordan guessed this one was 140 pounds, but he was something far short of a cougar expert. But at that size this was either a full-grown female or a younger male, but an adolescent would be unlikely to track prey this large, or so much of it. Her movements were fluid and silent, and there was no wasted motion or fear as she took the most efficient route towards the campsite.

Jordan took five steps forward to emerge entirely from the treeline, and raised the Glock, waiting for the right moment. The cougar also stopped and stared, and a long moment that Jordan could never estimate precisely passed between them.

The breeze stopped and the air was still, the cougar took one step forward, and so did Jordan. He was close enough now to see its eyes catching the light as its head tilted. Behind him, Cali rolled over and mumbled something in her sleep. The cougar's ears twitched and pointed toward the sound, and Jordan heard his right hand tighten on the grip of the pistol. Mountain lions were long-distance hunters and could follow a scent across days and miles; it was possible she had been tracking them since they stashed the bikes. Jordan watched the cougar drop its head and take another tentative step. Now he knew he had to fire, he had to add this shock to his children's current roster of trauma, and he had to risk revealing his location as the sound rippled down this valley and the one next to it.

As he lined up the iron sights on the center mass of the cougar, he saw another shadow move behind it, then beside it. And then he saw the pair of cubs, each less than half the size of Teddy – who was sleeping uselessly in Josie's hammock – emerge from between her legs. They circled her feet and tried to draw her attention in an effort to understand the tension that now hung thick in the air.

Jordan watched the cubs, their small heads rolling back and forth as they stared up at their mother and then stepped back underneath her when she hissed. He and the cougar met eyes again, and, for the first time he could remember, he took a breath. He took one more step forward, the gun still raised, and, at some primordial level, there was an understanding between them that may have been entirely in his head: At least one of us is going to die, and the children suffer either way.

The cougar sniffed the air, rumbled something low and serious to the cubs, and Jordan watched as they melted back into the dark. The sounds of the forest slowly returned. Had it not been for the throb in his forearm and the sweat on his forehead, Jordan might have convinced himself this was a dream of some great symbolic import.

In the morning Sienna would notice Jordan was already up as the sun was rising, and she'd notice how exhausted he looked. The strain of this much mountaineering, she assumed, was taking its toll on everyone.

34 Plates

1 JULY

In a brightly lit but nondescript office in northern Tehran (تهران), Lt. Firouzeh Jamshidi (فیروزه جمشیدی) leaned forward to read the small print on his computer screen.

The Ministry of Intelligence of the Islamic Republic of Iran (وزارت اطّلاعات جمهوری اسلامی ایران) occupied a large building in the Pasdaran (پاسداران) neighborhood of the capital city, and information from every corner of the Middle East arrived here to be examined and understood – and, more often than not, information from much further away ended up here, too.

Jamshidi was reading a report that had arrived overnight. It said that there were reports of a sudden and simultaneous increase in military chatter within both China and India – but, at the moment, it seemed these spikes were entirely unrelated. He had this report up on his screen next to another that contained a series of images captured from a surveillance camera monitoring the path of the high-speed cable that connected Tehran to Pakistan's capital city. The cable went up and over the natural barrier between the two countries – the Makran Range – a hot, dry, and rugged series of peaks which had been formed through the violent subduction of the Arabian Plate beneath the Eurasian Plate.

The photos and grainy video from a camera on the Pakistani side of the cable showed four adults, almost certainly men by the look of it, in clothing indicative of local inhabitants, climbing along the crest of a ridge parallel to the cable. This sighting had been flagged because human activity in this area was essentially nonexistent, and, long before reaching the field of view of this camera, there would have been multiple signs warning hikers or wanderers to turn back for "Safety

Concerns" – which is one way of saying "Go away" without attracting the unwanted attention of saying "A semi-secret internet cable is up ahead and we do not want you to hack at it with a hatchet in hopes of finding something valuable inside." This had famously – and almost certainly apocryphally – happened in 1850 when an Irish fisherman was said to have accidentally caught the first transatlantic telegraph cable in one of his nets, and, when he cut it open out of curiosity, he was thrilled to find that this new species of seaweed had gold running through its inner rings.

Jamshidi leaned in a second time to look at the footage.

By the time he had zoomed in enough to see anything useful, the image became hopelessly pixelated, and he knew some specialist would have already done this and flagged it if anything useful had been spotted. "If I were the paranoid type," he thought to himself, "I'd think that they knew where this camera was posted, knew how far this model could see, and knew where to walk to get a good look at the cable without the camera getting a good look at them." He stopped and thought about this. What anyone else called "paranoia" could, in his department, be called "proactive risk assessment." That, he concluded, was a good enough reason to have someone look into this, even if it was just something as simple as a few flyovers of the area to see if this cable's route had suddenly become a high traffic area, followed by a few passes at night to see where any campfires or caravans might be situated.

He began filing a report with his analysis and observations so that his commander could process it and then file a report of his own to get the flyovers approved. He mentioned in his report that he didn't yet see an immediate need to alert their Pakistani counterparts to this threat, although, if the recon did find something, sending that alert would be the next logical step. These items were always carefully handled with the Pakistani intelligence services, and a considerable dose of international politics always played a part. The fact that their respective strengths and weaknesses could, at times, render them as strange mirror images of each other only made this intricate dance more difficult. Both countries had nuclear weapons, for example, but Iran had better missiles to put them on and Pakistan had better guidance systems. Both had elaborate intelligence agencies, but Iran spent the majority of its focus on Saudi Arabia and Israel, while Pakistan preoccupied itself with India and

Afghanistan. Iran's army was huge but lagged behind in technical sophistication, while Pakistan's smaller population resulted in a smaller army with better technology. And, for the purposes of Jamshidi's focus at the moment, the intelligence services of these two countries were major sources of power in this section of the globe. The Inter-Services Intelligence group (بین الخدماتی استخبارات), or ISI, in Pakistan was legendary, and neither organization wanted to run afoul of the other.

He sent his report and began closing the open files on his desktop related to this cable and its recent visitors. As he did, he saw two additional alerts regarding materials shared through his government's formal contacts in the Russian intelligence service (Федеральная служба безопасности). The first was about a U.S. aircraft carrier – one of the monstrous "regime toppler" sized boats as they were called by allies and enemies alike – that had suffered an accident with a civilian aircraft in the South Pacific and was now heading back toward its home port in Japan. The purpose of this report was to share the observation of a Russian satellite which calculated that this carrier was traveling home at a preposterously high rate of speed. This speed appeared to exceed simple haste to repair a major military asset, but who could read the minds of American commanders? This datapoint about odd American behavior became particularly noteworthy, however, when it was cross-referenced with what the Russian analysts studying these satellite images of the carrier believed about its final destination. Based on the path it had taken over the last several days and the way it had maneuvered around a minor storm, the analysts believed there was a small chance it was heading towards the northern coast of Japan rather than its home port of Yokosuka on the southern coast. That unusual destination would require it to pass through the Korean Straight (대한해협), essentially directly between the cities of Busan (부산시) and Fukuoka (福岡市), which connected the East China Sea (東海) with the Sea of Japan. The report concluded by suggesting that assets in any of these areas be put on alert to gather intel about any American activities.

To Jamshidi this seemed more like a quirk of navigation rather than something indicative of where that boat was actually heading. But it did bear keeping an eye on in the meantime.

He heard the speakers outside his building begin the call to Dhuhr (ظهر), and he scrolled up to check the date of this original observation and saw that it was already three days old. By this point the ship was very likely back at its home port. The fact that there wasn't a follow up report indicated that this ship had probably made it back home without any further incident. An alternate reason for the lack of follow up could be that the ship had done something even more worrisome and then the Russians stopped sharing their information until they better understood its implications. At the moment, he had no way of determining which of these two options was the case unless he called the Iranian embassy in Tokyo to make a few inquiries about which U.S. warships had recently arrived back home – and something about that felt equal parts reactionary and foolish for such a simple report.

The second report was a lot more interesting, although equally inconclusive. The Russians had a handful of container ships that they surreptitiously used for open-ocean reconnaissance, and one of them had recently detected something very unusual. These 1,300-foot ships were all registered to legitimate shipping operations owned by obedient Russian companies who dutifully included a handful of generic shipping containers that were outfitted with an array of reconnaissance equipment and staffed by intelligence technicians dressed like maritime laborers. This setup, which was also used by the Americans, Chinese, and others, gave their intelligence apparatus the ability to gather data far away from home.

This report noted that one of these ships, enroute from Vladivostok to Tacoma, captured a reading bouncing off the upper atmosphere that was indicative of multiple stealth aircraft. The readings were definitely not naturally occurring, but the data amounted to little more than heat, echoes, and vibration – but there was enough of it to indicate four or possibly five stealth aircraft moving at high speed and particularly low altitude. That behavior was not only unusual, but there were no easily accessible bases for stealth aircraft in that area. There were a handful of F-22's at Kadena Air Base on Okinawa (嘉手納飛行場) to keep an eye on Taiwan, and there were another two dozen at Misawa Air Base on the northern edge of Japan's Honshu island (本州) – but to reach this specific point of detection from any of those airstrips would have require those planes to fly *over* the container ship from the south rather than elude it to the north. The only other possibility – and this was especially remote – were the F-35's at Eielson Air Force Base near Fairbanks, or the F-22's near Anchorage. It was impossible to think either of those aircraft would be operating so far away from home at the very fringe of their Aleutian Islands.

But that was it – there was no visual, no speculation on their flight path or intended destination, and no conjecture about the intentions of this sortie. All of that was impossible without something concrete, and right now all they had was, essentially, some loud sounds in the sky and the implication of things that were moving very, *very* fast.

* * * * *

It was the middle of the night, local time, somewhere 450 miles southwest of Sapporo.

Captain Goral watched on a screen in the electronic warfare department as another Chinese satellite passed directly overhead on a route it had never taken prior to 48 hours ago. Since then, it had made a habit of taking a long, slow look at them every six to eight hours. A Russian satellite that Moscow believed was cleverly disguised as a weather research craft had been following a similar schedule. Goral had to hand it to Major Horn – the George had certainly drawn the full attention of both countries. It helped that he'd brought the Peralta with him. This was a one-two punch that no one wanted to absorb. But that assumed the Russians or Chinese really believed either boat was here to find or cause trouble. And that type of assumption would have to be based on there being a reason for anything like that. A guilty conscience could be counted on to invent 100 reasons for why something unusual could be considered threatening.

"So," Goral said to himself, "who feels the guiltiest around here?"

He knew enough about international military protocols and reactionary thinking to conclude that the first government to contact his government was likely to be the one with the most to hide, lose, or eventually deny.

But, for the moment, he found himself on a calm ocean, in the pitch black, cutting a ferociously fast path toward Sapporo, with enough firepower to unseat most governments. No wonder they were getting their picture taken from the upper atmosphere so often.

By this time tomorrow they'd be close enough to start behaving like a salvage operation. They'd start putting spotlights on the water, they'd start pinging the bottom of the ocean loud enough for every other navy to hear, they'd drop buoys, they'd send out helicopters to fly low and slow over the water – and after three or four days, or whenever the intense gentleman from the Pentagon gave the go-ahead, they'd successfully find that sunk boat at the coordinates in his safe.

But, for tonight, just being here was a victory.

The plan that his navigation, engineering, and reactor team had worked out with the planners at the Pentagon had been simple: The George was going to run its reactors at about 130% of capacity in order to get here in 6.5 days. To call this ambitious was an understatement only a sailor could appreciate. The "official" top speed of a Nimitz-class carrier like the USS George Washington was roughly 32 knots, which worked out to approximately 34 miles per hour. Considering that the distance between Tauranga and Sapporo was 5,998 miles in a straight line – but closer to 6,600 after you took into account maneuvering around a few different islands on both ends of the trip, plus a squall – achieving that arrival time was technically and "officially" impossible. But Captain Goral had a couple unofficial numbers on his side that tipped these impossible scales in his favor. To start with, the "unofficial" top speed of the George was about 37 knots once you had the nuclear reactors running at 130%.

To the uninitiated it might seem strange that a 30% increase in power only supplied you with five extra knots, but the laws of physics hampered mariners with a non-linear relationship between power and speed. Said another way, increasing your power output by 30% didn't give you 30% more speed. The basic physics behind this dictate that, as the speed of an object increases, so does the resistance to the object moving – and, in water, this relationship is particularly extreme. In particular, the water resistance a boat encounters is the cube of its velocity. Furthermore, once you took into account the shape of a boat's hull, the geometry of its bow, its buoyancy, and a few other esoteric measurements – the max speed of a waterborne object could be calculated by multiplying the square root of how much of the boat's total area sat beneath the water at any given time by 1.34. The resulting number was the physical limit of how fast that object could move no matter how much extra energy you pumped into it. Historically speaking, reaching anything close to that maximum achievable velocity was purely theoretical since producing the requisite power was impossible – but, as Captain Goral was demonstrating right now, in certain circumstances that energy threshold could be achieved if you owned a boat with two nuclear reactors.

Once all the available reactor power was used, there was one additional, particularly aggressive step that could be taken with fuel injection to achieve 37 knots, or about 43 miles per hour. But that was something that you only did in wartime or if something was particularly dire. Or, it now appeared, this was something you did if someone at the Pentagon was executing a plan that had been approved at the highest possible levels.

"What the hell is going on up there?" he thought for the thousandth time.

These types of speeds were intended for exceptionally short durations, and the material science governing every component on the ship dictated that extreme stresses which reached or exceeded these ranges were not sustainable when extended across multiple hours, to say nothing of a day, to say nothing of a week.

There was no small amount of conjecture on the internet about how fast a boat like this could really go when the situation demanded it, but, despite all the hypothesizing, there were only four or five people on this entire ship who really knew the answer, and everyone else was simply looking out the portholes and marveling at how fast the world was flying past. This kind of output felt like something akin to the stories you heard about young mothers suddenly summoning the strength to lift a pickup truck off a child during an emergency.

By running flat out at 43 miles per hour around the clock, the George had covered 1,032 miles a day, and it kept that pace when an unexpected storm swept over them on the fourth day and they had to navigate a couple hundred miles around it. To its credit, the Peralta had kept up every step of the way. But those little boats have it comparatively easy, he thought to himself.

The Peralta was already making small adjustments to its course and heading towards its final destination an additional 300 miles northeast at an otherwise empty point of ocean directly between the far eastern coast of Russia and the island of Sakhalin (Сахалин). That point of ocean was very nearly bordering Russian territorial waters, but the Peralta wasn't exactly something you could show up and chase off, so it could probably hold tight for a few days. If reconnoitering the island was part of the job, they'd be there a long time – Sakhalin was three times the size of Belgium. The only instruction Horn had given the Peralta was to have every anti-aircraft system on alert while in the region and to wait for additional instructions which might arrive at any time.

Goral stared out at the flat, black sea and began making another mental list of things he needed his senior officers to check on before he sent an alert to Fleet Command and the Pentagon in the morning confirming his arrival. All the major governments in the region knew by now that they were here, but the sudden presence of something as massive as the George was sure to catch quite a few civilians off guard. He was still compiling his list when one of the counter surveillance officers approached to inform him about the impending arrival of another Russian satellite that was about to enter direct line of sight engagement over the horizon to the northwest. The George momentarily cut its engines to give this bird less of a look at its draft, although this wouldn't do much to fool the people studying these photos. At best it would just make their recent speed a bit more ambiguous.

* * * * *

The last three days had been far less eventful for Cyrus and the other five F-22 pilots.

The temporary hangars here on Kiska were serviceable, warm, and they had all spent a night or two in worse conditions than this. The Air Force had a well-deserved reputation for sleeping in warm beds far away from the action while the Army and Marines dug foxholes and slept in the dirt – but here in this tent there was something distinctly aggressive about secretly sleeping 40 feet from a fighter jet on a cold and deserted island in the middle of a vast ocean while awaiting the call to action. This feeling was multiplied by the understanding that the call would ask them to raid the airspace of at least two – but probably three – semi-hostile foreign nations.

Cyrus had spent the time plotting every possible approach angle to the region surrounding the Nizhneleninskoye-Tongjiang Bridge, as well as all the likely intercept points for the one or more of the Vigorous Dragons they were there to encounter. They had started referring to this landmark as "NTB" since, amongst all the pronunciations they were trying to use, they were realistic enough to know each of them was wrong

Considering what the Raptor was built to do, its pilots were never given simple missions, but this particular scenario had more variables than usual. First, there was the issue of surreptitiously refueling off the coast of Hokkaido and then dropping back to low altitude to weave through the national air defense radar of multiple countries at maximum speed. He'd likely make landfall somewhere over the Russian coastal city of Plastun (Пласту́н) and then almost certainly acquire the J-10 somewhere north of Hegang (鹤岗) – but just getting to that point would require weaving around anti-aircraft networks for 385 miles without being detected. In the best-case scenario, the mere presence of the F-22 would be so completely unexpected that the Chinese pilot would panic, break off its attack vector, and things would freeze while D.C. and Beijing had a long talk about it. By the time that phone call took place, Russia would have already pleaded ignorance, the North Koreans would have claimed they knew everything, and the U.S. would have answered any questions with a request to pursue diplomacy in parallel channels.

Who knows.

These outcomes were feasible as long as the J-10 pilot didn't fire on the train, he didn't try to engage the Raptor, and as long as the F-22 could make it back out of all this hostile airspace once that Chinese pilot sent word to the anti-aircraft batteries on the ground about his last known position and vector.

The monotony in the tents was interrupted by an update from the Pentagon. The news included information from within the Chinese Air Force that additional orders covering operational readiness had been sent to the airbase nearest the NTB and that these instructions came from the War Planning Department (战略规划办公室) not the espionage services. It appeared China was no longer expecting to avoid a conflict. But fighter pilots – whether in these tents or in northeast China – never expected to avoid conflict.

At least once each day since they arrived, Cyrus and his pilots had done a full walkthrough of their aircraft with the technicians to examine every possible mechanical requirement of the mission. Having been based in Alaska for so long, all the pilots were familiar with navigating over rugged terrain and using it when the situation called for it – whether that meant sneaking up on someone or evading something else. The pilots also examined how to account for any engine performance issues after traveling at low altitude over the ocean, as well as the fact that the mission parameters called for them to operate at speeds for extended periods that were typically used in small bursts. And they discussed the acceptable tradeoffs between speed, altitude, mileage, and stealth.

There were also long meetings with the Armament Officer who had outfitted the Raptors with their current complement of weapons. There are three internal compartments on the F-22 where missiles are stored – a major upgrade compared to past aircraft since having giant weapons hanging from your wings was the easiest thing for enemy radar to spot. Those internal storage bays could hold a wide variety of things, and for this mission the cocktail of weaponry had been very carefully selected. Since stealth and surprise were the foremost priorities for any possible engagement on this mission, the pilots' first choice would be the M61 Vulcan cannon attached to the base of the right wing. The Vulcan was a six-barreled electric gatling gun that fired a six-inch high-explosive incendiary round – which is to say it was designed to explode and fragment on impact and then set everything nearby on fire – and it could place 100 rounds per second on a target with accuracy up to 9,800 feet. When the importance of staying invisible was at a premium, the Vulcan cannon did not require the F-22 to expose its location by suddenly blasting an enemy fighter with targeting radar that could subsequently be detected by ground-based installations, and it also eliminated the easily trackable heat from a missile's motor. For the purposes of this mission, the J-10 was particularly susceptible to the cannon: Vigorous Dragons were designed to arrive quickly and throw a lot of punches, but it was not designed to *take* any punches. One solid burst of fire running perpendicularly across the fuselage between the wings and the cockpit would easily saw the J-10 in half, and each of the F-22 pilots in this tent knew how to approach and attack in such a way that the enemy fighter would never even see or hear the cannon. In this scenario, the J-10 pilot would suddenly find himself in a depressurized cockpit, shocked and confused, as he spiraled to the ground separate from the body of the fighter that had his name stenciled on the side.

But there was no chance this operation would remain entirely a gun fight. In the event a Raptor pilot lost the element of surprise, had compromised visibility, or couldn't get close enough to stick with guns, the rest of the weapons were chosen to solve those problems. Since they needed to make visual contact with the J-10 before taking any action, the long-range air-to-air missiles that could hit a target over the horizon were unnecessary – instead, each fighter carried a pair of AIM-9 Sidewinders. These short-range, air-to-air missiles were designed for close-quarters aerial combat and, in situations where there was limited time to maneuver or accelerate to safety, a Sidewinder that successfully acquired the heat signature of an engine nozzle was nearly impossible to survive. The Armament Officer and the pilots had debated how many of these to bring, but ultimately decided two were plenty considering that, once both Sidewinders were in the air, the one or two J-10s incurring Russian airspace would certainly break off and radio their headquarters that there were somehow F-22s on station. Those J-10 pilots were guaranteed to break off their attack on the train if it meant having to duke things out with a Raptor that had the element of surprise – even if they outnumbered it. After all, those pilots would reason, what were the odds that there was only one undetectable Raptor in the sky at that moment?

Everything else the Raptor was carrying in its weapons bays was for getting back to the coast so it could race back home over the open ocean.

This included four AIM-120D missiles which were specialized variants developed to engage naval vessels, and, as it turned out, any other target at ground level. The 120Ds also had their own radar systems, which meant they could hunt down targets on the other side of the horizon all by themselves. These would be used to punch holes in the network of anti-aircraft defenses that would be frantically hunting him after any type of interaction with the J-10.

The 120D traveled at Mach 4 – twice the speed the F-22 would be traveling as it ran for its life – and its guidance system had been adjusted to lock onto the radar waves an anti-aircraft missile battery would be pumping out and follow that beam of energy right down to its source. Some installations countered this by having their radar dishes separate from their weaponry, but the Chinese system did not and neither did the North Koreans. The warhead of the 120D was packed with ball bearings that would shred the delicate equipment of these outposts and their operators, and it would travel there fast enough to prevent countermeasures or attempts to go dark in hopes it sailed overhead.

The electronic warfare system on the F-22 was so complex that the pilots were fortunate that it largely operated itself. It would automatically track every threat in the observable region and incorporate live satellite data to suggest a flight path with the highest likelihood of survivability and highlight the installations they couldn't slip past and would have to destroy.

As brilliant as the Raptor was at rebalancing the scales this deep in enemy territory, however, no amount of technical sophistication was enough to render it invincible.

On this mission, hope would play an unusually large part.

But Cyrus was an optimist. It might have been ego, but it felt a lot like optimism.

"As much as we might be relying on the avionics to get us out of Dodge, the two primary ways we leave there alive is still good 'ol fashioned speed and stealth."

"In that order," added LaChappelle.

This morning's briefing had included quite a few bits of new information about the technical capabilities of the landscape they'd be covering, as well as a retread of an early briefing on everything there was to know about the J-10C.

Last night they'd been joined on Kiska by the intelligence officer they first met back at Elmendorf, and he sat with them in the semi-circle around a display screen that included their commander back in Anchorage.

"But you know," Cyrus said, thinking out loud, "if we don't shoot anything down, we might actually be able to gaslight the Chinese if they ever accuse us of anything." This made the intelligence officer grimace. "I mean, come on, do you want to be the Chinese diplomat who has to say with a straight face that some planes from Alaska were screwing around in Manchuria?"

This got a laugh.

"You could just get one of your boys at the State Department," now Cyrus was pointing at the intel officer, "to tell him, 'This kind of wild conjecture is deeply problematic,' and then change the subject to how 'The United States is deeply committed to the idea of regional stability.'"

Now the room was trying out different Presidential impersonations.

The commander was a busy man, and, as important as this mission was, he also had a base to run. He interrupted just enough to get the briefing back on track.

"Thank you, General, allow me to continue," Cyrus said, clearing his throat, but still smiling broadly. Luckily from this angle the General couldn't see that.

"In terms of how we exfiltrate from this theater in the event of an engagement of any type – no matter how poorly things are going, and no matter how many inbounds you have chasing you, if you can fly straight over the top of the Peralta, you are going to be ok. Those boys are already on station, and there isn't a single thing that China, Russia, or North Korea can summon at a moment's notice that can survive a flyover of a Burke-class boat."

The intel officer nodded and looked at the screen with the current location of the Peralta.

"If you reach the water without any major holes punched in you, you're going to be ok."

"We'll regroup here again this evening," the General said in a way that told everyone the meeting was over. "Thank you for staying sharp in the meantime."

Inside these giant tents, everything was *meantime*.

Under optimal conditions, an F-22 generally required 43 hours of maintenance from mechanics and specialized technicians for every one hour it was in the air, and that figure was well represented here – where wind howled, and a 4,000-foot stratovolcano loomed three miles to the north.

2 JULY

It was almost time to stop and take a long break for lunch, and Jordan could not remember the last time they hadn't been hiking uphill.

Earlier that day they had crossed the outer edge of the circle on the map, but even now that they were well within the boundary, there was nothing in the vicinity that looked particularly well suited to host a long-term shelter.

Arriving at this spot had happened with the help of some unexpected adjustments to the route.

During breakfast Scarlett told everyone what she had mentioned to Jordan the night before: The peak behind her was something she had "seen" in a "dream" – although, in this context, both of those words had flexible and non-traditional definitions. Jordan had already shared this with Sienna, but it came as news to the rest of the family.

"We hiked up this mountain because of a dream?" Blaise demanded, "If I knew you could do that, I would have dreamed about hiking downhill and ordering a pizza."

Only Cali seemed unsurprised. She finished her last bite of oatmeal, cleared her throat, and reluctantly shared an extra detail.

"On the other side of that peak, there's a long, high ridge that connects it to another peak, and on the other side of that peak is a forested valley with a lake. The lake isn't very big, and it has a pretty island-like thing on the far side of it."

Everyone stopped eating and stared.

"Did you see it in a crackle dream?" Scarlett asked.

"I saw just the lake two nights ago, and then I saw the whole thing last night. I saw that whole mountain wall," she said, pointing at the towering peak in front of them.

"I saw the island thing in the lake last night, too," Scarlett added.

"You girls saw this in dreams?" Sienna asked again, just to be sure. This part of the Signal was not something she had ever experienced.

"Yep," Scarlett said matter-of-factly.

"I don't know if it was a dream, but it was while I was asleep," Cali said.

She was right, Sienna thought, those are two very different things.

"And the Signal was definitely a part of the dream," she added.

"This is crazy, but I'll go along with it just to hit the lake," Blaise said.

While they talked, Jordan was swiping and tapping the GPS screen to follow the basic directions from Cali. It didn't take long to find it: Francis Lake was tiny, and incredibly remote – surrounded on all sides by towering granite walls and sitting at over a mile above sea level. He dialed in the specific coordinates and read through the route information. Of all the possible paths they could have taken today and tomorrow, this was among the less excruciating options, but it was still incredibly difficult; the elevation gain over the course of the day was, as the GPS noted, "extreme."

"I think your uncle's up by the lake," Scarlett said confidently, pointing far off into the distance.

"I actually think she's right," Cali added. "He *is* up there."

Sienna and Jordan met eyes and agreed that encountering this much certainty after so many days of indefatigable chaos felt incredibly strange to the point of being off-putting.

Blaise was still grousing about the new dream-centric navigational techniques.

"Ok, I'm a team player, so, 99 times out of a thousand, I would be totally willing to go along with –"

"That is actually a terrible percentage," Cali pointed out.

"Ok professor, but, seriously, no one else thinks it's weird we've gone from navigating by the stars, to a GPS, and now to dreams?"

"Who here is navigating by the stars?" Scarlett asked, genuinely curious.

"We're doing a combination of things now," Sienna said, pulling Scarlett onto her lap and mouthing the words "Stop!" at Blaise.

Blaise sheathed his knife and rolled his eyes.

They finished breakfast, topped off everyone's supply of trail mix, and began the process of another long climb.

The conversation picked up roughly where it had stopped the previous evening. Jordan shook his bag of trail mix, examined its contents, and groaned.

"Freaking raisins."

"Why do you hate raisins, Dad?" Josie asked.

"There is no excuse for raisins."

"'No excuse' to what?"

"Exist."

This started a family-wide discussion about the ideal composition of trail mix, and the consensus was that the mix available on this trail was dramatically sub-standard. Far too many cashews, far too few peanut M&M's.

Three hours and several trail mix arguments later, they could see the ridge between the two peaks in the distance, and Blaise took great care explaining that the technical term for this formation was a "saddle or a col, depending on the way the two peaks connect." Three hours after that, with the sun beating down on them and the temperature unusually warm, Jordan led the family down the opposite side of the second peak. They found some much-needed shade next to a creek that careened down the steep mountainside and eventually found its way into Francis Lake, which sat like a mirror halfway down the valley, about a mile away.

"That's the lake," Cali said without a trace of uncertainty when she laid eyes on it. "This is even the same angle I saw it from."

Scarlett stood next to her and nodded quietly. "This is the spot."

Sienna and Jordan shared another look. The weirdness here was deep.

"So what do you girls think we do now?" Sienna asked, very curious but still cautious enough to not put any pressure on them to keep supplying the family with answers.

"This is the place the Signal wanted us to find. Now we wait."

"Wait?" Blaise asked, saying what everyone was thinking.

Jordan noticed that Cali was now also attributing opinions to the Signal.

Long before they finally reached the creek, each Riley child had become particularly vocal about how overdue they were for a break and how late lunch was taking place today, but everyone was glad to find the shade beneath a large rocky outcropping. The aches and pains of nonstop hiking were wearing on everyone, and, with the heaviest pack of all, Jordan was acutely feeling the dull roar of compression in his lower back. Sienna had an especially hard job of her own – bringing up the rear with Josephine and Scarlett and finding ways to keep their spirits up in the process.

And today had been particularly difficult for Sienna, Calista, and Scarlett as the hum that Sienna remembered so well seemed to come and go in increasingly unpleasant waves.

For now, no one was complaining about Cali's belief that this was the final destination. That didn't necessarily get them any closer to Uncle Harvey, but that was apparently a separate matter.

The Rileys spread out on the cool stone, in the shade underneath the large outcropping – the remnant of some combination of glaciers and ancient landslides. The kids used their packs as pillows and pulled their hats down over their faces. Sienna poured everyone more trail mix and handed out meal bars, while Jordan checked their water bottles and fed Teddy. These bars had absorbed copious criticism over the last few days, but they were undeniably useful. This particular brand was a favorite of long-distance hikers because each relatively small bar contained 3,600 calories and featured all the essential nutrients – and everyone had hit the trail with 10 of these in their backpacks. They didn't taste amazing, but you could hypothetically live off of them for an extended period of time, and Sienna knew that almost anything would start to taste great if you got hungry enough. That point in time had not yet been reached, but it was at least nice to know the survival bars could eventually seem delicious, if it came to that.

Teddy had spent the day bolting in and out of bushes, eating ferns, and chasing small forest creatures he had no hope of catching and no concept of what to do next even if he did. Now he lay fast asleep between Scarlett and Josie. Cali had wrapped a sweatshirt around her head and was trying to sleep off the lingering nausea. Sienna and Blaise were leaned back against the stone while he busily carved something. Jordan was digging around for the uneaten half of this morning's survival bar when he and Sienna heard a sharp scrape on the ledge directly above.

They locked eyes and froze. Then they heard it again.

"You've been making great progress today considering you're traveling with so many children."

Sienna's head whipped around, and she craned her neck to look straight up the ledge but had to squint in the brightness of the perfectly blue sky.

A man with a rifle slung over his shoulder and a loose braid in his white beard was staring back at her intently. The voice and the posture were unmistakable.

"Uncle Harvey?" she asked, just to be sure.

"I knew your father was dead when no letter arrived two years in a row. Did he die well?"

"Are you quoting 'Braveheart?'"

"What?"

"What?"

They both stopped talking and stared. Both of them filled in the parts of three decades since they had last seen the other and reverse engineered what they saw onto the face and the person they remembered.

"How did you know to come here, to my little valley?"

"Grandma had a map in an old cabinet that had this area circled."

"And so you came here to, what, vacation?"

"No," Jordan said, walking slowly out of the rock's shadow to get a clear look at this unlikely relative, "we just needed a place that no one else would know about for a little while."

"It's because of the government and some stuff that's going on with them," Blaise suddenly added.

Harvey looked his direction and slowly nodded. This was an explanation that made sense to him.

He turned to look north toward the top of this valley, and a ponytail of bright white hair swung over his shoulder. He stepped one leg up on a big rock and rested his crossed arms on his knee as he peered down at this small, exhausted looking group. Sienna remembered him being tall and gaunt, and now he looked positively skeletal when a breeze blew his t-shirt against his frame.

"Any blood of mine that needs protecting from them is welcome to it." He spit the words out in a way that showed he meant it and laid bare a level of animosity that overcame whatever burden these six newcomers were sure to present.

A wave of relief washed over both parents. It was so wildly unrealistic to have hoped for this reaction, and yet they had staked everything on it.

"You can stay with me for as long as you need, but I'll warn you that the winters here are extremely difficult. Hopefully your troubles will have come and gone by then."

He leaned further over the ledge to see the rest of them, still on their backs, frozen looking up at this wild-looking, so-called relative. Calista was on her feet now, too, sizing up this stranger upon whom they had bet their short-term survival.

"And you must be Jordan," he said turning his attention back to him. "Years ago my brother sent me a photo of your wedding.

"Do you still have it?"

Now it was Scarlett's turn to talk, and she glowered up at him since defiance was all she had left now that the high ground and the element of surprise were both unavailable.

"No," Harvey laughed, "but I can show you where I have all your grandpa's old letters, if you want." He began to walk down toward them, and, as he did so, he pointed to what seemed like a random point on the mountainside in the direction of the lake. "When you've rested a minute, we can walk down to the cave." He made his way down from the ledge with ease, taking giant steps from one boulder to the next, his arms hanging long at his sides while he moved casually across such difficult terrain.

As the girls pretended to sleep, Harvey and Sienna caught up, and Jordan, Calista, and Blaise asked questions about how he had survived this long and where he had found a place to live. An hour later they were still talking, and the girls were now asleep, and this tiny family reunion might have gone on all afternoon if a buck hadn't started picking its way through the trees on its way down to the lake, followed by Harvey wasting no time shooting it. This served the dual purpose of waking everyone up and giving Blaise the thrill of a lifetime when he watched his great uncle gut and dress it right there on the spot.

"Do you know why you always gut an animal far away from where you live?"

"I do."

"And why's that?"

"Bears."

"Good boy."

Twenty minutes later they were each carrying half of it, and the trek to his home began.

The steep walls of this valley, like all the others they had passed, were covered in trees right up to the ridge. It was strikingly beautiful, and the bright sunlight shimmered on the glassy surface of the lake in a scene that would have enchanted any landscape painter.

After a few hundred feet they crossed a thin but well-traveled trail that Harvey explained ringed the valley and that he used to move from one side to the other to hunt, fish, or, on exceptionally rare occasions, go anywhere outside the range. The trail dipped low towards the base of the mountainside as they reached the lake and then pitched sharply upward again toward what looked like another rockslide overlooking the water.

Uncle Harvey took off his sunglasses as they made it into the shade of the peak. Sienna remembered the wild look he had in his eyes, and that fire had not dimmed after all these years in the mountains. Up close she could see a deep scar on his cheekbone that had needed stitches but never got them, and his hands were huge – rough like the stone of these walls, and red from constant use, countless frostbites, and what had to be the beginnings of arthritis. He moved with a slight limp that he either didn't notice or valiantly repressed, and at regular intervals he paused to point out spots along the bank of the lake where he had planted vegetables and beans.

"And here we are," Harvey said as they reached the pile of rocks.

Jordan noticed how inorganically jagged these rocks were, and the weathered marks of what looked like a jackhammer or cutting tool could be seen on almost all of them. Harvey walked behind one of the rocks closest to the mountain and disappeared for a moment. He popped his head out a moment later and waved them over.

"This is the front door, obviously," he said with a laugh.

Blaise and Calista were overcome with curiosity and were the first to enter. Sienna held the hand of each of the little girls and led them along. Jordan paused to take one last look around the surrounding mountains, suddenly caught by the need to check and make sure no one was watching as he disappeared into the safety of the hiding spot he had been unrealistically and fervently hoping for since punching in the code to close his garage door.

Behind these giant stones was what looked like a bird's nest of rebar, arranged in a dish-shaped covering of the entrance to a tunnel that stood about seven feet tall and four feet wide. The rockslide visible from the trail had clearly been equal parts triggered and then arranged to cover the entrance and its iron frame, and then obscure it from the casual observer. The tunnel went straight back into the heart of the mountain for another 75 feet in a wavy line until it split off in two directions – one dead-ended another 50 feet away in a pile of rubble with a giant tarp spread across it, and to the right the tunnel opened up a few steps later into a circular room, about 40 feet wide with a surprisingly high and gently domed roof. Depending on which area of the room you were facing, it alternated between looking like a natural formation or something that had been violently chiseled from the surrounding granite.

"Beautiful, right?" Harvey said flipping a switch that lit a small bank of lights in the middle of the room. Tiny reflective flecks of minerals embedded in the rock flared in the light. "Most of this side of the mountain is composed of Plagioclase Feldspar," Harvey explained as if any of them had ever heard either word, "and this room butts up against a giant vein of granite that was full of quartz crystals. That's most of what you see twinkling in the light."

"You've been here the entire time? Since you left, I mean?"

"Yeah, a lot of it," Harvey said, looking around the room and admiring it like a new homeowner might while hosting a housewarming party. "I knew from the survey that there was this big hollow pocket right here where we're standing, so once I burrowed my way through from the outside wall, I just kind of rounded it out to be a good sized room, and then kind of just kept the ceiling the way I found it."

"Thank you for taking us in," Sienna said quietly, looking him straight in the eyes. She had never really looked at her uncle from this angle; she could only remember looking up at what she remembered as a towering figure. "If you hadn't still been here, it would have been a rough next few days."

"No family of mine – whether it's my baby brother's children or anyone else – is going to get turned away, and *especially* if you're sideways with the government."

"It's not that we did anything wrong to get sidewa…"

"In my experience, you don't have to do anything wrong to be in trouble."

"Ok, but it honestly wasn't a matter of us doing anything wrong, it's that Jordan and I…"

"Girl, if you didn't do anything wrong but you were still scared enough to run – that tells you everything I could ever try to explain to you about the government."

Sienna didn't share all of her uncle's conspiratorial leanings, but this point was difficult to argue with after sneaking out of her own house and carefully disappearing.

"Fair enough," she said, "and we are very grateful. In a couple days Jordan or I will hike down to get some supplies and check in on civilization."

"It'll probably be about as gross as you left it."

"Probably, but we'll still need to check."

"It's a long hike, but I can show you how to make it."

"Thanks, Uncle Harvey."

Now that there was light in the room besides the small flashlight Harvey had used to guide them in, Jordan began to look around the room. There was a vintage-looking cot against the wall on one side, stacks of supplies in the middle of the room, and very little else besides what appeared to be cold weather survival gear on the opposite side. Jordan walked the perimeter of the room as Harvey pointed out various geologic formations in the stone, and the kids started climbing the natural handholds in the wall and following the occasional small trickle of water seeping through the rock. As he walked, Jordan saw the remains of what looked like a recent campfire.

"You light fires in here?"

"It gets really cold in from about October to March. And September sometimes, too. And that deer tastes horrible if you try to eat it raw."

"But how do you do that? Did you dig a chimney?"

"I drilled a chimney."

"Drilled it to where?"

"There's a big rock about 80 feet above us just sitting there, and with some basic trig anyone can figure out where that rock overhang is relative to where we're standing, so I drilled down at a pretty steep angle to arrive right about here, then I used a thing we called an auger to punch out something about the size of a fireplace right here."

He pointed to the spot on the floor where a five-foot by four-foot square had been cut about four feet back into the wall. It was unmistakably a fireplace, and the heavy buildup all around it told the story of years' worth of meals cooked right here.

Jordan looked across the room and saw Sienna holding Scarlett on her lap. They both looked miserable. The last 18 hours had been brutal, and it seemed to be getting worse. He saw steel hooks sunk into the stone of the wall at regular intervals and had an idea as he started estimating the distance between them.

"I hang supplies on those, but considering the hammocks I saw in your bag, you could string those up no problem if you have enough cord.

"That's what I was thinking," Jordan said, digging through his bag. It only took a minute to get three of them up, and he helped Sienna transfer the girls so all of them could rest in the cool air of the cave.

JULY 2

For an airbase that was traditionally quiet and focused on patrolling an interior mountain range, life had suddenly become quite hectic and consumed with oceanic topics.

Earlier that morning, two American naval assets – one of which was a carrier – showed up unexpectedly 110 miles off the coast of a tiny Russian village named Maksimovka (Максимовка).

The patrols Wáng Xuěméi and her fellow pilots had been flying for almost two weeks were now going to be far more frequent and the routes were now extended in a way that would allow them to skirt the waterline and get a reading on the carrier. The carrier had also arrived with a friend – a Burke-class guided missile destroyer, no less – that had a special capacity for shooting expensive things out of the air. The Burke vessel was currently 50 miles to the northeast of the carrier, which was well outside protocol for how these boats typically arranged themselves, particularly in a place where they knew their presence would escalate tensions.

The base commander had already held a meeting – and announced another one later – to emphasize that the unplanned arrival and the non-standard deployment indicated that the Americans had hostile intentions, though their objective was currently unclear. These meetings covered the strengths and weaknesses of both craft, their known or proposed vulnerabilities, and a half dozen different plans of action in the event the carrier started scrambling aircraft. There was an unconfirmed report that the carrier was currently unable to efficiently or effectively launch aircraft, but, as the commander explained, when a carrier is parked within striking distance you cannot assume it is out of commission no matter how much alleged damage you see on its flight deck. That didn't exactly sound like a Confucian aphorism, but it was wise, nonetheless.

These briefings also included the unusual step of presenting a tentative theory about why the carrier had arrived, and this conjecture was acknowledged as an attempt to provide the pilots and their mission planners with better insight into what to expect from any engagement with U.S. naval pilots. Considering the content of the previous briefing about the energy weapon the Russians were moving toward the Nizhneleninskoye-Tongjiang Bridge, it was easy to speculate about some level of coordination between these nations – but this supposition, in the estimation of the Ministry of State Security, was extremely unlikely. Both the Russians and Americans had decades of animosity standing in the way of this type of coordination, and the official analysis cast doubt on whether or not those two nations could coordinate an attack on any third-party which they had no pressing reason to antagonize. All evidence pointed to the Americans having an alternative reason for being here, although it was, at the moment, unidentified. The nature of the timing could not be dismissed, however, and this was no doubt keeping the intelligence gathering and the counterespionage teams in Beijing working around the clock and, predictably, shaking down every corner of their networks for information.

The pilots at Chaoyangchuan Air Base all felt the situation tightening around them as hourly updates arrived about the train, the carrier, and the carrier's unpleasant friend. Xuěméi stared at the photos in each briefing and was careful to nod gravely at all the right times. She recognized that, for any pilot, streaking through the Russian hinterlands to destroy a clear and present danger was a thrilling idea, but doing so while looking over your shoulder at two American weapons platforms complicated things in extraordinary ways. At a bare minimum it drew focus away from what should have been a singular mission. The Americans could certainly track every J-10 coming and going from Chaoyangchuan, but putting their own craft in the air at the same time as China's would be wildly provocative, even for western imperialists. Whichever pilot got the call to go destroy the weapon on that train would launch with the expectation of a soon-to-follow warning that the Americans had responded.

In an effort to not show a reaction to the American presence, the Chaoyangchuan base commander decided to only put two J-10's in the air at a time – one flying the same route they had all made at least 40 times now to keep an eye on the bridge, and the other to keep tabs on the carrier by flying along the North Korean border until reaching Yanji Airport (延吉机场) and then making a quick U-turn near the Sea of Japan. The North Koreans would not be happy about how the Dragons clipped the edge of their airspace during this route, but that was something the ambassadors could iron out.

Xuěméi was still concerned by what her flight commander, Huáng Yǒngjūn, had told her about what may or may not be on this train, but she did not believe this was a question for her or any other pilot to ask the base commander or any of his senior officers. This situation – both its circumstances and its consequences – seemed much larger than any one of them, and her belief in the PLA's ideas about loyalty and executing orders as they were given was still deeply ingrained, even if her reasons for being in the air were now much different than those of her comrades.

Her father had often talked about the importance of doing the right thing for the right reason and the strength of character which came from such behavior. What she was planning would not have pleased him – but, to be fair to both of them, he could not have foreseen this. She had been young the last time they spoke like this, and her mother had grown up poor enough to consider personal convictions a luxury. This left Xuěméi somewhere in the middle. After months of fighting a horrible cough, he had spent her 10th birthday at the hospital. He weighed 90 pounds on her 11th birthday. She celebrated her 12th birthday alone. She went 20 years without celebrating another – and only then to let Mínghuī help her blow out the candles.

Today's briefing with the base commander ended with the announcement that extra maintenance and mechanic crews would be arriving over the next three days to ensure they could keep three planes in the air at all times, as well as having two standing by and ready to launch at any given moment. The meeting ended with the assignments for the next 24 hours: Xuěméi would be the plane standing by on the tarmac in case of emergency, and Yǒngjūn would be flying the bridge patrol route overnight.

* * * * *

In his office beneath the Pentagon, Major Carl Horn watched a pressure cooker that kept getting hotter. On most other days it was just a map.

Data points measuring escalating levels of crisis were highlighted in multiple places, and this particular piece of cartography featured an extreme level of detail that presented all the geographic features accurately despite the notorious difficulty of representing a spherical object on a flat surface. But this achievement in projection was not nearly so complex as these interconnected and overlapping hot spots, and he was running out of time to resolve them all cleanly.

Just as predicted, the Iranians had caught wind of something happening right over their border with Pakistan and there were now patrols in that area actively hunting for a possible incursion. It appeared as if General Gupta had been particularly aggressive in his attempt to kill the weapon he believed was pointed at him, as well as any possibility of it being saved or reconstituted after his attack. He knew that Gupta knew that the data link between Tehran and Islamabad ran through those mountains. The General had been contacted by one of his peers in another section of the Pentagon and been urged to exercise caution, but from what Horn had seen over the past several days, General Gupta had only accelerated since the call. Horn had received a report this morning that somewhere near Karachi a small strike force was already in motion, *and* that the Chinese air force had pulled all but a skeleton crew of mechanics from an airbase in the far western Xinjiang province (新疆维吾尔自治区) and sent them to Chaoyangchuan on the Russian border. Rather than just watching things unfold, Horn now had a hunter-kill sub of his own watching for the possible arrival of an Indian submarine that might enter the waterway directly adjacent to Pakistan as a part of Gupta's apparent goal to start a war with as many neighbors as possible.

Elsewhere, the dress rehearsal for World War 3 was still charging forward along the Russian-Chinese border. Currently, he was successfully splitting the attention of both groups now that each was keeping a very close eye on the very sudden arrival of the USS George Washington and its unusually mean little brother, the USS Peralta. This was a fine initial response, but he would need both ships to do more than that – he needed them to draw a disproportionate amount of focus to the south such that Raptors in the northwest might go unnoticed. The George and the Peralta were the preferred alternative to having electronic warfare aircraft flood the area with interference to help cover the Raptor's escape. Putting that many radar-jamming planes in the air would immediately indicate that the Americans had an active operation underway, whereas having those two boats just floating there presented an uncertainty of purpose that worked to his advantage. And, of course, they could help cover what might become a highly contested trip back to Alaska.

But, ideally, it wouldn't come to that.

Amongst all this chatter, Horn was still surprised that Russia had so little idea about what was swirling around it. If and when China did execute a strike against that train, the Russians would be caught completely off guard and assume – somewhat correctly, it would turn out – that it was an act of unprovoked aggression.

This was a point in the planning process where a civilian might begin weighing the pros and cons by trying to figure out, "Well, what's the worst thing that could happen?" The military approach to this was essentially identical, although few professional soldiers saw any value in summoning the self-awareness necessary to notice this grotesque similarity. Despite all the training a man like Horn had undergone over the years, he was – just like every other military leader before him – still human and still a product of his environment, and this led his finely tuned intuition and hard-earned instincts to be joined by the stray pieces of folk wisdom he had been raised hearing. Today an antediluvian kernel of wisdom from his mother crossed his mind. She had been a sincere, god-fearing woman who met uncertainty with trust and chased away fear with even more faith – and, even as a child, he did not find her approach to life remotely appealing. Now he had lived three years longer than she had, and his mindset was further away from her than ever. In this line of work, in this basement room, he could not entertain the idea that "the worst thing that could happen" had a silver lining since it led to everyone ending up in a happy afterlife. He found something dissociative and cowardly about staring the worst-case scenario in the face and consoling yourself with the idea that, even if everything goes wrong and everybody dies, they'll be in heaven, so that's at least nice.

The actual way his mother would have thought about it wasn't so trite or dismissive, but the punchline was essentially the same. Horn could not find any comfort in the world ending but reaching paradise as a consolation prize for a life left unfinished. There was something defeatist and deeply compromised about doing his job with that belief as a fallback position in the case of total failure. His job did not afford the luxury of even considering that heaven might be real; his focus was on finding those ideal outcomes that occurred here on earth. He had tried and failed to picture an emptied planet full of strife and a heaven full of satisfaction. He couldn't imagine finding joy in the next life when everything had failed here. Whatever his mother believed about God, surely she didn't think He wanted his creations getting wiped out and moving back in with him prematurely.

He picked the fragment up off the table and put it back in his pocket as he checked his watch. In 20 minutes he had a briefing with the Secretary of Defense on every move that had been made up to this point. The number of nuclear-armed countries planning to retaliate against nonexistent threats had surpassed everyone's comfort level, and the President needed to be told in simple terms all the things that were being done to defuse as many of these tensions as possible. The worry was, of course, that any proactive de-escalation might make things worse in-real time, and, conversely, that any decision to *not* act might be judged harshly by history.

But, Horn thought to himself, if things worked out just right, no one would ever know any of this ever happened – each of these nations would simply consider that their worst fears had been unwarranted and the problem had worked itself out naturally.

* * * * *

One of the hot spots on that giant screen Major Horn watched as he prepared his briefing for the Secretary of Defense represented a grid search Captain O'Shea and his crew had been relentlessly pursuing for the last 19 hours. Searches like this were almost always fruitless, but the subtle hint of a foreign sub sneaking into this region for no good reason was enough to get everyone interested, in particular this pugnacious captain.

There was a belief in the armed forces that no one "normal" chooses to spend their career hundreds of feet underwater in a metal tube built by the lowest bidder – and, in many respects, the laughter that came along with this premise was nothing more than interdepartmental jokes with little truth behind them. But, in other respects, this analysis had millions of proof points attesting to the reality of that assessment. The submarine corps – from the bosuns to the captains – were, unequivocally, the most *colorful* group the U.S. Navy had to offer, and the crew of the USS Arizona did nothing to dispel this notion.

O'Shea had slept very little since getting the order to conduct this search, and he had been present as one square in the grid after another was searched, cleared, and then adjustments were made to move to the next one. His Chief Navigator and Tactical Officer had carefully plotted all the approach points the Indian sub could make, and it was now patrolling the choke point that each of those routes would move through based on the local currents and bathymetry – the very official and rarely used word for the topography of the ocean floor. Now they were just waiting and watching. This might have appeared tedious to an outsider, but for the captain of a hunter-killer sub, this was, quite literally, the hunting that preceded the killing.

O'Shea liked to say that a hunter-killer sub such as the Arizona was an inherently violent apparatus, but, first and foremost, it had to be a great listener. This sounded thoughtful, but the next sentence was usually, "Because you can't kill what you can't find."

He was unquestionably correct about the Arizona's ability to hear things. On its nose was a giant sensor that could listen without giving off the tell-tale pings that revealed its own location in the process, and three fiber optic panels mounted on its outer hull added extra listening power on top of the mile-long cable it could tow behind it. That tail acted like a giant funnel for the stray sounds that other subs hoped went unnoticed.

Twenty minutes before a shift change on the bridge, the senior sonar operator quickly ran a follow up scan on a small, hazy image that popped up 6,500 meters directly east of their current position. While the operator waited for the software to process and recompile the image, he asked the new sonar technician seated six feet away to do a check of her own. This young lieutenant had recently been the star pupil of the same unforgiving professor who had once taught him the finer points of sonar at Annapolis, so this was the perfect chance to test whatever it was they were teaching kids at the Academy now.

They both got the updated result at about the same time, and, in unison they both said "contact" loud enough for the XO to hear it and suddenly appear over their shoulders. "It's inside 6,400 meters, and just emerged from behind a thermocline layer, otherwise we might have caught it six... make that seven minutes ago," she explained.

Right now, the sonar readout was showing them a quiet spot in the water that was quieter than all the naturally occurring ocean noise around it – but the algorithm and the operator both knew what that meant. The XO called for the Captain and considered that the Indian navy really deserved a lot of credit for getting a diesel engine to run that quietly.

O'Shea was there seconds later and, as soon as he spotted it on the display, the sonar operator heard his hand reflexively tighten into a fist on the cushioned headrest of the chair. The captain picked up the phone mounted to the wall above the monitors and called down to the engine room. He told them to be ready for new instructions and to power down anything nonessential.

"No big moves and no big noises down there until you hear otherwise, ok Dan?"

His next call was to start coiling up the towed array at the highest possible silent speed.

By now the Weapons Officer had made his way over, and as soon as he saw the screen he knew what to do without being asked. He'd already been asked to put two torpedoes in dry tubes and have them standing by for whatever showed up. Both torpedoes were now given that murky spot on the display as a target, and the weapons technician plotting the firing plan would keep updating that target as it got closer and clearer.

This contact was already well within range of the Arizona's torpedoes, however. The Mark 48 Mod 7 CBASS torpedo had a 25-mile range, traveled at 65 miles per hour, and used its own on-board sonar system to pursue its assigned target. This torpedo had been designed to single-handedly kill the destroyers and aircraft carriers of every other navy, along with their nuclear-capable submarines, and, once it was in the water, there was simply no escaping it. There were no reports – rumored or otherwise – of a Mark 48 not reaching a selected target, and nothing it touched had ever survived. The Chinese navy was pinned against its own coastline because a dozen subs exactly like the Arizona carrying this exact torpedo kept it there. This tiny sub from Mazagon (मझगांव डॉक शिपबिल्डर्स लिमिटेड) didn't have a chance.

"I want to know if our new neighbor does anything weird, ok?" he said to the sonar team. "If he changes course or speed or whatever, tell me first."

Then he walked across the bridge to talk to the navigator and helmsman.

"If this captain is smart enough to creep in behind a thermocline layer, then he's already accounting for the fact someone might be looking for him."

"Why would he expect us to be here, sir?" the navigator asked.

"He probably doesn't expect it to be *us*, but if he's sliding in here planning to hit Pakistan in the back of the head with a pipe, then he's going to show up extra careful."

"Roger that, sir."

"When he's confident he's here alone he'll find a spot he likes to post up and wait to do whatever's next." He turned to the helmsman, "Once he settled in, I want you to put us beneath his layer and 2,000 meters directly to starboard."

"Aye, sir."

"I know we can get a lot closer than that, but I want to be just a little extra careful in case their flank array or one of their technicians running it are better than we expect."

He leaned in close to double-check the readings of the surrounding layers of ocean water and the boundaries between them. This was where O'Shea became particularly dangerous. Much like the layers of sedimentary rock visible at the Grand Canyon, the ocean itself is composed of 200-foot-thick layers of water that differ in their temperature, salinity, and density – and a savvy submarine captain knew how to use these differences to his advantage. As a sound wave moved from one layer to another it was bent and warped by those different densities and temperatures, and this created a "sonar shadow" or a dead spot in the water where they could hide while taking careful aim at a passing ship or sub. Right now, a pair of seasonal phenomena were making the differences between these layers more pronounced than usual: The summer sun was overheating the layers closest to the surface, and the monsoon season was dumping enormous amounts of fresh water that wreaked havoc on the Arabian Sea's otherwise predictable salinity. Both of these things were making the borders between each layer particularly sharp, and sounds crossing those various boundaries were significantly distorted, if not lost entirely.

O'Shea's mastery of these layers gave him several tactical advantages – including his current order to drop beneath the Vagsheer's layer so that it could be followed with maximum stealth.

As he stood to leave, he slapped the helmsman on the shoulder and said, "Robin, as soon as they pass, please bring us around 290 degrees and maintain that distance of 2,000 meters." He tapped a point on the screen showing the center of the thermocline layer beneath them. "That's our spot right there."

O'Shea walked back to the sonar station with one additional instruction for the senior officer that had just occurred to him.

"I want someone on your team to focus entirely on finding anyone who might be bringing up their rear to check and see if anyone like us is lurking around – they could either be right on their six watching their back, or, they could be doing a big flanking maneuver to see if there's anyone hiding in the fringes."

"Aye."

"I mean, that's what I would do if I was storming into an enemy shipping lane, but who knows if they had time." He trailed off to think about this and was convinced the extra effort and focus it took to watch for this was the right move. "If you spot anything, no matter how remote, I want to know right away."

"If they brought a friend, we'll know, sir."

"Good man. Oh – and wherever they end up parking, I want to know if anyone or anything leaves the port (کراچی پورٹ) with a heading that directly intersects them."

Three hours later, as expected, the Vagsheer took up position 11 miles off the coast of Karachi at a depth of 420 feet.

Now O'Shea watched and waited.

JULY 2

With everyone safe, accounted for, and out of sight, Jordan had the luxury of being able to think about things not immediately related to survival – like, this semi-man-made cave he was standing in.

"Harvey, how did you make this? And how did you even get here?"

Harvey laughed and rested his hand against the cool stone above the fireplace. The story took the better part of 25 minutes to tell.

It began with Harvey as a much younger man, working as the foreman of a team drilling a path for telephone and power lines through the Cascade Range. The job spanned multiple years, and they had actually started work in the Sierra Nevadas, just a few hours from where he had grown up. After finishing a series of projects in northern California, the company offered him the chance to keep working in Washington, with the understanding there would be even more work available in Alaska after that – and, at the time, ending up somewhere as far away and untouchable as Alaska sounded perfect. His company had developed a handful of novel drilling techniques that attempted to avoid the chronic corrosion these lines suffered in an exposed mountain environment by running them through the mountains themselves. A tube that was carved through stone predating the dinosaurs would, the company's founder explained in his sales pitch, probably outlast the civilization that needed it.

In the late summer or early autumn of 1976 – he was fuzzy on the dates but knew the locations down to the millimeter – his crew had finished punching through the mountain on the opposite side of this valley and were preparing to begin their next hole about 300 yards north of where he would eventually drill a chimney and spend the rest of his life. Earlier that summer he had given up on ever going back home; he chose these mountains instead. He had a lot of reasons, and, where reason wore thin, he had a lot of feelings to fill the gaps in the logic. He had gone his entire life without ever feeling comfortable, but here he found love in what he interpreted as the tranquility of the emptiness. As far back as he could remember, he had detested the never-ending expectation and consequence that came with the so-called advantages of the modern world, and he decided to stay here and *exist* while everyone else scrambled haphazardly to *survive*.

But even before he got to this valley, and before he was anywhere near it, something was already different. Ever since he started this work in Placer County, deep in the Sierra Nevadas, he had dreamed every night about the freedom this job would finally bring – the faraway places his work could take him and the world he could leave far behind in the process. But the move to Washington found him dreaming about finally finding a home – and when he was awake, he started to feel like this was it. His dreams grew more vivid and more specific until, after several months, he started to picture the actual place he'd live. And then, a week after seeing it, he climbed up over the eastern rim of this valley and saw it.

"I felt this place calling to me," he said solemnly.

By the time he laid eyes on his future home, however, company politics were beginning to threaten his plan. The day before his team entered the valley, a supply shipment had showed up to keep the camp fed and paid, and along with it came a note from his friend at the corporate office who passed along a rumor that the company was about to be bought by a much larger conglomerate that already had lines routed across these mountains a couple hundred miles south. If that was the case, the letter reasoned, he should keep tunneling until the very last moment and then collect a nice check at the end which would be prorated for all the distance he covered.

For Harvey, this was the last piece of the puzzle, and the last straw, and his last bite at the apple – all in one.

He started giving his crew Fridays off with the reasoning that they were doing as much in four days as anyone else did in five, and so he'd write up the weekly progress reports in such a way that they were paid accordingly. If anyone on the crew noticed that their average four-day progress was actually pretty average they didn't mention it – they happily accepted the extra day off and same pay.

Every Thursday night, as the men on his crew headed into town – and almost always with his permission to "be back by brunch" on Monday – Harvey spent every possible moment of the next three days digging something for himself. This went on for weeks. He wasn't quite as proficient with every piece of heavy equipment as the men on his crew, nor could he work as fast or keep his lines as straight, but he made steady progress as they spent their weekends in various states of incapacitation in the tiny town of Whittier – which was about two hours away once you accounted for the hike down the mountain, the slow ride along the logging roads, and then the quick stretch of interstate through the mountains.

It took over a month worth of weekends to slowly chew and cut the rock out of the main tunnel, all in an effort to reach the hollow bubble which sat deep inside this peak – it was something his company's geologist had spotted weeks earlier while surveying the ground penetrating radar results collected for this valley. The company, as a rule, made every effort to avoid any naturally occurring pockets or openings in the rock – the reasoning was that only by drilling through solid stone could they reliably predict the structural integrity of the pathways they were drilling. Furthermore, the company's insurance could refuse to cover a claim that was the result of a naturally occurring phenomenon, like a collapsing pocket in the stone.

This pocket, the geologist casually explained at the time, was likely the remnant of an old magma flow through the mantle that had been pulled up amidst all the standard tectonic uplift which created these mountains several hundred million years ago. Harvey had that report from the surveyor in his pocket the entire time he dug, and as soon as he reached the edge of that bubble, he began widening it, boring out a vented tube for the fireplace, and grinding out whatever extra space he'd need to make a life here. He knew enough to put a bend in the tunnel so that no one could see the light from inside, and also to minimize the wind howling directly at him. Beyond that, he figured it out as he went.

When everything seemed finished, it occurred to him that a lot of winter days would pass without it being possible to go outside – even with the hidden, avalanche-proof door he'd fabricated with rebar and all the rubble he'd pulled out of the tunnel – and he sure didn't want to have to use the bathroom in the same room where he slept and ate. It didn't need to be big – it was just going to be a bucket sitting on the ground, after all – so he picked a spot along his tunnel and branched off in the opposite direction. He couldn't help but think he would be the only man outside of Lascaux with a bathroom carved this deep into a cave.

The dig for this bathroom, despite being comparatively short, turned out to be far more difficult than the main tunnel or the room. After several hours of negligible progress and considerable wear on the drill bit of this particular machine, he stopped to look at the stone. It was the same familiar granite, but for several feet in every direction it looked warped – as if it had been exposed to some extreme geologic heat or pressure. When he got close to the stone and followed its wavy texture with his hands, it looked as if this vein of stone had been melted and then reconstituted – and this process had now rendered it extremely hard. This caused him no small amount of concern as he considered his options now that his time was limited; a message had arrived with the last resupply that the negotiations for the sale of the company were nearly complete, and, as soon the terms were finalized, this project would be called off. Harvey figured he had, at most, two weeks left, and that accounted for how slowly the news would make its way up to him. He reasoned, probably incorrectly in retrospect, that he didn't have time to start a new branch of this tunnel, so he doubled down on the current direction he was already headed. He shifted his trajectory just slightly to the left and continued to drill parallel to this warped vein of granite. This made the digging easier, but it was still considerably harder than usual. Normally he would have worried about how hard this was on the equipment, but he knew that anyone who might complain wouldn't be on the company payroll by the end of the month.

He kept working, made a lot of progress, and by late Sunday night had nearly carved deep enough to put his bathroom sufficiently far away from his living room. He had 50 feet as the magic number for this branch of the tunnel, and, at about the time his instruments were reading just shy of 47 feet, the tungsten carbide drill suddenly stopped in its tracks – going instantaneously drop from 790 RPM to zero. The motor behind it was still pushing at full power, so he scrambled to shut things down before it blew out and took him with it. He pulled the drill back and leaned in to see what impenetrable obstacle he had suddenly encountered.

"And *that* is when everything changed," Harvey said with a flourish.

"What do you mean?"

Harvey let out a long breath and rocked back on his heels, as if bracing for something. He shrugged and gestured for Jordan to follow him outside.

"That's kind of enough for Day 1 in the cave, isn't it? Why don't I help you get settled in, and I'll show your boy how to cook a deer."

"He would love that, actually."

"It seems like he has a good feel for the woods."

"If he ever heard you say that, I don't think his ego would ever come back to earth."

"I remember being his age," Harvey said with a smile, "all I wanted was to be somewhere like this."

"Where did you learn how to survive out here? I don't think I ever heard Sienna's dad say a word about hunting or camping."

"No, I'm sure he never went; none of us did, growing up. I had to figure it all out, a piece at a time, over 17 years working in the mountains, and then, once I was here, I had to hurry and figure out the rest of it."

"And you had to figure those last parts out alone."

"Pretty much."

"How tough did that get, all these years out here alone on a mountainside?"

"Well, in my defense," he said with a smile, "it's not like I'm some kook out here talking to myself and the rocks all day."

"I know that; I didn't mean it like that."

"Kevin will tell you I'm not some freak."

"Who's Kevin?"

"You're standing on him."

Jordan looked down at the long flat rock under his feet.

"Harvey, I didn't mean –"

Harvey roared laughing and pointed a long finger at Jordan.

"Your face! I can't believe it – you actually thought..." he was wheezing laughing. "That is probably going to be the highlight of the summer!"

"How was I supposed to know what level of weirdo you've become up here?"

Harvey was still laughing, and now it had turned into coughing. This story was definitely going to be retold to his kids later.

"Naming rocks is only the 40th or 50th weirdest thing a dude can do out here after being alone this long."

"It will be a couple more years before I go full hermit."

"Ok, so what *do* you and Kevin do, then?"

"You might not know this, but the Pacific Crest Trail runs just a few miles from here."

"Right."

"And anytime I want to hang out and spend some time with humanity for a couple days, I dress up like a long-haul hiker – you know, dirty shorts, beat up boots, faded hat, and an internal-frame backpack that has seen better days – and I just go hang out at a campsite that all the hikers use to rest and send mail and pick up supplies."

"And there's just people always there?"

"During the peak months you can count on a minimum of seven or eight people, and some years it will be triple that – and it's nice, everyone is having a good time, there's a fire going, there's a couple joints circulating, and you just kick back and talk for hours."

"That does actually sound fun."

"It's great, and way out in the woods when you get to talking – you'll talk about the deepest stuff you can imagine. You just talk while you stare at the Milky Way directly above your head. It's profound, man. Some of the smartest and some of the best people I've ever met were at that camp."

"Do you keep in touch with any of them?"

"No, there's no way to do that. I just go over, fill up my need for human engagement, then I work my way back here."

"And that's enough to never get lonely?"

"Son, there are people living in the suburbs who will go a year between saying a word to the neighbor on either side of their house. I've heard a thousand men pour out their hearts next to an open fire and a midnight breeze. I'd say my social life is probably above average in terms of cumulative words spoken to others."

Put that way, it did seem nice if not still a bit lonely in between.

"And then, when all the yapping is done, I come back here and pick up where I left off. And pretty much everything I need is here."

"I still can't believe you have a bathroom."

"A cave with indoor plumbing – not bad, right?"

"Does a bucket count as plumbing?"

"Speaking of the bucket, I try to limit my use of that to winter or rainstorms for obvious reasons – but, trust me, there are a lot of good spots outside. And you can't beat the view."

JULY 2

At 7:14 am residents in three cul-de-sacs running parallel to a greenbelt received an e-mail from their cable and internet provider alerting them to a temporary service disruption. These interruptions were rare but not unheard of, particularly for this provider, and the e-mail noted that multiple maintenance crews from around the area had already been dispatched. The provider noted that service should be restored "within 3 hours."

E-mails like this were typically automated and should have arrived much sooner since the service to these homes had actually dropped off at 6:32 am. Or, looked at a different way, the area's internet connection had dropped about 25 minutes after the first member of the Tactical Cyber Operations Team got to her desk and began sifting through the list of requests her team had received overnight. Kara Clark noticed that the top spot on the task list had already been deferentially given to a major at the Pentagon, and, when she pulled up the specifics of that request on her terminal, she saw a note her boss had added saying that this particular request should be accommodated with all possible haste.

The request was simple enough: Knock out cable and/or internet access to every home inside an outlined area on an attached map. The total area wasn't particularly large, and, at a glance, it didn't look like more than 25 houses. She kept reading the request and saw that the major needed something that would require multiple hours to fix as well as "more than 3 to 4" on-site maintenance trucks and crews to adequately resolve the situation. Knocking out internet access was easy – she could do that from her phone while on the treadmill – but making things bad enough to require multiple work crews rather than some network administrator at the corporate office essentially hitting reset on that neighborhood's router? That did take a bit more time to put together, but it was still a common enough operation that its execution was much closer to a paint-by-numbers than the creation of a unique cyber masterpiece.

She spent the next 10 minutes programming a series of parameters that would do a few different things at once – the combination of which would generate a major red flag at that local provider's headquarters once she put it into place. First, she arranged for the local network switch directing digital traffic to these houses to overload and then crash, then she installed a program that would make it appear as if a massive cascading system failure had been triggered by this, and then, with some genuine artistry, she laid in an additional layer of misdirection such that when the response team determined that there wasn't actually a cascading failure afoot they would instead "discover" that having this much disruption in the local area indicated that the fiber optic cabling must have been compromised somehow. Water, construction, or a very determined burrowing animal were the most common reasons for this. This problem would present the very real chance that a critical mass of overloaded switches could knock out service for the entire subdivision. That concern would prompt the dispatch of multiple work crews to go address this as quickly as possible, and the executive in charge of infrastructure maintenance could reliably be predicted to move quickly on this.

For a neighborhood this size, it would take around three hours to check the wires, perform diagnostics on the hubs, and test every inch of insulation and piping – only to discover that everything was fine. After three hours, Kara's program would pull back, delete all its fingerprints, and service would resume. Whatever thing the crews had most recently touched would get credit for having been the fix. Later, there would almost certainly be an audit within the technical team at headquarters to find any underlying problems or signs of tampering to explain this mystery outage. But, by the time that audit had proven inconclusive, this would all be a distant memory to Kara, the TCOT, and the moderately shadowy major from the Pentagon.

She took one last look at the finer points of her programming, double checked the orchestration and timing of each wave, and hit "enter." It was 9:31am and there were nine other requests in the system, and both Jon and Eric were on vacation this week instead of helping.

At the same time he'd submitted the request for this outage, Major Horn had also contacted a forensic investigative unit stationed at Joint Base Lewis-McCord, about an hour south of this neighborhood. The briefing document sent to this forensic team was also short, straightforward, and light on nuance – but the mission itself was unambiguous: Outfit a maintenance truck in the livery of the region's internet provider, arrive at a specific spot at a specific time, do not be surprised by the presence of other maintenance trucks, and then await further instructions.

At the appointed time, the truck and its three occupants arrived, outfitted with generic coveralls and toolbelts. They turned off the truck and waited. A moment later, the phone held by the senior officer began to ring.

"Which house are you in front of?"

"7722, sir."

"Are the other crews already working?"

"Yes, there are five of them," he checked his rearview mirror, "and they seem to be getting after it with the local access boxes, and we have a couple other guys looking at some kind of meter on the side of a house, and it looks like four to five other technicians going from house to house."

"Work your way around the back of 7722, these other crews should offer sufficient cover to move about freely. Once you've made your entry and assessed it, call me back with what you find."

Horn expected the house to be empty, but he had no idea why, and he could not yet guess at what they would find inside. The sudden evaporation of a very average family of six was inexplicable.

It would have helped to get here sooner.

Over the last 24 hours he'd had a surveillance drone fly over this house three times to look down through it. Rather than finding six warm blobs scattered around the residence the infrared scan found zero, and, from the looks of it, both cars were in the garage. There was no data coming or going from the house, aside from a trickle of WiFi activity which meant they had an Alexa or a smart fridge. This confirmed what he'd already learned about the family's four phones being suddenly turned off – essentially in unison – the night of the 28th. In parallel to this, a search of all known contacts had been executed with nothing to show for it.

None of this made sense.

This family had appeared on his radar after one of the research departments upstairs passed along a voicemail received from a former NRO program director. The caller worked in an office complex in Alexandria which the Defense Department set aside for old scientists with old secrets, and this particular old scientist had apparently sat on this information for two days while he tried in vain to get in touch with a former program subject.

From what Horn could tell, this family had simply blinked out of existence sometime around the night of June 28th or the morning of the 29th. There had been a steady churn of credit card activity, cell activity, and data consumption reaching back over 20 years – and then it went to zero instantly.

Six people just dematerialized.

This was incredibly strange to the point of being particularly suspicious. But what, exactly, did he have to be suspicious about? What did *they* have to be suspicious about?

As soon as the first scan of the house showed it was empty, Horn had ordered an unusually intense download of this former program subject's entire background. He read through every piece of available information on "Riley, Sienna Barrett" and her husband, but the only thing even remotely interesting was the classified testimony she had given at a Senate Intelligence debrief in 2018. But even that testimony was uneventful, although the program itself had sounded interesting. The family's financial information did not raise any flags either, although a large cash withdrawal from an ATM, followed by a bigger one at a bank, were called out in the report – but similar moves had been made in the past, so they weren't total outliers. The amounts withdrawn also weren't the amounts you'd need to go on the lam long term.

He kept thinking about a footnote in her Senate Intelligence file noting the existence of an addendum report which was held by the NRO. In an effort to be thorough his team had requested it, but the

NRO typically took a week before responding with a standard, "We cannot provide the requested material at this time." He hoped a call from the SecDef would cut that down to one day, but the likelihood that file had anything new or helpful in it was incredibly low. But an operation like this was willing to look underneath every stone.

While walking back to catch up on the air traffic in Manchuria, Horn ran through these details again in an effort to conjure up the missing connection that had eluded him and the rest of his team: How could this Sienna Barrett possibly be connected to this electromagnetic interference? She had no ties to the international community or her old program director, the program itself had ended inconclusively 30 years ago, and an exhaustive background check that leapt over every privacy law on earth had found nothing in her life history that was remotely noteworthy for the purposes of this mission. Unless this jail where she worked had a particle physics lab on campus, there would be no way for her to even know this interference had returned.

This was a very normal woman who had disappeared with her very normal husband and children at the precise moment governments around the world were secretly gearing up for war – and at the same moment her own government happened to come looking for her.

But, just in the nick of time, she vanished.

Something here didn't add up. His gut told him that Barrett knew something about her old program that he did not.

He also needed to talk with the director of that old program, but that would have to wait until he could figure out what on earth Gupta was trying to do in Karachi, and he still needed to get things settled with the George and Peralta. Adding to this was the update from the Arizona which was still up on his screen; the overview he got from that cowboy of a captain had turned up the temperature several degrees amongst his staff. For now, he was left to think about the phone call he had just ended with the R&D colonel who had spent seven hours talking to this Dr. Torquemann. The colonel's blunt assessment of the conversation was, "The old man is sharing about 1 out of every 52 things he knows." Horn needed to look this Dr. Torquemann in the eyes and see if he could pierce through whatever defenses had fended off the colonel.

His phone rang.

"They're not here, and they haven't been for slightly more than 36 hours."

"How can you tell?"

"There's an incredibly fine surface level of dust on the countertops. I'd estimate the airflow here hasn't been interrupted for at least that long.

"What else?"

"There are dishes in the sink, and a few more on the table. That can indicate a couple possible things: It can show you that the people who used to be in the house did not know they were leaving, it can mean that they left in a hurry, or it can mean that they are not planning to return."

"Do you have an assessment of which one of those it is?"

"There's no sign of any struggle or haste, there's no chairs left askew around the table, and all the stools are pushed in around the kitchen island, so it doesn't seem like they dropped everything and ran. But what's odd is that both cars are still in the garage. With what little I know about this situation, it's hard to explain how that fits into this, and if they had used Uber or a car service, you'd already know about it."

"So, they walked away?"

"There's a bike rack here with no bikes in it, but that doesn't necessarily mean there's been bikes in it lately."

"Understood. Anything else?"

"Two things. First, you probably already know this, but all four cellphones are here, so they have the trifecta of off-grid disappearing acts: No car, no phone, no credit cards."

"The credit cards are there, too?"

"His wallet was in the master closet, and her purse was in her car."

"Are their ID's there, too?"

"Yeah, both ID's were there in the wallet and purse, and one of my guys found a small safe in the master bedroom's closet that had an empty gun lock and five passports in it.

"So, we can narrow down their whereabouts to the lower 48."

"That's a reasonable bet, sir."

"What's the second thing?"

"Next to the door into the garage is a calendar with the family schedule on it, and they have June 28th through July 4th penciled in as a road trip.”

“That they took without a car?”

“It could imply they are riding with someone else.”

“What do you make of it?”

“My gut says it feels deceptive, but I don’t have any evidence for that right now.”

“Go on.”

“The caution against jumping to the conclusion that it’s deception is that, if it *is*, it demonstrates a level of premeditation and coversion which speaks to something *much* more sophisticated than what I’m seeing from the happy suburban family pretext that’s showing up here on the surface.”

“Understood. So, if you had to begin assembling a short list of places for them to go, what’s at the top of this list?”

“Sir, 98 times out of 100, when I come across a sudden disappearance that’s this unexpected and this drastic, everyone I’m looking for is already dead. It’s typically because one of them ran across something they didn’t understand or couldn’t avoid – and that was it. If you told me that no one in this family has any connection to the type of work your organization is doing, then maybe I drop that number to 50-50. That’s how extreme this looks on our end. I’m standing in a living room that had a family in it less than two days ago. I can see the crush marks in the couch where they like to sit. The bread in the pantry isn’t stale yet. The dirt in the potted plant next to the kitchen window still isn’t dry. There’s a big framed photo on the wall of six people who either dropped everything perfectly and disappeared in a way that no special operator could be expected to do with five civilians, or an assault team showed up so suddenly that they didn’t even have a chance to try to escape or put up a fight. In that case, they’re all zipped into bags, and you don’t need to waste the effort trying to track down which pieces are in which landfills.”

“Understood.”

“I recognize this may not be the news you’re after. There just isn’t a better explanation for what we’re seeing here, and your average family just can’t pull off a disappearing act this thorough.”

“I appreciate the context, captain. Is there anything else?”

“In the event my hunch is wrong and they’re still out there, they’re running from something they desperately want to escape. You are going to need a very special kind of manhunt to find them now. I'd start looking somewhere in the surrounding woodlands. There's a couple million acres of it here."

"Understood. Thank you again for your fine work on such notice. I will send my regards and thanks to your commander at JBL."

The investigator was right, Horn thought to himself, this was wildly unordinary. Whatever it was about Sienna Riley that had sparked that old program director's memory seemed justified now.

Wherever she was, and whatever she knew, it was worth disappearing.

JULY 3

Jordan shifted his weight in his hammock and, for the first time in several days, wasn't woken by the dawn sunlight. It was exceptionally easy to lose track of time in this cave, and he checked his watch to figure out if he should still feel this tired.

It was 7:10 am, and he could hear Sienna and the girls talking nearby.

The entire family had been up late – lateness was as impossible to determine in a cave as earliness, it turned out – listening to Uncle Harvey tell stories about their grandpa and their great-grandparents, as well as a few about their mom running around causing problems at family get togethers.

For her part, Sienna had already been awake for over an hour with Calista and Scarlett. The hum had been rising in their ears all yesterday, but here in the tunnel it had changed. It had moved from static to something that just pulsed in the background. Both girls had climbed into her hammock at some point in the middle of the night, and when they woke up again around 6:00 am she started telling them about all the techniques Dr. Torquemann and Dr. Tunis had taught her to quiet her mind, to focus in on the Signal, to get inside it, and to see and hear what was there.

It only took a few minutes for both of them to start talking through what they could see and hear. There were sounds and sights they described so clearly that she could recognize them from her own time in the research cabin, and she couldn't help but think what one of these girls could have done with an ESR. When Scarlett hopped out of the hammock to go get a bar from her backpack, the sudden drop in the clarity of the Signal was unmistakable, even for Sienna who wasn't picking up anything nearly as acutely as either girl.

Uncle Harvey was over on his cot, snoring loudly, and Blaise was sure to keep sleeping in his hammock nearby, so they decided to go walk down to the lake while everyone else slept. A landslide the previous winter had cut this area off to hikers, so they were certain to have the entire place to themselves. They found their shoes in the dim light of a dying headlamp and headed outside. On their way out, Scarlett's curiosity took over and she dashed off to the right to see what was at the end of this short tunnel. There wasn't much. At the end of it was a pile of rubble with an old tarp stretched across part of it – and she wasted no time climbing this rock pile, figuring she'd go up, touch the ceiling, and come back down. The ceiling was much higher here than in the rest of the tunnel, and, as she picked her way across the rocks, she stepped on the edge of the tarp and noticed it was wet from the water leaking through the stone above it.

As she walked, some small, loose rocks shifted slightly, and the tarp began to slide and pull away at the edges as the weight of the water which had pooled up in the middle dragged it down. After a few more steps the right half of the tarp fell away entirely.

Jutting out from within the wall of the tunnel was a long, smooth metallic surface, about 12 feet long, subtly arching in a half-moon shape from one end to the other. It had a beveled edge and a mirror-like quality, and it was covered in grit and dust.

They all stared.

Calista walked up and hovered her hand over it, as if checking to see if it were hot. When she laid her palm on the surface all three of them suddenly heard the dull hum of the Signal snap into silence – it was the type of silence when a radio goes from static to a perfectly tuned station. It was unmistakable. The change would have been jarring if it was not such a sudden relief. The peace washed over all of them. Sienna walked closer to see the surface, and Scarlett slid down the rocks to get a closer look.

Cali was the first one to consider moving the other half of the tarp, and, in a single motion, she pulled the rest of it to the floor.

Sienna took a small, sharp breath at the site of it.

Cali stood, staring, the tarp still in her hand.

The half circle of metal they had touched gradually sloped toward a much larger teardrop-shape. It was embedded in the solid stone of the tunnel wall, and it was impossible to guess what the rest of it might look like or how big it all was. The exposed section was at least 30 feet long. Looking back down the tunnel you could now see an unmistakable ripple through the rock as if it had arrived here violently and then left the mountain to heal behind it. Up close, where it wasn't covered in dust, it looked as if it was made of black glass, despite its unmistakably metallic feel. There were no seams or rivets or panels, there was not a mark or scratch, and it now hummed and pulsed.

Sienna knew precisely what this was.

And now it was time for Jordan to get the rest of her story – the part she had left out because she hoped the retelling would not offer any value or play any role in what came next.

She quietly took two long, deep breaths to calm down enough to make it sound casual when she asked Cali to run and get her dad.

A minute later Jordan arrived at the fork in the tunnel, and he reflexively cursed at the shock of it.

He turned to Scarlett and apologized.

"It's ok Dad, I've already heard mom say that word. It happened when she dropped the cake at Josie's birthday last year."

It was so matter-of-fact that it wasn't funny yet.

"I think my uncle has a lot more to that story he was telling before dinner" Sienna said flatly, still staring at it.

"It explains the weird spot he chose for the cliffhanger," Jordan added, rethinking in the moment if this was the best time for levity, and whether or not he had control over when comments like this were made.

Jordan went back to the hammocks, grabbed a few things from the backpacks for breakfast, and took Sienna and the two girls out into the bright morning light to eat. Blaise and Josie were both heavy sleepers, so they'd likely to be out for at least a couple more hours if no one went and woke them up.

They sat on a long-fallen tree and felt the warm sun on their faces as they ate.

"What do you think it is, Dad?" Scarlett asked.

"What does it look like?" Cali snapped back at her.

"It looks like the reason Uncle Harvey never wanted to leave,"

Jordan offered.

"You know what it is, Dad, we all do," Cali said, annoyed that this wasn't being confronted directly.

"It's… a lot," Sienna finally said.

They sat stunned, still chewing, for a long moment.

"It's probably from space," Scarlett finally said to fill the silence.

"It's *obviously* from space – and just… what the crap is going on here?" Cali snapped again.

"I'll let Uncle Harvey sleep for now, but then we have to connect a few dots."

"Do you think it is here in peace, Dad?" Scarlett asked. She was now fully invested in the concept and the shock had given way to curiosity.

Sienna was the first to notice the sound of footsteps in the tunnel and the scratch of steps across the gravel near the opening. Harvey walked out and waved, he was shirtless, with cargo shorts and his faded SuperSonics hat.

"Good morning," he said smiling. "I see you found Stella."

"You call it 'Stella?'" Scarlett asked, even more curious now that it had a name and backstory.

"Yes, it's short for…"

"Don't say 'interstellar…'" Cali interrupted.

Harvey wasn't amused at being beaten to the punch of his own joke, but he respected the intellect. "Yes, it's for 'interstellar' – because I'm pretty sure it was built a long way from here – and I don't mean Hong Kong."

"Definitely not Hong Kong," Scarlett said, nodding thoughtfully. She had wandered a few feet away to attempt a handstand, with an old stump to brace herself.

"So, your story last night – I get why you ended with drilling out the bathroom and breaking your drill – so, what happened next?" Jordan asked. There was something about this story he was dreading, but he wasn't sure why.

Harvey settled in next to the Rileys and sat down on the ground to lean back against the log. He paused to take in the entire valley and absorb the calm in the same way they had been doing for the last 10 minutes.

"Well, there we are in early December, and it is fully freezing out by then, and so we are wrapping things up for the season, and the company's going to be sold before we come back in the Spring – and that's when I hit Stella."

"You literally hit her with your drill?" Scarlett asked, now upside down.

"I did," he said nodding slowly, "and then things were kinda weird for a lot of years."

"And why were you drilling at that exact spot?" Cali asked.

"Well, the short answer was I needed a bathroom for when it was too cold to come outside. But, really, to be honest, geez…" he swatted away a hovering insect and thought about it. "I guess I just felt drawn there – and not just to the valley, but to this exact spot on the mountain," he pointed back over his shoulder to the doorway to his cave.

"I thought you said you had a geologic survey that you used to pick your spot?" Jordan said.

"I did, but pockets like that in the rock aren't terribly uncommon – and besides, the spot I drilled was the first thing I set eyes on when I found this whole place, and *this* exact spot on the mountain was the spot I knew was going to be home right away. I knew right away I was going to drill right damn here even if I had to chew through solid pig iron to do it."

"Wait," Sienna jumped in, "go back to what you said – what do you mean things got weird for a bunch of years?"

He dove back into the story, and, after a few reminders, was able to pick up where he left off.

When his drill had first stopped there had been several thousand volts powering it, and Harvey had assumed that was more than enough to get through this shiny black patch.

"At the time I figured it was something like obsidian or hematite, even though any geologist would tell you that's crazy."

"True," Scarlett said, still balancing.

"So, I lined up the machine again, set it to max power and about 2,000 RPM, and I went straight at that black mineral deposit – I figured I'd just wipe it out with equal parts high speed and brute force."

"And?"

"The entire front of this huge industrial drill disintegrated on impact. Just – poof, annihilated."

As he went on to explain it, smoke immediately filled the tunnel, and he struggled to see what had happened as blood poured out of a deep cut above his left eyebrow where he had been hit by a piece of shrapnel that was once a part of the drill's transmission. He paused to run a finger across the long scar. With the drilling assembly gone, the remaining half of the machine was now pressed up against the wall, still billowing smoke and violently throwing sparks. With his one good eye he found where to cut the power, and, as the smoke began to clear, he noticed that the copper coils and the exposed writing from where the electrical supply reached the motor were both glowing white hot and had tilted over to lean up against that same patch of obsidian.

"I don't know how long Stella has been here, but I know just enough about the geology to tell you that nothing much has changed here in 300 million years, give or take – but between two heavy strikes with the drill and then an extended electrocution once the motor flew apart, well…"

"What?" Cali asked, leaning forward.

"You know…" he said, gesturing in a way that seemed unrelated to any actual verb.

"What?" Scarlett asked eagerly.

"It woke up."

"It what?" Jordan asked.

"It started talking."

"*It what?*" Sienna burst out.

"Not *talking* talking, but it definitely had its switch flipped."

He explained that several thousand volts of electricity – or maybe it was the two collisions with the drill, he wasn't sure, but probably the former – had kick-started Stella after years spent encased in the mountain. At first, all he could see was a nine-inch-wide patch of metallic black glass. But then, over the next several hours, the material seemed like it was flexing or pulsing. He admitted that at this point a lot of his sensory input was being influenced by the obvious concussion he was suffering from – but he still ran to find a jackhammer and set to work along a few cracks that seemed to radiate out from that patch of black. After a couple hours of work a big section crumbled away and exposed what is still there today. He couldn't tell if it was broken, and he had no idea how to fix it if it was, but whatever he had done with the drill certainly got a reaction. He could feel a periodic pulse come from it. Lights in abstract patterns lit up under the glassy surface and moved around it. Sometimes the walls creaked at regular intervals as if it was trying to rotate or shift on its axis.

It didn't seem alive, per se, but it did seem to want to do something.

"By the end of that weekend, right as the guys were coming back, we got word that this week rather than the next week would be the last one of the season, so we were told to pack everything up and bring it back to the warehouse in Seattle. This meant I was out of time to drill much of anything else."

He paused to stretch and touch his toes. He threw a pinecone at Scarlett who was still holding her handstand, albeit with flagging balance.

"Mid-way through the next week the company drove three four-wheelers up to the valley and my guys began loading the wagons they were towing with gear. There was a semi-truck parked at the trailhead, and they were going to ferry everything there one wagonload at a time. We never even got back to drilling anything, so I didn't even need to use the story I'd made up for why one of our biggest drills exploded while they were gone for the weekend."

He explained that he had strategically loaded all their gear so that these first several rounds only hauled away the things he didn't need. Once only the best stuff was left, he sent everyone home and said he'd make the last couple trips himself.

"As soon as I knew everyone was off the mountain and on their way back to Seattle once and for all, I took our two best drills, the two newest diesel generators, a bunch of car batteries we used for powering smaller units, and all the fuel we had left – and I dragged every piece of it down into my tunnel. I figured I could make that fuel last several years if I rationed it just right. I knew the company that bought my outfit used entirely different and much newer stuff than we did, so all of our old and busted gear was just getting sent straight to the dump. No one was ever going to do an inventory and see what was missing. So, once I had loaded everything into that room where your hammocks are, I drove that four-wheeler back down the trail, threw the last couple things in the semi, and told the driver he could leave; then I went and checked in at the office in Seattle to say everything was done, and picked up my last check; then I emptied out my bank account and asked for it in $20 bills, and I was back here by lunch the next day. And that was it.

By now Blaise and Josie had woken up and wandered out into the warm sun. Jordan caught them up on the main points of the story and Sienna filled in the details.

"And it's in your *bathroom?*" Blaise asked.

"Crazy, right?" Harvey said, laughing.

"So did you try to free it from the rocks?" Josie asked. She was concerned it was alive.

"I did. I used both of those drills that I stashed here, and I kept cutting and carving until I'd used up every blade I had and way more fuel than I ever thought it would take. But that rock in there – it's something fierce. I chewed through every drill bit I'd stashed away and only exposed a few extra feet of Stella."

He seemed defeated by this, and he slumped back against the log again. His curiosity had been piqued to the highest possible levels and then, alone in a cave of his own making, he had been forced to come to terms with both an incredible secret and the fact he would never really know anything about it.

"But, it kept me warm a really long time," he concluded.

"You slept on it?" Scarlett asked?

"Slept? Ha! No! No, there was a time when I was drilling with one of the smaller drills and, as one of the car batteries was getting low on juice, I went to switch the cables, and, without really thinking about it, I laid the cable that I had just disconnected on Stella's bumper..."

All six Rileys cocked their heads to the side.

"...it's a bumper to me, at least – it's the part you climbed up on this morning, I saw the wet footprints – and as soon as I set it down, the drill started running again. So now I'm thinking to myself, 'Woah, free electricity?!' And, sure enough, I ran one of the jumper cables over to the space heater and the rack of lights in the main room, and both of them turned on."

"You used it as a battery?" Jordan said, surprised. And impressed.

"Don't misunderstand, it was not a lot of power – it was like I was catching the bare minimum of something it was just kind of giving off. The best way I can describe it is that it kind of seemed similar to electromagnetic induction."

"I'm nine, Uncle Harvey, please explain," Scarlett interrupted, "and it's hard to hear because all the blood has rushed into my ears."

"Yeah, so, you know how if you stand underneath those really tall high-tension power lines you can hear the electricity crackling? And you know how if you stand under them and hold a fluorescent light in your hands it will start to glow? Not super bright like if it's in a light socket at your house, but it will glow enough to read a book or something."

None of the Riley kids had heard of this. Jordan had heard about this in junior high but never actually seen it happen. Sienna thought it sounded like an urban legend.

"Oh yeah, it works. The science, which maybe they aren't still teaching in your public schools, is pretty straightforward: If you take one of those long fluorescent lightbulb tubes – the ones that look like lightsabers – and you stand underneath a high-voltage power line, the electrical field generated by the lines passes through your hand and the glass of the bulb and it starts spinning the atoms that make up the gas inside the bulb. And when those atoms start spinning, they ionize and that makes the gas start to glow."

Josie knew where a box of these light bulbs was in the garage back home, and she made a mental note to take them to the power lines that ran next to the park she passed on the way to school.

"So, if I had to guess, I'd say I was just catching the tiniest wisps of electrons as a byproduct of whatever actual power source Stella has – but who knows. I don't exactly have the tools up here to scientifically diagnose this. But whatever was going on in there, it was a lot of help and it made my life a lot easier. And it kept on working for 15 or so solid years. The lights under the surface would flip on and move around every so often, sometimes I'd hear it spin up and then spin back down after a few minutes or an hour, and maybe a couple times a year, or every other year, there was something almost like a tone or a resonance that would come out of it – and that would always match up with the lights really starting to dance on it. And then it would just go dead silent again."

"And then it broke?" Josie asked.

"And then it just went back to sleep once and for all."

He had another pinecone ready to throw at Scarlett, but this part of the story obviously made him sad, and he tossed the pinecone over his shoulder instead.

"Did you try to wake her back up?" Josie asked, trying to lead him toward what she hoped was a happy ending to this story.

"No, not really. I still had some fuel for the generators, and I had bought a solar panel a few years earlier that kept the reading light on at night and charged a few flashlights, so I was able to get by well enough. And besides, Stella had a good run. It seemed greedy to go bang it with a hammer or something and hope to get some more juice out of it."

"So, what did you do?" Sienna asked, suddenly starting to put a few pieces together.

"For a while, life just went on. And then…"

He paused for a long time as he checked through all his pockets and finally found a pocketknife that he used to start sharpening a stray stick.

"And then what?"

"I got a little greedy."

"How so?" Jordan asked.

"Well, it's actually good I did because, a week later, here you guys are – and trust me, if you're still here this winter, you'll be glad that space heater is keeping your backside warm while we all sleep facing the fire."

"Wait, when?" Sienna asked. Now she was deathly serious.

Harvey squinted at her – half because of the sun, and half in surprise that she was suddenly so tense.

"Well, I guess it would have to be two weeks now that I think about it, give or take a couple days."

"And what happened?"

"What happened was I had an honest conversation with myself: My days of hiking into town and bringing back a couple gallons of fuel are long behind me, so I decided to go back to the gift that used to keep on giving."

"So you did… what?" Sienna asked slowly and deliberately. Portions of her life were starting to flash before her eyes, and, unconsciously, she put her hand over Cali's.

"Well, like I said, it started talking again."

"*Talking* talking?" Scarlett said, hopefully.

"No, not words, but I started getting this feeling that I hadn't had since I was little, like almost your age," he pointed at Josie. "See, when I was in 2nd grade all I wanted to do was play baseball, and my mom, your Great-grandma Megan, she signed me up for little league, and five minutes into the first practice, I lean down to re-tie my shoe and a ground ball hits me right behind my left ear, and my lights go out. I wake up at the E.R., my mom is crying, but I'm pretty much fine. But the headaches I had for years after that were just horrible – it felt like I had a railroad spike in my head."

The girls grimaced at the metaphor and Blaise nodded approvingly.

"So, my mom got a referral to a doctor that dealt with chronic pain and stuff like that, and I must have gone and seen this guy for a million visits – it was this creepy doctor and he pointed some kind of X-ray at the back of my head that he said would help regulate the pain. I'd lay there and I'd start to see and hear stuff – like a chatter or a warble or like a broken TV back when TVs had to have antennas."

"Like my mom?" Josie said.

"What?"

"Nothing, sorry – keep going," Sienna interrupted just quickly enough to make it slightly weird, but just in time to not interrupt the flow of his story.

"So, yeah – it was like when I was a kid, kinda. And not to get off on a tangent, but I know for a *fact* that something about that doctor was off – just being near him would freak me out. I would cry the entire ride across the bridge to his office and beg my mom to bring me home. But then I'd get there and just lay flat with this weird sci-fi-looking, robot-looking machine lined up next to the side of my head. And back then nobody had any idea about the dangers of this crap – and sure enough, 15 years later I'm still getting headaches, and when I make an appointment to get my head scanned, they find a tumor that's pretty much exactly where he used to put that weird looking machine. And, of course, I'm scared and mad, but the doctor doing the scan tells me, 'Oh, but don't worry, this growth is benign and it's not going to grow or hurt you, so you don't need surgery.' Ok, sure, if you say so, doc. And then, later, I was getting the same headaches and I felt like my vision was going bad, and I had it checked a second time, but all I got from that doctor was another version of the same thing about how everything was 'fine' in the 'but you still have a tumor hanging out on the back of your brain' sense of the word."

"And you never had surgery?" Blaise asked.

"Nope, never did. A few months after that trip to the doctor I got offered a job here in Washington, and I took it and just kinda forgot all about it. But I'll tell you I didn't forget how it happened. Whatever that doctor was doing was shady, and I know it. It was definitely a government operation, I just don't know what it was doing."

Jordan and Sienna made eye contact.

"But the more I thought about it over the years, I just *knew* that this was one of those experiments that the government does on the population just to see what happens – and this guy was an agent of that type of operation. I mean, listen, when you kids get home," they shared another look, "use the internet and just look up the word 'Tuskegee' or look up 'Operation Sea-Spray,' or type in 'human plutonium injection 1946.' That last one was when the U.S. government went to random hospitals and injected patients with radioactive waste just to see what would happen to them."

"What happened to them?" Scarlett asked.

"Exactly what you'd expect."

This had taken a grim turn, and the kids were fascinated.

"How did you figure out the doctor was a spy?" Blaise asked.

"Not so much a spy, but definitely some kinda government agent. So, check this out – over the years at those doctor appointments, every once in a while this other guy would be there – this guy in a dark suit who would just hang out while the doctor set up the machine next to me, and then they would talk over in the corner while it was running and look at the screen. Then one day after one of my appointments, my mom and I were both hungry, so we pull over at a McDonalds on the same road as the clinic, a couple miles away. The drive-thru was packed that day, so we go inside, and we get in line, and guess who's at the front paying for his food? That dude in the suit. He walks right by us, didn't even notice us 'cause he was digging around in his bag for fries, and he goes out the door, and I watch him the whole way as he walks out into the parking lot. So, I sneak out the door to see where he's going, and he gets in this car, and when it pulls out, I can see the "U.S. Government" license plate. I mean, I already knew, but back then we didn't know not to trust the government yet."

They shared another look.

"I know what you're thinking. I know it sounds crazy. But I know what happened – and I know it in my bones."

The family was silent. Uncle Harvey had a sound in his voice that was a lot like their mom's the night she told them about her time at the camp. That seemed like months ago right now.

No one spoke, but they stole glances at Uncle Harvey who stared into the distance while he relived the parts of the story he didn't have the strength or closure to say out loud yet. They heard a breeze move through the trees and then reach their faces a moment later.

It was finally Sienna who spoke up again to ask a question that, for the sake of her daughters, she had to know.

"What happened to start it back up?" she asked.

"To start it? Oh, yeah, Stella, right. So, I had my little solar panel recharging a couple of the car batteries that I use to run those lights down in the room, and I knew I was just going to be recharging them again in a week, and it looked like we had a couple storms on the way, and that means nothing gets charged for a while, and I just couldn't stomach the idea of sitting there in the dark, so I took the two batteries, I put the jumper cables on Stella and… you know, tried to prime that pump again."

"You tried to jump start a UFO?" Sienna started the sentence as a shout but pulled it back almost immediately to present it as a question.

"That seems like a crass term for my Stella, but, essentially, yes. One thing to consid–"

He was interrupted by the loud and surprisingly odd bugle of an elk, and he stood bolt upright to scan the ridge of the valley to find it. Half a mile away he spotted a pair of antlers maneuvering through the trees. Harvey dropped back down to his knees and whispered to the Rileys, "That's dinner for the rest of the Summer and Fall. And breakfast and lunch, too. I gotta go."

He ran into the cave and was back out less than 20 seconds later with a rifle.

"Stay here and stay low, I'll be back in an hour, and I'll probably need Blaine to help me carry him back."

Blaise nodded enthusiastically and did not correct him.

He took off like a flash and didn't lose speed until after he dipped out of view.

Sienna looked at Jordan and then back to the kids. This was her opportunity to tell the rest of an un-tell-able story.

"I know this is going to sound crazy, but this is where the Signal comes from."

"That thing?" Jordan said, pointing back at the cave in total disbelief.

"Yes."

"But how do you know that? We just got here, there could be a million –"

"There's no mistaking what the Signal sounds like and looks like, and when the girls and I got up close to Stella today... that's definitely where it comes from."

"Right *here*, in *that* tunnel?"

"I don't understand it either, but that's the Signal."

"I thought it was the Russians," Cali said.

"Yeah, that's what they told us."

"Did you know it was Stella?" Cali asked.

Sienna paused and felt the lightning strike of panic that came from indecision. The urge to unburden herself of the secret that had altered her life and left it permanently incomplete was so strong that it was a physical sensation.

"I didn't know anything about Stella, and neither did anyone else who I knew."

Jordan watched her eyes.

"Whatever Harvey did," she said, "it turned Stella back on, and that turned the Signal back on – and that's what started things with both of you."

While she was talking, Sienna began piecing things together. She finally understood the conversations she overheard when the scientists and technicians spoke quietly in the research cabin and thought no one could hear them. She remembered the way they would talk so fast and say things that startled her even though she didn't understand them. But Sienna Barrett had always been an infinitely curious creature, and her failure to find anything of substance in the Signal left her with an obsession to understand *it* and understand *why*. And so Sienna Barrett listened to everyone and everything, and she learned how to look bored and distant and aloof in order to hear even more. It was a strange facade to use in a place that prized performance, and it was a clever cloak to wear for a child with so few natural gifts.

The basic math she was doing in her head checked out. The dates, as hazy as they were in Uncle Harvey's recollection, lined up.

By now the sun was overhead and it was hot enough to make the lake below irresistible.

"Let's grab something to eat for lunch and go get in the lake," Sienna suggested. "Tonight, after dinner, you girls and I can spend some more time with Stella."

"I have to get another look at this thing," Jordan said, getting up and heading back toward the cave. The strangeness of everything about this had still not sunk in enough.

"I'm going with dad," Blaise said, running to catch up.

"I can show you where the trail down to the lake is," Cali said, standing up and stretching her legs.

Sienna had a very strong idea about what she and the girls would do tonight, but she needed a few hours to build up to it.

JULY 3

It was early afternoon in New Delhi, and General Gupta finally noticed that he was exhausted. Noticing this was something of a luxury that had eluded him up until this moment.

Every day prior to this, for the last week, at least, had been so tense that there was nothing to compare it to in recent memory. He had met regularly and around the clock with the Prime Minister and his cabinet, and parallel to this, he had put the Para commandos in place with all the supporting collateral they would need to exfiltrate themselves – and, in parallel with *that*, there was the paramount importance of preparing his military in the event Pakistan guessed correctly and lashed out with a reprisal of their own. This preparation was made particularly difficult due to the fact that he had to move his military into a state of readiness without it looking like they were being told to expect something. Sending 100,000 troops to the Pakistani border three days before an EMP went off on a military installation was the easiest possible way to admit guilt *and* be branded a war criminal at the same time. Getting the military situated onto its front foot and making it seem random to have cycled so many various units into a general state of readiness had been no simple task, and, if such things were measured, that alone would be an organizational achievement worthy of praise. But this, like everything else about the present situation, was done in the darkest of shadows. Remarkable measures had been taken to ensure nothing about this mission was typed, written down, or even spoken in whispers anywhere outside this room of this building.

This was a mission that truly did not and could not exist.

The luxury that allowed him to feel the grip of exhaustion that he'd been fighting for several days came from the finality of what he had just done. Six hours earlier he had given the Para commandos the go-ahead to commence their attack, and he had just received confirmation that the team had passed their checkpoint halfway between the Baloch village and the site where they would launch the drone. In terms of any bearing he had on the finality or effectiveness of this strike, his work was done and, without thinking about it, he had already transitioned to speaking and thinking of it in the past-tense.

He had just received word from the office of the Chief of Naval Staff that his order had been delivered to the sub waiting off the coast of Karachi and it was now standing by on high alert for the next phase of its mission. The sub would now move from a safe and relatively anonymous 11 miles off the coast to a mere 4.5 miles. The admiral sending the order also included the instruction for the sub to come up to a depth of about 150 feet so that they could quickly ascend a few extra feet to reach the Para team once they were in the water and swimming down toward them. This order had the double purpose of granting a request from the prime minister to gather a before-and-after reading of the area's electronic activity. This latter request was an example of the country's leadership attempting to salve their conscience by telling themselves that they didn't entirely send a nation back into the Stone Age – just its most important airbase. And a chunk of its biggest city.

This would also allow the sub to remain completely motionless before, during, and after the attack – and then just slip away silently under battery power once the Paras were onboard.

The order to get that close to shore while being that close to the surface was certain to raise the blood pressure of several officers on that sub, but it was a reasonable risk to take. He had received the feedback that this move violated the protocols of normal operation in these settings and that subs generally only got this shallow to do reconnaissance or launch a cruise missile – and, in both cases, it only stayed at that depth very briefly – but this was an extraordinary circumstance, so he had insisted. The sub had reported that its sweep of the area confirmed it was alone and had entered the region undetected – so now was the time to act.

This was a type of combat General Gupta was trained to facilitate, but he was still a product of an era where you could see what you shot at more often than not, and you usually got a good look at who you killed.

He had been lost in thought for several minutes when the throbbing in his right hand shook him from it. The arthritis in this hand had been getting bad, and this extended period without sleep or exercise made it much worse. On another classified mission, as a much younger man, his rifle had been shot out of his hands during a firefight, and the brute force of it had broken every bone in that hand between his knuckles and his wrist. This particular firefight continued unabated and, unfortunately, there was soon a considerable number of available weapons scattered amongst the dead for him to use in place of the one he had lost. Everything between his fingertips and elbow soon went numb and became grotesquely swollen, and he spent the following three days shooting with his left hand and leading four separate counterattacks to scatter the steadily advancing enemy. For his courage under fire and his successful efforts to organize his men in the face of an overwhelming enemy force, he had been awarded the Param Vir Chakra medal – essentially the Purple Heart and the Silver Star combined. This honor had been bestowed only 15 times prior to his own ceremony, and all but three of those distinctions had been posthumous. He considered himself lucky to have survived, particularly after having returned to this special operations division while the scars on his face and neck were still healing from the Indo-Pakistani War.

This job hadn't been a part of that young soldier's plans. He had simply raised his hand every time something desperately needed doing. What he knew then but truly understood now was the extent to which this instinct had so many compounding effects on the future. "The problem with the heroic impulse," he had once explained to his son, "was that most heroes die, and then the guys who stayed behind and hid make it back home and start running things."

Two years from now he would be retired and resisting requests to write a memoir. Fearsome engagements with Pakistan had now book-ended his career and punctuated his life with the same regularity that they had punctured him. He would remain here to supervise the fallout from this operation and then navigate the proposed and threatened reprisals, followed by the begrudgingly offered and accepted assistance to rebuild, and then the inevitable return to a tense status quo. After that was done, he would formally resign, accept the thanks of the Prime Minister and Parliament, and then seek out the comfortable retirement befitting a formerly powerful man.

With enough time and unconditional love from his dozen grandchildren his karma might one day pass Yama's inspection such that he could find a small place in Svarga (स्वर्ग).

* * * * *

Over the last two weeks Major Horn had slept in his own bed only four times. Perhaps three. His constant presence had moved from "critical" to "mandatory" early on, and he had been in this same operations center as the state of international affairs had moved from "critical" to "existential." As he walked between meetings with his senior staff, he thought about his first day here. During the four minutes of orientation, he noticed the showers down the hall, and that told him everything he needed to know about this job.

The news he had just received guaranteed that today would be the worst one yet in this current unraveling of world affairs. "Worst," he thought, is too pejorative a word for such important work. Certainly it would make today the "most dangerous."

The phone call in question had been followed by all the screens in the room snapping to a real-time satellite feed from eastern Russia. An operative monitoring the train reported that its crew had just received their long-awaited instructions. The crew was instructed to head toward the Nizhneleninskoye-Tongjiang Bridge and use a railway turntable about a mile from the river to turn around and then resume course to Ozersk, roughly 4,000 miles to the west. Horn acknowledged the information, set the phone back in its cradle, and immediately picked it back up to ask three follow up questions.

It was impossible to ignore that the mental fatigue was becoming acute.

The information he needed was specific, however: How long would it take this train to get moving again after having powered down and parked for such an extended period? Were any of the Chinese fighters currently patrolling nearby? How long until the next Chinese satellite passes overhead and notices the train's engines are running?

The answers were not heartening. He was told it would take approximately an hour to get the engines warm and the pre-trip checklist completed before departure. That seemed about right to Horn, and he added this to his list of several hundred things to keep an eye on. There were no Chinese fighters in the immediate area, so that was good. But a Yaogan reconnaissance satellite (遥感系列卫星) would crest the horizon in 8 minutes, and that was bad. Despite being nearly 20 years old, it had a thermal camera that, during its last pass 11 hours ago, was observed to be actively gathering data. The first thing the Yaogan would do as soon as it achieved line-of-sight contact with the train was take heat readings 10 to 12 times per second during the entire 22 minutes it spent overhead. This satellite, and all the people monitoring the readings back at the People's Liberation Army Strategic Support Force (战略支援部队), would immediately notice the engine car was warm for the first time since they began watching it, and they'd know that the temperature was increasing by the second. The last Chinese satellite had passed overhead nearly 2 hours ago, and it had seen nothing but a cold train and colder hills.

Horn looked at his watch and back at the plot of the satellite headed directly toward the city of Birobidzhan and its surrounding area. Within 10 minutes of getting that first measurement, an update would arrive in Beijing, and it would be in front of the Central Military Commission another 20 minutes after that. The verdict of that group would have been, in typical fashion, decided in advance: They would give the order to strike the train after what they believed was a suitable amount of time for an earnest discussion to have taken place. Assuming there were no delays with this information criss-crossing China, he had about 70 minutes until the Chinese high command gave the order to kill the train.

Too many of the scenarios on the table right now ended with one country responding to a threat or an attack – or the threat of an attack – with a nuclear weapon. And nobody thought rationally about nuclear weapons. The least rational of all those irrational thoughts was the idea of surviving them. TV and movies make people think they'd be one of the lucky few who survive, and the countless portrayals of post-apocalyptic life on Earth all avoid the fact that almost no one lives long enough to begin sorting through the practical concerns of surviving in the burned-out husk of the planet. In reality, almost everyone dies right away, and the unlucky ones die shortly after that. Anyone within 100 miles of an urban center – which is most people – won't be around for the "One Year Later Retrospective Candlelight Vigil" commemorating that fateful day. Anyone still alive at that point will be more concerned with finding medicine to treat their radiation sickness and avoiding the cannibal gangs who wander between settlements. But, Horn reasoned, it was probably unhelpful to tell people that all those concerns are misplaced since, after the flash, they will have nothing left to worry about.

He could feel the shard digging into the palm of his hand. He needed a way to extinguish this problem so completely that there was no chance a hot spot could flare up again later when he wouldn't be here to fix it. He walked over and set the fragment next to one of the two framed photos in his small office. It was Dorian's enlistment photo, taken four years before they first crossed paths. It was the same photo and the same frame that had been placed within the wreath next to his casket. He had sat silently staring at it while the pastor kindly shared words he couldn't hear and read things he'd never remember. He sat there next to Marta and listened to her one-week-old daughter breathe in small, rasping breaths left over from a sinus infection. Horn knew what a difference 70 minutes could make. He knew how much blood could be spilled and how much blood could be lost simply because you couldn't move fast enough.

He called over his communications officer and asked for a connection to the pilots at Kiska. It was time to get those planes in the air.

* * * * *

Ninety-three minutes later, the commander of Chaoyangchuan Air Base received the order to strike the Russian train.

The train was already in motion and slowly building speed as it headed south toward the Amur River crossing, and the order called for it to be destroyed at the earliest possible intercept point.

The timing could not have been better – Captain Huáng Yǒngjùn was just minutes away from the bridge at the moment the order was relayed, and he was especially accurate in air-to-ground engagements. He received the message to intercept the train but did not reply. The order was sent again 15 seconds later, and this time he toggled his microphone.

"I cannot complete this mission. I am returning to base."

The base commander flew into a rage and screamed the orders into a microphone for a third time. This specific type of dereliction (失职罪, 擅离职守罪) was considered especially egregious, and both men knew it. The commander did not need to tell Huáng that his exceptional career was now over, but the more immediate need was still the train. The seething commander paced across his command center and gave the order to scramble the backup fighter waiting on the runway – just as a roar from outside filled the room.

Xuěméi had heard the entire exchange on the open channel in her earpiece. As soon as she heard Huáng's silence, she ordered all of the flight support personnel to get away from her aircraft and began taxiing toward the runway. At first, she had thought that, perhaps, Huáng was in trouble and needed her help, but she knew better. By the time she heard his voice refusing the order she had already asked the flight control tower to confirm there were no other aircraft in the vicinity which might hinder the type of takeoff she was planning. When the commander finally made his way into her earpiece, she was already headed down the runway. This preemption would almost certainly earn a reprimand; the commander couldn't tolerate two pilots not following protocol, after all.

Her acceleration and overly aggressive launch angle violated every operational principle of responsible piloting. She flashed past the sound barrier while still low enough to shatter the windows of every jeep and maintenance vehicle at the end of the runway, and, in an instant, the entire region disappeared beneath and behind her.

She was still accelerating when the voice of the Commissar suddenly appeared and began explaining that the entire 61st Fighter Brigade had been betrayed by the "individualist tendencies and imperialist sympathies" of Huáng and that the safety of her nation was now her responsibility.

She could already see Huáng's jet on her long-range scope. She knew that she would never have the chance to say goodbye or ask what happened. But she knew. And he would know that it was her who raced past at full throttle to go do the exact thing which he believed to be wrong.

"Goodbye, Yǒngjūn," she said in her heart, swallowing a lump in her throat as his Vigorous Dragon passed in the opposite direction, seven miles to the north.

The base commander was now in her earpiece, telling her things she already knew like her present speed and estimated arrival time on target. A moment later she heard him repeating this information – and that meant more listeners were being patched into this channel to observe the mission in real-time. She could hear the commander's voice echoing – which meant a large room, likely somewhere in Beijing, where people with household names and faces were watching this play out. She had nothing to add and would wait to be asked a direct question, although that seemed unlikely to happen.

The Chaoyangchuan base was just 315 miles away from the bridge, and at 1,512 miles per hour, the train would appear on the horizon in less than 15 minutes. Flying this fast wasn't great for fuel efficiency, but it wasted no time.

As she crossed the border into Russian airspace, Xuěméi scanned the instrument panel again and ran her thumb over the fire-controls on the control stick. She knew exactly what to do and she knew exactly how to do it. She stared hard into the radar that showed her every inch of the surrounding area and took some comfort that, despite having just crossed over into a foreign nation inside a war machine with violent intentions, China's air superiority here was a given. There wasn't another aircraft anywhere near these skies that could compete with the J-10, and she would be among the first to know if that American carrier started launching aircraft.

As if on cue, she got another update from her base commander that there was currently no activity on the deck of the carrier. The smaller vessel, however, had begun moving an hour ago and was now holding position at the very edge of territorial waters. It had checked in with a Russian coast guard vessel and explained it was retrieving malfunctioning scientific equipment that had drifted into the area.

She double-checked the rangefinder displayed on the cockpit glass in front of her; at this speed she would be within range to fire over the horizon in two minutes, but her instructions were to get eyes on the target before shooting and then visually confirm the kill. Visual range was still four minutes away. There was nothing to do now but allow that time to pass.

During the pre-flight checks, no one had noticed the small lump behind the zipper that ran vertically down the left side of her torso, just below her collarbone. She reached over and unzipped it just enough for two ears made from soft brown felt to poke out such that she could see them from her helmet.

Inside of her gloves each fingertip was black. This morning she had been startled awake by a sudden premonition that today was *the* day. There had been something in the briefing last night which made it seem certain, and there was something about the winding down of time that left her with no doubt. She checked her calendar book, wrote the letter, and then rubbed the ashes into her hands so that it might travel with her, so that she might wrap this grief around the controls of her aircraft. This had been the day Mínghuī had proudly shown his mother how he sorted the peas, beans, and carrots into separate piles on the tray of his highchair during lunch.

> *Little Bear, this is the last day I will wonder. It is the last time I will wonder where you are. The last time I will wonder if you are happy. The last time I will wonder if you remember me.*

> *Today I will fly away from here, and when I wake up again, I will be far away. I'm leaving what is left of you to find what you have become.*

> *I don't know how to find you, but there is nothing that can keep me from you. Wait just a little longer for me.*

When she was done writing she leaned close to the paper and let the smoke drift up. She breathed it in and could still smell it in her hair. It was a funeral pyre which carried away what she knew would be her last moments with her son.

But first, this flight.

She was still looking at those ears when suddenly she heard a microphone switch on in her earpiece. She glanced at the transmitter to her right, but this wasn't coming from Chaoyangchuan – this was from the air-to-air comm link that the J-10 pilots used to talk amongst themselves while flying together. But that link could only transmit at very short ranges.

* * * * *

About 3,900 miles away and 50,000 feet lower, Desmond O'Shea watched as the Indian sub rotated to point its nose at Karachi and slowly rose to within 165 feet of the surface. It had been parked a few hundred feet lower and about 7 miles further out until a couple of hours ago when it started moving.

This depth meant one of two things: Picking something up or dropping something off.

"Drop off," he thought to himself, was a very pleasant way of saying "cruise missile."

He called over to the sonar operator for the third time in the last 20 minutes.

"Is there anything at all in the water headed their direction?"

"No, sir, nothing at the moment."

The sonar operator would keep answering this question all day, but the captain would also have been the first person who he told if something suddenly changed.

Captain O'Shea stared at the data on the screen and strained to see something that made sense. There was no good reason for the Vagsheer to make this move right now. There was hardly any traffic in the area, and they were getting way too close to the coastline.

He cursed under his breath because the only conclusion was that they were about to start flying cruise missiles toward the city of Karachi in the middle of the night. It didn't make sense, it was a bad tactical move, this whole setup was poorly conceived – but now it was happening.

O'Shea figured they were within a minute of being correctly positioned to fire. He would need four times that long to get a message to and from his contact at the Pentagon, and that was after he took the particularly dangerous step of elevating toward the surface without being heard by his target.

The Vagsheer had put him in a position to have to make this call himself.

After keeping a safe distance of 2,000 meters, the Arizona had crept to 1,200 once the Indian sub started rotating to face the city. O'Shea wanted to be right on top of the Vagsheer so that any strike would be quick and clean, but this also made them susceptible – however infinitely unlikely – to a counter punch if they made any mistakes. They were too close to shake the Vagsheer's hull with a sonar ping and scare them into aborting whatever they had in mind because, at this distance, if they responded by just firing back without asking any questions, the Arizona would have an exceptionally difficult time avoiding it. O'Shea had already considered and dismissed the idea of shooting to disable their engines and propeller – a shot like that left open the small possibility of the Vagsheer shooting back as it sunk, and he could not accept that.

Shoot to kill was the doctrine here.

He had checked and re-checked the depth of the ocean floor at this exact point. It was just within the survivable range, and he'd begin rescue operations the moment it touched the ground. The torpedo was programmed to strike right beneath the tower and sever any connection between the bridge and the areas controlling its propulsion and weapons.

During their grid search he had flooded two torpedo tubes so that they were ready to shoot at a moment's notice. Flooding those tubes and putting a torpedo in them was one of the noisiest things you could do on a sub, and his gut had told him he might very well arrive in this current scenario where he'd want to keep the firing protocols silent until the last possible second when the outer tube doors opened – and that was a sound that the Vagsheer wouldn't miss.

Traditionally, submarine captains had chosen to not flood the torpedo tubes until it became obvious that the likelihood of needing to shoot was extremely high. The next step was to open the outer tube doors hand expose your weapon to the open ocean – and you only did that once the order had already been given to shoot. Anyone who had ever shot a pistol recognized the process: Flooding the tube was akin to flipping the safety to the "off" position; opening the outer doors was placing your finger over the trigger. The traditional reason for not flooding those tubes was, in part, due to the fact that torpedoes were complex pieces of electronic equipment that, according to the manufacturer, needed to be kept dry until the very last second. But, in an era when smartphones could be left to soak in a bathtub overnight with no ill effects, these new Mark 48 torpedoes were not affected by a few days spent in room temperature seawater.

O'Shea checked the range again and did the math. He called his Weapons Officer over and had him do the same – again. At a distance of 1,200 meters, that Mark 48 torpedo would arrive on target inside of 38 seconds. The Indian sub would have no chance to evade or survive. O'Shea had taken every step perfectly up to this moment and now everything was done except to pull the trigger.

That Mark 48 was as ruthless a piece of equipment as existed in the U.S. Navy. It was 20 feet long, it traveled 65 miles per hour, and it carried 650 pounds of high-explosive in its warhead. It even incorporated the unused fuel from its engine into the detonation. It had been developed to sink the largest surface ships as well as the elusive nuclear submarines, like the Typhoon-class Russian subs which were 600 feet long and stocked with nuclear warheads. But the Mark 48 didn't actually hit its targets – instead it used a specialized proximity fuse that detonated directly beneath a ship to snap its hull in half. This meant the ship was instantly in two pieces rather than having a hole punched in its side that slowly filled with seawater. The Navy called this a "quick sink" and it ensured that there was no time for an evacuation. Each of these torpedoes cost over $5 million, but that was a bargain considering it was cracking $2 billion worth of enemy ships in half.

The gunslinger in him knew exactly how the next few seconds would play out even before he reached for his revolver.

First, any sonar operator worth the title would hear the outer door of his missile tube open and immediately be alarmed – but because there hadn't been any sound of tube flooding, they would pause for just a moment and listen apprehensively. They would likely alert the officer on the bridge at the time that the tell-tale sound of an outer door had been detected, but with none of the accompanying audio signatures that should have preceded it. This pragmatically paced response would eat up every available second in the tiny window of time they had to react and survive – and O'Shea knew they'd waste it tinkering with their instruments and evaluating this strange new contact. By the time the officer asked to see the data for himself, the window would have closed, and they would already be dead. Once the Mark 48 hit the water, however, there would be no mistake what was happening, and that first flash of confusion would instantaneously turn to visceral terror. The Indian Navy was not among the short list of countries given access to the Mark 48, but the sound of its swashplate piston engine and its two contra-rotating propellers was unmistakable.

The screen in front of the sonar tech would immediately light up and diagnose the starting point, range, trajectory, and ever-increasing speed of the torpedo, as well as assessing its make and model. That last bit of news would be unnecessary, and, during the three seconds the sonar tech listened, the Mark 48 would have already leveled out, aligned itself with the Vagsheer, and reached its hellish top speed.

O'Shea knew that by the time the captain could get to a screen to see the incoming path and then shout orders for evasive maneuvers to the helmsman, that torpedo would have already covered at least 500 meters. The submarine would lurch suddenly into action, and the noise would make the Mark 48's job even easier. A boat like the Vagsheer wouldn't be able to respond quickly enough while sitting so shallow, and, as the torpedo crossed the halfway point its active sonar would start pinging and every sailor onboard would hear it getting louder. Terror would turn to panic. These Kalvari-class subs did not have huge crews, but even a small group of men who know they're about to die is an ugly thing. The captain would order another evasive maneuver, and as the sub pitched wildly, he would order a distress call that would not be completed in time.

The last thing anyone heard from the Vagsheer, if anyone even knew to listen, would be the shockwave of an instantly depressurized hull.

* * * * *

Just a few miles to the north, Captain Amit Joshi and his team were at the tail end of a brutally hot trip through the coastal desert that stretched for seemingly countless miles to the west and north of Karachi.

These sand dunes, scattered with rocks and only sporadic vegetation were crisscrossed with winding and often impassable ravines that made progress treacherously slow. Without their Baloch guides this trip would have been impossible, or at least it would have taken six or seven times longer.

This area was famously inhospitable despite its proximity to the ocean. "Coastal desertification" was the name for this phenomenon, and it arose from high temperatures leeching freshwater out of the soil just long enough for ocean breezes to carry it away and leave behind enough salinity to prevent anything from growing. The term "wasteland" can be used casually, Captain Joshi thought, but here the term didn't quite do the landscape justice.

To ensure their approach was cloaked in the highest possible secrecy, they had left in the late afternoon and traveled through the night. When daylight came, they erected a camouflaged shelter inside a ravine and waited. The shade did nothing to alleviate the extreme heat, and sleep was largely impossible. When darkness fell again, they set out to cover the remaining two hours of distance between their ravine and the location they had determined to be the ideal launch point for the drone. That point was yet another ravine within sight of Masroor Air Base, and this winding crevasse continued for several miles in the direction of the ocean, giving them an excellent way to exit the area undetected while they made their way to the bridge and their extraction.

Despite the darkness, it was still so hot that breathing was uncomfortable, and a thick layer of dust covered everyone's goggles, masks, and helmets. The moon was bright enough to make the night vision goggles unnecessary, but the Paras were still scanning the horizon with their infrared lenses.

According to Joshi's GPS coordinates they were on schedule, albeit just barely. He had not believed they would need so much time to travel this far by ATV, but the Baloch people knew this terrain and this specific route intimately, and they had estimated things precisely, so far.

All communications for this mission had been cut before they left the village; the next time he'd talk to Chatterjeee would be after he was aboard the sub that was already out there waiting. Even Indian satellites were cleared from the area for fear they might be accused of watching the mission unfold.

Everyone back in New Delhi would learn of the mission's success or failure on the news. The first words from the television anchor would either be "Early this morning, an unprecedented attack in Karachi..." or "Overnight the Pakistani military captured several suspected terrorists..."

Joshi did not know how either of those stories might end, but he knew how to finish this.

41 Talking

JULY 3

Sienna spent the day with the girls in the small lake below their uncle's cave. It was everything they could have wanted from a vacation.

The water was clear enough to see all the way to the bottom, and it was a mirror for every cloud and bird overhead. The water was freezing, but today was so unusually hot that the girls welcomed the chance to escape the heat.

Throughout the day they had hiked around the perimeter of the lake, finding places to play amongst the trees and the tiny, rocky beaches scattered around it. Josephine was both the youngest and the most fearless when it came to getting too far up a tree or leaping off rocks – and this wilderness playground presented an unusually high number of opportunities to make her mother nervous and her sisters swear they would never try such a thing. At lunch they found a small waterfall on the far side of the lake, and spent the rest of the day climbing up, down, and underneath it. Teddy followed them to the top of the waterfall each time they jumped and then ran down to the water's edge as they swam back to shore.

Around the time Sienna suggested going back to eat dinner, Josie and Scarlett found a particularly old log in the brush and rolled it into the water. It floated just enough to be useful, and they proceeded to paddle it across the lake with their arms and legs until finally meeting their mom and Cali on the other side. At several points along the way both girls stood up to show that they could "surf" on it, and then promptly lost their balance and fell back into the water. Jordan saw this performance from high above, and, as per usual, he was more impressed than concerned.

Around the time Blaise returned with his uncle carrying another several dozen pounds of elk, Sienna and the girls trudged back up the trail to the tunnel entrance – wet and tired and happy after a day spent exploring.

Harvey and Blaise built a fire near the entrance and the seven of them relaxed while sections of yesterday's deer and today's elk deer roasted over the flame.

Uncle Harvey was, it turned out, an excellent addition to the dinnertime banter, even if most of his stories were about government treachery, hunting, and whether or not income tax was constitutional. But the stories the kids really liked hearing were the ones about the times bears had chased him, or the avalanches he had narrowly avoided, and the mountain lions who had attempted to take up residence in his tunnel. What went unnoticed in these stories was the fable-like subtext that contained a lesson about the trades he had made in order to make this life possible.

After dinner the family took a field trip to the shelter Blaise had built nearby and intended to sleep in for the duration of the visit. He took great pride showing them how he had chipped the logs to fit together with his hatchet and lashed them together at key areas for structural support. Inside was a raised bed, the walls were filled with moss to protect from the wind, and a tarp was sandwiched between the boughs on the roof in the event of rain. Tomorrow he'd go get clay from the southern end of the lake to make a fireplace. It really was impressive work for someone whose previous bushcraft experience was almost entirely YouTube playlists and a couple dozen campouts. He would see a remarkable number of remarkable things from this otherwise humble structure.

By the time Blaise's open house was over the sun was starting to set; darkness came fast once the sun slipped behind the mountain range out on the peninsula. Everyone was exhausted, and, as they made their way past the fork in the tunnel, Josie called out, "Goodnight, Stella!" and then made a series of beeping noises – to which she then replied, "Oh, thank you Stella, you too. See you in the morning!"

While Jordan helped Josie get ready for bed, Sienna quietly pulled Scarlett and Cali aside and led them back down the tunnel to visit their ancient roommate.

It had taken her all day to process her immediate reaction to seeing it, and it had taken that entire time, minus a few welcome distractions, to finally put the words together in her mind to form a complete sentence about what this was.

"This is what the Signal was looking for," she finally said to herself. Everything she had ever seen or heard was talking to, looking for, or hoping for *this*.

Something about the scattered pieces she had seen and heard in the Signal, something about the pull she felt to it, some odd kind of kinship or misplaced attachment – it made her certain about what to do next.

She led the girls to the side of Stella, and she told each of them to place their palm on the long smooth panel arcing out from within the wall. She did the same and put her other hand on Scarlett's shoulder. Calista stood close to her mom, and Sienna rested her head against the top of hers.

The Signal's hum immediately wrapped around them, as if they were completing some type of electrical circuit. An object appeared in Sienna's mind, as if emerging from a fog. The image was far clearer and closer than anything she had ever seen from the Signal before.

"Girls..." she started to say.

"I see it," Calista said.

"It's already talking," Scarlett added.

Sienna stood perfectly still and silent. A wave of recognition washed over her.

As she felt it, she knew that her daughters felt it, too.

As the Signal passed through their minds, the emotions and the impacts of the mind best trained to work within it spilled over and moved across all of them. The girls caught bits and pieces as Sienna thought back on the many long months she spent peering into it, and the many long years she had spent thinking about it after.

As her mind searched back 30 years, the feel of the smooth arc beneath her hands reminded her of the 100-million-year-old stone around it.

"How old has all of this got to be?" she wondered.

The girls heard this question, and, as it was asked, they felt Sienna's sudden recognition of a voice she had heard so many times, in such tiny fragments.

> Compared to you, we are very old.

Sienna remembered the sudden bolt of realization from that summer day in the research cabin, and now the girls felt it, too.

> You have looked and listened
> to the stars for such a short
> time, it would be nearly
> impossible to find something
> younger than you.

Sienna felt the relief come through. It was the feeling of having found something lost.

The feeling of looking and listening through the Signal with such clarity was familiar and strange in equal measure. She could feel her girls struggle to find their bearings within the power of it.

> This energy is no different than
> what organizes in your mind as
> time and memory and
> intelligence.

> You are a pebble that only
> notices it is wet.

> You do not yet consider the
> depth of the river flowing over
> you. And where it has come
> from. And why.

No one had moved. Later, none of them would even remember breathing. And now they began to understand, because Sienna had begun to understand, what this was.

> There is a time and a way to
> reach the surface and navigate.

> Incompleteness is the
> misunderstanding of a

beginning and a
misinterpretation of an end.

It was this, not Stella, that she had been hearing in the distance for so long.

Her passion, left incomplete as a child, now drifted back to her in finished form. She felt herself begin to tremble as the emotions flooded. It was the relief of conclusion, of finishing what had started, of finality of purpose. This finality, she knew, was her contribution to this Universe. This was the connection point between two distant forms of life. It was not the simpleness of two biomechanical structures connecting at long distance, but the confluence of intelligence. Her life was the small wrinkle that connected two folds of the Universe; an imperceptibly small part of this dimension, and an invisible part of the next.

She had not architected some great innovation; she was simply the current step in a great process that preceded her by eons and would extend past by even more. She was the innominate, final electron added to a vast molecule which created a new lifeform. She was the last piece of the machine which created the future.

Her daughters felt this, and, in time, Sienna would tell them why. For now, they kept thinking the same word. What struck each of them, however, was how familiar this felt despite there being no conceivable similarities anywhere.

We are both small pieces of the
same very large thing.

You do not yet have the right
word to describe it.

And neither do we.

We are no more alien to you
than a stream is alien to a river.
Both flow towards each other,
then converge, and make their
way toward the ocean.

In her mind, Sienna now understood the stretches of time that had elapsed, the time spent looking for what was stranded in this mountain, and the scale of this time.

You cannot yet imagine that
things exist where you cannot
look. Your planet changes often
enough to hide your past.

You are comparably brilliant, but,
amongst all possible conclusions,
you have found so few.

There are civilizations that have
lived a thousand millennia
within one of your rotations.
Others see brief moments
during the lifetime of your sun.

Your fear comes from being
small in an infinitely large
place. You dread that
intelligence is common while
you misunderstand why
consciousness is rare.

This was the ending to a conversation she had never been able to start. Her heart lifted for the first time since she was a child. Her daughters felt this sense of continuation. Calista reached up to her cheek where she felt the cold glass of the passenger-side window in her grandmother's station wagon.

On two unique sides of the Signal, each recognized the other.

You no longer cry now, Rabbit.

Sienna remembered her last day in the research cabin. She recalled the first day she heard the scratch and hiss in her ear. She remembered leaving that small campsite in San Mateo. She remembered sliding out of the MRI and the meeting that followed with Torchy. She remembered everything left unfinished, and why. She remembered the fear of beginning something that could not conclude. The fear of ever discovering the distance between what you might have been and what you are.

The memory flashed before Sienna's eyes, and all the additional questions from Cali and Scarlett suddenly vanished as they watched and understood. To Scarlett it was happening too fast, and the memory itself was coming back in pieces that were too abstract for a ten-year-old. She was reeling from the sensation of charging through three decades of emotions in seconds. But Cali *saw*. Her eyes squeezed even tighter, and a wave of understanding washed over her. It was something different than relief, but not quite joy either. In that moment she understood her mother in a way no one else would. That connection would be the great joy of her life – to be the only person who ever had the pleasure of knowing Sienna Barrett.

JULY 3

Cyrus had been lying awake in his cot when he heard the satellite phone ring, and he knew immediately in his gut that this was it.

The message from the Pentagon wasn't even 10 minutes old before he was taxiing away from the makeshift tent where his Raptor had been waiting patiently for action these last five days. Once his back tires reached the pitted concrete of the 80-year-old runway he put the throttle down and essentially leapt off the concrete and out of sight.

When Cyrus took the call, he had acknowledged the order but interrupted the major from the Pentagon with a request to get filled in on any additional details once he was airborne. Now that information came like a firehose, and he listened carefully as he cruised a few dozen feet above the waves.

Just getting into this cockpit had come with its own bit of potentially internecine conflict, however.

After setting down the phone, he had run to get his flight suit and was soon joined by the other five pilots who began doing the same. Now he had the hard conversation with them that he'd been planning in his head since they'd first been told the basics of this mission.

"Stand down, gentleman; I'm flying this mission solo."

They all turned and looked at him, some confused and others incredulous. He knew these men better than his own siblings. Greg Dunfee, Rex Quandroh, Will LaChappelle, Nate Graffin, and Eric Gurewitz. This would be a battle of wills that could last forever, so he was going to end it quickly.

"This objective does not require six birds in the air, even if a couple of them are just covering the retreat. A single aircraft is the only thing that gets in there undetected. That's it."

The other five pilots went back to suiting up.

"This is an order, all of you will stand down."

"You can't give that order," Dunfee responded, zipping up his pressure vest.

"I'm the senior officer, Greg, all of you will stand down, now."

"You might be the senior officer, but we were all told what to do by the same guy at the Pentagon," Graffin said.

Cyrus took a step closer and lowered his voice so the mechanics and technicians scrambling nearby couldn't hear him.

"If all six of us are up in the air, we're all going to die. If there are even two of us up there, the odds some lucky radar tech sees something is too much – and then we're both in evasive maneuvers instead of catching that J-10. And what then? One of us goes and catches a rocket so the other one can stay on target? *Hell no.*" His intensity was, for a moment, overwhelming. "You can say I assaulted you, or slashed the hose to your mask, or whatever you need to say – but I can't live with a mass suicide mission."

The five pilots shared looks. They hated this.

"If I do this right, I get in, I scare off the Dragon, and then I follow the gaps in their air defense all the way back to the coast. The windows are all going to be so tight that there's no way all six of us fit through them."

He was right. The available counter arguments were all focused on how strength in numbers guaranteed a successful outcome – but what "success" meant for this mission was hard to pin down, especially when it meant accepting that someone was almost guaranteed to get shot.

They stopped what they were doing and stared back at him. They knew he was volunteering to die by himself to prevent them all from dying as a group.

"Radio silence about this until after I'm long gone – like, until I'm at the refuel, at least. I don't want someone important ordering the rest of you to scramble once I've left. As far as anyone knows we've all gone in with our transponders off. If the Pentagon calls back, just..." he picked up the satellite phone and shattered it on the ground. "...Just tell them I dropped the phone."

Two minutes later he was done suiting up, LaChappelle handed him his helmet, and he settled into the cockpit.

It occurred to him that he had better die on this mission because he was almost certainly going to get court-martialed. At the very least he'd get knocked down a rank. He could live with that.

But he might not have to.

"I've always been an optimist," he said into his mask.

He kept his altitude low the entire way, and after the refuel, he dropped back down to skirt the topography as he made landfall. When only one plane showed up for gas the Pentagon figured out what he had done, but, to his credit, this major didn't even mention it. At this point in an operation, you roll with the punches.

Right now, the middle screen in the cockpit showed him every enemy radar installation and where they overlapped, as well as the ideal path around them. Next to that was another screen that showed him the satellite and radar information tracking the J-10. It was moving at its absolute top speed – plus a little, Cyrus noticed – toward the train. An intercept course was locked in, and all that was left to do now was determine the final course of action. Cyrus kept his subjective observations off the radio, but it was clear to him that he wasn't closing in on a recon mission – that Dragon was on its way to shoot something.

The briefing he'd gotten in his ear after takeoff was from the same, intense guy at the Pentagon, and he confirmed that this Chinese fighter was a non-scheduled departure, that its trajectory had not altered since it took off, and that its course was pointing directly at the train. Its current trajectory was, in fact, a classic attack vector that followed all the standard operating procedures of the People's Liberation Army Air Force.

Cyrus had said simply, "Copy" to every datapoint up until this last one.

"It's a bad day to be in charge of Russian air defense, right? I mean, getting infiltrated by two countries on the same day? Damn."

A long pause had followed and then a simple, "Indeed," from the Pentagon.

It sounded as if no one had considered the diplomatic fallout which would arise from Russia being exposed as incapable of protecting its airspace. Combining the anger at being attacked with the humiliation of how it happened was a dangerous amalgamation of international emotions.

Cyrus was pushing the Raptor at the extreme limits of its speed and taking full advantage of the fact that the radar cross section of the Raptor was so tiny and so impossibly difficult to detect that he'd already passed seven air defense checkpoints and was 170 miles inland. As he counted the last few anti-aircraft installations in front of him, he got an alert that some portion of his fuselage had been read by enemy radar.

"These fuel tanks..." he thought to himself, cursing the extra weight and exposure.

The extra fuel carried by these 600-gallon tanks were what made it possible to get in and out in one shot, but they were not a standard part of the stealth design, and if he were going to be seen today, it would be these things that got him spotted.

One of the cockpit screens suddenly lit up as every radar tower in the region surged in energy and intensity trying to determine if what had just been seen was an aberration or something real and dangerous. Few things could make a pilot's heart race quite like seeing this, but, ironically, there were only two major radar installations between here and the Chinese border, and, as soon as he reached the unaware radar operators in Chinese airspace, he would be safe again.

Cyrus wove through the last of the Russian air defense and slipped unseen into China. The J-10 was still headed toward him and their projected flight paths were now perpendicular in a way favorable to the Raptor's surreptitious approach. He checked the J-10's speed again and picked a spot on his map that he'd use to engage. The plan, carefully choreographed at Kiska, was to sneak up behind and below the J-10 unnoticed. This was a tactic F-22 pilots had shared amongst themselves over the years, and its intention was to reduce the need to start shooting while maximizing the lethality if the shooting started.

When the J-10 was about 125 miles away, he reduced altitude, dropped speed, and watched, from 5,000 feet below, as the Dragon blew past like lightning. He then accelerated and climbed toward it from underneath.

He closed the gap smoothly and quickly and was now so close to the J-10 that the sound of its engine shook his cockpit. His microphone was already programmed with the classified frequency the Chinese pilots used to communicate between cockpits, and now he toggled that frequency on his own radio.

He had been told to try this approach only as a last resort, and he had a card in the chest pocket of his flight suit with a prepared statement from the State Department – spelled out phonetically to help with the Mandarin – that he was supposed to make. He did not give the official statement of friendship and diplomacy a second thought – he already knew what he was going to say instead, and he knew this was going to be another strike against him if he got home.

He cleared his throat, pulled the control stick hard to the right, and the F-22 instantaneously leapt up alongside the J-10. For the opposing pilot it would look as if the Raptor had suddenly materialized. No pilot was prepared for this. It should, technically, be impossible.

"I have no idea how I would react to this," he thought, the moment before he did it.

Xuěméi did indeed feel her heart stop for what should have been several beats. Her mind raced trying to comprehend the impossibility of it and she felt her head begin to swim from the shock and sudden dump of adrenaline.

Cyrus was impressed when he noticed the dark helmet looking back at him didn't flinch or react after whipping around to face him.

He turned his head toward the pilot and, in the Mandarin he'd been practicing in the tent on Kiska, said with almost perfect pronunciation the most direct thing one trained warrior could say to another:

"Turn around and go home. I do not have to kill you."

Xuěméi might have been taken by surprise, but she was not as helpless as this American presumed. And she knew the J-10 could do quite a few things their CIA still didn't know about.

She immediately did what the American least expected: She shot straight up toward the operational ceiling of the J-10, knowing the Raptor would give chase, lose contact in the scattered clouds, and this would give her the few thousand meters of separation necessary to dive back down and engage the train. By this point the Raptor would be right back on top of her, but she was happy to face the inevitable consequences once she put her two missiles in the air. This American pilot was blinded by his interest in surviving this mission, and that was why he would fail.

She never paused to consider why this Raptor was here, where it came from, or the nature of its objectives. Her focus had shrunk entirely to the rapidly shrinking space between her Dragon and the train. Her course hadn't changed for several seconds, and the Raptor was now beginning to drift directly behind her at an attack distance. She quickly opened a channel back to Chaoyangchuan. "There is a rogue American aircraf–" was all she had time to say before pulling into a vertical climb once the Raptor lined up directly behind her and prepared to fire.

Her body crushed back into the cockpit seat and her voice went with it. As the Dragon raced skyward she craned her neck back to see when Raptor's nose began to tilt up in response to her sudden ascent. The J-10 reached its 60,000-foot operational ceiling and passed through two layers of cloud cover along the way, and then kept climbing. As she slipped out of sight into the first cloud bank, she painted him with her targeting radar and thus highlighted the Raptor for every anti-aircraft battery in eastern China.

Cyrus heard that alert the moment her laser touched his aircraft. He knew this was always a possibility – but he pushed this terrible news into the back of his mind in order to finish the task in front of him. He silenced the alarm and watched as the J-10 reached the lower levels of the stratosphere and then executed an evasive corkscrew descent. It was a genuinely masterful piece of flying, and when it passed back through his current altitude, he'd knock it out of the sky.

His targeting computer had never lost track of the J-10, and he was still so close that he could finish this manually with the cannon and avoid the additional heat and radar noise of firing a missile. Just that tiny extra amount of operational stealth would boost his likelihood of escape a slim few percentage points.

The J-10 missiles that were already within range of the train; he was surprised it hadn't already fired. He reasoned that the pilot had been instructed to have eyes on this target's destruction and report back personally, rather than let the satellites sort it out. This pilot would be able to see the train within the next 40 seconds, so he decided to wait half that much before firing. As he watched his instruments, he casually dropped the external fuel tanks, and the Raptor immediately regained its full stealth. The tanks were still tumbling through the air when his threat detection system brought the news he had been dreading: Three anti-aircraft sites on the ground had coordinated quickly and effectively to determine that he was somewhere within their triangle, and they had fired in unison such that now his Raptor had incoming threats from three unique vectors, thus providing him with no remaining avenues for evasion. It was a brilliant tactical move, and standard airborne warfare doctrine did not have reliable counter-maneuvers for such a scenario.

Xuěméi was now within 100 miles of the train. Her radio was crackling with demands that she complete her last transmission, but she was currently resisting 10 G's as she wrestled the Dragon down through the cloud cover to line up on the train. The radio would have to wait a few more seconds.

Right at the 20-second mark, the J-10 accelerated again, and Cyrus gave up on using the cannon. In one smooth motion he selected both Sidewinders and let them fly. He had never lost missile lock on that huge, hot engine and it would take less than two seconds for them to cover this distance. As the missiles left the weapons bay, he was already banking hard to avoid the fireball that was about to replace the J-10, and he turned his attention to the screen mapping both the radar installations hunting him and the three active SAM's that had already engaged. The scope said the nearest one with the best angle was 12 seconds away from impact.

He checked his scope to see how far away he was from the coast and from the Peralta a couple hundred miles past that. If that boat was going to offer him any cover it would have already put birds in the air, and there were none on the way. That was the right move, he thought. This airspace didn't need any extra fireworks right now.

Out the window he could see the flame pushing the nearest missile his direction. His realistic diagnosis of the situation presented no chance of survival, but he was going to make them work for it.

The deafening alarm of the Missile Approach Warning System came as no surprise to Xuěméi, but she appreciated that it drowned out the sound of the commander back in Chaoyangchuan. She did not need to steel herself for what came next. This was her last action, and she found pride knowing it would be successful. She selected both KD-

88 missiles she was carrying and confirmed their radar was still locked on the train.

She braced for impact.

"I love you, Mínghuī," she gasped.

No one in the tower at Chaoyangchuan knew what that meant.

* * * * *

In the sand dunes outside Karachi, Captain Joshi watched as the last pieces of the drone were snapped together and Lieutenant Sharma did the last check of the battery and superconductor.

After a few moments he stood up and looked at Joshi.

"It's ready," he said dispassionately.

Sharma gave the electric motor two quick pumps from the throttle and the blades spun fiercely in response.

Joshi took one last look at the nearest warehouse on Masroor Air Base through his binoculars and gave the order.

"Send it, Sharm."

The drone leapt off the ground and streaked toward the airbase. It disappeared immediately in the darkness and the sound of its propellers was gone a moment later.

* * * * *

Captain O'Shea ordered the Weapons Officer to dial in the final data points instructing the torpedo on its path toward the sub and the precise point where – down to the millimeter – he wanted it to detonate in order to achieve his preferred combination of crippling and recoverability.

Being this precise wasn't always an option available to captains, but he was happy to take advantage of it.

The Indian sub wouldn't have the heads up of hearing a torpedo tube flood, but it wouldn't miss the sound of the tube door opening or the launch itself. The policy of the Indian Navy dictated that in this scenario a sub would stay powered down unless one of two things occurred: A craft was headed toward them and they needed to avoid it in order to remain undetected and on station, or if they detected evidence that they were being tracked or targeted. O'Shea had made sure the latter item never entered their mind. The fact that the Vagsheer had powered down to its most basic functions in order to be as quiet as possible meant that it would not have a chance to take an evasive maneuver of any real consequence when he fired. They would send out some baffling, but that was easy to defeat, and by the time the engine could send an adequate surge of energy to the propellers, things would be all but over.

The targeting was all set. Now was the time. O'Shea was not the type to wait with his finger hovering over the trigger.

"Fire."

Everyone on the Arizona felt a small, sharp vibration in their feet. Twelve-hundred yards away, a sonar officer's eyes went wide at the noise he had finally relaxed enough to stop dreading. The XO behind him saw the alert over his shoulder and called out an evasive maneuver he knew would not work.

JULY 3

The three women had not moved from where they stood at the end of the dark, damp tunnel.

Sienna's mind was now bordering on the transcendental – in the sense that she was thinking about how thinking about something like this would be inconceivable or unbelievable if you thought about it in any other way. And that, she reasoned, was why the Signal existed. To believe or conceive of this required a way to communicate that was not reliant on persuasion or logic.

It further occurred to her, or, more specifically, it occurred to Scarlett, that it wasn't a human explaining this to them. It wasn't a human way of explaining anything. It wasn't even English that was putting these ideas together. This was something incredibly different. But it accommodated them by being similar enough.

But, Calista noted, "similar" was, perhaps, too strong a word.

Sienna now had the same question as both daughters: What now? What happens after this? What does something this powerful do?

It does not require power to do
this.

You mistake power as the
ability to destroy.

Destruction is just the addition
of chaos. It pushes something
forward through time to replace
its natural undoing.

> But creation is very difficult.
> And consider what you created.

Calista thought to herself how fortunate they were to have found the benevolent type rather than the conquering type.

> Everything you fear from life
> outside your galaxy is what you
> fear from life inside your world.

> The things you fear from great
> power displays what you would
> do with it.

> But violence is far more rare
> than you will believe. The effort
> to seek something out is
> opposite the urge to destroy.

Cali felt something that she would later label as "a reason to rejoice" that they had found "the good ones." And she would often think that "found" wasn't precisely right.

This idea hadn't even occurred to Sienna beforehand, and she wondered if the human instinct to fear the unknown would be one more reason to make altruistic content seem unbelievable.

> Your physical form is unique,
> and its paramount rarity is the
> architecture of your mind.

> You evolved on a planet whose
> surface was filled with dangers.
> Your brain evolved while you
> did anything necessary to
> survive.

> The impulse to survive at all
> costs continued long after you
> survived at all costs.

This was a comment all three of them would later reflect on many times. It made them feel stunted at the same time it made them feel powerful enough to overcome their natures in pursuit of something better. It was that pursuit, they were learning, that preeminently mattered.

> Life is rare in the Universe, but
> it is far more rare for it to
> survive a place so hostile
>
> You assume this planet is ideal
> because you exist.
>
> Nearly every other life form has
> grown very differently. On
> planets where survival did not
> precede struggle and did not
> incentivize destruction.
>
> On different worlds there are
> different forms with different
> minds.
>
> They do not share your
> instincts. They could not
> understand your motivations.
>
> Your idea of power has no
> value in the vast emptiness of a
> Universe.
>
> Gaining power over things is
> infinitely small relative to
> completeness.

This was why, Sienna understood, the Dark Antennae program was never going to work.

They were trying to find another version of themselves to study and understand and, if possible, direct and control. No one in the program had ever understood how the Signal drew from the words and intentions of the sender in a way that could land in the mind of the receiver with both the intent and the closest possible words packaged together into a data stream that could be heard without your ears and seen without your eyes. A long series of linguists had explained, to both the staff and the kids, that additional meaning and information might be found if they could look past whatever words were heard to the meanings behind them. The first rule of translation, they would explain, is that no two languages have perfect synonyms, and that five or six words in one language are necessary to arrive at the deeper meaning of a single one in another. For a camper who was struggling, this was difficult advice; while she strained to find fragments of sentences, the astrolinguists encouraged them to draw deeper textual significance from the spaces between the letters, and they proposed that there might be treasures of meaning in the vast, empty expanses separating one phrase from another.

This concept had largely been lost on Sienna at the time, and she had continued to charge into the Signal looking for words and pictures, but never meaning. But now she could hear the way the words landed strangely as crude avatars of principles that her brain did not yet have the shape to understand. But Sienna and the girls now knew what it meant to have a brain with a rare shape and what just a few cells out of place could do.

> Your mind has evolved to think
> that safety is only possible with
> power. Every consciousness in
> the Universe has a weakness
> tangled in its strength.
>
> You mapped the stars and
> created a means to calculate the
> observable Universe before you
> had electricity.
>
> You are simply phenomenal.
>
> Your weakness is believing the
> end of violence is the success of
> power. And now you are
> powerful enough to abandon

your strengths in despair.

Your form is unique, your brain is unique, and thus your logical conclusions and most robustly studied beliefs are unique creations all your own.

But they are only yours.

The evolution and shape of your brain chains you to your most carefully constructed beliefs. You cannot know when it is incomplete.

This was the point, Scarlett reasoned, that the secrets of the Universe were about to get unlocked. Cali found this idea funny. Sienna found it scary. But each one felt there was one last thing that, thus far, had been left unsaid.

There is no single perfection to aspire to. There is no single pinnacle we can offer you. Those heights are only reachable through continuity.

Every particle has a common source. Everything shattered, everything scattered can be reformed.

The pinnacle is hidden in pieces.

The possibility of perfection is only reachable through completeness. The search is for every missing piece of that completeness.

This is the opposite of
conquering. It is the reciprocal
of conquering.

It is the idea of completeness
through the total offering of
our totality.

Sienna and the girls all felt peace wash over them. They had stared into something that looked back at them, and now there was a last concept communicated which defied the ability of the Signal to land in their minds with the vocabulary they had available.

Scarlett asked the question they were all thinking: "How soon can we meet you?"

We exist where space and time
are no longer dangerous but
lovingly crafted.

We will be easy to find when
you know what to do with that
meeting.

You have already sensed us;
you simply cannot yet see. Your
eyes and your instruments are
made from a material that can
only see itself. Like a mirror
that only catches its reflection
in other mirrors.

We did not anticipate you being
here, we did not foresee you
hearing us.

Right now others like you have
found their worst fears in the
things they fear most.

We will prevent the additional

chaos it has wrought.

The Signal suddenly faded away, the air pressure in the room seemed to change, and the hum that had wrapped around them was gone. After so many days, the sudden silence felt strange. Sienna opened her eyes and saw Cali and Scarlett looking back at her. Sienna had no idea how much time had passed, but it hadn't been long – she could hear Jordan still telling a story to Josie in the main room.

"How do you girls feel?"

"I'm fine," Scarlett said matter-of-factly.

"I'm fine, but is that what you did every day at your program?"

Sienna laughed, "No, never."

Both girls looked back at her incredulously.

"No, I'm serious, not once ever. The closest I ever got was…"

She trailed off, and started again, "The closest…"

"Was the one time, the rabbit time," Scarlett said, wrapping her arms around her mother's waist, trying to hold her tight enough to protect her from the memory.

"It was the time right before you left the camp," Cali said softly, "and then again when it tried to find you while you…" she stopped to think about it, "…drove."

Sienna pulled both of them close. "Yes, those two small times. But I could never do it right by myself."

JULY 3

In three different rooms inside military headquarters spread across India, China, and the United States, notes containing the same essential message were handed to commanders who refused to believe what they were reading.

The American and Chinese leaders even had high-definition footage to watch from the cockpits of their aircraft, and they demanded to see playback while they were patched in to question the pilot.

The first message had come from an American submarine commander who had fired on a target in the Arabian Sea, and then watched his torpedo suddenly disappear less than 100 feet from impact. When he called for the second torpedo to be fired, there was only a pile of finely grained powder in the secondary torpedo tube, and more of the same in the room where the rest of the weapons were stored.

The Chinese pilot had fired two missiles and almost immediately both of them also disappeared. A split second later, her cockpit window was momentarily shrouded after she flew through a cloud of particulate. The American pilot chasing her had also fired, lost contact with his weapons, and then passed through a separate cloud.

In India, the young soldier flying a drone suddenly lost the signal and the remote control went dead in his hands. His commander, watching it travel through night vision binoculars, saw it evaporate in what looked like a puff of smoke, and then ordered a hasty move to their extraction point.

These three military commanders were equal parts dubious and incredulous, but attached to each of those notes, in one form or another, was an additional datapoint that was noteworthy but not necessarily related:

The electromagnetic interference they had been tracking had suddenly disappeared.

JULY 3

Sienna and the girls made their way down the tunnel, moving slowly in the pitch dark toward the entrance.

As they made their way around the concealed entrance, they felt the hum through the air and saw a beautiful, massive object that dwarfed their mountain.

It hung in the air like a mist, so close it could almost be touched. It looked like a giant, crystal chandelier shrouded in a cone of light. Its glow washed the surrounding valley.

Your world, the things you can see, the things that are real to you, are strands to be woven together.

Your interpretation of the Universe and its laws is uniquely accented, in the same way your speech draws boundaries between regions.

You have not seen your own world the way we have seen it. You do not yet know what it is, what it had, who you are.

You will learn what your joy and sorrow mean. You will discover how to use what those things have built for you.

We are from the same.

Sienna knew her part in this was done.

She knew there would be countless other experiences like this, and none of them would be hers

She knew that there had been many before, and now her link in this chain, the piece she had been missing, was in place.

The hum drifted and the voice went with it.

Scarlett craned her neck and watched the light fade.

"We didn't even have to hold hands that time."

EPILOGUE

TOP SECRET

<pre>
The Pentagon
Global Operations Center
Washington, D.C.

August 28
</pre>

REPORT FOR THE SECRETARY OF DEFENSE

Re: Final analysis of the DODONA Incident

Pursuant to Executive Order 82712-b received from POTUS on July 5 to gather and evaluate all data related to the DODONA phenomenon, this report includes final forensic conclusions of the materials recovered on-site, investigative results and interpretation of witness accounts, and an examination of presently applicable strategic interests that are geopolitically relevant.

As noted in the report sent to SecDef on July 18, intercepted communications and clandestine assets within the Russian, Chinese, and Indian militaries indicate significantly elevated levels of confusion within the senior ranks, as well as extreme pressure from political leaders to provide adequate explanations for the chain of events on/around July 3. Presently, each of these nations has reacted to the fallout in predictable ways: Russia is investigating the failure of its listening systems such that it was unaware of these escalations in real time, China is scrutinizing how its proactive response was neutralized, and India is pursuing information regarding how its own series of countermeasures were interdicted on two fronts.

In the 6 weeks since the initial report from this office, reviews in each of these military organizations have led to considerable changes in both their personnel and data collection practices. This indicates that their independent analysis discovered considerable vulnerabilities and potentially evidence of our penetration into their communication networks. Their conclusions regarding operational vulnerability and various tactical weaknesses are in line with our own assessments of their situational readiness.

Information about these administrative and operational changes were covered in greater length in the report dated August 22. These changes have also been evaluated in parallel with two additional data points regarding the internal functions of countries falling within the operational areas of DODONA. First, on July 10 a senior Air Force pilot in China was given the results of his Court-Martial which adjudicated him as being disqualified from future combat service. The sentence called for him to be stripped of rank and reassigned to a factory which fabricates fuselage components near the remote city of Ürümqi in western China. Sources indicate this discipline was related to the pilot's refusal to participate in air-to-air engagements taking place on July 3 near the Chinese city of Hegang.

This violation of a direct order from a general officer supports previous data indicating uncertainty amongst both the senior leadership in Beijing and local forces regarding the justifications for direct action against an ostensibly civilian target within Russian territory.

The secondary item relates to reports of four Indian nationals captured by the Pakistani military after a brief firefight near the Masroor Air Base outside Karachi. Information about this incident has not yet reached the news media in either country, and India is presently pursuing diplomatic channels aggressively to return these unidentified individuals, one of whom sustained serious injuries during the exchange of fire but is expected to survive. The Indian ambassador nor the cabinet of the Prime Minister have offered any reason for their presence, and Pakistani sources have not yet stated how their presence was ascertained. Our sources within both governments indicate that these four individuals are highly trained members of the Indian military sent to eliminate a target at Masroor. The parameters of their mission were developed based on the Indian government's interpretation of the data precipitating DODONA.

The recommendation at this time with regard to India-Pakistan has not changed: No U.S. action of any kind is necessary, pending any unforeseen developments or connections to domestic interests.

The recommendation at this time with regard to China has evolved in recent days pursuant to their continued questions about the presence of American warplanes in their airspace on July 3.

This office recommends initializing Operation Twin Sister as documented in the August 20 briefing, vis-a-vis: Drop from low-Earth orbit a poorly rendered copy of the F-22 (sans advanced avionics or radar-defeating coatings, but with some components rendered in proprietary alloys used in the J-10 and J-20) into a remote canyon on the Chinese-Siberian border, at which time reconnaissance photos of the crash site will be placed in a database that Chinese cyberwarfare teams are known to have penetrated. This will confirm suspicions already rampant within Chinese political circles that a small collection of PLA Air Force generals have been quietly and independently developing aircraft in preparation for a potential coup. Until this operation has been executed, U.S. ambassadors should continue dialog with the Chinese government through diplomatic channels in order to emphasize that there has been no U.S. aircraft in Russian or Chinese airspace.

Once the decoy plane is found and our sources connect key military leaders to it, the resulting reorganization of Chinese military leadership will serve the multi-pronged purpose of further weakening its strategic posture, significantly reducing its number of senior leaders, and also clearing the U.S. of any supposed involvement in the alleged airborne conflict of July 3.

On September 5 this office will present a report to SecDef regarding the blackout of all EMF frequencies for the 90 minutes following DODONA. Comprehensive analysis is still ongoing to determine the means and motive of such an action, methods of execution, potential defenses, and the specific ways in which the spectrum has and has not returned to normal in the interim.

Based on feedback from SecDef following our previous report dated July 27, extensive work has been done to verify the accuracy of statements gathered from the sole witness of the only known case of DODONA in U.S. territory, as well as additional analysis of its connection to the aforementioned situations in China, Pakistan, and Russia.

This observation in U.S. territory occurred on the night of July 3 at approximately 47°37'50.8"N 121°25'13.5"W, which falls within a remote section of the Mt. Baker-Snoqualmie National Forest in Washington state.

Initially there were no known witnesses to this event – and the existence of it, its location, and its connection to DODONA were unknown. Subsequent to DODONA, however, an ongoing surveillance operation in the Seattle suburb of Sammamish, WA resulted in contact with a family of six individuals who the G.O.C. Director had prioritized for contact and data gathering based upon reliable HUMINT that they were potentially connected to the larger phenomenon outlined in our previous report dated July 11. Contact with this witness was made on July 7 as she and 5 family members approached their home after an extended and unexplained absence.

This individual, Sienna Riley (née Barrett), had been part of the Dark Antennae Program described at length by Dr. Julius Torquemann in the POTUS briefing on July 14, and previously summarized in our initial report on July 5. Riley voluntarily participated in 11 hours of comprehensive debriefing on July 8 and July 9 in exchange for a written guarantee her children and husband would not be questioned. Reports from this initial encounter describe Riley's husband as an "exceptionally problematic" figure for our agents upon their arrival, and in short order it was decided that the debrief would be conducted in their home rather than the FBI Field Office in Seattle.

In this debrief, Riley corroborated Torquemann's account of the program and her participation in it. Riley was also questioned at length regarding her whereabouts before/during the period of time her house was surveilled from July 1-7. Riley explained that the family undertook a last-minute camping trip and was able to identify on a map the route they traveled over the course of several days. Biometric readings of Riley during this conversation recorded high levels of deception in her answers despite her thorough recall of the relevant topography and her overview of the travel - all of which was later corroborated by a detachment of Operators from JBL's 75th Ranger Regiment who were sent to track her course through the mountains (more on this below).

Among the many unsatisfactory responses offered by Riley, two stand out in particular and have not, as of yet, been adequately resolved: First, her family had no previous experience with extreme outdoor conditions and thus there is no reasonable explanation for such a sudden endeavor. While her purported deception remains a topic of study, the Ranger team who retraced her indicated route found campsites, food remains, waste, and evidence of recent fires at each of the approximate areas she indicated on the map provided by our agents. There is currently no doubt she was present at these locations on the dates indicated.

Second, the connection between her participation in the Dark Antennae program as a

child and her current status as a witness to a
DODONA-connected event remain unexplained but
extend far beyond any statistical probability of
coincidence. More rigorous investigation will be
required to determine this connection, but no
such work is currently underway due to her
present status as a nonparticipant in the
DODONA-related events of July 3. Additional
research into this connection may be warranted
once geopolitical concerns have abated or if
factors related to DODONA reemerge.

Riley further explained that she and her
family were camping at the approximate
coordinates noted above (based on her own
estimation of their campsite's location when
shown a satellite image of the area) late on the
night of July 3 when she was the sole witness to
an event that is, based on current evidence,
conclusively linked to the DODONA phenomenon.
According to Riley, she witnessed what she
believed to be volcanic activity from a small,
nearby peak. Specifically, she reports seeing a
bright pillar of light suddenly emerge from the
mountainside perpendicular to the mountain
itself. After an extended period of brightness,
the light appeared to move away from her
location and continue upwards through the
atmosphere and out of sight.

Upon receiving this information, the G.O.C.
immediately dispatched a forensic team and
tactical unit to the area and arrived via
helicopter within 18 hours of the information
being shared. Several hundred pieces of evidence
were retrieved from the area, and a small
shelter built by Riley's family near the site
was also found at the approximate location she
described. At the site, investigators discovered
a long cylindrical cavity in the mountain where
Riley described seeing the projected light. The

TOP SECRET - PAGE 7 OF 10 - TOP SECRET

cavity was approximately 85 feet deep and 23 feet in diameter. The size and ultra-precise uniformity of the cavity was noted as being highly unusual by the forensic team, but additional laboratory analysis presented the most noteworthy finding from this location: The granite within the cavity was uniformly coated in an ultra-fine microscopic residue which was found to be an exact match for particulate matter recovered from the air intake ducts of the F-22 present at the engagement in Chinese airspace, as well as a sample collected from the torpedo room of the USS Arizona after the unexplained loss of their tactical weaponry. All three incidents appear to have occurred within the same very narrow timeframe, potentially simultaneously. Sources inside the Pakistani military have also reported an unknown substance found inside a satchel carried by one of the Indian nationals captured near Karachi, and reports of their initial study of the substance indicate it will match the three samples currently in our possession.

Samples of this material have been studied exhaustively to determine a place of origin, manufacturing technique, and purpose of use. Multiple tests have demonstrated conclusively the initial finding related to this material: Namely, that it is not composed of substances which are presently understood or recognized on our periodic table. This substance does not have identifiable magnetic or isotopic signatures, nor does it react normally to gravity, magnetism, or radioactivity. The studied opinion of this office and its science division is that the substance has an extra-planetary origin and is manufactured with a technology that is currently unavailable. Additional research is underway to determine how this material played a role in DODANA and how it was distributed to 4

TOP SECRET - PAGE 8 OF 10 - TOP SECRET

disparate locations. Our report from August 2 details the ways in which DARPA is currently pursuing this line of inquiry.

When Riley was questioned on July 9 about the residue or the source of it, she had no additional information and referred to her earlier statement from July 8 about a sudden beam of light which she believed was part of a volcanic event.

This answer also registered "incredibly high" levels of deception, although our investigators cannot at this time determine the purpose or motivation for misdirection or duplicity. Considerable scrutiny was applied by the investigators to these areas tagged as deceptive, but no additional details were ascertainable from Riley. Other areas of her debrief that registered as "high" or "incredibly high" for deception included her observation of Russian communication practices while a part of the Dark Antennae program, her understanding of the purposes of the program, her state of mind during the time her family spent in Mt. Baker-Snoqualmie National Forest, and the reason they remained at the location for approximately 24 hours after witnessing what she believed was a volcanic event.

Of additional note: The cylindrical cavity left in the mountainside near her campsite represents approximately 35,000 cubic feet of granite, which totals approximately 6 million pounds of stone, yet none of that material is present in the surrounding area. There are no known geologic processes that adequately explain how such a precise cavity could be formed without creating readily identifiable detritus in the immediate area. Although a volcanic event has been ruled out as the cause, this is further evidence of an advanced technology source which is presently not understood. After a lengthy study, the cavity was collapsed with explosives

TOP SECRET - PAGE 9 OF 10 - TOP SECRET

to eliminate public discovery and speculation as to its origins.

Also of note is that around the site of this cavity there was evidence of long-term human habitation. The Rangers who first arrived at the site found no one else present, but, upon further reconnaissance, discovered a trail leading away from the area into the surrounding wilderness. Attempts to follow it were discontinued after several miles. The size of the footprints and the length of the stride indicate an adult male of above-average height, and the gait pattern and pronation of the left foot indicate a person of advanced age. Riley claimed to have no knowledge of anyone matching that description.

Further analysis of materials and tactics will continue for the foreseeable future based on the response by POTUS and the Joint Chiefs to our two previous reports and the accompanying implications for international relations, geopolitical stability, and national defense. However, at this present time, there are no other immediate direct actions recommended outside those outlined above. POTUS does retain the option to pursue any of the five courses of action outlined in the report dated July 21, and this can be achieved by invoking PEAD #7 and #9. In lieu of any PEAD orders, this office recommends authorizing funding and resourcing for periodic diagnostic checks of all systems affected before/during the DODONA phenomenon, and the foundation of a scientific sub-division dedicated to studying the exotic materials currently in our possession.

--END--

TOP SECRET - PAGE 10 OF 10 - TOP SECRET

ACKNOWLEDGEMENTS

The idea of writing a book had never seriously occurred to me before this plot came rushing at me late one night after getting home from a concert. I am so grateful that it did, and I am so glad I started dictating notes into my phone right away; so many of the most important parts of this book came tumbling out that night. Pushing every other hobby and interest to the side in order to focus entirely on writing and rewriting this book has been one of the great joys of my life, it has been endlessly entertaining, and simply completing this project is the most satisfying possible outcome. I hope the half dozen people who read this book find it as interesting as I do.

Throughout the process of writing, my family was exceptionally patient (and also not) whenever I talked about what these characters had done that day as if they were real people, and they were quick to notice when I borrowed one of their characteristics to make a character more lovable, or, at least, believable.

After I finished my first rewrite, I trepidatiously showed a very small circle of friends what I had put together in hopes they might have some feedback. That early draft bears very little resemblance to this finished product, and they have my greatest gratitude for investing the time and energy to read something so significantly incomplete and unpolished. Greg Shriber was the first to finish it, and, over the course of several lunches he offered ideas and asked open-ended questions that dramatically improved what you are now holding in your hands. One lunch in particular found me madly writing notes on a burrito wrapper and several napkins as our conversation sparked new ideas – all of which translated into over 100 pages of new material once I started exploring and expanding upon what we had discussed. Greg also helped me design the front and back cover, and he dramatically improved the ideas I was trying to pull together. Joanna Bell was the first person besides me to ever lay eyes on the text, and she was kind enough to talk on the phone for several hours about what resonated and where gaps in the story might exist. Throughout the second rewrite I kept thinking about the advice she shared, and I think I finally got around to making all the changes she recommended. Carl Gustafson was another reader who kept e-mailing me questions that hit me in such a way that I just kept writing and going deeper to find where those things might lead. Some of my favorite sections of the book came from those exchanges, including a handful of passages I can't imagine publishing this book without.

Between the last and second-to-last rewrites of this book, I paused long enough to read Steven King's "On Writing," which is essentially a manual for how to be a great novelist if you happen to already be wired like a brilliant author. Despite lacking a lot of the fundamental tools, I was fascinated by the book, and, despite being a very slow reader, made my way through it in just a few days. One concept that stuck with me from King was the idea that every novel is really just an attempt by the author to write a letter to someone about a topic that is important to them. I already understood this on some intuitive level, but seeing it there in print, and discovering that other people already knew this, was startling. That principle is certainly true of this book, but it wasn't until after I had finished writing, and the copy editing and layout had begun, that I finally understood that the intended recipient of this letter was me. It was only at that late stage that I could finally appreciate how much of this book was a coded and metaphorical meditation on a half dozen issues I have been sorting through for years. And, yes, that's kind of weird.

I would also like to thank Daniel Dumille, Tariq Trotter, Malik Smart, Daymon M. Smith, Bradley Nowell, Sean Daley, Anthony Davis, Gregg Gillis, Brian Jacques, Greg Graffin, Brett Gurewitz, Christian Jacobs, Chad Larson, USA Triathlon, Kenny Blankenship, Vic Romano, Jay Buhner, Edgar Martinez, KGRG, Adam Yauch, Adam Horovitz, Michael Diamond, Nate Merrill, Bill Wurtz, Alan Capron, Patrick McManus, Mitch Hedburg, Suzy Izzard, Tom Dolan, Ted Theodore Logan, Bill S. Preston, Esq., Mountain Dew Kickstart Pineapple Orange Mango, Monster Energy Rehab Watermelon, Dan Carlin, Roy Casagranda, Neal Maxwell, Jeff Campbell, Tanner Kay, Nate DiMeo, Roman Mars, Anthony Ray, Alex Sivers, David

Letterman, Richard Arthur Assman, Bryan Atchison, Neil Olstad, Robert Van Winkle, my copy editor Theresa Moffit, Wayne Hancock, Roger Alan Wade, Andrew Rousso, Frog Socrates, Jordan Peterson, Bill Waterson, Dave Barry, Peter Zeihan, Richard & Claudia Bushman, Sandy & Eric Wengreen, Matt & Mike Chapman, Dave Niehaus, Rick Rizzs, Michael Walsh, Lawrence Cohen, Clark Devereaux, Richard Wang, Brandon Walsh, Andrea Carmichael, Stephanie Steinbrenner, Lotney Fratelli, Rosalita, Chester Copperpot, Rod Kimble, Carl Spears, and also Bronwyn Blair.

And I want to end these acknowledgments with a callback to an earlier section of this addendum. There is in each of Sienna and Jordan's four children some small pieces of my own. While the Riley children fall far short of being "based" on my four kids, I did draw something beautiful and positive from each of them that now shows up on the page – and the book, much like my life, is far richer for it. I am a better person, and this is a better book, because of them. In the first draft of this book, I also based parts of Sienna on my wife, but, in the subsequent rewritings, those direct connections were almost entirely lost as the story took things in many different directions. However, Sienna's innate convictions, the indefatigable elements of her nature, and what she does with the tenacity of her love for her children are all drawn from what I have observed of my wife over these last 20 years.

I don't know if I have another book in me, so I can only hope this one turned out ok. I still think about the characters and the settings often. Every time I see a distant mountainside I think about the Rileys, and I am so grateful for the year I spent with them.

Ben Hawken is the award-winning creator of several beloved video series and a small handful of children. Previously, he was the author of zero other books and graduated with honors from a community college, as well as a real college. He lives outside Seattle with family.